PICTURE PERFECT LIES

A WATERFORD NOVEL #3

MIA HAYES

FINNSTAR

Cover Design: RBA Designs

D.S. ~ for our many adventures past, present, and future

1

"Where are you going, Veronica?"

Dark clouds dot the pale May sky, and humidity clings to my skin. Most people would complain that it's uncomfortably hot, but I enjoy the steamy heat. I don't even mind the little beads of sweat rolling down the base of my throat and into my cleavage because I'm greedily soaking up the first real day of summer.

On the patio below, people laugh and talk while kids run from the bounce houses to the face painting station set up on the golf cart path. I love Memorial Day – it's the start of long summer nights, pool parties, and sunshine – and it sets the tone for the rest of the season.

"What do you mean?" I turn toward my husband and smile warmly. "I'm right here."

"In your mind." Pete softly touches my bare upper arm before reaching out and pushing a piece of hair behind my ear. Chills race down my spine. He peers into my eyes and lightly taps my forehead. "Where are you going in there?"

With a slow shake of my head, I push away from the metal railing. I had come up here to get away from the crowd. I can only take so much bitchiness before I need a break, and Pete and our friends have been going hard, drinking since the morning. I'm tapped out and tired of their antics.

I hold up my empty, plastic cup, exposing the red paper bracelet encircling my wrist. A lie slips off my lips. "I wanted to get another drink."

Pete tilts his dark blond head, and his blue eyes search my face like he's trying to see my thoughts. "They closed the bar up here."

"I know." I gaze at the river, and a comfortable silence settles between us. We don't need to say much these days, not after twenty-plus years of marriage. Both our kids are in college, so our days of active, daily parenting are long behind us, and Pete often can't discuss his job. Sometimes, we gossip about neighbors, but mostly, there's silence.

I'm okay with it. Pete understands I need alone time, and that despite my reputation, I'm actually an introvert. Or maybe I'm an extroverted introvert. Either way, I need alone time after a busy week of social obligations.

After a few minutes, he lays his hand on mine. It's warm and comforting. "Let's get back to it. People are going to wonder where you are."

"Would that be so bad?"

Pete shrugs, and I try to decipher what exactly that small gesture means. He doesn't realize the power he has over me – how just one word or look from him can make me feel amazing or like utter crap. "You're the one who's always concerned with our image."

"Maybe they'll think we're having an illicit encounter," I tease. I place my free hand on his broad chest. "Maybe we should?"

"Sweetheart," he says, "you never cease to amaze me." Pete grins, and the dimple in his left check deepens. He's boyishly handsome with dark blond hair, golden skin, and gorgeous blue eyes. But most importantly, when he talks to me, I feel like no one else exists in the world.

Since Elizabeth Mavery blew up Waterford, I've been batting clean-up, trying to repair the damage she did to our reputations. And while attention spans are short in Waterford, memories are long. Fortunately, enough time has passed, and people have finally stopped whispering about Pete's involvement in the Ashley Madison scandal and Elizabeth's insinuations. We're once again Waterford's golden couple.

I roll my empty cup between my hands. "No one's up here, we could--"

"Veronica!" Stacey McLeod shouts from below. She waves her hands over her head like she's guiding an airplane into the gate.

I roll my eyes at Pete.

"You're being summoned," he says, pecking me on the forehead. "To be continued."

"I'll get rid of her." I squeeze his hand before glancing down at Stacey. "What?" I shout not bothering to hide my annoyance. "I'm busy."

"Come down! Eve is going to do the bronco."

Of course Eve wants to ride the mechanical bronco. She gets trashed and tries to ride it every year. It's her thing. "So?"

"She won't listen to any of us." Stacey flails wildly. "She's wearing a dress!"

Eve has no shame. She wants to be the center of attention so badly that she'll do anything for people to notice her. I sigh. "We won't see anything we haven't seen before."

"You need to help us." Stacey puts her hands on her hips. "C'mon. There are kids here."

Pete leans into me and whispers, "Go save the day."

Annoyed, I lean over the railing. "Fine. I'll get her home," One thing I'm very good at is averting disaster and getting people to do what I want. "But this is the last time. I'm done saving her ass this week."

"Hurry!" Stacey says. "She's third in line, and I think she may take a kid or two out to cut ahead." When I don't move fast enough, Stacey adds, "The husbands are watching."

I glance at the peaceful river. Overhead, the clouds have become thicker and darker, but streaks of sunlight break through and glint off the water. I really don't feel like dealing with a drunk. "I'm coming."

Stacey waits at the bottom of the stone stairs. Despite the humidity, her highlighted chestnut hair is perfectly frizz-free thanks to expensive keratin treatments. A few years ago, she had a complete body transformation and makeover, and somehow, it was enough for her to worm her way into my social life. Most people have forgotten what she was like before – when she was an unpopular social climber – but I haven't.

"Can you believe her?" Stacey giggles as Pete and I descend. "She's such a drunk."

"She should know better," I say. Eve is the definition of neglectful mother. She'd rather drink, party, and ignore her kids than play board games or go to sporting events. Not that I was "Mother of the Year" when my kids were small, but at least I played one in public. "She does this every year. It's so predictable."

"I know, but she's wearing a *dress*." Stacey is basically salivating and making no secret of how badly she wants Eve to crash and burn.

"That was intentional." I purse my lips. "Eve never does anything without forethought. She's the most calculating bitch I know."

Pete makes a funny face, and I chuckle. "I'll find you," I say to him. "Give me ten minutes."

"I'll be waiting." He winks before wandering off.

"Oh my God! You two are the cutest couple ever!" Stacey squeals. "Total couple's goals."

I dip my head in mock modesty. Truth is, Pete and I have been to hell and back over the past few years. We're in a good place now, but our marriage has been stressed and tested more than anyone in Waterford knows. I've spent a lot of time and energy making sure it stays like that.

"Let's deal with Eve," I say.

Stacey claps her hands in excitement and bounces on her toes. "This is going to be so good!"

And that's why I don't really care for Stacey: she gets too much pleasure out of other people's humiliation.

We weave around groups of people and food trucks toward the bronco. There's a line of kids waiting their turn, and Eve stands off to the side with Jenn, Kate, and Julia. Thank God they at least got her out of line. "They should be taking care of her," I say to Stacey. "She's their friend. Not mine."

"You know how she is," Stacey answers. "Eve thinks she's the head bitch in charge, and they're all afraid of her."

"Well, she's about to be very afraid of me if she doesn't sober up." I'm eager to get back to Pete, so this better not take long.

Eve's pale blond hair is a mess. It looks like she ripped her ponytail out and forgot to run a brush through the ends of her hair. Her Lily Pulitzer dress has an A-line skirt, and realistically, she could ride the bronco and not flash anyone until she fell off. I'm not going to fight her too hard. If she wants to ride that thing, who am I to prevent her?

"Hi, girls." I step into the circle of women surrounding Eve. "What's going on?"

Eve waves a manicured finger. "I'm riding the bronco, and no one can stop me!"

Panic shoots across Kate's face. Clearly, no one knows what to do with Eve – which is why I'm here.

Good God, why can't they function without an adult in the room?

Julia, the only one I really like, says, "Eve, honey, you can barely walk. Why would you want to make yourself sick by riding that thing?"

Eve teeters in her Tory Burch wedge sandals. They give her about three inches on me and make her thin, toned legs look longer than normal. She points at me. "Veronica, you'll do it too, won't you?"

"No, I'm not dressed right. Neither are you." I run my hand over my spaghetti strap sundress. Hazy sunlight beats down on us, and I squint behind my sunglasses. "Let's get you some water."

"Boo! You're no fun." Eve glares at us. "None of you are!"

People constantly compare the two of us – sometimes going so far as to say Eve's a younger version of me. Yes, we both have long, blond hair and are about the same height and weight, but I'm refined while Eve is a drunk, social-climbing bully. Everyone knows it.

Out of the corner of my eye, I spy Pete watching us. He stands with a few of his friends near the trees, beer in hand. He brings the Solo cup to his lips while keeping his focus on me. I give a small wave; he lifts his chin but doesn't smile. My heart sinks. I made the wrong decision. I should have stayed up on the verandah with him and told Stacey to let Eve's friends handle her.

Damn it.

As I'm about to walk away, Eve leans against Jenn. She must be dead weight, because Jenn staggers into me, and I brace her. I'll never understand how these girls can drink so much and function the next day. When Karen and Alexis lived in Waterford, we drank, but not sloppily like this.

"Water." I point toward the drink booth. "And shade. The heat is probably making her buzz worse."

Eve sticks out her tongue. "Who died and made Veronica the boss?"

I have a strict rule about not fighting with drunks, so I ignore her. "Kate, can you help Jenn? Stacey and I will get a bottle of water."

As they drag Eve away, Stacey chuckles. "You should let her get on the bronco."

"I'm trying to be nice," I snap. My irritation has grown exponentially. This is taking longer than I thought, and Eve is being a bitch. "I don't want her spraying vomit all over some poor kid."

"Since when does *Eve* do nice? You should let her get on the bronco. She's fighting you, after all." Stacey has a point. Eve wouldn't stop me from making an ass of myself. In fact, she'd probably encourage it. But I'm not Eve, and I still believe in not kicking people when they're down – even if they are social climbing ingrates.

"*I* may be a bitch, Stacey, but I have limits," I say curtly. "And puking on unsuspecting kids is my limit."

The patio is more crowded than when I came downstairs, making it difficult to walk a straight line. I glance left, to where Pete was standing, but he and his friends are gone. Voices and laughter mingle with music, and little kids dart between legs. Summer is in full effect. There will be a barbecue and an after party somewhere, and Pete and I will roll home in the evening tired, but content. Despite the current Eve drama, this has been a very good day, and if I can salvage my rendezvous with Pete, it may even push into excellent territory.

"One water," I say, holding up my finger to the bartender.

He eyes my wristband and empty cup. "Any wine?"

Why not? Unlike Eve, I can hold my alcohol. "A glass of white."

I set the cup down, and he gives me a generous pour. I collect the water and wine and head toward the shade with Stacey in tow.

"What are Pete and Eve doing?" she asks.

I swivel my head. "What? Where?"

She points. "Over there. With Jenn. It looks like they're fighting."

Eve grips Pete's arm and shouts something garbled. Pete pulls away from her, but she lunges and catches his leg before sliding to the ground.

"Oh, Jesus." I hurry toward them, and wine sloshes out over my hand. Ugh.

A group has gathered around Eve, blocking her and Pete from view, and I have to force my way through. If there is one thing the women of Waterford love, it's watching one of their own fall.

Eve kneels before Pete. Her already messy hair now has a stick in it, and mascara streaks run down her face. She's a complete, blubbering mess.

I run to her side, kneel down, and place my wine on the ground. "Let's get you up. I have water." I offer her the bottle.

"Fuck your water." Eve slaps my hand away. "And fuck you, Veronica White."

7

I recoil in confusion. "Where's Mike?" I look up at Pete. "Where did he go?"

Pete clenches his fists and sets his lips tightly.

"Pete?"

"He left. Said he couldn't deal with her."

"So we have to?" It's so like Mike, or really, all the guys in Pete's group. They're a bunch of piss-head losers who disappear when things get tough. "Help me get her up," I say. "Can you carry her up to the verandah?"

"Yeah." Pete leans down to scoop Eve up, but she swings at him.

The crowd has grown, and whispers and funny looks float around us. I can't save Eve from herself, but I'm not going to let her bring Pete down too.

"What should we do?" Jenn asks.

"Leave her." I set the bottle of water next to Eve and straighten up. "Drink that. You'll appreciate it later."

Eve moans and wraps herself around Pete's leg. Her skirt bunches around her thighs, exposing her black, lace thong. With a sigh, I lean over to pull her skirt down. "Eve, you need to get up. If you do, you can ride the bronco."

She rolls her head up and back to look at me. Rage fills her glassy, unfocused eyes. "Really, Vee? That's the best you've got? You'll *let* me ride the bronco?"

No one but Pete calls me Vee, but I let it slide. "Would you rather go home? Because those are your two options."

Eve grabs my wine cup and tries to throw it at me, but it splashes onto the ground.

"What is wrong with you?" I snap. "I am trying to help you."

Eve stumbles to her feet and presses herself into Pete's side. "How about *you* go home. No one wants you here, Miss High-and-Mighty."

I blink. "Excuse me?"

Kate and Julia step between us, and Jenn holds my shoulder.

"Walk away, Veronica," Jenn whispers. "She's drunk. You can't take anything she says seriously."

Why am I even involved in this? All I was trying to do was be a good person. I couldn't give a care about Eve, and yet, here I am being verbally assaulted by her. I snap my fingers and point toward the clubhouse. "We're out."

My husband tries untangling himself, but Eve latches on harder. "What?" she slurs. "I'm not good enough now?"

The color drains from Pete's face. "Shut up, Eve."

Heat builds in my ears and burns my cheeks. "What did you say?"

Eve fake smiles. "Pete doesn't want to go with you."

"Of course he does." I walk over to them. I yank Eve's hand off my husband and shove her aside. She bumps into Kate, who catches her. "Now, you can go ride the bronco, pass out, or go home. I really don't care, but leave me and my husband alone."

Jenn tries pushing Eve through the crowd, but she stiffens. "Do you want to tell her, Pete? Or should I?" Eve crosses her arms and raises her eyebrows. "Of course you won't. You never do."

I dart my gaze around the crowd. Hundreds of eyes stare back at me. My heart pounds, and my throat tightens.

"What do you need to tell me, Pete?" I whisper. *Don't break my heart. Please, don't break my heart.*

He shakes his head. "Nothing. Eve's drunk. We should go."

"I'm not drunk," Eve screeches. "You like to fuck me. Me. Not her. Tell her."

There's no air, and the little bit I can pull into my lungs burns. My chest heaves. I stare at Pete, waiting for him to deny it, but he won't meet my gaze. The whooshing of blood in my ears drowns out all the noise. I'm in a tunnel, trapped in some nightmare and can't get out.

"Veronica?" Stacey grabs my hand. "Come on." She yanks me through the crowd. My leaden feet clamp hard against the ground. "We need to get you out of here."

How am I walking? How am I breathing?

"Where's Pete?" I need to talk to him. I need him to explain what just happened.

Scorching air rushes out of Stacey's SUV, and she shoves me inside. "I don't know."

My mouth drops open, and I want to say something, but my voice lodges itself in the back of my throat.

"I'm so sorry you found out like this. I...we all thought you knew." Stacey tries to pat my hand.

"What? You knew?" I hit her bare arm. "You fucking knew! What is wrong with you?"

I fling the car door open and jump out into the empty parking lot. Where is Pete? Why hasn't he come to find me? I spin in a circle. My breath comes hard and fast.

This can't be happening.

My sandals fall off as I sprint across the burning blacktop toward the golf course and away from the party. The short grass pricks my feet, but I don't stop until I reach the 11th green. It backs up to the river, and for a brief moment, I consider throwing myself into the water and letting the current carry me away.

I lift my head. The dark clouds rumble; heavy raindrops hit my skin. I could sink to the ground and cry. Or I could keep going.

I need to make a decision.

I close my eyes. I've ignored and dismissed the rumors so many times before. I've trusted and believed Pete over and over again.

He's humiliated me, and he let Eve publicly embarrass me.

It's like my skin's been turned inside out.

My hands tremble in rhythm to the thunder, and I inhale the earthy smell of the rain to calm myself. As I drop to my knees, a guttural roar rips free of my lungs. "What. The. Fuck!"

I stretch out on the soggy ground and roll onto my back. The rain pounds me, but I don't care.

I howl.

2

A half-empty old-fashioned glass sits on the counter with the ice cubes still in it. I pick it up and run my finger around the lip. I bought these glasses for Pete on a whim a few weeks ago, and he thanked me with a chaste kiss on the cheek.

I should have known.

Water drips from the ends of my hair and off my clothes, creating a slick puddle on the hardwood floor. The cavernous house – the one Pete insisted we buy – is eerily silent. He either left or is hiding from me. I wouldn't be surprised if he ran out the front door when he heard the garage open. I would too.

I twist my leg to look at the cuts on the bottom of my foot. It's black and crusted in mud. I walk to the sink, hoist myself onto the counter, and stick my feet under the faucet. Lukewarm water rushes down my legs, and my hair hangs around my face, creating a stringy, soggy curtain.

"What are you doing?" Pete says from behind me.

My molasses brain churns. "What?"

"Why are you on the counter with your feet in the sink?" He

11

moves closer to me with his hands held out like I'm an injured, wild animal. "Let me help you down."

Pete reaches over me and turns off the water, then tears off a piece of paper towel, and lifts my foot to dry it. "You're filthy. Did you fall?"

"Don't touch me." His touch burns, and I yank my leg away. "Don't ever touch me again."

His shoulders sag. "Vee, let me help you down. You're being irrational."

"Is it true?" I choke out. "Stacey said everyone knew." Tears form in my eyes. "Tell me it isn't true."

"I can't do that."

My stomach rolls. "How could you let Eve humiliate me like this?"

"I couldn't stop her."

The physical distance between us is nothing compared to the emotional distance engulfing us. I cup my hands over my ears. "Stop. I don't want to hear more of your lies."

"Okay then." Pete takes my phone from his back pocket. "Stacey gave me this." He holds it out. "Here."

I'm terrified that if I accidentally touch him, I'll lose my cool demeanor. "Put it on the counter."

"It's been ringing non-stop. Can you at least mute it?"

I snatch my phone from him and flick the volume button. "You could have done that." I slam it face down on the counter and swing my legs out of the deep farmhouse sink. "It wasn't hard."

I slide off the counter and face Pete. Neither of us speak.

The unbearable silence breaks me, and I crumple to the ground. "You found someone else. She's younger and prettier. Is that why?"

Pete folds himself over me, like he's trying to shield me, which is ridiculous because he's the one I need protection from. "It was one time, and it meant nothing."

Snot bubbles in my nose. "That's one time too many."

"Vee, please, I'm sorry. We don't need to do this." Desperation seeps from Pete's voice.

His touch repulses me. I slap him away. "I said, 'Don't touch me.'"

Pete sits back on his heels. "We're going to pretend none of this happened. Can you do that?"

My cotton-ball mouth makes it hard to form words, so I shake my head in disbelief.

"We can fix this." Pete's blue eyes study me carefully. "It *is* fixable."

So many times I've lost myself in his eyes, and I always wanted to believe he couldn't hide personal things from me – work yes, but not personal things. I tilt my head. "I can't do this." My raspy voice betrays my fragility. "I love you, and I thought you loved me too."

"I do love you."

"Funny how you show it." Tears stream down my face, and I bury it in my hands. I can't believe a word he says. "What am I supposed to do?" I gasp. "I need someone to tell me what I'm supposed to do."

Pete wraps me in his solid arms. "I didn't mean to hurt you. It was selfish of me, and I'm so, so sorry."

I float over my body, watching the scene unfold. Pete created a total cluster fuck, and I'm breaking into pieces while hoping he puts me back together. It's insane. I curl deeper into his arms. "I can't do this."

He rests his chin on my head. "What do you mean?"

"The less I know the better. Don't say anything else." How can I forgive him if I have an endless loop of images of Pete with Eve playing in my mind?

Pete inhales like he's trying to soak me up. "We're going to be okay."

"Are we?" I whisper, despite the anger building in me. "Are we really? Everyone knows, and I'm a humiliated, clueless wife."

"It may take time for us, but we have to go to the McLeod's for dinner." He leans back and stares down at me. "Let's put on a brave face. It will blow over."

I glare at him. "You want to go to the McLeods' for dinner? And pretend everything is okay? Are you serious?"

"Just try," he pleads, reaching for my hand. When I clench my fist, his fingers tighten around my wrist, and he pulls me back into him. "We'll deal with this privately. There's no need to make it into a thing."

I snatch my hand away. I've done this too many times over the years. Pete screws up, and I pretend everything is fine. It's like how I handled the Elizabeth Mavery situation all over again. I ignored it and worked hard to convince people that things were fine between Pete and me when it was obvious to everyone that things were anything but.

"This is a thing," I shout, "because you did it, and you let your whore tell everyone."

Pete shrugs. "Eve was drunk. No one will take her seriously."

I stop short of smacking him across his calm face. "Are you an idiot? Stacey was shocked I didn't know. What does that tell you?"

For the first time, Pete looks rattled. "You were being serious?"

"Oh my God. Are you that fucking naïve? Eve runs her mouth."

"Damn it." Pete slams his hand on the floor. "One time, Vee. One time. I was drinking, and she kept throwing herself at me. It wasn't anything. I swear to God."

My vision dims. I want to believe Pete. It's easier than accepting the alternative. "Only once?"

"Yes." The color drains from his face. "I swear."

My body shakes, and I wrap my arms around myself. "Are you sure?" I sniff. "It was a drunk mistake?"

Pete runs a hand through his blond hair. Red rims his blue eyes. He looks as miserable as I feel. "I love you." He gets on his knees. "I'm so sorry. Tell me we can get through this."

I want to kick him. I want to punch him. I want to rip his eyes out. I want to do a million things, but none involve absolving my cheating husband. And yet, I allow him to embrace me, and I bury my head into his armpit while sobs wrack my body. Pete rubs my back.

"We'll fix this, sweetheart. I swear. No one will remember it in a month." Pete's voice shakes.

I lift my face and stare at my husband's distraught eyes. I've always known Pete's weak spot is his own whims and wants. And right now, he wants me to put on a united public face and cover for him again.

"I can't pretend anymore," I say through my tears. "And it's unfair of you to ask it of me. Everyone knows, and I look like a fool."

Pete tangles the ends of my hair around his fingers. "Sweetheart, we're a team. We can make it through this." He glances over my head at the wall behind me. "It's almost six-thirty. We need to get ready."

As much as I want to hurt and humiliate Pete, I know that in order to survive in a place like Waterford, I have to put on a brave or nothing-is-wrong face. The fastest way to kill a scandal is lack of information. So if Pete and I don't say anything or acknowledge it, this nightmare will go away. It's a lesson I learned from that awful "Surviving the Suburbs" blog.

I untangle myself from Pete and stand. I scoop up Pete's old-fashioned glass and deposit it in the sink with the amber liquid still inside. I spin around with my heart banging against my ribs and my breath ragged. "I'll go," I say. "But only if you can swear that if Eve's there we will leave."

Pete rushes toward me and rests his hands on my shoulders. "I swear."

When he releases me, I run my hand over my face. I can do this. I can keep up appearances. After all, that's what I do best – create a perfect image from the messy fragments of my life.

"I need to get ready," I say, evenly. "My hair is a mess, and I'm covered in mud."

Pete's eyes soften. "You look beautiful."

I hold up my hand, silencing him. "Too soon. And no, you can't sleep with me in the master. I'm not forgiving you. I'm doing this for me, not you. I need to be able to go out in public without people whispering and staring like they do after things like this happen."

"It will die down. It always does," Pete says calmly.

I focus my cool gaze on him. "Don't worry, I'll make it go away. Just like I always do."

"Vee--"

I hold up my hand as I stomp away. The first person I need to convince is myself. If I can do that, then maybe everything will be okay. "You should get ready." I glance over my shoulder. "We have a performance in thirty minutes."

I trudge up Stacey's driveway carrying a handle of Tito's. If I need to make a positive impression, vodka is the way to go. Low carb, low cal, and every woman in Waterford's favorite drink. Plus, if they get drunk enough, maybe they'll forget the whole thing.

Pete stays right at my side. When we reach the door, he lifts his hand to ring the bell, but I shove the door open. A riot of laughter floats past me as nausea hits hard. I brace myself against the door frame.

"Vee?" Pete whispers. "What can I do?"

"Keep your dick in your pants?" I hiss under my breath. "Start there."

With resolve, I step into Stacey's house. My nerves tingle as I walk toward the kitchen and great room where everyone is gathered. I draw air into my burning lungs and plaster the biggest, fakest smile I can muster. "Hey!" I say a little too perkily. "Sorry we're late."

Everyone stops and stares at us, but my eyes rest on Eve. She's cleaned up from earlier and looks gorgeous with her long, ice blond hair perfectly curled and a faint pink tinting her lips. She's changed into a spaghetti strap maxi dress that accentuates her fake boobs.

Really though, she's unbelievable to show up here. And why

hasn't Stacey thrown her out? I eye the doorway. Pete said we could leave if she was here, but now that I'm in the moment, I know I can't. I draw a deep breath and fight the urge to unload on Eve.

Pete slips his hand around mine. "I've got you," he whispers before taking the vodka from me. He lifts the bottle to chest level. "We brought this."

Stacey tries to hide her excitement as she rushes toward us, but it's there in her too-wide smile. Like everyone else, she's dying to see what's going to happen.

"That's definitely not enough for this crowd!" She takes the Tito's. "Do you want a drink, Veronica?"

I side-eye Eve. Did she really believe she can humiliate me?

"Veronica?" Stacey says again. "Drinks?"

I blink. "Oh, yes. I'll have a vodka tonic." Pete drops my hand and heads toward a few of the guys near the TV blasting the Nationals game. I hate baseball. I hate how long it takes. I hate how nothing really happens. But mostly, right now, I hate it because of how much Pete enjoys it. He should be miserable, but instead, he's smiling with the guys. Bastard.

I wander toward the coffee table, grab the remote, and turn the TV off.

"What are you doing?" Pete asks.

"It's too loud."

Steve Nims scowls. "Then turn it down or mute it, but leave the game on."

I clench my jaw. "No. I hate baseball. Put on a decorating show or something."

Eve's husband draws his brows together, but before he can say anything, Pete plucks the remote from my hand. "Why don't you go talk to the women in the kitchen?"

He turns me and pushes me slightly. I stumble forward in my strappy sandals, but I recover gracefully even though my legs tremble.

The women stand around the kitchen island where Stacey has a spread of fruit, cheese, and crackers along with bottles of wine and my Tito's. She spies me lurking behind everyone. "Veronica! I have your drink."

All conversation stops, and ten pairs of eyes stare at me. No doubt they were all taking bets on how long it is until Pete and I announce our divorce. *Breathe, Veronica.*

I plaster my best 'everything-is-fine' smile on my face, and slip between two women and accept the glass. Like everyone I know, I hate vodka tonics, but it's low cal, so I drink it.

Eve leans against the far end of the marble island like she doesn't understand the turmoil she's caused. The sticks and ratty hair from earlier may be gone, but the crazed look in her eyes tells me she's pissed. What did she expect? That Pete and I would immediately file for divorce, and she could swoop in? And what the hell is wrong with her husband? How can he not throat punch Pete?

"How nice of you to show up, Veronica," Eve drawls and swirls the red wine in her glass. "I mean, I don't think I could."

I fight the urge to lunge at her. "Given that *you* are at my friend's house, I'm amazed *you* are here."

Jenn Brooks whispers in Eve's ear and pulls her toward the French doors leading to the deck. "We'll be right back."

I've known most of these women for years, and not one of them thought to tell me about Pete and Eve. In fact, they seem more than okay with it. I clench my jaw. How could no one tell me? How did they let me run around thinking my life was pretty damn good?

Stacey elbows Christina Morris. I narrow my eyes. "What?"

"Nothing," Christina says, heat flushing her cheeks.

"It seems like something," I snap and set my glass on the counter.

Christina shrugs. "You're making Eve uncomfortable."

My heartbeat thunders in my ears. "You can't be serious." Before I can stop myself, the words I'm trying to hide slip out. "Eve is a tramp that slept with my husband."

"He's at fault, too." Christina purses her lips. "Why aren't you mad at him?"

The French doors swing open, and Eve saunters back inside with Jenn behind her. She smirks.

Oh hell no. She's not winning this one. "What goes on between Pete and me is private. However, if Eve can cheat with my husband, I'd be worried about what she may do with yours – especially since most of them make more money than mine."

"Don't be crass," Jenn says rolling her eyes. "You couldn't keep him happy."

"Says the adulteress who stole her husband." I shift into mean-girl mode. "No one has forgotten how you got knocked up by Ellison's husband." I grab my vodka tonic off the counter and barrel through the crowd toward Eve. Everyone backs away from me, but she holds her ground.

When I'm inches from her, Eve laughs. "What are you going to do, Veronica? Kick my ass? That would get you an assault charge."

I jiggle the glass in my hand. "Stay away from my husband and me."

"Isn't that up for Pete to decide?" She cocks her head, and a coy smile snakes across her face.

"Pete," I scream, "doesn't get to make a decision! This is--"

Someone grabs my upper arm and pulls me away from Eve. "Stop," Pete whispers in my ear. "You're feeding the situation."

I spin on him, and my drink spills down my arm. "I'm feeding the situation?" I push firmly on his chest with my dry hand. "You're the one who wants to pretend everything is normal."

Pete tears the glass from hand and yanks me toward the front door. I stumble after him, tripping over my feet. "Ladies," he yells. "Thanks for the entertainment. We're leaving."

"See you soon," Eve says loudly. "I'm sure we're all dying to see you again, Veronica."

I break free of Pete's grasp and charge Eve. I slap her before I can think anything through.

She recoils in horror, and a red handprint stains her face. "You fucking hit me! You all saw it."

"We're leaving. Now." Pete grabs me around my waist and throws me over his shoulder.

He isn't seriously carrying me out, is he? I flail, pounding my fists into his back and kicking his chest. Stacey holds the front door open for us and doesn't bother to say goodbye. Pete hauls me in the light drizzle to the car and drops me next to the door. He pins me to the side of the BMW. "Stop acting like a crazy woman."

I gape at him. "You did this! Don't put it on me!"

"Lower your voice. The neighbors will hear."

"Does that fucking matter?" I shout louder. "Everyone already knows the rumors are true."

"And they'll forget if you stop acting like a maniac."

I shove him out of my way and brush past him.

"Where are you going?" Pete asks. When I don't stop, he yells. "Veronica! Stop! You're going to ruin your hair."

I pivot. "I don't care about my goddamn hair!"

"Come back." He doesn't move toward me.

Every moment of the Memorial Day party replays in my mind: Eve wanting to get on the bronco; her wrapped around Pete's legs; his refusal to deny her accusations. I stare at Pete. Water drips off his face, and he holds out his arms. "Vee, please. Stop acting like this."

I hug myself, but it doesn't do anything to still the thoughts racing through my brain. The urge to run as far from Waterford as I can consumes me.

"I'm leaving," I say. Out of the corner of my eye, I catch a glimpse of Eve standing victoriously in Stacey's window. "Since everyone thinks this is my fault, I'm leaving."

As I say the words, I realize how much I really need to be away from Waterford. I can't face any of these people – not now, and especially not knowing how every one of them betrayed me.

"Where are you going?" Pete asks as if I'm planning a vacation.

My stomach quivers. Where *am* I going? I haven't been on my own in my entire adult life. I step toward the car. "Take me home."

Pete's eyes soften. "Thank you." He opens my door like the chivalrous jerk he is. "Let's work this out at home."

I'm exhausted and have no fight left in me. Pete shifts into reverse; I rest my head against the cool window. The manicured lawns of Waterford blur together as Pete speeds down the street. The houses are so perfect on the outside, but they hide the truths of what goes on behind the brightly-colored doors.

I need to get out of here. I can't take the whispers and gossip, and I can't bear having to look at Pete.

After we pull into the garage, I race into the house. I need to execute my plan before Pete's sweet talk convinces me to stay. With determination I head toward the finished basement.

"What are you doing?" Pete asks with concern.

"Getting my suitcase. I need time away."

"I thought...I thought we were going to work on this." Hurt flows from his words.

I pause with my hand on the doorknob. "Don't you dare play the victim. Don't turn this around on me."

My husband frowns. "So this is it. You're leaving, and I don't get a say?"

"Did I get a say when you decided I wasn't good enough?"

"That's not it."

"Then what was it?" I scream. "What drove you into Eve's willing arms?"

"You're never available, and your friends matter more than me." Pete crosses his arms and stares me down. "Why don't you accept some responsibility?"

"Responsibility? For the choices you made? Don't you dare blame me for what you did. Don't *you* dare."

"We wouldn't be in this mess if you cared about our marriage as much as you do about drinking and new handbags." Pete sets his jaw. "Admit it, Veronica. You suck as a wife."

I tear the basement door open and run down the stairs. The stack of suitcases tumbles when I slide mine from the center. I don't bother to pick up the mess. I tear up the stairs and beeline for the safe.

"What are you doing?" Pete asks carefully as I spin the lock. All our important documents are in here. I dig through the file folders until I find my passport.

"Getting my passport." I stomp out of the office, grab my suitcase, and walk up the second-story stairs to my room.

"Don't do this." Pete leans against my closet doorframe and doesn't make any sort of effort to stop me. "I'm sorry for what I said. Stay. I'll go to counseling. Whatever you want."

I drop two bathing suits into my suitcase. "Sure you will."

"Vee, please." Pete's voice hitches. "Don't go."

I turn my head so that he can't see my lip quivering. "You don't get a say in what I do, or don't do, anymore. I'm tired of living a lie."

"Our life isn't a lie," Pete chokes. "I love you. Despite my actions, I do. I don't know how to live without you."

I fight the urge to wrap him in my arms. To comfort him. To make him stop hurting.

He did this, not me.

I zip my suitcase, take my phone out of my pocket, and call an Uber. "I'm leaving."

"Where?"

That's a good question. Where will I go? What's far enough away from Waterford to help me put my head back on straight?

"Does it matter?"

"Yes, it matters. I'm worried about you." Pete blocks my exit. "You matter to me."

"Funny how you like to show it." I yank the handle of my rolling bag up and shove past him. My phone buzzes. "My Uber is here. If I come back, I'll see you then."

"Vee, wait. Don't do this. Don't--"

But I'm already out the door. I'm done with Pete humiliating me. And I'm done with Waterford.

3

Marrakech stretches beyond the plane's wingtip, a flat expanse cradled by the sloping Atlas Mountains. The plane circles the city, giving aerial glimpses of the red-roofed medina's souks and minarets. I press my fingers against the cloudy window. An adventure like this should have me buzzing, but I feel nothing.

The plane sinks lower until the landing gear connects with the runway, and we bounce.

We taxi past shanties, and I half expect goats or wild dogs to run alongside the puddle jumper. Pete's job has taken us on assignments all over the world, and I'm no stranger to culture shock, but I'm suddenly questioning my decision. After all, I know Europe. It would have been a safer choice.

When I left yesterday – or was it two days ago, it is hard to tell with time changes – I had no idea where I wanted to go, but I'd always had a fantasy of walking up to a counter and buying the first available ticket on the first airline I saw. So I did it. I bought a one-way, business-class ticket to Morocco on Emirates.

Pete's going to die when he sees the credit card statement, but why should he care? It's my money. And right now, I'm being indulgent and running away.

The plane stops short of the terminal, and a crew pushes a set of stairs toward the door. Unlike my cozy Emirates flight, this short flight from Casablanca to Marrakech is bare bones. I gather my bag from the overhead bin and follow the other passengers to the stuffed buses that carry us to the terminal.

Maybe it's jet lag, or more likely the two Xanax I've taken, but the shattered feeling from earlier has subsided a little. I haven't allowed myself to cry, which is good, but my mind races, trying to make sense of everything.

How did this happen? How did I not know? I fight the lump forming in my throat. Everyone must have been laughing at me behind my back the way we once did at Ellison Brooks. Someone elbows me in the back, and I glance over my shoulder at the tall, black man behind me.

"Sorry," he says, in a thick New York accent. "It's crowded, ya know?"

I don't respond because I'm terrified that if I open my mouth, I won't be able to keep my anger trapped inside. The bus lurches again, and I tighten my grasp on the overhead leather strap. So far, Marrakech isn't meeting my expectations, but being here and forcing myself to focus on something other than my humiliation is good.

One step at a time. Just get through this moment.

In a drugged-up haze, I drag my roller bag through the terminal. A driver is supposed to meet me at baggage and take me to my hotel. When I booked it using the shoddy internet at the Casablanca airport, I tried to find a nice riad inside the medina. However, it proved too difficult for my current mental state, so I defaulted to the Four Seasons. My plan is to stay there a few days, get my bearings, and maybe move into a luxury riad later.

Since I have no luggage other than my carry-on, I breeze through Customs and head toward the pick-up area. The crowd churns around me, pressing me closer and closer to the exit. Dark-suited men holding signs line exterior sidewalk, and I scan them, searching for my name. Nothing. Nothing. Nothing.

Finally, toward the end, a small man holds a professionally printed sign. "Four Seasons, Mrs. White."

I want to rip the sign from his hands and tear it up. I don't want to be Mrs. White right now.

"*Bonjour.*" I force myself to smile. If I smile, everything will be okay. "*Je suis* Veronica White, *mais appelez moi* Veronica."

"Welcome, Mrs. White, to Marrakech! I am Mohammed." The man ignores my request and reaches for my bag. "May I help you?"

His English is heavily accented, but so is my French. Perhaps he didn't understand me. I'm not Mrs. White, I want to scream. I'm Veronica White. There's a difference now.

I step aside so that he can take my luggage.

Mohammed guides me outside to the parking lot where a sleek, black Mercedes sedan waits. He rushes ahead to hold the car door open. "It's not a long drive, but I have water and light snacks for your comfort."

I collapse into the backseat and close my eyes. The uninvited image of Eve wrapped around Pete's leg hits me, and the tears I've held in slide down my cheeks. The more I try to fight them, the harder they fall, until a guttural sob rips through me.

"Mrs. White? Are you okay?" Mohammad asks from the front seat.

"No," I shout, slamming my fist against the seat. "I'm not okay! I may never be okay again!"

Mohammad watches me in the rearview mirror. "Should I stop?"

"Just drive." I don't need his pity – or anyone's for that matter. I may not understand what's happening with my marriage, but I know that I don't want people saying, "Poor, Veronica, she couldn't keep her husband happy."

Because I did. I worked hard at my marriage, and I thought Pete did too. We were happy and had reached a comfortable place where we enjoyed being together. But all the while, he was running around with Eve. No matter what Pete says, I have had seven hours on a plane to think about them together, and I know it wasn't a one-time thing. *Everyone* knows it wasn't a one-time thing.

God, how stupid was I?

Mohammad hits the brakes hard, and I jolt forward. My handbag flies into the back of the passenger seat. "Oh my God! Be careful!"

"Sorry, Mrs. White."

I grip the leather seat and pray I don't die because Mohammad's driving is frightening. Or maybe, more correctly, Moroccan driving is terrifying. There are no apparent rules or lanes, and everyone seems to move however and wherever they want. And the cars are either high-end models or barely drivable. There's no middle ground.

We pass expanses of desert dotted with seemingly random, luxury developments, followed by more shanties, and then fields of roses. Camels graze in the median. As we draw nearer to civilization, a motorbike path runs along the side of the street, and dozens of scooters zoom past – many carrying entire families on one small, strained frame. I'm especially alarmed at the family of five balancing on a bike while carrying cartons of eggs.

Where am I? How is this my life?

Mohammad lays on the horn, and I jump.

"Sorry," he says while looking at me in the rearview mirror and not at the road. "These people do not know how to drive." He hits the gas, and we jerk forward. "Will you take a taxi in Marrakech?"

I scrunch my brows together. "I...I don't know."

"If you do, do not go with anyone until you get the price you want. These drivers will take your money. You are a Western woman with light hair. Do not over pay."

I nod. I don't have the energy to discuss what a good price would be.

We enter a roundabout, and Mohammad takes a sharp right into a driveway. A guard station surrounded by lush greenery sits off to the side, and an ornate metal gates blocks our path.

Mohammad pops the trunk while a man searches the underside of the car with a mirror. The guard leans in through Mohammad's window and says something in brisk French that I don't fully hear. Mohammad answers with a nod, and we're waved through.

As we drive up the long, winding street, I try to focus on the flowering gardens on each side. On anything that will ground me in being here, and not reliving Pete's cruelty. But I can't erase Eve's drunk, sly smile from my mind or the way she tauntingly called me Vee.

How long? I need to know how long it's been going on.

My door swings open, and miraculously, I stand without my knees giving out. My luggage is retrieved from the trunk, and I'm shown through a metal detector.

You just have to get to your room. That's all you need to do. You're almost there.

"This way, Mrs. White," a tall, thin man says. "The reception is this way."

No one knows me here. No one can see my embarrassment. No one knows.

"Mrs. White," a pretty, polished woman says with a smile. "Welcome to Marrakech! Did you have a pleasant flight?"

"Yes," I lie. *Please stop calling me Mrs. White.* I dig into my bag and present my passport.

"Would you like some mint tea while you wait? It may take me a few minutes to process everything." She takes my passport and gestures to a low tea table behind me. "Please, sit."

I arrange myself on a large cushion while a young man pours tea from a silver pot over sugar cubes. "This is good after a long flight," he says. "It helps settle you."

"That's exactly what I need." I smile weakly as I hold out my hand to accept the tiny glass cup.

"Hold it like this," the attendant says, arranging his fingers so that his thumb rests on the bottom of the cup, and his index pinches the lip. "It will burn your hand otherwise."

I take the cup, cradling it as he did, and bring it to my lips. The smell of sugar and mint hits my nose. I've never liked mint much, and I don't do added sugar, but I sip.

It's delicious.

"Good?" the attendant asks.

"Very." I take another sip of the sweet, hot tea. The attendant must be satisfied because he smiles and walks away, leaving me sitting by myself. I'm never alone. Never. At home, I'm always with Pete or my friends, or before they went to college, my kids. But here, I'm completely and utterly alone, and I can't even text my friends to keep me occupied.

My burning breath lodges in my throat. There's no air. I set my cup down and lower my head. My shoulders round.

Breathe. You can do this.

But can I? I've never traveled on my own, and Pete's always arranged everything for us. It's his hobby – planning elaborate trips for us – and I've always been happy to provide the money and go in whatever direction he points me.

But now I'm alone. My breathe hitches again.

I chose to leave. Pete and all my so-called friends laying into me and defending Eve – it was too much. I couldn't stay and maintain my self-respect. I know this, so why am I having such a hard time?

I need to text Eve and find out the truth. If Pete won't tell me, she will. She wants me to hurt. I fumble with my phone and find her number. My finger hovers over the keyboard. What do I say? How do I start this?

"Mrs. White. You are set. I'll have your bag sent to your room," the desk clerk says gently, like she's aware that I'm not completely of sane mind. "Here are your keys and passport. Would you like a tour of the property?"

I shake my head. "No, thank you. Just my room, please."

28

She motions to the attendant. "Jamal will take you."

As we move through the entry courtyard, Jamal rattles on about car service to the medina and something else, but I've tuned out. He leads me past a giant basin of orange roses, and I pause.

"Those are beautiful," I say.

"Yes. They're fresh every day."

We continue down a walkway flanked by two ponds toward a set of glass doors.

"Welcome to Marrakech," the greeter says, swinging the door open.

I nod.

Giant birdcages filled with songbirds sit on each side of the entry way, and a fragrant multi-tiered display of red roses greets me. A light breeze coming through the retractable ceiling sways gauzy white curtains. We turn right, past an open-roof seating area and dining balcony, and then left down a hallway. Jamal steps into a short hallway and stops outside a non-descript door. "This is your room. Would you like me to show you inside?"

"No."

"Then please enjoy your stay, Mrs. White."

When the door closes behind me, and I'm all alone – really alone – I lean against the bed and slip off my shoes before crawling over the fluffy, white duvet and planting myself face down in the pillows. I don't have any energy left to scream; my tears are dry; my throat sore.

I'm not Mrs. White anymore.

I wake to an alarm. At least, that's what I think it is. But as I lie in bed and focus my groggy brain, I realize it's the call to prayer. I roll off the bed and stumble toward the sliding balcony door before shoving the blackout curtains aside.

An orange and purple dusk has settled over Marrakech. I step onto the wide balcony that overlooks a lush garden, and hot, dry wind licks at my skin. Everything feels raw – my skin, my bones, my heart – and it takes all I have not to succumb to my shaking legs.

The haunting prayer consumes the city, echoing from different mosques, and I settle onto the patio couch to listen. From my limited knowledge of Islam, I know this is the time of day when practicing Muslims are supposed to stop, face Mecca, and pray, and that it happens several times a day. I am not religious. Not even close. And yet, the sound of the singing, or chanting for a lack of better description, reaches deep into me. I draw my knees to my chest and bow my head.

Don't think. Don't think. Don't think.

What am I doing? Millions of people are cheated on, and most can't afford to run away like I have. I'm luxuriating in the ability to wallow.

When the call to pray is over, I rest my cheek on my knees. I need a list of things to do, like message my kids so they don't worry about me and text Eve so that she realizes she hasn't won even though I left. I frown. If I do that, though, she will show everyone, and I could come off as desperate. No, best to not give her the attention she craves.

My phone rings, and I turn slightly toward the interior of my room with a scowl. I want to be alone, so I can sort out what to do next, and talking to anyone right now seems like too enormous of a task. If they really want me, they can text, and I'll answer on my own time.

But then my phone rings again. And again. And again.

Worried something is wrong with one of the kids, I re-enter my room take my phone off the nightstand. Message alerts and missed calls fill my screen – all from Pete.

--Where are you?--

--Vee, call me.--

--Come home. We need to talk.--

--Why am I getting a foreign ringtone on your phone? Where are you?--

And so on. I stop reading and don't bother to listen to his voicemails. I can't bear hearing his voice right now.

But I do need to tell him where I am, if only for the kids' sake. I don't want them to worry. Pete can spin my sudden trip to Morocco however he wants, but I'm sure they'll hear through the wonderful Waterford grapevine what happened. In fact, they probably already have.

The sun sinks below the horizon, darkening my room except for the glow of my phone.

--Vee, please call me. Please--.

Pete's begging unnerves me. What game is he playing?

Screw him. I focus my annoyance and begin typing.

--I told you I had to leave. You don't need to know where I am. I will come back when I'm ready.--

Three dots appear on the screen followed by a message:

--You took all the money.--

I clench my jaw.

-- I did. I forgot in the midst of jet lag and misery to fill you in.--

--And bought a ticket on Emirates?--

--Yes.--

At least he cares enough to do a little research.

--Vee, this is crazy.--

I stare at the screen. Crazy? No, what's crazy is the way I've given him the benefit of the doubt for so long. That's what bonkers.

--Come home. We can work this out.--

Going home is the last thing I want.

--No.--

--Then let me come to you.--

I hover my finger over the screen. He could come here, and maybe we could figure things out away from the prying eyes of Waterford. But no, I can't. Not right now and not without trying to kill him.

--I don't want to see you.--

I stare at the phone for five minutes, waiting for some sort of response, but my phone goes dark. Has he given up that easily? Why isn't he responding?

Well, I'm not going to reach out to him.

From my handbag, I retrieve Xanax and dry swallow one. I honestly have no idea how many I've taken in the past twenty-four hours, but I'm still awake and still anxious, so clearly it hasn't been enough. I reach for the hotel phone and call room service.

"How can I help you, Mrs. White?"

"I'd like to order a bottle of champagne."

"We have Veuve," the operator says. "Would you like that?"

"Yes." I hang up.

Moments slip into minutes, each one slowly ticking by. I pace the room, waiting for room service or for Pete to text me. Finally, when I'm about to explode, there's a knock on the door. The waiter stands outside with an ice bucket and a chilled bottle of Veuve. "May I come in?"

"Of course." I step aside. "I'm sorry it's dark in here. I can't figure out the lights."

"I will help you." He sets the bucket and bottle on the table. "The switch next to your bed operates the reading lights. This one," he flips a switch near the closet, "turns on the main lights." He smiles. "Would you like me to open your Veuve?"

I nod.

He expertly removes the cork and pours me a glass before placing the bottle in the bucket. "Is there anything else you need, Mrs. White? Turndown service, perhaps?"

I shake my head. "No, I'm fine."

After he leaves, I take the bucket and my phone back onto the balcony. Pete still hasn't responded, and my heart plummets. Was he only pretending to care? Or was it really just about my money?

I down my first glass of bubbles and stretch out on the all-weather couch. The warm breeze dances over my skin, reminding me that I am, somehow, still alive.

Damn it. I have no idea what I should be doing. I've lived in Waterford and know countless people whose marriages were destroyed by affairs. You would think that I'd at least have a clue on how to handle this. I guess this is what I get for laughing behind Ellison Brooks' back and lying to Elizabeth Mavery. It's karma for all those days I gossiped with Eve and Karen. I deserve this.

As I close my eyes, one thought stands out amongst the rest. No one has called me or reached out. No one. Not even Stacey, who no doubt wants the inside scoop to boost her standing with the bitches.

With a frown, I pull up Facebook, and my heart races as I scroll through my so-called friends' feeds. Looks like they all – Eve included - went to the pool together. I scroll back until I find pictures from the Memorial Day party. There are dozens, each one more stomach-churning than the next. And the captions! Stacey actually posted a group shot with Eve and me and wrote, "Love these girls!"

It's like, by me leaving, everything Eve and Pete did is okay, and all is forgiven.

Part of me wants to block all of them, but the other part of me knows that social media is a powerful, useful weapon. If I can make it look like I'm having the time of my life, if I can pretend to be happy, then I can control this situation. And maybe, if I pretend hard enough, I can make it a reality.

In the past, when Pete and I had our differences, everything went back to normal after a few days. But it's never been like this. There's never been concrete evidence of an affair, only whispers and gossip. And no one has ever blurted it out for everyone to hear. I can't pretend it never happened when everyone heard Eve say it, and Pete did not deny it.

How long do I need to run around Morocco pretending I'm fine before people forget the Eve situation? And how long is it going to take me to swallow my pride? Because as I once told Elizabeth, women like us don't get divorced. We suck it up and put it behind us. But how? How do I actually do that?

I refill my glass. My heartbeat slows as my breath levels out. My eyes grow heavy, and my brain stills a little. The Xanax is kicking in at last. If Pete wants to work things out, I can do it, but not until he suffers for his actions. I'm going to make him sit in our home and reflect on what he stands to lose. Then, when he's as miserable as me, I'll forgive him, and everything will be better.

4

Sunlight pours through the open curtains, and I groan. My pounding head and the dry, ashy taste in my mouth remind me that I finished an entire bottle of champagne on my own.

I push up onto my elbow and look at my silent phone. Last night, Pete couldn't stop calling. Now, it seems he's vanished.

He has enough info to find me if he wants, and really, all he has to do is check our joint credit card. Plus, I'm sure some of his so-called secret government training could lead him to me.

God, I wish he would at least try. I wish he'd pick me. Not some other woman. Not his job. But me. I want him to put me first the way I've always done with him – not even our kids took priority over him despite his claims to the contrary.

Breathe. He'll come. He has to.

Except, maybe he won't. Last night, I searched through the thousands of photos on my phone and counted all the ones with Pete and Eve in them. I stopped when I got to 183 and sobbed into my champagne glass. But here's the thing: I'm better than them, and I'm going to show the world. I mean, it would be so easy to post Eve's info on *She's a Homewrecker*, but what will that really accomplish? It won't fix my marriage, and I have to fix it even though Pete isn't making an effort.

I blink back burning tears. At some point you'd think they'd dry up, but no, my eyes are leaky faucets that I can't control. I stubbornly wipe my eyes with my fingertips, but it doesn't stop the tears.

As I lie here, the unbearable crush of indecision overwhelms me. In my forty-five years, I've never been completely alone, but here I am, sitting in a hotel room in Marrakech, able to do whatever I want, and the only thing I want to do is order another bottle of champagne and take some Xanax. But that's not going to accomplish anything except give me another pounding headache and more self-pity.

You're in Marrakech, Veronica. Do something fun. Make Pete realize what he's missing.

I know perception is sometimes more important than reality, and I am an expert at smiling and pretending. But how do I sell it when everyone knows I'm not okay?

I roll onto my back and stare at the ceiling. I want Eve and Pete and everyone else to see that nothing brings Veronica White down – even if I hurt more than I've ever hurt before. That means I need to take dozens of spectacular pictures of me having fun and post them on every social media site.

I drag myself from bed and to the shower. First step in my crisis PR plan: make myself look presentable. No one will believe my photos if I look like an unwashed, deranged animal.

After scrubbing my hair and shaving, I give the handle a hard crank and shut off the water. Cool air rushes into the shower when I crack the door open to retrieve my robe. I wrap my hair in a towel and walk to the double vanity where two bloodshot eyes stare back at me. I look every bit of my forty-five years. It's going to take a ton of makeup to fix this mess. However, I may be an emotional wreck, but I certainly don't need to look like it.

Once I finish my beauty routine, I move to the walk-in closet and select a knee-length sundress from my suitcase. At some point, I should hang things up, but I don't have the energy right now – and I only booked myself for three nights, so what's the point? I grab a light scarf to wear over my shoulders and my white sunhat. Thankfully, I've had enough travel experience to know how to pack for any situation.

One more look in the full-length mirror convinces me that I don't look like a beast, but before heading to the restaurant, I practice my different smiles – delighted, amused, excited. Each expression requires a little tweak, and once I'm satisfied, I leave my room with a soft smile sitting on my lips.

The restaurant is on the lower level of the three-story building. Outside tables fill the space around a fountained pool, and white umbrellas cast shade, giving some relief from the early morning sun.

"May I help you?" the hostess asks.

"A table for one. By the pool, if possible," I answer. I've never dined alone before, and it feels surreal – like I'm watching myself do things.

The hostess nods. "Yes, of course. Right this way." We glide between white cloth tables. "The breakfast buffet is in that room." She points to the left before stepping down the two steps to the patio. "Your waiter will take your drink order once you're settled." We stop next to the table closest to the pool. "Is this satisfactory?"

There is minimal shade, but it's early and not too hot yet. "It will do."

She smoothly pulls out my chair. "May I ask your room number?"

I don't know my room number, and stare at her blankly. "I..."

"It's on your key."

"Right." I retrieve the key sleeve from my bag. "319."

"Thank you."

Black and white mosaic tiles decorate a bubbling pool that has to be fifty yards long. Palm trees flank each side, and a gorgeous two-story building sits at the far end. I snap a shot and filter it. If nothing else, the Four Seasons has amazing Instagram spots.

Even though it's not a picture of me, it's still a nice first picture. Something to let everyone know where I am, and what I'm doing. I caption the photo, "Breakfast by the pool," and hashtag it with every possible combination of words I can come up with. Then, I set my location to Marrakech and post. Within seconds, the likes come pouring in – mostly from accounts I don't recognize.

"Tea, coffee, or juice?"

I jerk my head up. "Oh. Ummm...tea. It's the mint kind, right?"

My server, a young, beardless man in his early twenties, nods. "Yes, but we have others if you prefer."

"Mint is fine." I'm not hungry, so I don't bother with the buffet. Being out here, listening to the fountains and watching the birds calm me. And I need calm right now.

The server holds the tea pot at shoulder height and elaborately pours it over the sugar cubes in a tiny cup. Not a drop splashes out. The glass cup is hot, so I hold it the way I was taught at check-in and sip. The fresh mint leaves tingle against my lips.

What does one do in Marrakech? I've heard of the souks, and I love shopping, so maybe I should spend some time there? I search 'Marrakech' on Instagram and study the photos. Beautiful shots of brightly colored tiles, spice markets, and women posing against dramatic backgrounds fill my feed.

I need to do that. I wave at the hostess who hurries over. "Yes, Mrs. White?"

"I want to go into the medina and souks. Is there a guide to take me?"

"Let me ask the concierge."

Today, I'm going to be okay. I'm going to take hundreds of smiling pictures, and I'm going to plaster them on every social media site I'm on. I may even tag Pete and write something like, "Missing you!"

Satisfied with my plan, I relax against my chair and study the other guests. Most people happily chat, but next to me, a Middle Eastern man smokes a hookah while his kids color and his wife looks on with boredom. They don't speak, and my heart grows cold. He's probably cheating on her because that's what all men do: fool you into thinking everything is okay, and then BAM! You find out about their mistress when she literally throws herself at their feet.

"Mrs. White?" A man in a smart suit says. I assume he's the concierge. "You would like a medina tour today?"

"And the souks, if that's possible. Dinner at a trendy, picturesque restaurant, too. I don't know anything about Marrakech, so I'm going to need help."

"Yes, of course." He folds his hands in front of him. "What time were you thinking for both."

I hadn't been thinking at all. "Oh. As soon as possible for the tour. I don't want to be too hot, and maybe 8:30 for dinner?"

"Please come to the reception after your meal. I'll work on this for you."

I flash my excited smile, but it feels foreign, like I've never done it before. "Thank you."

If I keep myself busy with activities, then maybe I won't think. And if I don't think, I won't hurt. And if I don't hurt, maybe this will all go away.

Anytime we step out of the shadows of the souks, the late May sun pounds us mercilessly with a blinding white light. The Excedrin I took before leaving the hotel hasn't done anything for my headache, and my hat feels too tight, but I don't want to take it off because of the sun.

"Mrs. White, do you need to stop? We could take a refreshment." My guide, a lovely, beardless older man with a bald head, watches me closely. His gold embroidered white robe glows in the harsh light, and I wish I also had on a flowing robe instead of a bra, underwear, and fitted sundress with a scarf draped over my shoulders.

"No, I'm fine. I'm not used to this type of heat."

"Ah, yes, the sun in Morocco is strong." Amine pauses outside a small leather goods shop. We've been winding our way through the crooked streets and alleys for nearly three hours, and I have a back-pack stuffed full of merchandise: leather shoes, scarves, and a hand-bag. Along the way, Amine has pointed out various points of historical interest, and I've made sure to get as many pictures as possible. When I get back to the hotel, I'll strategically select my favorites to post.

A man rushes from the shop across from us with a leather satchel. "Hello, lady. Have a look? Do you like?"

Amine rattles off something in Arabic, and the man sulks away. Thank God, I have a guide. If I tried to visit the souks on my own, not only would I have gotten lost, but I probably would have been swindled.

I dig in my backpack and find an unopened bottle of water. It's warm and not refreshing, but I don't care. I just need to drink something after sweating so much.

"Would you like to go back to your hotel?" Amine asks. He's been so patient with me and my constant picture taking. He's definitely earning his tip.

I shake my head. "Actually, I'd like to see the square now. Can you take me there?"

"Of course, but you must come back at night when the food markets are set up. It's a wonder."

I cap my water and place it in my backpack's side pocket. I'm sticky and hot and feel filthy, but I absolutely cannot be alone. Not right now.

"You understand Marrakech is very poor," Amine says as we walk. "Not everyone, but many people. Some families live on," he pauses. "Five euros a day. But you should not over tip. It's bad manners. Some people see Westerners and try to take all their money. Never take the first offer they make."

We walk down an alley with bright, multi-colored Berber rugs hanging overhead and more lining crowed stalls. We turn a corner and pass delicately etched tea sets until popping out onto a wider street teaming with people.

"Stay to the right," Amine reminds me as a scooter nearly runs me over. "And avoid the puddles."

Apparently, people pee in their workshops and throw it out into the street, but Amine has assured me that every night, the souks are cleaned. It doesn't make it seem any more hygienic.

We walk until he abruptly stops and claps his hands. "We are here."

I can't take in the entire square without moving my head from side-to-side. Several football fields could easily fit inside it. The square is oddly vacant of smells, or maybe my nose is fatigued after the stench of leather and delightful spices in the souks. But there are monkeys. And snakes. And throngs and throngs of people. The din of foreign languages blurs together, and I can't make anything out.

"In a few weeks, you won't be able to walk," Amine says. "Too many people."

"Then I came at the right time." If what I'm seeing right now is considered light traffic, I can't begin to imagine what high season is like.

During my tour, Amine disregarded the hordes of Instagrammers posing for the same pictures. He had no qualms stepping through their shot. "They ruin everything," he had said, while still agreeing to take my picture and waiting patiently while I checked them.

"Soon the restaurants in the Square will open." He guides me toward an open expanse and points down. "They will make the restaurants here. See?" He taps metal flaps embedded in the ground. "These are for electricity and gas."

"I'll need to come back."

"Yes, but Mrs. White, it may be best if you are not alone." Amine shakes his bald head. "Marrakech is very safe, but some men..."

I hold up my hand. "I understand."

But I have every intention of coming back with or without a guide. I will not sit in my room, alone with my thoughts, waiting for Pete to text or call me.

"Amine, will you take my picture again?" I hold out my phone.

He's been a good sport despite his obvious disdain for other people's photos. "Maybe over there, by the monkey?"

"Oh, no, Mrs. White." Amine says firmly. "They will demand money."

"I'll pay." I start off toward the men with the monkeys. "Do you think I could hold one?"

Amine nods. "Yes. I'll arrange it." He hurries ahead and speaks animatedly with one of the monkey handlers. After a minute, he motions me forward. "He agrees to twenty dirham for one picture with the monkey."

I smile modestly at the monkey handler, making sure not show my teeth. In some cultures, it's considered overly friendly. "I agree."

"Very well. Stand there." Amine points at a spot next to the monkey handler. "Hold out your arm, and the monkey will sit on it."

I do as I'm instructed, and a monkey wearing a red fez jumps from the handler's shoulder to my bicep. His cool feet dig into my skin, and he cocks his head and studies my face.

"Well, hello there," I say, resisting the urge to pet the monkey. "What's his name?"

"He has no name. He's a monkey." Amine laughs. "Please. I'll take your picture now."

I turn my face so that the monkey and I look directly at each other. Amine walks over with my phone. "Very nice. I think you will like it."

The monkey handler clicks his tongue, and my furry friend hops back onto his shoulder. I take the phone from Amine and study the picture. It's cute and looks like I'm having a conversation with the monkey. Definitely worthy of social media.

"Mrs. White?"

"Yes," I look up from my phone.

"Our tour is done. Would you like me to help you find a taxi back to the hotel?"

My heart sinks. I can't go back. Not yet. It's only four o'clock. "I think I'm going to explore more on my own."

Alarm creeps into Amine's face. "Do you remember what I told you? Do not go down *derbs* – dead ends -- unless you know what is there. Stay on the main streets. And please, never take anyone's first offer. Walk away if you must."

I nod. "Yes, I'll remember."

He bows. "Then Mrs. White, I will say good-bye."

I reach into my crossbody bag and discretely count out my money. "Thank you, Amine," I say handing him the dirham. "I appreciate your help today."

"Thank you." He bows again. "The taxi line is that way. It is easy to find if you are in the Square."

As he melts into the crowd, panic nibbles at me. Now what? My dinner at NOMAD isn't until 8:30, and to be honest, I'm terrified of going into the souks alone – even to find a quiet place to get a drink. I do need to shower off all the grime encrusted on my feet and the sweat that's rolling off me.

I stare across the square, past the monkey handlers and snake charmers and am paralyzed by indecision. What do I want to do? Why can't Pete be here to tell me what our next adventure is?

Oh, right. Because he's a cheating asshole. I sigh loudly. I guess I'll go back to my room and clean up. Plus, the hotel serves wine, and I could really use a glass right now.

I wind my way across the square to the taxi stand. It's not so much a line but rather a group of Moroccan men haggling for passengers without any order.

It's safe, I tell myself. *Act confidently*. I walk up to the first car, and the owner comes running. "*Puis-je vous aider?*"

"*Oui*," I answer.

Another man comes over, and the two speak loudly in Arabic with dramatic hand gestures. Finally, the second man says in English, "This way, I'll take you."

Remembering what Amine said, I ask, "How much?"

"Where are you going?" he asks.

"The Four Seasons."

"Fifty dirham."

I mentally calculate the amount. I think it's about five dollars, but I'm not entirely sure. "*D'accord*," I answer in French. The man leads me toward his car, a dusty, beat-up-looking thing. I slide into the ratty, torn backseat. There are no seatbelts. I try not to think of what that could mean as he steers the car onto the busy street. We zoom past a tall minaret and through traffic circles. Scooters putter next to us. My driver keeps yelling out the window while grinding the car gears.

It's incredibly stressful.

Finally, we arrive at my hotel. I pay the driver and get out, making sure to gather all my belongings. The valet takes my bags and instructs me to pass through the metal detector. I wait as he inspects my backpack and goods.

Once I'm cleared, I pass by the lily ponds, and the door attendant greets me with a hearty, "Welcome back!"

It's a world apart from the souks. The civility and serenity compared to the hustle of the markets are jarring. My shoulders sag, and I meander toward a cushioned chair in the open atrium where I drop my backpack on the ground and take off my crossbody bag. My feet ache now that I'm no longer walking.

"Would you like a drink, or perhaps, a snack?" a soothing voice asks.

I don't have to think here. Every little thing is taken care of for me. It's comfortable.

"Can you bring me the wine list?" I ask.

The hostess nods. When she returns, I scan the menu. "I'll take the Pinot Grigio." It's not something I'd normally drink, but it's so hot that I want something light.

As I wait, I get on the hotel WiFi and open Facebook. The first picture I see is Eve. She's laughing with Kate and Stacey. I hover my finger over the block button, but decide against it. I want her to see my pictures, and she won't if I block her. I continue to scroll, taking special interest in Eve and my friends' posts. I click like on a few, but don't comment. I'm literally stalking them and obsessing, yet I can't stop. I need to see what everyone is doing. Do they miss me? Why hasn't anyone called or texted me? Am I that forgettable?

Maybe they need a reminder that I still exist. I flick open my photo album and click the picture of the monkey and me. The photo is classic, and everyone is going to believe I am having the time of my life. I play with filters before settling on one that makes my hair and skin glow. Then, I post it on Facebook with the caption, "Thank you, Pete, for the best trip ever! Miss you!"

I hit share and regret immediately washes over me. Was my caption too much? Should I have posted the picture with just the date and place? Maybe I should edit it?

But then the likes and comments start.

"Oh my God! Jealous!"

"Best husband ever!"

"You look so pretty!"

I do look pretty. And happy – that's the most important thing: that I look happy.

Needing more validation, I post the same picture to Instagram, only this time, I caption it, "Had an amazing time in the souks today. Met this little guy. Going to NOMAD for dinner tonight. I'll let you lovelies know how it is." I hashtag it with every Marrakech and travel tag I can think of and hit share. The most successful Instagrammers use the platform like a micro-blog, and if I'm strategic and grow my followers during this trip, I may hit influencer status.

As I stare at my phone, waiting for comments, Pete's smiling face flashes across the screen. He must have seen the picture. Good.

"Hello?" My voice waivers, and I don't sound confident. Not at all.

"Vee, sweetheart, we need to talk." Pete's voice is scratchy, like he's been smoking, which he absolutely doesn't do. Or does he? I don't know him as well as I thought.

I shift the phone so that it's closer to my mouth. "I'm listening."

"I'm sorry," he says. "I'm so sorry. I didn't mean for any of this to happen."

I pause, waiting for something more, but when he doesn't offer anything else, I say, "Well, that's a start."

"Come home," Pete says.

The waitress sets my wine on the glass side table. I'm very aware that I'm sitting out in the open and having an emotionally-charged conversation with my unfaithful husband.

"I don't feel like it. Marrakech is amazing." I lift my wineglass and sip. A sense of cold calm settles over me. I am not a hysterical woman, and I'm not going to break down.

"Everyone thinks we're divorcing."

My heart quivers. "Are we?"

"We don't have to." Desperation seeps from his words. "I don't want to."

"Then why did you do this?" My voice catches. I will not cry. "If you're so happy with me and our marriage, why did you cheat?"

"Do you want me to come to you?" Pete asks, ignoring my questions.

"Yes," I choke out before I can stop myself. So much for being collected. "I didn't think I wanted to see you, but I do."

There's an awkward silence.

"Are you going to come?" My pulses races. If he says no, what does that mean?

"I can, but I need money if I'm going to buy a ticket."

It's a gut punch. My voice ticks up into an angry whisper. "Is that why you called? You want my money?"

"Vee, I need to see you. I want to work this out." Pete keeps his voice level and calm while ignoring my accusations.

A tear slips down my cheek. "How is this going to work? You humiliated me. You threw me away. Everyone knows. Everyone."

"I know, and I'm sorry. It shouldn't have happened like that," Pete says.

"It shouldn't have happened at all!" Pete doesn't say anything. "Are you still there?" I ask.

"Give me the money, and I'll come."

Anger bubbles inside me. "You can't figure it out on your own? You really need my money? Is that the only thing I'm good for?"

"I didn't say that." Pete speaks louder now, which means he's agitated. "Stop putting words in my mouth."

I bristle. "Why are you upset with me? I haven't done anything wrong."

Pete blows into the phone. "You're being irrational. I can't talk to you when you're like this."

I grit my teeth. "Don't bother coming. I don't want to see you."

Before I can change my mind, I hang up and drop my phone on the cushion next to me. I cover my face with my hands while taking a deep breath. I'll be damned if he's going to make this my fault.

5

The medina's streets and alleys are dizzying, but even more so in the settling dusk. My driver dropped me off as close as he could to NOMAD, but I have to make the rest of the trek by foot, and my GPS doesn't work in the labyrinth of souks, riads, and restaurants.

The hotel concierge printed directions for me, but I'm hopelessly confused and have backtracked three times already. Remembering what Amine told me – to never ask directions from a random shop keeper or a "helper" who roams the streets preying on tourists – I pop into the first restaurant I see. I do feel bad asking where NOMAD is, but they kindly point me in the right direction. To my relief, once I turn the corner, there are arrows painted on the wall directing me the rest of the way.

Like all other restaurants in Marrakech, a well-dressed man stands outside the door, encouraging would-be patrons inside. He's clean shaven with light eyes. Moroccans are fairer than I expected, more like those who dwell along the Mediterranean, and could easily pass for Spanish or Italian.

"Would you like to taste the most delicious food in all of Marrakech?" the man says to me in perfect English.

I step closer to him, but not so close as to be immodest. "I have a reservation."

The man motions me inside. "Please. They will help you at the desk."

NOMAD isn't as large as I thought it would be. The waitress leads me through a tiny, crowded dining room to a staircase. The scent of unidentifiable spices chases after me until we reach the rooftop, and the fresh Marrakech air blows it away.

A 360-degree view of the sun setting over the city greets me. The tall minaret I pass to and from the medina dominates the skyline, and the uneven, red rooftops of Marrakech stretch out in every direction. It's that hazy, purple time, right before dark, when the city lights glow dimly against the sky.

The hostess shows me to a corner seat, and I settle into the dozen brightly woven pillows that line the banquette. "The menu," she says, producing a small, narrow piece of paper. "Your waiter will be with you in a moment."

The postage stamp-size space holds thirty people or so and has an absolutely beautiful view. I glance at my fellow diners. There's a large, rowdy party on the other side of a low partition and a few couples lost in conversation nearer to me. Next to me on the banquette, a young man reads a book.

I stealthily observe him by pretending to take a selfie, but really, I'm checking out the young man. He has the faint stubble of a beard and floppy, light brown hair – like he hasn't had a haircut in weeks. His sunglasses sit low on his nose, and he wears a plain, faded green t-shirt and jeans with man sandals. There is only one set of silverware, so like me, he's alone.

I wonder what his story is? How did he end up on a rooftop restaurant in Marrakech, dining solo?

The waiter places water and bread in front of me, and I look up, but the waiter has already walked away without asking if I need anything. I frown. I hope the questionable service isn't an indicator of the food.

I creep my fingers toward the bread and stealthily tear off a piece like I'm doing something wrong. Normally, I don't eat carbs, but the bread smells delicious, and I need nourishment beyond wine and the handful of nuts I picked at during happy hour. I nibble off a corner of the doughy, yet crusty flatbread, and my taste buds sing.

I flip my phone over and study the photo of the young man. It's a great picture even if it's only a profile shot. He's completely lost in his book, unaware of anything around him and comfortable, like he doesn't find eating alone at all strange. I don't have that luxury. Sitting here by myself only adds to the constant pounding in my chest. I'm alone because my husband cheated on me, and not one of my friends has reached out to see if I'm okay.

I sigh, the sound covered up by the large party's raucous laughter. The waiter spies me and looks away. I stare at him until he glances at me again. I wave him over.

"Are you ready to order?" Outside of America, no one hurries you through your meal. Waiters don't depend on tips, so you can take your time and sit for hours, and I plan on doing exactly that so that I stay out of my room as long as possible.

"Just a drink." I scan the menu. Since the restaurant doesn't serve alcohol, I settle for a Coke - not even Diet, just a regular old, made-with-real-sugar Coke. "Can you give me a few more minutes to decide on my entrée?"

"Of course."

Next to me, the young man's food arrives. He stops reading and takes off his sunglasses. He dog-ears the page and sets the book next to him on the bench. I would never abuse a book in that manner, but to each their own.

"Thank you. It smells delicious," he says in a flat Midwest American accent. Interesting. I would have sworn he was from the West Coast with his laid-back, educated-surfer look.

His food looks delicious. I scan the menu. He must be having the Moroccan Gazpacho. When I lift my head, he catches me watching him as he slurps the soup, and I quickly turn away.

"It's excellent," he says in a friendly, conversational way. "I highly recommend it."

"It does look good," I answer and give my small talk smile. He caught me staring, and there's no shame in that. I was ogling the food, not him, after all.

The young man nods. "This is my third time eating here, and every time I try something new, but this," he pauses dramatically, "this is by far my favorite appetizer. Whoever thought to put melon in gazpacho? Genius."

"What else have you had?" I want to keep the conversation going. "I'm having a hard time deciding."

"The lamb shank and Spring chicken are both amazing, but I prefer the lamb."

I frown at the menu. "Those do sound good."

The man goes back to eating the gazpacho, and I stare out at the skyline. Lights dance below us, like little fires – which they very well may be. This is the perfect photo spot, so I snap a few selfies.

"Do you want me to take one of you?" the young man asks.

I hold out my phone. "That would be great."

He takes it, and I kneel on the banquette so that my arm rests on the top of the railing. "Turn your head a little this way," he says. "Look more at the camera."

Ah. He knows how to take a good picture. Very nice. I smile at the camera, and he fires off a few shots.

"Let me know what you think. I can take more if you want." He hands the phone back before taking his seat.

I swipe through the pictures. "These are great," I say, hoping I sound thankful and not like a desperate housewife. "You have an eye for photography."

"Well, I guess it's a skill you acquire after traveling around the world for a year." He sticks out his hand. "I'm Oz, by the way."

"Veronica."

"It's nice to meet you, Veronica." He sips from a glass of lemon water. "What brings you to Marrakech?"

I purse my lips. I haven't thought of my story yet. Do I blurt out the truth, or make myself seem interesting? "I spontaneously decided to come."

The left corner of Oz's mouth ticks up. "What exactly does spontaneous mean, if it's okay to ask?"

"Oh, it's fine." I wave my hand like it's no big deal. "I drove to the airport and bought the first ticket on the first airline I saw."

Oz's brown eyes grow wide. "That's some story."

I nod, content that I haven't lied and created exactly the right amount of mystique. "How about you?"

The waiter interrupts us. "I saw you waving. Are you ready to order?"

"Oh! Yes." I check the menu again, like I forgot what I wanted. I may have eaten the bread and had a Coke, but that means I can't go wild. "I'll have the lamb shank and cauliflower."

He scribbles my order on a well-worn notepad. "Do you need another drink?"

"No. I'm good." Too much soda will bloat me, and I hate feeling bloated. "But a bottle of water with a lemon would be nice."

When he walks away, Oz leans closer to me and says, "I'm traveling the world."

"Interesting." I study him again. There's a navy backpack at his feet, and a black hardback notebook on the table under his book. I can't see what he was reading because of how he's positioned it, but it looks well-loved. "Have you been anywhere interesting?"

"I have." A big, lopsided smile shows off years of orthodontia work. "Would you like to hear about it?"

"Sure."

He leans back into the throw pillows. "I started backward because I'm chasing Summer. I went to New Zealand and Australia, then up to Asia. I came from Tanzania, and before that I was in Dubai and Egypt."

I raise my eyebrows. "I'm impressed. You're doing it alone?"

"I am." He pushes his empty bowl away. "How long are you here?"

"I have no idea." I shrug. "I bought a one-way ticket."

"That's great!" Oz lifts his water glass. "Here's to adventure!"

"To adventure," I say, clinking his glass.

We chat until my food arrives. The tantalizing scent reminds me of how little I've eaten over the past several days, but try as I might, I can't stomach more than a few bites. Oz, meanwhile, works his way through a giant piece of cardamom orange ginger cake. When he's finished, he looks over at me.

"Hey, Veronica?"

"Yeah?"

"I met some people at my riad, and we're four-wheeling in the desert tomorrow. Want to come?"

Is he flirting, or just being nice? No. I'm much too old for him. He's being nice. "I'd love to. What time?"

"The bus leaves at 8am from the Square. You can meet us by the taxi stand." He picks up his bill before counting out some cash and setting it on the table. His waitress swoops over and takes it. "I think it'll be fun."

I nod, but I wonder if my heartbreak shows. Is that why he's being kind to me? "I can't wait!" I say, forcing enthusiasm into my voice. "Is there anything I need to do?"

"The tour guide said to wear pants and light-weight long sleeves."

The waitress returns with Oz's change, and he shoves it into a worn, leather wallet. He takes a pen from his backpack and tears a piece of paper from his notebook. "Message me through WhatsApp if you need anything. Here's the phone number for my account."

I have no idea what WhatsApp is. "I'm staying at the Four Seasons. Veronica White."

Oz's eyebrows tick up. "I thought for sure you were staying at La Mamounia, but the Four Season is pretty swanky, too."

"La Mamounia was full," I say without irony. "And I couldn't find a decent riad on such short notice."

He chuckles. "I should get your cell number so I can message you if things change."

I don't want to sound old and out of touch not knowing how WhatsApp works, so I take the pen and notebook he offers and scrawl my number on it. My data bill is going to be insane.

"Well, I guess I'll see you tomorrow morning at the taxi stand." He collects his things. "It was great meeting you."

"You, too."

His tall, lanky frame towers over my table. He must be about 6'1" and still growing into his body. Pete was like that until he hit thirty, then he suddenly lost the awkward gangliness of youth. Oz gives me one last smile before disappearing down the spiral staircase and into the belly of the restaurant, leaving me to myself again.

I sit back and stare at his contact info. Guess I'll be downloading WhatsApp.

My alarm bleats at 5:35am, but as tempted as I am to turn it off, nervous excitement courses through me. Am I completely insane to spend the day four-wheeling with complete strangers? Probably.

Last night, I downloaded WhatsApp. I open it, but there are no messages. My excitement wanes a little, but Oz didn't seem like the kind to invite someone on an outing and ditch them.

I shower and do my makeup, taking care to slather my body in sunblock. I only have jeans and white linen pants, so I choose the jeans. I'm going to roast, but it's better than getting sunburned. I button my loose linen top and slip on tennis shoes, then I gather my hair into a low ponytail and head to breakfast.

The sun sits low, and orange streaks the sky. I take my breakfast on the patio again, but this time, I have a slight appetite and nibble on a chocolate croissant. Delicious mint tea tops off the meal. At 7:30, I make my way to the valet and negotiate a ride to the medina.

For a Thursday morning, the streets are surprisingly empty.

Maybe Moroccans sleep in and start their day later than Americans? My driver breezes through the traffic circles and past the minaret whose name I still don't know and deposits me at the near-empty taxi stand.

Oz stands a little way down the sidewalk with a group of twenty-somethings. Doubt rears its head. I'm definitely too old to be with them. They're around my kids' ages, and my kids never want to spend time with me anymore.

"Veronica!" Oz shouts, spying me before I can run away.

Despite my misgivings, I walk over to him and his group. There are two young women and a slightly older man. Standing with them, Oz seems older than I previously thought.

"You made it." His smile is somehow both charming and mischievous. How many women have fallen for him?

"Of course!" I answer. "I never turn down an invite." I size up my new companions. "Hi," I say, extending my hand to the young woman nearest me. "I'm Veronica."

Amusement dances across her face. Great. I was right. I am the old lady of the group, and they don't want me.

"Taylor," she says with a healthy dose of vocal fry. "And this is Emmy and Grant."

I shake everyone's hands. "Thanks for letting me tag along."

Grant nods. He's on the shorter side and shaped like a square, but he has lovely, deep-set green eyes. "We didn't get much choice."

"The more the merrier!" Oz says, obviously trying to smooth out the situation. "And besides, the first rule of solo traveling is that you look out for others."

Wonderful, I'm old and a charity case. I turn to Taylor. "Are you all traveling alone?"

"No." She plays with her long, pink-streaked hair. "Emmy and I are only here for the week. What about you? Oz said you're in Marrakech for a while."

"I'm on my first solo trip," I say.

Emmy shrugs. "I guess there's a first time for everything."

Normally, I would bite back with a stinging remark, but I don't have it in me. Besides, who fights with children?

A black Mercedes van pulls up to the curb, and Oz greets the driver. After confirming that he is indeed taking our motley crew to the desert, the driver opens the sliding door, and we pile in: Taylor, Grant, and Emmy in the back and Oz and me in the middle row. The girls chatter between themselves in their annoying uptalk, and every once in a while, Oz rolls his eyes at me. Grant doesn't make a sound.

The desert sits on the outskirts of Marrakech, and it takes nearly an hour to get there. We pass impoverished developments and gated communities; camels and mopeds; and acres of roses. Finally, a grove of palm trees appears, and the driver turns down a narrow, dusty road. He stops in front of a ramshackle, thatched shack surrounded by dirty ATVs.

"Wow," Taylor says sarcastically. "They really go all out, don't they?"

I raise my eyebrows. "It's the desert, and we're on an adventure. Par for the course."

"I like your attitude," Oz says.

"I'm trying." I exit the van and wait for the others to climb out. A tall man who may or may not be the owner rushes forward. He's wearing a backward New York Yankees baseball cap and a *djellabah* – which I learned from Amine is not a called a kaftan when worn by a man.

"Five?" he says, counting us. A frown forms on his lips. "The reservation is for four."

Oz flashes his disarming smile. "What's one more? A little extra money in your pocket?"

This seems to appease the man. "Very well. Give me a moment to prepare another vehicle."

While we wait, Oz and I try to engage Grant in conversation, but either he's the silent type or a mass murderer. I can't quite tell yet.

The merciless early morning sun beats on me, and I move closer to the shack so that I'm in the tiny sliver of shade it casts. Emmy and

Taylor pose next to the ATVs, snapping pictures. They must not have gotten the memo about appropriate clothing, because they both have on tiny jean shorts and crop tops. It's travelers like them – and their complete disregard of cultural norms - that give Americans a bad reputation.

Oz wanders over to me and turns his back on the others. He gives me a conspiratorial look. "Okay," he whispers. "I may have invited you so that I wasn't alone with them."

I chuckle, and our companions stare at me.

"Are you laughing at us?" Taylor says, pouting out her bottom lip. "Because if you are, you shouldn't."

Oh. Poor thing. She's trying to act vicious. Little does she know. "Why would I laugh at you?"

Taylor scowls. "I don't know. Because you're, like, my mom's age."

I'm sure she means it as an insult, but I shrug it away. "And you act like my bratty nineteen-year-old daughter, so I guess we'll get along well."

She huffs. "Whatever."

Grant has wondered off to inspect the ATVs, and the girls join him. When they're out of earshot, Oz leans close to me, giving me a whiff of his shampoo. "Hey, I'm sorry. I thought they were cooler than this, but I guess my judge of character is off."

"I wouldn't go that far," I tease. "You still chose me, after all." Oh, no. Was that too flirty? I hope he doesn't take it as flirty because I'm completely not flirting with someone his age.

Oz holds out his fist, and I bump it. "We older solo travelers need to stick together."

I stick out my tongue. "Seriously? You are what, maybe thirty?"

Oz pretends he's straightening a tie. "Actually, dear Veronica," he says in an imitation of a stuffy British accent, "I'm one hundred and three and wonderfully preserved."

He does not ask how old I am, which I appreciate. Not that I have an issue with my age...okay, yes. I do. I totally do. Most days I feel as if I'm still in my twenties, but I've aged. My skin isn't as elastic, and my hair isn't as thick as it was. I spend a fortune on Botox and fillers and peels, and I exercise like crazy to keep my figure. And none of it prevented Pete from cheating with the "younger model."

My heart pounds, and my throat goes dry. Damn it. I will not cry. I'm here to have fun.

"Veronica?"

I plaster on a smile. "Seriously, though, you're not a vampire, right?"

Oz shakes his head. "No. I'm thirty-three, which makes me ten years older than Tay-Tay and Emmy, and in their eyes, positively ancient."

"At least you're not their mothers' ages." I cross my arms.

The baseball cap wearing attendant motions us over to the ATVs. When we're all assembled, he goes over basic operating and safety instructions. Our ride takes us through the canyon to a waterfall where we'll have a traditional Berber lunch before returning back here.

"How long are we doing this?" I whisper. I really should have asked earlier, but it never occurred to me that we'd be gone for more than two hours.

"Five hours roundtrip." Oz turns his head toward me. "Do you have somewhere you need to be?"

"No. I'm completely free." Saying it out loud sounds so final, but there's nothing holding me to this earth except a desire to go on. In this iteration of my life, I'm no longer a mother, a wife, or a member of the so-called Bitch Brigade. I'm free-spirited, solo-traveler Veronica, and I'm fine with that.

We mount our ATVs and set-off for the mouth of the canyon. We pass through gorgeous red rock formations, lush green spaces, and tiny creeks that must be rushing rivers after the winter mountain snow melts. When we come across goats grazing next to a small stream in a gorge, I stop. Since Oz is behind me, he stops also.

I remove my helmet. "It's pretty, and I kind of want to pet the goats."

"Do you think that's wise?" Oz asks. His brown eyes hold concern, and he crinkles his forehead.

"I've been to a petting zoo." I climb off my ATV and place my helmet on the seat. "It can't be much different."

Oz follows my lead, and we approach the goats slowly. Grant, Emmy, and Taylor have disappeared from sight, which doesn't bother me at all, and Oz seems okay with losing them as well.

The goats bleat as we approach, but go back to eating the meager grass lining the stream. I spy a cute baby one and walk over to it. Another goat, maybe it's mother, lifts its head, but doesn't come near me. I turn toward Oz. "Can you snap a picture?"

"Sure." Oz takes out his phone. "Stand a little to the left so that I can get the canyon wall behind you."

I scooch over and crouch next to the baby goat. It ignores me. "How's this?"

"Perfect." Oz holds up his phone and takes a few pictures. "I think they're good."

"Come over here. I want to see them. " I beckon him toward me.

He holds out the phone, and I take it. "These are so cute!" I hand the phone back. "You need to send them to me." The baby goat nudges me, and I reach down to pet it. "We should get a selfie."

Oz shakes his head. "I'm not really into being the subject of pictures. Much rather take them."

"Oh, c'mon! Just one?" I bat my eyes and pout. "Please?"

He laughs. "How can I say no to that?" He gets on the other side of the goat. "What should I do?"

I take out my camera. "I'll take the picture. Make sure you're in the frame." We kneel next to the goat, and I shift so that all three of us are on the screen. When I hit the button, the goat headbutts Oz, and he topples over onto the dusty ground.

"Hey!" I say to the naughty goat. "That wasn't nice."

Oz laughs. "Did you get the picture?"

I touch the phone screen. The photo is cute, even if you can't fully see Oz's face because he's looking away. Definitely Facebook worthy. Pete's going to wonder who exactly I'm with, which gives me a small tickle of satisfaction.

"It's perfect," I say, holding it out to him as I dust myself off with my other hand. I point toward the other end of the gorge. "Should we find the rest of our group?"

Oz shrugs. "Do you want to?"

"Not really. Taylor is a bit of a brat, and Grant may be a serial killer." I pause. "Please tell me they're not your close friends."

"No. Like I said, I meet them at my riad, and I'll probably never speak to them again." He mounts his ATV, pushes back his hair, and puts his helmet back on. "But you, Veronica," he points at me. "I think we're going to be great friends."

6

For three long days, I've waited in Marrakech for Pete to make a grand gesture. Three days. It's plenty of time for him to pull himself together and find a way here. I guess I shouldn't be too surprised, I hung up on him after all, but damn it, he needs to make some effort. He needs to show me that our marriage matters beyond telling me that he wants me to come home. Can't he at least do that?

I shrug out of my clothes and place them in the polished wooden locker. After my ATV adventure yesterday and the medina on Wednesday, I really need a me day. I've booked my first-ever hammam and plan on sitting next to the pool for the rest of the day.

As I wait for my appointment, I lounge in a white terry cloth robe next to the splash pool. I left my phone in the locker and feel jittery without it. What if Pete calls when I'm offline? Then what? Would he leave a message?

My chest tightens. *Push it away, Veronica. Push it all away.*

"Mrs. White?" The attendant calls my name, and I stand and follow her down a marble hallway to a beautifully-tiled, private sauna.

I begin sliding off the rubber sandals the front desk gave me, but the woman stops me. "You'll burn your feet," she says in a husky voice. "Put your robe here." She points at a coat hook on the back of the door. "Leave your slippers on."

A small hole in the floor spews steam along the back of the 10x10 room. Heavy, humid air surrounds me, and each breath is a struggle.

"First time having hammam?" the woman asks. She hasn't given me a name, and it seems weirdly normal that I would strip down naked before her.

"Yes," I say, turning around, showing off my very exposed self. "It's hot."

"Just wait." She arranges a towel on a marble table that runs along the left wall and pats it. "Now you steam."

I am completely naked, but she seems unbothered by it, so I relax and climb onto the table. She looks at me strangely. "Lay down."

"Oh, right." I stretch out on the table. A week ago, I never would have thought I'd be lying naked in a hammam with a strange woman. No, I would have wagered that I'd be having drinks with Stacey or maybe even Kate. We'd dissect life in Waterford and pass judgement on those who had committed sins. There would be parties and fun and drinks...

"Wait five minutes," the woman says before disappearing through the heavy, wooden door.

All those hot yoga classes must have paid off because even though it's boiling hot in the room, I'm now able to breathe deeply, and my mind feels clearer despite not feeling at all calm. If Eve or Pete were anywhere in my vicinity, I'd probably throw a right hook at them.

Maybe it's a good thing I ran away because I'd most likely be in jail for assault.

The door swings open, and the woman reappears. "Stand here."

I move closer to the steam-spewing hole, and she dips a bucket into it. Before the horror of what she's about to do hits me, she dumps the entire thing over my head. It's burning hot, and I sputter as I push my dripping hair out of my face.

"Oh my God!"

The woman laughs. "Now I scrub. Get rid of the dead skin. When I am done, you will feel like a baby." She has a bar of black soap and a mitt. She points at me. "Turn around."

I do as I'm told, and she roughly exfoliates my shoulders and back with what feels like sandpaper before spinning me around and scrubbing down my front. When she really gets up between my legs, I stand still like it's no big deal that she's closer to my private area than anyone but Pete has ever been.

I close my eyes as she works, and I let the hot air surround me. I flutter my eyes open when she stops scrubbing. She has the bucket again, and this time, I'm prepared.

"Jesus!" The ice cold water shocks me. "You need to warn me!"

The sadistic woman laughs. "Please, follow me."

I nervously put on my robe and follow her into the hallway. First hot water, then sandpaper, followed by ice cold water. What wonderful thing is next?

She leads me into a smaller room. This time, a towel is already stretched over the marble table. It's not as hot as the other room, and there's a shower. She positions me on the table, slathers some sort of clay mask all over my body and places towels over me.

"You wait," she says before leaving.

I try laying still, but my brain is too chaotic. The thing that upsets me most is that by posting amazing pictures, I'm making things easier for Pete at home. After all, if it seems like I've forgiven him, why shouldn't everyone else?

And that's the thing: I have to forgive him – at least publicly. I have to pretend it never happened. I clench my hands open and close as I consider my shitty situation. If I don't pretend, it becomes an even bigger thing.

The door creaks open. "You're ready now."

I turn my head to better look at the attendant. Thank God she came back. I need distraction. I eye her suspiciously. Getting the clay off is going to require another blast of water. Whether it's hot or cold is anyone's guess, so I'll prepare myself for both.

She removes the towels and helps me off the table before leading me to the hand-held shower. "We clean you."

She aims pleasantly warm water at me and uses her free hand to remove the clay. When she's done, she squirts a blob of shampoo into her hand and scrubs my head. "So pretty," she says as she rubs the ends of my hair. "Like straw."

Normally, if someone told me my hair looked like straw, I'd be offended, but I think in Morocco, it's a good thing. After she rinses me, she says, "We are finished. You can use the hot tub or splash pool if you'd like."

I don't dare tell her that I feel a little violated, and the last thing I want to do is lounge naked with other women. "I think I'll change into my clothes."

"All new," she says, running her hand over my arm.

If only it were that easy to scrub off my old life and rid myself of memories of Pete.

I touch my arm. It's like silk. "I'm so soft!"

She nods. "Like a baby."

After I put my robe on, she leads me back into the hallway past the splash pool and to the locker room. Several other women stand in various states of undress, and not one looks at me as I change. No one ogles my amazing body or casts furtive, envious glances. I'm simply another middle-aged woman getting a hammam.

This must be what if feels like to be invisible.

There are two pools at the Four Seasons: the adult pool and the family pool, and there is no way in hell that I'm going anywhere near the family pool. The last thing I want is shrieks and splashes while I'm trying to be Zen, so I veer to the left, toward the more serene area.

A beautiful blue mosaic lines the bottom of the adult pool, and dozens of empty sun loungers surround the perimeter. Toward the far end, there is a covered restaurant, and to my right, a pool hut selling sunblock and other necessities.

The pool boy rushes toward me. "Would you like a bed?"

"Yes. Something with an umbrella."

The pool isn't overly busy, and he easily finds me a front row lounger. I wait while he arranges my towel and adjusts the umbrella.

"This is the menu," he says, handing me a laminated paper. "I will bring water for you."

I toss the menu to the end of the chair and strip off my Trina Turk cover-up, exposing my sleek, white one-piece suit with a plunging neckline. Since I didn't know where I was headed when I ran away, I packed this modest suit and a skimpy bikini, and looking around the pool, it was the right call. I normally wouldn't wear this in Waterford as I instead stick to string bikinis. But here it feels just right, in an Old Hollywood way.

The pool boy returns with a soft-sided cooler. He opens it. "Your water." There are six glass bottles of Vittel inside. Fancy, fancy. "Please let me know if you need anything else."

When I was young, my family spent two weeks every summer in the south of France, soaking up the sun on the pebbled beaches. My favorite memories involve my dad and mom drinking champagne at a private beach in Nice. I would lounge the day away eating strawberries and ordering soft drink after soft drink until the sun set. This reminds me a little of back then.

My parents. I haven't spoken to them in a week, and I'm sure they're wondering why. Neither have social media, so unless Pete's told them what's happened, they're blissfully in the dark. My heart sinks. I've never told them about my marriage problems, and they love Pete like a son – which he is since I'm an only child.

Reluctantly, I take my phone from the straw tote I bought in the souks the other day, and it rests heavy in my hand. If I can't confide in my parents, who can I tell?

But how do I tell them Pete's a philandering jerk?

With a deep breath, I call my mom's cell. She picks up after three rings.

"Hello, sweetheart! It's early for you isn't it?"

"Hi, Mom. And no, it isn't. I'm actually in Morocco." My pulse races. Disappointing my parents wrecks me, which is why I keep my marriage issues private.

"Oh?" Surprise oozes from Mom's voice. "Is Pete on a new assignment? I don't remember you mentioning it."

"No. I'm alone. Pete's back in Waterford. We're having some problems." My words tumble out in a long, breathy sequence.

"Problems?"

"He..." How do I say this without ruining my mom's perfect image of us. There's no way. "He had an affair, and I left."

Silence. Long, empty silence.

A sob erupts from the other end of the phone. "Are you sure?" Mom asks. "Are you positively sure?"

"Yes," I whisper while keeping my own tears in check. I can't cry in public. "He confirmed it."

"Are you divorcing?" Mom asks, her voice trembling. "Tell me you're not. It will break your Dad's heart."

And this is exactly why I've put up with Pete's less-than-perfect behavior all this time: I can't disappoint my parents. They've been married for fifty years and believe divorce is an easy out.

"No," I say. "We're not divorcing. I'm taking some time to collect myself."

Mom blows into the phone. "Good. That's good, Veronica. Your marriage can bounce back from this if you both work at it."

Too bad I'm the only one working on it. "Mom?"

"Yes?"

"Don't tell Dad. If Pete and I work this out, I don't want him knowing."

"I won't. He doesn't need the stress right now, and you know how much he loves Pete and you." She pauses. "How long are you planning on staying gone? I know the kids aren't home this summer, but don't you think you should be with Pete if you want to fix this?"

I fidget with latch of the cooler. "I don't know yet. I'm still too angry to really talk to him."

"You need to go home soon, Veronica. The sooner the better. This is salvageable."

"I know." My shoulders fall. My mom has confirmed my suspicions: she is 100 percent in favor of me staying with Pete. If I don't, she and Dad will be devastated. "I have to run. I'll talk to you soon, okay?"

"I love you, Sweetheart. Hang in there and call as much as you need."

"I love you, too. Thank you."

"Bye."

I hang up and stare at the underside of the white umbrella shading me. All my life I've done exactly what my parents have wanted. I went to the University of Virginia and got my MBA like Dad dreamed. I married the man they loved. I had two kids and stayed home because Mom said it would be best. I've lived my life by their expectations. Will it ever end?

Needing distraction, I take a magazine from my bag and mindlessly flip through it. Because my messy brain can't concentrate long enough to read even one article, I check my Instagram feed. But my heart isn't in it this morning, and I can't bring myself to think of any worthwhile comments, so I only like a bunch of things.

I flick the screen and check the time. It's 8am at home. I could call Pete, but then what? What exactly do I say? All is forgiven? Because it's not. Not even close. But Mom expects me to make more of an effort – she made that clear -- and honestly, I miss Pete with the deepest ache my heart has ever experienced. A slice of my soul has been torn out, and I have no idea how to repair it when he's unwilling to work with me.

Against all reason, I open Facebook, where I know I'll see Eve, and begin scrolling. I don't know why I insist on picking this scab and hurting myself, but I can't not look. I immediately regret my decision.

Picture after picture of my so-called friends flash across the screen. They're all having fun, and not one, not a single one, has reached out to me. Out of sight, out of mind, I guess. I should have expected that; it happened with Karen and Alexis, and of course, to Elizabeth. Once you leave Waterford, you cease to exist.

Or do you? Maybe that's when you're given your freedom, and you never look back.

I'm about to put my phone aside, when I see it: a picture of Pete with Mike, Eve's husband. The two of them smile at the camera and hold up beers.

What the actual fuck?

My stomach rolls as I read the comments. Eve had a party and invited Pete? After publicly announcing their affair? And Mike is okay with it? What the hell is wrong with these people?

Have I even crossed their minds? Is it really like Pete said? Has everyone moved on to a newer scandal, and I can come home and go back to how it all was? Can Pete and I simply kiss and make up and sweep the whole situation away?

Mom would like that.

Tears sit in the corners of my eyes, and I try to blink them away, but the stubborn bastards roll down my cheeks. I reach under my sunglasses and wipe at them. I absolutely cannot cry in public, not after my outburst in the lobby yesterday. In fact, I shouldn't be crying at all with the way Pete is ignoring me. He's sending a clear signal.

I stretch out on the lounger and hold my phone above my face, so that I'm looking directly at it. I wrap my fingers around the PopSocket and use my free hand to scroll. So many damn pictures. Pete's in the background of many of them, and I study them like an FBI agent looking for clues.

No wonder he hasn't called – he's been too busy having fun.

Well, I'll show all of them.

I roll onto my stomach and prop on my elbows so that I can still see my phone. I find the photo of Oz and me with the goat and edit it. It's a great picture, and I look happy. That's what's most important, that I look happy even if I'm not. It also helps that Oz is attractive even if you can't fully see his face. Not exactly my type, but attractive, and the women of Waterford will salivate over him.

I carefully craft my message: *Who's cuter: the goat or the guy? Having a blast in Marrakech!*

Pete doesn't have social media, at least not officially, but I know for a fact that he has secret accounts that he uses to spy on me, and I hope to God he sees this and feels as awful as I do.

I post and wait. Nothing.

I try refreshing my feed. One like. From Stacey. Okay, it's a start.

I have 1,143 friends stretched around the world. It may only be 8am in Waterford, but it's afternoon in Europe and maybe tomorrow in Asia. Someone has to be up to see my post. All I need is a few likes and comments to get it pushed up in people's feeds. If that happens, there's no way that Eve won't see it. And she'll tell everyone – including Pete.

But what if Pete takes it as meaning I'm done with him? What if he thinks I've moved on?

Okay, isn't that what I want? For him to feel as miserable as I do?

I try wasting a few minutes flipping through my celebrity trash magazine until I absolutely need to know if anyone else has commented.

Twenty-two likes and three comments, and not one – other than Stacey – are from my so-called Waterford friends.

Well, fuck it.

I pull up Google flights on my web browser. If they can't remember me, I'm going to make them. I'm going back to Waterford and show all those bitches just who is boss. And I'll show Pete and Eve too. Like Mom implied, I've already been gone too long.

As I plug in my return date, a message from Oz pops up on my screen. I swipe it away and study the flights. I could leave tomorrow morning and be back in Waterford by tomorrow night. I hover my finger over the 'select' button.

Oz's message pops up again.

--Hey Veronica, I'm headed to Bo Zin tonight. Want to come?--

I have no idea what Bo Zin is, but it sounds infinitely better than sitting around my hotel driving myself crazy while waiting for my flight.

--Sure. What time?--

I stare at the screen, trying to decide if I want to buy the ticket or not. What's my end game? To fix my marriage and preserve my dignity while making Pete beg for forgiveness? Or am I only doing this because it's what's expected of me?

--8pm-- flashes on my screen. *--Want me to pick you up or meet there?--*

--Meet you there--.

--Awesome. I'll make a reservation. See you at 8. No Tay-Tay this time.--

The brilliant afternoon sun has shifted, and the umbrella's shadow no longer covers me. It's damn hot. I wave at the pool boy. "Can you move the umbrella?"

"Of course."

While he does that, I dip into the pool. A seat runs inside the edge, and I immerse myself. The cool water is a welcome respite from the heat. Across the pool, a young couple takes turns rubbing sunblock on one another. The woman is stunning. She has those Middle Eastern good looks that I would die for: silky, dark hair; gorgeous skin; and a willowy frame. Her bathing suit looks designer – maybe Chanel? I'm not close enough to see if the interlocking C's grace the suit.

The man she's with is clean shaven and lean. He's overly attentive, doting on her. They could be on their honeymoon, or they could very well be illicit lovers.

God, why do I keep going there?

I get out of the pool and return to my lounger. The shade once again covers it. I retrieve a water from the cooler and glance at my phone and the flight info. I am not an indecisive person, but I can't figure out what to do. Not even talking to Mom helped.

I put my wide brim sunhat on and sink lower on my chair.

I'll get the ticket. I can always change my mind later.

Bo Zin is a nightclub. Or maybe it's a restaurant. It's not exactly Asian, but it isn't Moroccan either. It's a fabulous mash-up, and I positively love it.

Oz and I sit at the corner of the sleek, well-stocked bar, people watching and making up stories about the other patrons. A DJ spins from behind the bar, and music thumps around us. Dining tables and low couches create an intimate atmosphere for a mix of British tourists and locals. Paper lanterns sway over head and candles flicker around the open floor plan. Beyond the French doors is a dining garden with cacti and a fire pit.

Unlike the rest of Marrakech, short skirts, bare shoulders, and gorgeous kaftan-wearing women sit at the same table. Everyone, every single person, is well-coifed and polished.

It's like stepping into a well-curated Instagram feed.

Oz lifts his old-fashioned and holds it out to me. Pete drinks old-fashioneds with the best whiskey available; Oz drinks his with what he can afford.

"To new friendships, adventure, and living out loud," he says.

I barely know this man, and yet, somehow, he has a way of saying what I need to hear. I clink his glass with my champagne flute. "To fun!"

A half-eaten platter of dim sum – Oz ate most of it – sits between us. Bo Zin's menu is decidedly Asian-Moroccan fusion, which is something we don't have in Waterford. We've ordered dim sum and a lamb tagine, and even though I've only nibbled, both are excellent.

The music switches from American pop to something Middle Eastern sounding, and even though I can't understand the words, the beat is hypnotic. I playfully shimmy my shoulders and sway my head from side to side.

"Do you want to dance?" Oz shouts over the cacophony of music and voices.

"Not out there." A few British girls have taken over the space next to the bar and throw their arms around each other as they rock back and forth. "I don't think there's room for us."

Oz shrugs. "If you really want to dance, we'll make some."

Pete never dances with me. At home, it's always my friends and me that take over the dancefloor while the husbands stand near the bar drinking. "You would dance?"

He nods. "Only if you're not embarrassed by me." He bops around in his seat to the rhythm. "I'm not too shabby, I swear."

I want to dance, and honestly, dancing with Oz sounds fun. But first, I should have him make a video of me. Something that shows me laughing and having an amazing time. "Okay," I say. "I'll dance, but can you take a quick video?"

He shoots up his eyebrows. "It's probably not my business, but what are you doing with all these pictures and videos?"

A small smile forms on my lips as I sway in my seat to the music. "Oh, you know, Facebook and Instagram and stuff."

"Are you an influencer?"

I laugh. "Hardly. I only have 2,000 followers on Instagram."

He takes my hand and yanks me to my feet. "Forget the pictures for once. Let's live in the moment and dance."

I'm wearing strappy sandals and totter a little, but Oz keeps me upright. "It's the shoes, not the champagne," I say. "I'm not drunk."

"Didn't think you were." Oz clears a small area next to the dancing British girls for us. He moves rhythmically to the music, and I'm pleasantly surprised by his ability to dance while still sober and without 80's rock – the only music that gets Waterford husbands away from the bar.

I pull my phone from my Tory Burch bag that doubles as a clutch. "Just one?"

He frowns and shrugs. "Sure."

Oz takes my phone, and I strike a pose. He holds up his finger while looking at the screen. When he points at me, I laugh and twirl to the music, and when he lowers the phone, I stop.

"It locked," he says, holding it out.

"16-45-73," I say.

He aims the phone at me again, and I pose while he snaps a few more pictures.

"Do I look like I'm having fun?" I shout over the pounding bass and squealing British girls.

"*Are* you having fun?" Oz asks. "Because, and forgive me if this is blunt, it seems like you're trying to convince someone you are."

I snatch my phone from him and study the video. "I was enjoying the company, but if you're going to be a little bitch, I may have to rethink that."

Oz recoils. "Whoa. All I'm saying is that you seem a little sad, like you're forcing yourself to have a good time."

I don't need his pity, so I stomp back to my barstool and pound the rest of my champagne. My head feels woozy and my lips loose. I shouldn't lash out at Oz, not when he's been nothing but kind to me, but I can't yell at the people I *am* angry with. I slump against the bar and rest my chin on my hand. "I'm sorry, Oz. I am trying. It isn't easy."

He climbs onto the stool next to me. "What are you running from, Veronica?"

How does he do that? How does he know?

"I'm not ready to talk about it," I say. "Maybe later, but not right now. I don't want to kill the vibe."

He seems okay with that because he picks up a piece of *har gow* and devours it. For the amount of carbs he eats, he should weigh at least fifty pounds more than he does.

"Have you decided how long you're staying in Marrakech?" he asks.

I sigh. "I bought a ticket to go home tomorrow morning."

Surprise flickers across his face. "Oh."

"Are you disappointed?"

Oz sets the dim sum down. "I thought you were a traveler like me."

"No, just a woman who needed to get away." I unshell a pistachio, but drop it back into the bowl. "When are you moving on?"

He gives a half-smile. "Actually, I'm leaving for the Sahara tomorrow. A little camping excursion to the Algerian border."

"Interesting. How did you arrange that?"

"The guy who moved into Grant's old room at my riad told me about it. Said it's a life-changing experience, so I thought I'd give it a go."

"And after that?" I ask.

"On to Europe. I don't suppose you have recommendations?"

His voice fades in and out with all the club noise, so I lean closer and give him a devious smile. "Why would I know anything about Europe?"

Oz chuckles. "Tell me you've never been."

I look away. How much should I reveal about myself? Oz and I are parting ways after tonight. Does it really matter what he knows about me anymore? "I've lived there a few times."

"A few times? Don't most people save up their entire lives, visit once, and then go back to real life?"

"I don't know, Mr. World Traveler. You tell me."

"Where did you live?" Oz spears a green olive with a toothpick.

The DJ switches to something calmer, and the dancefloor empties. Oz no longer needs to shout for me to hear him.

"Zagreb, Croatia mostly. But I grew up in Zurich. My dad was in finance." After Pete got his first job with the State Department, I was elated to move back to Europe. I've always felt more comfortable there, maybe because I've only really lived in the U.S. in spurts as an adult. But I'm not going to tell Oz that – my old life with Pete is too raw right now.

"Croatia? Really?" Oz says with surprise.

"Really."

He nods slowly. "I want to see the Dalmatian coast and maybe hop over to Sarajevo and Belgrade."

"The coast is gorgeous," I say. "It's been a few years since I've been, and I hear the tourists are overrunning it. But if you can, try to get out to the islands." I loved living in Croatia. Things were simpler and slower. It was by far the happiest time in my marriage.

Oz takes a cellphone-sized notebook from his pocket and scribbles something.

"What's that?" I ask.

He holds up the black, leather notebook that I noticed the first day we met. It's slim with a piece of black elastic holding it shut. "My travel notes. When I get home, I'm going to turn it into a book."

"And where is home? What Midwest town are you from?"

"Awww, man. I had hoped I was an international man of mystery." He wiggles his eyebrows. "Did my accent give it away?"

I nod.

"Well, I'm from a small town outside Omaha, Nebraska. Ever been?"

I shake my head. Admittedly, most of my travels have been abroad and not around the U.S. except to places like New York and LA. "Sorry, I'm a big city girl."

"You'd be surprised, Veronica. Omaha is hopping. Lots of tech moving in, creating a boom." There's a note of pride in his voice. Wow, he actually likes being from Omaha.

"I see." I finish my champagne and reach for the bottle, but it's empty. "Looks like I'm all out." I shake it.

"Probably for the best if you're leaving in the morning." Oz flags the bartender. "Can we get the bill?"

Am I leaving in the morning? Do I really want to?

The bartender places a cup holding the check next to Oz. He picks it up.

"How much do I owe?" I ask, reaching for my wallet.

Oz waves me off. "I've got it."

"But I drank an entire bottle of Veuve! You have to let me at least pay for that." I try to tug the bill from his hand, but he holds it up over his head. "Oz, come on. Let me pay my part."

"I'm paying for the company – even if you did get snippy with me." He hands the bartender the bill and a silver, not platinum, credit card.

The check has to be nearly $200 which must be much more than a guy from Omaha who's traveling the world can possibly afford. "Well, if you're ever in DC, I'm taking you out."

Oz cocks his head. "You're from DC?"

"Northern Virginia, actually – about twenty miles outside DC."

"Hmmm. I was positive you were a gay divorcée from LA or something."

I'm not sure whether to be insulted or not. "And why did you think that?"

"You have that look – bleach blond and fit. And there's that air of sadness around you."

I study the wall of alcohol behind the bar. "We're not going there, but no, I'm not a gay divorcée."

Oz offers me his arm. "I'll help you get a cab." We walk toward the exit. Or more correctly, I totter and bump into Oz, and he keeps me upright. "Do you want me to drive back to your hotel with you?" he asks. "Do you feel safe going alone?"

I think it's well after midnight. I'm in a strange country, and while it feels completely safe, you can never be too cautious. Especially since I'm tipsy. Plus, some taxi drivers have a habit of picking up additional riders along the way. However, I don't want Oz to think I'm inviting him back because I'm absolutely not. I don't like him like that. "If you could ride with me, that would be great."

Our cab is a vintage Cadillac. Once again, there are no seatbelts, and even though the streets are relatively empty, driving like this feels reckless. When we pull up to my hotel's guard station, Oz lets out a low whistle. "Maybe I should have let you get the bill."

I playfully slug his arm. "Told you."

At the valet, I lean into Oz and hug him. He smells wonderful, like a manly aftershave. "Thank you for inviting me out. I hope the rest of your journey is wonderful."

He touches my arm, not in a sexual way, but more like he needs to say something. "Are you sure you want to go home? I mean, there's an awesome adventure to the desert that I know about."

I smile softly. "You've already taken too much pity on me."

He shakes his head. "It's not pity. It's just…"

"What?"

"I think we get each other," he stammers. "Not romantically. No, not like that, even though you are a beautiful woman." He flushes. "I'm being selfish."

"Why?"

He runs his hand through his mop of hair. "Sometimes, being on the road is lonely, and I'd really like your companionship."

"You want me to come with you?"

The driver turns around in his seat. "Are you going to get out or not?"

"Come inside with me," I say to Oz. "We can talk in the lobby or at the bar." I slip out of my seat, but he doesn't move. "Are you coming?"

"I think maybe it was wrong of me to say that." He doesn't move.

"Come inside." I pull on his arm. "I want to talk."

Oz pays the driver and opens his door. We stand in the dim moonlight, staring at each other. For him, this may be about loneliness, but for me, if feels more monumental. If I don't go home, I'm going against everything I've been taught and my parents' expectations.

I lead Oz into the hotel.

We're not supposed to be in the pool area, but I figure, if we're very quiet and don't get in the water, no one will say anything. I recline on a lounger and stare at the stars while Oz stretches out on the one next to me. It's nearly 2am, and I'm not at all tired. However, my flight leaves at eight, and I haven't packed.

Oz has been regaling me with stories from his travels. He has a gift with words, and his descriptions make me feel like I've experienced it too: camel races in Dubai, surfing in Australia, an impromptu safari in Tanzania. He may have started life in small-town Nebraska, but he's a seasoned traveler now.

One thing that strikes me is how neither of us talk about the lives we've left behind. It's like all that matters is the journey we're each on. I've also noticed that Oz is an expert at guiding the conversation to where he wants it to go, and he doesn't want to talk about growing up in Omaha. I don't feel he's being cagey, just reserved, and in all fairness, I haven't exactly dropped the my-husband-cheated-and-I-ran-away card.

My phone vibrates. I glance at it, and seeing Pete's picture, my heart sinks.

"I have to take this," I say to Oz. "Excuse me for a minute."

I stand and walk toward the vacant restaurant. When I'm positive I'm out of Oz's earshot, I answer.

"Yes?"

"Vee?" Pete's baritone voice floats out of my phone. "Can we please talk?"

I glance across the pool at Oz. He's staring up at the sky with his arm tucked under his head. He's so comfortable being alone. I hope I can get that way.

"It's two in the morning. We can talk later," I say quietly in case Oz can hear me.

"Why are you whispering?" Pete says. "Who's with you?"

I press my lips together to hold in the verbal lashing I want to give him.

"Vee?"

"I'm standing by the pool in the middle of the night." I take a deep inhale to prevent myself from losing it. "You are projecting."

"Is this the end?" Pete says softly. "Tell me it isn't. I can't lose you."

I snort. "You should have thought of that before you fucked Eve."

"I know."

My heart drops, and I search for the right thing to say.

"Are you there?" he asks.

"Are you admitting that you cheated because you wanted to, or are you still blaming me?"

"No...that's not what I'm saying." Desperation oozes from his voice. "I was wrong. I know that, and I want you to come home, so we can work everything out."

"Has my mom called you?"

"Well, we spoke a little. And she's right, Vee. This can be fixed. You have to give me a chance. Can you do that?"

Of course Mom called him. She's always taking charge of my life. I inhale deeply. "Well, you're in luck. I bought a ticket to come home."

"When?" There's an uptick in Pete's voice.

I stare at the sky. I bet the stars are amazing in the desert. "Tomorrow."

Pete lets out a whoosh of air. "That's good. Send me your info, and I'll pick you up."

There's victory in his voice, and it stings. If I come home, all will be forgiven, and life will move on as if nothing has happened. I've done that too many times before.

The truth is, I don't want to go back to Waterford. I don't want to be a big fish in a small pond. I don't want to be only Pete's wife and my kids' mother. And I definitely don't want to be a founding member of the Bitch Brigade.

But I do want to see the desert and find out where my journey takes me; maybe that's back to Pete, but maybe it isn't. I have to do this for me, not for my parents.

"Vee?"

"Pete, I can't come back. Not now. I can't go back to that cesspool." I pause. "I don't want to see Eve, and I don't think I want to see you."

"You don't want to see me?" Hurt drips from his words. "Are you saying we're done? You just said you were coming home?"

Oz rolls onto his side so that his back is to me. I study him. Like me, he's running from something. I'm sure of it. But unlike me, he has a plan.

"I changed my mind. I need to figure things out," I say with no emotion.

"Without me." Pete's voice shakes.

"On my own," I answer. "So, yes, without you."

There's a commotion on Pete's side, like he's dropped the phone. "Are you still there?" he asks.

"I am."

He blows into the phone. "If you're going to stay gone, at least give me some money. I need to pay the mortgage."

"I'll pay it," I answer. "But that's it. You can live off your paycheck for once." When we married, my parents put my money into a trust for me. It pays me out each month, and Pete signed away his rights to it in our pre-nup. But oh, does he love spending my monthly stipend. It's how we afford our house in Waterford and take lavish vacations. It's how he's able to drive his BMW sports car on a civil servant's salary.

"Do you love me, or do you love my money?" I ask. I've never doubted his love; never believed he only stayed with me for financial reasons, but I can't deny his behavior.

"I love you. Only you. I want you to come home. This is madness."

I shake my head even though he can't see me. "I'm going to the Sahara tomorrow. I'll be offline for a few days."

"What? Veronica, --"

"Good-bye, Pete."

8

I want to puke. Or die. Or both. I slide as far away from the left-hand side of the bus as I can until I cross the aisle and sit on the other side. I try not to focus on the sheer drop on the edge of the road, or that we're on a twisty, two-lane mountain road and passing cars - in a bus.

Oz stares at me quizzically. "Are you okay?"

I don't dare open my mouth, so I shake my head and make my eyes wide.

"Are you afraid of heights?"

I nod and force myself to speak. "How long are we in the mountains?"

"I'm afraid we're here for at least four hours, but after that, it's six hours on flat ground."

I hold my breath before letting it all out. "I'm going to die."

Oz moves so that he sits next to me. There are others on the bus, but everyone else is either talking quietly or listening to headphones. Apparently, I'm the only one who is terrified.

"We'll be okay," Oz says softly, touching my hand. "I've been on worse rides."

"You do realize that he keeps driving us down the wrong side of the road, and the cliff is right there. Oh, and there's no shoulder." Panic wells inside me, and I can't let that happen. No one needs to see me blubbering in the corner. "I need Xanax."

"Is it in here?" Oz scoops down and lifts my backpack. "Take one, and I'll wake you up when we stop."

"Are you sure?"

"Take your medicine. You're going to be a mess if you don't."

I place the pill in my mouth and swig some water. "Thanks."

After I settle into my seat and put my headphones on, I close my eyes. The bus sways and jerks then sways again. I grip the seat's armrest. This is going to be a long ride.

At some point, I must have fallen asleep because my eyes flicker open, and Oz softly shakes my arm. "Veronica," he says. "We're stopping for lunch. Are you hungry?"

I bat him away and groan. My motion sickness hasn't abated, and I feel like crap. "Are we out of the mountains?"

"Not yet."

Another groan. I straighten up and delicately rub my eyes so that I don't smear my makeup. "I think you have it in for me. That's the only explanation I have for this bus ride."

Oz laughs. "C'mon, you." He wraps his hand around mine, and I don't pull away. In fact, holding his hand feels safe and comfortable. "Everyone else has gone in."

I have drowsy, Xanax brain and can barely hold my eyes open. "Can't you just bring me something? A water at least."

"We can't bring food on the bus," he reminds me. "But I can sneak a candy bar for you."

That wakes me up. "Ewww! No! Do you know how much sugar and carbs are in one candy bar?" I push myself to standing. "I'm coming because you clearly can't be trusted with nutrition." I drop his hand and gesture at his lanky frame. "After all, you're over thirty, eat like a machine, and look like that."

"I'd love to be able to put on some muscle," he says. "But, alas, my metabolism is crazy high."

We exit the bus. "Be thankful. It goes downhill after forty."

"You're over forty?" Oz sounds surprised. "Really?"

As much as I want to deny it, I frown and nod. "Forty-five, actually. Ancient, right?"

He crinkles his face. "Veronica, I honestly thought you were only a few years older than me. Maybe thirty-eight."

My heart sings. "Really?"

"You look amazing." Oz turns his head away. "What do you think of the restaurant?"

The roadside restaurant is little more than some picnic tables under a pergola. "Posh."

He laughs and strolls toward the table where our bus mates are gathered. He pats the seat next to him, and I sit. Someone passes us a menu to share.

A waiter comes out, takes our orders, and soon piles of rice and meat are set before us. Mangy cats roam between the tables, begging for scraps, and flies swarm us. The heat isn't oppressive, but it's enough to make me sweat. I quickly eat, chug some water, and head back to the air-conditioned bus.

"That was great!" Oz says, taking the seat in the row across from me. "Total hole in the wall, but awesome."

I don't eat for enjoyment. I eat for fuel. And if I keep eating like I just did – loading up on carbs – I'm going to gain ten pounds. "I'm glad you liked it."

My backpack sits at my feet half-unzipped, and I rummage through it to find my phone. I was so out of it when we got off the bus that I left it behind. I hold it up next to the window, but there's no cell or data service out here.

"There's WiFi," Oz says. "I saw the sign at the restaurant. I think the password is 'Busride'.

"Thanks." I log in and am immediately bombarded with dozens of emails – mostly from shopping sites. But one catches my eye, and my stomach rolls.

"Veronica?" Oz says. "Are you okay?"

85

I need privacy to read this email. "I'll be right back."

I exit the bus and find a quiet place away from the diners. My hands shake as I open the email. It's from someone saying they're Pete's attorney. I try to wrap my brain around that. Pete has an attorney. My husband who wants to work things out has hired an attorney.

Mrs. White,

We've been retained by your husband, Peter White, to begin divorce proceedings. Please respond to this email to acknowledge receipt. A copy of the documents has been attached. Please sign them and return to us. Your attorney may also contact us for more details.

Thank you,

Ashley Byers

Byers, Cunningham and Davis, LLC

I grit my teeth and angrily pull up Pete's number. Thankfully, there's a weak cell signal. I don't care if it's early, he needs to hear from me.

"You motherfucker," I hiss. "A divorce attorney?"

"You left me."

"Are you running off with Eve?" A sob lodges in my throat. "Is that what you're doing? Suing me for my money and running off with her?"

Pete sighs. "I've told you, I don't want Eve. I want you, but you left."

"To figure things out!" I shout. A few diners turn toward me, but they go back to eating when I drop my voice. "I need some time and space."

"Vee, I don't understand what's going on with you." He pauses. "I love you, and I want you to come home. But instead, you ignore my texts and calls, and I have no idea where you are."

"I'm on the way to the Sahara to have a life-changing experience.

I told you that." Tears slip down my cheeks. "Why are you making this so damn hard?"

"Because I messed up, and I'm trying to make things right, but I can't if you're a continent away."

"You think filing for divorce is the right way to go about that?" I huff. "And you say you love me?"

"Yes. Only you."

"You don't cheat on someone you love." My shallow breath comes in gasps. I glance at the bus where people are filing back on. Oz stands outside, watching me. He waves at me to hurry up. "I have to go, but I'm not signing anything until I can meet with my attorney, so get that out of your mind."

"You don't need to sign anything. Just come home."

"So everyone can laugh at me?" I ask.

"No one's laughing. In fact, everyone has moved on to the latest scandal: Melissa Foster's wardrobe malfunction at the pool." He makes a forced laugh. "And I swear to God, Eve will leave you alone. We can even quit the club, if you want."

"I get penalized for your mistake?" I snap. Everyone except Oz has boarded. "I really need to go. My bus is leaving."

"When can we talk again?" Pete asks.

Do I want to talk to him again? Pete's like a comfortable, but ratty sweater I can't part with. I love him, but he's disgusting. "A few days. There's no signal in the desert."

"Okay, be careful," he says. "I love you."

"I'll talk to you soon." I hang up and lift my head. Oz waits near the bus. I turn my back, wipe my face, and compose myself. Thank God for sunglasses.

"Everything okay?" Oz asks when I get closer to him. "You look shaken."

I flash my everything-is-okay smile. "I'm perfectly fine, but if we could get out of these damn mountains, I would be excellent."

Oz doesn't push the issue, which I appreciate. "The driver said it's only one more hour until we're out of the mountains. He wants to make up time in the valley, so be prepared for more kamikaze driving."

I roll my head back and loll my tongue to the side. "Will it ever end?"

Oz slings his arm over my shoulder, and it's not at all weird. "Just think, we get to do it going back."

"You," I say, shaking my finger at him, "aren't helping things."

He shrugs. "This is an adventure, Veronica. Embrace it."

We board the bus, take our seats, and settle in for five more hours of driving. The desert better be the most exquisite thing I've ever seen.

I need it to be.

The bus lets us off behind a decrepit building on a street that looks like it came straight out of Mos Eisley spaceport in *Star Wars*. It's dusty with a few azure blue-robed figures sitting in the shade of rickety-looking porches. Red sand stretches out before us in every direction.

I'm still jittery as I wait for the driver to unload the luggage from the underside of the bus. I've been replaying my conversation with Pete for the last five hours, and I can't decide how I feel about it. Part of me wants to try to make things work, but the other part of me is furious that he retained an attorney. How could he blindside me like this? He professes to love me, but none of his actions show it.

Several eight-passenger vans are parked nearby, and everyone from my bus heads toward them. I collect my rolling bag and set off, half dragging it, half carrying it across the sand.

Oz runs up to me. "I have a surprise."

"Oh?" I stop and turn toward him.

When he grins, a flutter of excitement builds inside me. "Over there," he points at a tall, dark-skinned man wearing a brilliant blue robe and turban standing next to a beat-up car. "I think that's our ride."

"Why aren't we going with the others?" I ask, drawing my brows together.

"C'mon." Oz motions for me to follow him. He stops before the man. "Are you Ali?"

"I am! Mr. Oz? Ms. Veronica?" He waits for confirmation. "Welcome to the Sahara!" His voice is loud and boisterous. He pops the car trunk and takes my bag before I can protest. "Is this your first time here?"

I'm not entirely sure what's happening. "Oz? Why aren't we going with the others?"

His smile swallows his face. "I wanted to really see the desert, and those group tours drop you off right next to the road." He nods at Ali. "But this man, he's going to take us to the real Sahara, right Ali?"

"I am!"

Unease rolls through me, but I push it aside. "Ummm. Okay?"

Ali holds the back door open for me. "You will love the desert! Come!"

I climb into the back, and Oz joins me. The car is an ancient manual, and there's no air conditioning. Ali has the windows down, and I worry about all the sand getting inside.

"*On y va!*" Ali says in French, shifting the car into first gear. We lurch forward across the sandy parking lot until we hit the start of the desert. Ali doesn't pause and drives straight into it.

"Where are we going?" I ask, turning around to watch the buses chug behind us, along the road.

Ali gives a hearty laugh. "To see the real desert. Not the tourist nonsense."

Wind batters me through the open windows, and stray pieces of hair wipe at my face. The car shifts and slides across the red dunes. As we go, Ali points out nomadic Berber encampments. "We know the sand," he says. "It changes every day, but we know how to go."

There is nothing around us, and fear nibbles at me. I'm alone in the desert without cell coverage with one man I don't know, and the other who is a newish friend. They could take my passport and abandon me. I could be sold as a sex slave – or even murdered.

I study Oz. "Are you sure this is okay?"

"I booked it through the Four Seasons Experiences," Oz answers. "Just wait."

I furrow my brow. "How did you do that? You weren't staying there."

He shrugs. "I said I was your assistant and booked it for you."

"You did what?" I exclaim. "Oz, that's..."

"Brilliant?" he laughs. "Just go with it, Veronica. Don't think."

We drive deeper into the dunes, and after half-an-hour, Ali turns and moves the car around a towering dune. We crest another hill, and a white-tented camp comes into view.

"Welcome to my home!" Ali booms.

I gawk. A cluster of three wide, white tents encircle a low table, cushions, and firepit.

Oz raises his eyebrows and bobs his head. "Good, right?"

"Some random guy told you about this?"

"Not this camp. That I did my own research on, but yeah. We travelers are excellent about sharing stories."

Ali pulls up to the encampment. "You are our only guests tonight, so the camp is yours. Please, pick your tent. You will be the King and Queen of the Sahara!"

I shake my head. "Oh, we'll need two tents. We're just friends."

Ali claps his hands. "Ah, yes." He guides me toward the middle tent. "This will be nice for you. It has a shower and electricity. See?" He flicks on a light switch. How is this even possible? I search for generator, but there is none. Ali laughs. "There's a real toilet too."

A king-sized bed dominates the tent with plush pillows and a white duvet. My eyes skip over the other furniture to the left side where an open curtain exposes the well-appointed bathroom.

"If you like, I will bring your bag." Ali takes a step toward the tent's door.

"Yes, please. This is incredible." I turn around, and face an excited Oz. When Ali is out of earshot, I ask, "How much is this?"

"A few thousand dirham, so maybe $500."

"For one night?" Again, I'm puzzled as to how he can afford all this. "Is that per person?"

"Yes, and it's worth it. Don't you think?" he asks.

A tremble of irritation grows inside me. "Did it not occur to you to ask if I could afford $500 a night for a desert trip?"

He cocks his head. "I'm paying. All you need to do is relax and have fun."

How in the world is he bank rolling all this? "Oz, I can't let you do that."

He holds up his hands. "I invited you. It's my treat." He turns his back. "I'm going to pick out my tent."

I follow him outside. One of the tents is fully opened, exposing a dining table and chairs. "Your private dining room," Ali says from the other side of the camp. "Tonight, you will feast." He points at a collection of beautifully woven rugs that lay on the sand in the middle of the encampment. A low table sits in the middle and a few cushions are scattered around. "This is where you can have dinner under the stars if you'd like."

"All this is ours?" I ask. Pete and I have taken amazing vacations, but this surpasses all of them.

"Yes," Ali's wide smile lights up his face. "You like?"

I nod. "It's incredible."

"Then sit." He points at a cushion. "I will have my assistant bring out snacks and drinks."

This is the Morocco I wanted to see when I sat in the Casablanca airport trying to decide what to do, and Oz has made it happen. If it weren't for him, I would still be ensconced in the Four Seasons, crying and fighting with Pete. Or I'd be on a plane back to Waterford to resume my life.

Oz steps out of his tent and joins me on the carpets. "So?"

"Amazing," I answer. "I have no words."

"You're welcome." He laughs, and the sound fills my heart with happiness. Being with Oz is easy, and even though we just met, it feels like we've known each other for years.

A teenaged boy, carrying a tray of lidded dishes, scurries down the side of the dune. He arranges the dishes on our table, lifting the top of each pot to show us what's inside: dates, nuts, and bread.

"After you eat, you will take a camel ride to watch the sunset, okay?" Ali beams at us.

"Great!" I answer. All my early apprehension has disappeared. I'm safe in this desert oasis.

9

Stars glitter overhead like tiny dots punched into an inky black sky. The sliver of moon casts light on us and no shadows. I lay on my back, palms pressed into the ornate rug covering the sand, and stare at the heavens. Every constellation I've ever heard of is visible in high definition.

A faint murmur drifts over the dunes from where Ali keeps his camp. Every once in a while, his hearty laugh rings out, but mostly, it's eerily silent. No crickets, no cars, no white noise. Only silence.

"You going to stay out here all night?" Oz pads across the sand, the soft earth hiding his approach. He lays down next to me on the rug.

"Maybe." Being out here, alone with the stars and a faint breeze, I oddly feel less isolated than I did in bustling Marrakech. I lift my phone and snap a few pictures of the heavens, but they don't do the sight justice. "I never want to forget this."

Oz cradles his head in his arms, and like me, turns his gaze upward. "Wow," he says with awe. "I haven't the faintest idea how to describe this."

"I know, it's stunning." I roll onto my elbow and face him.

Against the glow from my tent, Oz is a dark blur. "I wonder what else we miss living in cities."

"So much," he answers. "The world is full of amazing things, but I think we get too comfortable in our little bubbles and stop seeing everyday miracles."

"Is that why you left Omaha?" I ask. "To get out of your bubble?"

"No. I left because I needed more than what Omaha offered." He waves his hand at the sky. "It wasn't until I visited the Great Barrier Reef in Australia that I realized how much wonder is in the world and how fast it's disappearing."

"What do you mean?"

He draws a circle in the air, like he's enveloping the heavens. "All this was once visible where we live, but light pollution drowns it out. We're killing the Earth: the polar ice caps are melting; the Great Barrier Reef is dying. It's all because of us."

I roll my eyes. "Are you're a radical environmentalist?"

"No, but I've seen things that prove to me something has to change."

I don't feel like debating right now, so I tease, "I bet you've seen this kind of thing living in Omaha."

"Actually, no. But in Tanzania, the stars were almost as pretty." Oz's warm, disembodied voice floats around me like a cozy blanket.

"I bet."

"This is better though." He pushes up to sitting and leans slightly over me. "No lions to worry about."

I snort. "I thought you were going to talk about the present company."

"That's better, too." Oz is a hazy outline against the dark. He's close enough for me to see, but I can't clearly make out his facial expressions. "It's late," he says softly. "Almost eleven. Do you want to turn in so we can get up for the sunrise? Ali said it's at 5:45. We could take the snowboards out and dune surf before breakfast."

I'm a skier, not a snowboarder, but that doesn't mean I can't try.

"That sounds fun, and I'm in, but I think I'm going to stay out here a little longer."

"Okay," Oz stands and walks away before circling back toward me. "Veronica," he says in his raspy voice. "I know it's not my business, but what happened at the bus stop today? You were rattled."

Damn it. I thought I'd done a great job of pushing my emotions aside. "Husband stuff."

"Ah," Oz says with a bit of disappointment. "So there is a husband."

What do I say to that? I haven't mentioned Pete at all since meeting Oz, so it's probably obvious something is off with us. "There is, and he's home in Waterford."

"With your kids?"

I trace my hand across the sand and let the grains pour between my fingers. It holds the residual warmth of the sun despite the temperature dipping since sundown. "No. My children are college-aged, and both decided to stay at school this summer and work."

Oz kneels next to me. "If you don't want to talk, I'm not going to prod."

I sit upright and face him. Keeping everything inside is eating me up more than I want to admit and talking to Oz, a person who has no skin in the game and doesn't know Pete and me as a couple, may be therapeutic.

"It's complicated," I say. "Lots of layers and baggage."

"I assumed so," Oz says. "I mean, you're here and he's at home. It seems like you need some distance."

Wind dances across the sand and gently brushes over my skin, like a rough, little cat tongue. I close my eyes. "He cheated on me. Probably more than once, but I don't have any evidence."

Oz remains silent for a long time – maybe that was more than he wanted to know. I wait for him to say something, and when he doesn't, I offer, "You know, I am tired. I'll see you in the morning for the sunrise."

"Don't go," Oz says softly and grabs my hand. "I'm shocked, that's all. You're witty and fun and gorgeous. Men probably throw themselves at you. Why would any sane man cheat on you?"

"Really? You think I'm all those things?" My voice sounds ragged, like I may cry – which I may. "I don't feel that way. Not after what Pete did."

"Your husband is an idiot." Oz rubs the back of my hand with his thumb, and my heart pounds. "Anyone can tell you're too good for him."

"He wants me to come home, and I almost did until you invited me on this trip. But I can't run away forever, and I need to go back at some point."

"You're going back to him? After what he did?"

My chest heaves. "Cheating isn't that big of a deal where I'm from. All the guys do it."

I don't mention that I'm pissed my so-called friends are continuing on like nothing happened; that Waterford operates in a strange bubble of upper-middle-class indifference; that I'm not sure I can ever show my face again. "It's the way things are. I can either suck it up, or I can leave."

Oz drops my hand. "What do you want to do?"

"I don't know." My chest squeezes tight. "Neither option is particularly appealing."

Oz sits next to me, and his knee brushes my thigh. I don't pull back, and he doesn't move. He takes my face between his hands and turns my face up toward his. "Veronica, I'm going to tell you a secret: not all guys cheat. In fact, I bet the majority don't. What your husband did is shitty, and you absolutely deserve better."

I press my lips tightly together and pull my knees to my chest. Maybe I'm trying to hold myself together. I don't know, but I do know I'm off kilter. "He's my best friend," I choke out. "How can I walk away from someone I've spent over twenty years with?"

"Best friends don't hurt each other, and it sounds like your husband took advantage of your trust."

A lump forms in my throat, and no matter how hard I swallow, I can't force it down. Everything Oz has said is true. I deserve better. And Pete absolutely took advantage of my blind loyalty. My eyes burn, and I ball my fists into them. A sob escapes, and Oz pulls me against him. His arms encircle me, and I bury my face in his arms.

"Why did he do this?" I cry. "I've done nothing but support him and love him, and this is how he treats me?"

"That's not love," Oz says, rubbing my back. "I don't know what it is, but I promise you, it's not love."

"He's an asshole." I pull away and dab at my eyes with the bottom of my shirt. "I'm sorry. I shouldn't dump on you."

"I don't mind." In the dark, Oz's smooth voice calms me.

I flop onto my back and stare at the sky again. There are over seven billion people in the world, and I chose a man who breaks my heart over and over again. How did I end up with him? He promised to love and honor me, but I doubt he ever did.

"I don't know what to do," I say out loud, even though I didn't mean to.

"What do you mean?" Oz asks.

"There are so many variables: stay, leave, go home, divorce, work it out; I don't know where to start." I sniff and rub my burning eyes.

"Why make a decision now? Can't you wait and process?"

I swallow away the sob caught in my throat. "He sent me divorce papers even though he says he doesn't want to divorce." I cover my face with my hands and mumble, "Damn it, I do love him."

Oz strokes my hair. "Look, we don't get back to Marrakech until late tomorrow night. Why don't you sleep on whether you want to go home or not? There's no need to make a decision right now."

He's right. I have time. I told Pete I was going to the desert and that I'd be offline for a few days. There is no rush. I roll onto my side and push up to sitting. Oz stands and offers me his hand. "Thank you," I say. "For everything."

"No problem."

Before heading back to my tent, I wrap my arms tightly around Oz. "I don't know what I would do without you right now."

He runs his hand down my back and rests it on my hip. My chest presses against his until he pulls slightly away. "You're amazing. Don't think that you're not."

Cool air rushes between us when he steps back. What have I become? Veronica White doesn't cry on strangers' shoulders, and she certainly doesn't air her dirty laundry. Will Oz look at me with pity now that he knows my story? And if he does, do I care?

I hurry toward my tent. The yellow glow from within causes me to squint, and a whoosh of warm air escapes into the comfortable desert night when I pull back the flap. I enter and zip the door shut to keep the bugs and sand out. Once I'm sure everything is secure, I strip off my clothes. Then, I crawl into bed naked and pull the light sheet over me. I flick off the side table lamp and stare into the blackest black I've ever seen until my eyes grow heavy, and somehow, miraculously, I sleep.

My alarm goes off at 5:25, and I bolt upright. It's still unsettlingly dark in my tent, so I flick on the nightstand light. Sand blasts the side of the tent, creating a soft, shush-shush sound. I had to have been exhausted to sleep through that. I didn't even need Xanax, so maybe I'm improving?

With a yawn, I slink out of bed and toward my attached bathroom. The shower is simple, but Ali has assured me it has plenty of hot water. I'm not going to find out right now, though, because I promised Oz I'd dune board with him which sounds like it could be slightly dirty.

I brush my teeth and pull my hair into a loose ponytail. Day-old make-up rings my eyes, so I find a makeup wipe and clean my face. Little crow's feet line the area next to my left eye. Ugh. I tug on my skin to smooth out the wrinkles. I frown. My forehead isn't as taut as it should be either. In all the chaos of the last two weeks, I've forgotten about my Botox appointments, and now it shows.

As I stand there staring at myself, I debate reapplying my makeup. I never even go to the gym without mascara and eyeliner, but walking out of my tent makeup-free feels oddly liberating, and I'm pretty certain Oz won't be horrified if I'm not wearing mascara.

I turn my head from side to side. I'm really not that ugly without it.

Satisfied with my decision, I quickly dress. When I unzip my tent, darkness greets me. At some point in the night, Ali must have blown out the camp's lanterns, or they burned out. As I blink my eyes to adjust to the dim light, I notice Oz sitting at the low table on a cushion.

"Good morning!" he says. "Did you sleep okay?"

I nod. "I did. How about you?"

"Like a baby. The bed is really comfortable, isn't it?"

I laugh. "It's like the Four Seasons of the Sahara Desert." I take the cushion next to his. "I have to apologize for last night. Crying is not like me, and I'm sorry if it made you uncomfortable."

Oz shakes his head. "I don't mind at all." Then, as if he doesn't want to talk about it, he jumps up. "Let's grab the boards and head that way." He points toward the entrance of the camp and the highest dune. "We'll get a workout climbing up."

I follow him to the dining tent where the boards sit propped into the sand. "Do we need shoes?" I ask, glancing down at our bare feet. "Like snow boots or something?"

Oz inspects the boards. "I don't think so." He flips the board onto the ground and stands on it. "Nope. We're good barefoot."

I pick up my board and follow him across the rippling sand toward the large dune. The sky has turned gray, and slivers of dusky purple slice through it. We walk in silence until reaching the top of the hill. When I peer over the top, a flat valley stretches before me, and on the other side, there is a sheer cliff.

"Ali told me Algeria is over there." Oz sets his board upright in the sand and takes a seat. "We're right on the border."

"So the sun's going to rise that way?" I point toward the cliff. My

African geography isn't the best, but I'm sure Algeria is to the east of Morocco.

Oz nods. "Yeah. Probably in a few minutes."

The purple streaks have turned mottled orange, and while it's still dusky, I can see clearly. I flop in the sand next to Oz and study his profile. He has a straight nose and a strong, square jaw, and even though he's lean, his biceps bulge beneath his t-shirt. I'm fairly certain he has a six-pack. If he walked into the Waterford pool, the women there would ogle him and act like school girls.

Does he know how good looking he is?

"You know," I say, trying to get myself to focus on something other than Oz's looks . "I told you about me, but I know nothing about you. What's your story?"

"You didn't tell me much." He leans forward and, resting his forearms on his knees, turns his head toward me. "But I guess you could say I'm a fellow heartbroken traveler."

"Divorced?" I ask. He's old enough to have been married...and have kids.

"No, nothing like that." He stares off into the distance. The corners of his eyes crinkle, and he presses his lips together. "My dad died last year."

That wasn't at all what I expected. "I'm so sorry."

Oz's closes his eyes, and when he opens them, I'm taken aback by the immense pain he shows. "I'm coming to grips with it," he says. "This journey I'm on is helping."

"That's good. Anything to help us heal, right?" I want to pull him into an embrace, like he did with me last night, but if I did, what would that mean?

He gives me a small smile. "I'm not sure I'm healing, but it definitely helps me not think."

That's something I understand: the desire to keep moving so my brain doesn't dwell on unpleasant things. "Most people don't uproot their lives over a loss," I say. "Maybe we should start a club."

The corner of Oz's mouth pulls up into a lopsided smile. "You know, my dad always wanted to see the world, but he never got out of Nebraska. He worked construction his whole life, and we never had enough money to travel beyond an occasional campground. But he had a world map, and he'd put pins in all the places he dreamed of visiting. He always told me we'd do a world adventure after he retired." Oz gives a little shrug. "Dad was going to sell the house to fund it."

Our upbringings couldn't have been more different. My childhood was spent jetting around Europe while he was camping in Nebraska.

"What happened to the map?" I ask.

"It's in storage, but before Dad died, he sat me down and made me promise to get out of Nebraska and see the world. We made a list, and I've been checking it off."

"Oz...that's..."

"Yeah, I know. Sad, but cool, right?"

"Amazing." I glance at the horizon. The sun dances over Algeria, moving higher in the sky. "I think it's great that you're doing this for yourself and your dad."

"I'm almost done. Just a few places in Europe to check off," Oz says.

"What will you do after?"

With a sigh, he says, "I don't know. As much as I like Nebraska, I don't think I belong there anymore." He brushes his hands together like he's ridding himself of something. "Maybe I'll apply for a work visa in Europe."

I've never stopped to think about Oz having a job. "What do you do?"

"Computer stuff."

"Like?"

"Cybersecurity." He clenches his jaw and looks away.

"You're a hacker?" I ask in surprise.

Oz shakes his head. "No. I stop the hackers. I'm a good guy."

He clearly doesn't want to talk shop, and years of living with Pete have taught me to respect that. "Hey," I say. "Is Croatia on your list of countries?"

"Yeah." He turns his head and his brown eyes lock onto mine. My heart flutters. "That's why I was asking you about it. Dad wanted to visit the land of his ancestors."

"He was Croatian? What's your last name?" I sound more composed than I feel. Oz is too young for me, and yet, I can't help but remember how comforted I felt in his arms last night.

"I don't know what it was," he says. "My great-grandparents came over, but my dad never met them. We're really only Croatian in ancestry."

"Maybe Novak? That's a common last name in Croatia. In fact, I had several neighbors in Zagreb named Novak." I will focus on the conversation and not on how badly I want him to touch me again. "Do you know where in Croatia your family is from?"

Oz shrugs. "I don't think it mattered to Dad."

"I could help you," I say a little too enthusiastically. "I could come up with a list of things to do and places to see." Helping Oz may be the temporary distraction I need...or it could be a way to keep him in my life.

"Really?" he sounds hesitant, like he doesn't want to put me out. "You'd do that?"

"Of course! I'd love to." I let sand pour between my fingertips. The sun hovers over the horizon now. "Like I said, it's been a few years since I've been there, but I'm sure things haven't changed too much."

Oz pushes a hand through his mop of brown hair. "That would be great."

We sit there for another minute taking in the sunrise, before I ask, "What about the rest of your family? Your mom? Is she okay with you leaving Nebraska?"

Oz frowns. "I don't know her. She walked out when I was two and never contacted us again."

The shock of what he says hits me before I can stop myself from blurting, "What kind of mother does that?"

"The selfish kind," he answers without pause.

The sun hangs over the horizon. "My kids are older," I say. "It's not the same. I haven't abandoned them."

"Oh, I didn't mean it like that."

Sunlight pours down on us, and Oz stands up and grabs his board. He straps his feet in and motions to me. "C'mon. Enough of this depressing conversation."

I awkwardly place my feet on the board and adjust the straps until they're tight against my feet. "Ready?"

Oz flashes me the cutest grin, lifts his eyebrows, and lets out a whoop as he pushes himself over the edge of the hill. He cuts back and forth across the face of the dune until he reaches the bottom. For someone from Omaha, he certainly does know how to snowboard. He hops around until he's looking up and facing me. The sun blazes at his back. "Your turn, Veronica!"

I study the descent. Oz made it look easy, but I know better. I'm going to land on my ass.

And still, against every sane part in my body, I leap.

10

We arrive back in Marrakech after midnight. Shortly after finishing our breakfast, Ali had loaded us into his beat-up car and drove us back to the bus. I was exhausted and not in the mood to ride through the winding Atlas Mountains again, but it is the only way back. We drove across the sun-drenched valley until lunch, then again until we stopped once more for a quick dinner before heading up into the lush, green mountains.

Luckily, I slept this time, only waking when I heard shrieks. Apparently, the driver had to veer toward the steep drop-off and onto a narrow shoulder where he nearly hit a man walking. All this because another bus passed into our lane, and we nearly had a head-on collision. Thank God I slept through that.

As we wait for the driver to open the luggage compartment, I take in the thrumming Marrakech Square. A thousand people or more fill the space, and the strong scent of spices from the make-shift food stalls tickles my nose. Men selling goods toss whizzing balls of light into the air while trying to tempt unsuspecting tourists.

"I know we need to find places to stay, but are you hungry?" Oz points at the restaurant area. Long, communal tables fill the space before it, and despite the late hour, it's packed.

I promised myself I'd explore this place at night, and now seems like the perfect time to do so. "Sure," I say. "Let's see what they have."

Oz and I retrieve our bags and melt into the crowd. Our first stop: a booth selling snails. Having lived in Asia, I'm no stranger to odd foods, so I place an order at the high counter. The man yells at someone unseen and a paper plate piled high with snails is handed to me.

"You're going to eat that?" Oz says, making an ugly face.

"Yes, and you are too." When he shakes his head, I add, "It's basically Moroccan escargot. A little like oysters. Do you like oysters?"

Oz shrugs. "Never had them."

"Then try." I glance around for a free spot at a table and lead Oz to it. "You can pick the next item."

We tuck our luggage under the table and squish between a family of six and some other travelers who are speaking what I think is Dutch. They're both blond and easily in their late thirties, if not a little older, which makes me happy.

The family keeps to themselves, but the Dutch woman smiles at me. "Hi," I say. "Do you speak English? *Parlez-vous anglais ou français?*"

"Both," she says with a British accent. "I'm Janna and this is Hans."

"Veronica and Oz," I answer.

My traveling partner eyes the plate of snails with revulsion before nodding hello. "Are you in Marrakech long?" Oz asks.

"Only three days before visiting Fez," Hans answers. Like Janna, he speaks British English. "And you?"

Oz perks up. "We just got off the bus from the Sahara. If you haven't been, you should go. It was amazing."

"Yes, we spoke of it, but the drive is too long for our short trip." Janna sizes us up like she's noticing the gaping age difference between Oz and me. *Oh, hell, please don't think I'm his mother.* She draws her brows together. "Is this your first time in Marrakech?"

"Technically, it's my second time," I say. "I was here a few days before leaving for the desert, but it's my first trip to Morocco." I pick up a snail and dig the flesh out. Then with my eyes fixed on Oz, I pop it in my mouth and smile as I chew. The flavor explodes across my taste buds with spices I can't quite identify. They taste nothing like escargot, but are every bit as delicious. "Want one?" I tease, waving a snail at Oz. "They're amazing."

Janna and Hans share a platter of shaved meat and pita that smells heavenly, and Oz points at it. "Where did you find that? It looks a lot better than Veronica's snails."

"Whatever," I say, disappointed that he won't even try.

Hans gestures to a food booth behind us. "Right there. One of the best things I've eaten on this trip."

Oz stands and climbs over the picnic bench. "I'll be right back."

When he's gone, I eat a few more snails in silence before pulling out my phone. Out here in the Square, I have decent reception so I turn on my cellular plan. My phone begins dinging incessantly as messages and texts pour in, and embarrassed, I turn off the ringer.

Janna glances at me, and despite my desire to read all my messages and catch up on social, I drop my phone back into my bag. "Sorry," I say. "I was offline for three days."

The family has left the table and a group of young guys has replaced them. They're loud and boisterous, but ignore us. With unease, I shift my crossbody bag to the other side, away from them. Can't be too careful. Pickpockets are everywhere.

Oz approaches carrying a towering plate of meat, and grins. "This, Veronica, is real food."

"Says the guy from Omaha." But admittedly, the meat looks incredible with a white sauce squirted in a zig-zag across the top. Pita is tucked around the edges.

"Then I'm not sharing. You can have your snails." Oz digs in and chews slowly. His eyes twinkle in amusement.

Janna leans close to me. "Are you staying in the medina?"

"Actually, I don't have anywhere to stay yet. I forgot to make arrangements before I left for the desert." Despite having nowhere to stay, I'm not worried. Worse case, I go back to the Four Seasons. "What about you?"

"We're staying at a riad," Janna says. "The medina is confusing, isn't it? I hope we can find our way back." Her blue eyes hold concern, but Hans shrugs.

"It's an adventure," he says. "We'll find it."

"I like your spirit," Oz says between hearty bites of food. For being so thin, he can certainly pack it away. "I stayed at Riad Rose Blanche my first few nights, but Veronica stayed at the Four Seasons."

Confusion floats into Janna's eyes. "You're not married?"

Oh thank God – she didn't think he was my son. "No. We actually met a few days ago. We're both solo travelers."

"Oh." Janna smiles tightly. "Like souls always find each other."

"Yes, they do," Oz answers and winks at me.

My heart pounds. What did that wink mean? Is he flirting with me, and if he is, what would it mean if I flirted back?

"Where will you stay tonight?" Hans asks.

Oz puts his fork down. "I thought I'd go back to my riad. If they don't have room, I don't know. Veronica?"

"I'm going back to the Four Seasons. I don't want to deal with the hassle of trying to find a place." I whip out my phone and pull up the hotel's website. While Oz talks to our new friends, I type in my dates and to my surprise, it comes back as unavailable. "Excuse me," I say. "I need to call the hotel."

For privacy, I step away from the table. I never thought about possibility of there being no room for me. After the third ring, the receptionist answers. I tell her my story, and she very regrettably informs me there is no vacancy.

Panic bubbles in me. What now? I can't spend the night wandering the medina, looking for lodging.

"Veronica?" Oz calls. "You okay?"

I stroll back to the table and calmly say, "I need to find a place to stay. The Four Seasons is fully booked."

"Oh." Oz grimaces. "That's not good."

Hans purses his lips before saying, "I believe there is a room in our riad - a single."

"Can you take me there?" I ask.

Janna laughs. "If we can find it."

"We'll find it," Hans answers. "And if not, the three of us can camp out here."

"What about you, Oz?" I ask. "You going back to your riad?"

For the first time since I've known him, worry flits across his face. "I don't know."

"We didn't plan this well." I push the half-eaten snails aside. My appetite has evaporated. Janna and Hans have finished eating, but Oz's plate is only partially cleaned. "Do you want us to wait for you to finish?" I ask.

He shrugs. "I'm a solo traveler. I'll be fine."

I can't leave him alone in the Square with nowhere to go, and self-ishly, I don't want him to leave me. "At the very least, come with us. Maybe Janna and Han's riad has two rooms."

Oz turns up his hands. "What do I have to lose?"

The four of us clear our table, and Oz and I collect our bags. "I think it's this way," Hans says pointing at one of the larger arteries leading off the square. "At least, I believe that was where we came out."

Janna studies the routes before us. "I don't know. I should have paid better attention."

I cast a quick glance at Oz and raise my eyebrows. What if these people are con artists? What if they're going to take us into the medina and rob us. What if--

"We will go this way," Hans declares, moving toward the artery that's second to the right. "The riad is just inside and to the left, so if this is not correct, we will retrace our steps and try again."

"Seems logical," Oz answers. I want to shake my head and warn him that I have a bad feeling, but I can't figure out why.

We cross the Square until standing at the mouth of the souk entry. Hans goes in first, followed by Oz. Janna walks side by side with me. "Oz seems nice," she says. "How did you meet?"

Some of the fear growing inside me subsides. This is a kind woman. She didn't target us; we sat down next to her. "Oh, at NOMAD. We're were both having dinner there, and Oz offered to take my picture."

"And you've been traveling together since."

It's strange to hear her say it like that. "I guess. I mean, we're not together, but we are on an adventure together."

"Ah. So where will you go after Marrakech? Home?"

"I don't know yet. My trip is a bit open-ended." The souks have closed for the night, and it feels deserted despite there being maybe a dozen people walking about. I'm so thankful I'm not doing this alone.

"The two of you are American?" Janna asks.

"Yes. I'm from DC and he's from Omaha, Nebraska."

We turn to the left, and Hans holds up his hand. "Ah ha!" he shouts. "It's here." He points at a beautiful blue wooden door. He says something in Dutch, and Janna laughs.

"Forgive me," she says. "Hans is extolling his manliness."

Hans and Oz disappear through the door, but Janna holds me back. "Have you traveled alone before?"

"No."

"Please be careful. You do not know that man."

"Oz?" I ask. "He's harmless. If he wanted to kill me or kidnap me, he could have easily done it in the desert."

Janna drops her hand from my arm. "You trust him, then?"

"I do." And it's weird, but I do trust Oz. He's done nothing to raise my suspicions, and in fact, has been a source of comfort. I lucked into finding such an amazing travel buddy.

Oz sticks his head out of the doorway. "They have a room, Veronica. Two actually. We're in luck!" He darts back into the riad.

"See," I say, more to myself than to Janna. "Harmless."

I wake mid-morning. At check-in, the receptionist told us that there would be a light breakfast, so I make myself presentable and head down to the ornate courtyard. Hans sits alone at a bistro table near a tiny, tiled pool.

"Good morning!" he says in his hearty voice. "Did you sleep well?"

Not really. "It was fine," I say. "Thank you for helping me find a room."

"Of course."

"Where are Janna and Oz?" I arrange myself on a semi-plush cushion at the low table next to Hans. Nearby, an orange tree, heavy with fruit, scents the air.

He folds the paper he was reading. "Janna went to shower, but I believe Oz wanted to explore a little."

"Oh." A pang of disappointment hits me. He didn't wait for me. But of course he wouldn't. I slept the morning away, and it's not fair to make him wait. "Did he say when he'd be back?"

"No."

A woman brings over a pot of mint tea and a selection of pastries. I stare at them. So many carbs. This trip really is going to make me balloon up.

"Try the orange and chocolate one," Hans says. "It's divine."

Reluctantly, I point, and the woman places the questionable pastry on my plate with tongs.

Hans resumes reading his paper as I attempt to eat my breakfast. I flip my phone over on the table. It's not rude to browse if you're at your own table and the other person is reading a paper.

Most of my messages are shopping spam, but a few are from Pete begging me to check in. I'll deal with him later. I read my text from

Stacey – she wants to know when I'm coming home. Good, someone in Waterford has noticed I'm MIA. It's about time.

I type out a reply, being careful to sound happy, and hit send. Then, I scroll through Facebook, catching up on everything I've missed – mostly parties and pool days. Oddly, I don't long for any of it. I was having an adventure in the Sahara sand surfing and watching the sun rise while they were doing the same old thing with the same old people.

Hans pushes away from his table and stands. "If I don't see you again, have a wonderful remainder of your trip."

I smile. "You too. Tell Janna thank you again for helping us last night."

"I will."

After he's gone, I open the photos from the desert. I had Oz take dozens of pictures, and my favorite is one of me making sand angels. The way the sun hits me casts a beautiful glow across my face. And I'm laughing. That's the most important thing.

I manipulate the cropping and filters until I'm satisfied with the results. Then I create an album on Facebook and post the pictures with carefully-crafted captions. Let the Women of Waterford and Pete see how much fun I'm having without them. I wish Oz and I had taken a few together. I furrow my brow. Do I have any pictures of him other than the goat one? I scroll and scroll through my Goggle Photo app, but can't find anything.

We're going to have to fix that. I want Pete seething with jealousy. I check the time. It's nearly 5:30am for Pete, and he'll just be waking up. I can't avoid him forever, and he deserves to know that I'm alive. Before I can chicken out, I hit his number. There's a pause before the phone rings. He answers immediately.

"Vee? Are you okay?" he says drowsily.

"I'm fine. I wanted to tell you I survived the desert." I rest my elbow on the table and hold the phone to my ear.

He sighs. "Are you coming home now?"

"I don't know." I pick at the flaky croissant before me and drop the crumbs onto the table. "I don't know how I can. Not after what you did; not after Eve's outburst." Anger builds inside me, and I inhale to calm myself. "How am I supposed to face any of those people ever again? Everyone knew." To my surprise, my eyes don't sting with tears. In fact, I feel calm. "You embarrassed me."

Pete breaths heavily. "No one is talking about it. What they are asking is when you'll be home. Your disappearance is more interesting than my...my indiscretion."

"Right because all the guys there are cheating assholes and the women gossipy bitches."

"We'll move," Pete says. "If you come home, we can move. But Babe, I miss you, and we can't work this out with you an ocean away."

Oz walks through the riad door with brown paper bags in hand. He holds them up and gives them a shake. "Hey, Veronica!"

I lift my chin and smile. "Give me a minute."

"Who are you talking to?" Pete demands.

"Housekeeping."

"A guy housekeeper?" Pete asks. "Who are you with?"

"A fellow traveler, that's all." Despite my earlier thought about the photos, I can't bring myself to lie and say I've meet someone.

I wave to Oz, and he saunters over.

"Are you hungry?" he whispers.

I lift my finger, shushing him. "I'm on the phone with my husband. I'll find you in a few."

He lifts the brown paper bags again and nods. Without saying anything else, Oz walks away.

"Veronica," Pete pleads. "Come home."

"I'll think about it," I say, but really, I am ready to leave Marrakech. I feel like I've seen everything worth seeing. It's a beautiful city, but small. "I have to go."

"To see that guy?"

"It's not like that."

"Then explain it to me."

"If you came here, I could explain it to you," I say, not hiding the sadness in my voice. "But you can't even do that. Instead, you stay in Waterford, go to parties at Eve's house, and pretend like nothing happened. What is wrong with you? Don't you care that I'm hurting?"

Pete huffs. "Of course I care. That's why I want you to come home. I--"

"Then come to Marrakech. Come here, and let's work on fixing us." I glance around the courtyard and to the upper level. No one is around.

"I can't up and leave. I have a job."

I shake my head. "Then take a vacation. Say it's a family emergency. I don't care what you do, but you need to be here with me."

"You're being ridiculous. I can't stop my life because you decided to run away." He pauses. "I can see this conversation is going nowhere. Why don't you call me tonight?"

"Why? So we can yell at each other again and rehash the same issue?" My hands tremble, and I swallow to wet my parched throat. "I have nothing left to say. Either you come here, or you don't, but I am absolutely not coming back to Waterford until we figure things out."

I hang up and collapse against the low wall running around the dining area. Frustration rages inside me. Pete has shown me how unimportant I am to him. Work and friends come first. They always have, but I've been good at framing our life so that we looked happy and perfect.

It was all lies.

Oz leans over the upper floor balcony. "All clear?"

"Come down," I say, pushing my thoughts on my marriage aside. "I want to see what you have."

Oz walks down the wooden stairs and into the small, but pretty courtyard where I sit. He skirts the edge of tiny pool and ducks under the orange tree's low-hanging branches. He lifts the paper bag. "Guess."

"I have no idea."

He hands me the bag. Inside are dark, red, shiny cherries. "I went to the market this morning and thought these looked delicious. I don't know if you like them..."

"Oh!" I exclaim. "Cherries are actually my favorite. Very good guess." I pluck one from the bag and chew at the sweet yet tart fruit. "Oh my God! That's the best cherry I've ever had!"

Oz grins. "I thought so, too." He pulls out the chair Hans had been sitting in, turns it around backward, and straddles it. "Hey, sorry I interrupted you earlier. I didn't know you were on the phone with your husband."

I wave my hand. "It's fine. Nothing new on that front." I eat another cherry. "What's the plan for today?"

Oz bites the side of his lip and rests his forearms on the top of the chair's back. "I'm leaving this afternoon. I went to the airport this morning and bought my ticket."

My heart drops. I knew he'd move on at some point, but I wasn't expecting it now. I force enthusiasm into my voice. "Where to next?"

"Split, Croatia."

"You're going to do it?" I say evenly despite my lungs tightening in my chest. "Good for you." The room sways slightly, and I brace my hand against the cushion I'm sitting on. I had hoped...what had I hoped? Oz told me he was passing through, and maybe, it's time I move on too. Wasn't I just thinking that I'm tired of Marrakech?

"My flight's at four."

"Split's lovely. One of my favorite places, but Hvar Island is even better. You can take a ferry to it for a great day trip." As I speak, images of my old life in Croatia flit before my eyes. One summer, Pete and I took the kids to the coast for a holiday. We splashed in the cool Adriatic and lounged on pebbled beaches while the kids ran wild. We stuffed ourselves on *cevapi* and seafood, and in the evening, we'd walk along the promenade and get gelato for the kids.

I miss my old self. Somewhere along the way, I turned into a mean, suburban woman who cared more about fashion labels and parties than her family. That's not giving Pete an excuse, but rather looking at reality. He didn't just pull away from me; I forgot about him. We're both at fault in this situation. But that doesn't change the fact that he's not willing to do whatever it takes to repair things, and fixing it can't be my sole responsibility.

"Veronica?" Oz says. "You still with me?"

"Yeah." I blink. If I can't go home, and I don't want to stay in Marrakech, what should I do? My chaotic mind stills a little. Croatia. I could go back to where I was happy. "Oz, would you think it's weird if I went to Croatia too? I want to see some old friends in Zagreb."

He grins. "Last flight to Split is at 8pm. You better get packing."

11

Unlike when I landed in Marrakech, flying into Split causes butter-flies in my stomach. I peer out the window, marveling at the glitter-ing, blue sea and the red-tiled roofs. It looks like I remember, and that's what I need right now: good memories.

Oz and I couldn't get flights together, so he's going to wait for me near the baggage claim. I flew to London first and had a short layover before boarding Croatian Airlines for a two-hour flight to Split. Oz left earlier, so we didn't see each other in London.

I spent the time browsing magazines, scrolling through pictures, and kept coming back to pictures of Pete and me. We look so damn happy in all of them, but we weren't. We were disconnected, and I spent so much time trying to frame my life perfectly that I somehow started believing my own BS.

Obviously, I learned nothing from Elizabeth Mavery.

The plane bounces upon touchdown, and like in Marrakech, we stop short of the terminal. Two busses wait near the stairs as I climb down. I inhale deeply, savoring the smell of jet fuel and ocean air. *Oh, Croatia, I've missed you!*

After exiting the plane, I squeeze onto a standing-room only bus.

The man next to me lifts his chin in greeting, and I look away. I don't feel like having a conversation with a stranger.

The bus chugs toward the terminal, and once it stops, everyone pushes their way off toward the terminal door.

I pull my bag up the gangplank and into the airport. It's small and surprisingly crowded. I guess what I heard was right: Croatia has been discovered by the traveling masses.

Oz and I haven't discussed what we'd do once we arrived in terms of accommodations, and I have no idea if we're going to part ways or hang out more. My heart pounds. He wouldn't have allowed me to tag along if he didn't want to spend more time with me, would he?

I get out my phone and WhatsApp Oz.

--*Just landed. Headed to customs now.*--

There's no response.

I shove my way past a group of Asian tourists blocking the walkway. Their tour guide holds a stick in the air with a red flag attached, and each of them have on headsets. She speaks Chinese into a microphone, and the horde moves en masse toward customs. I need to get ahead of them.

The customs line stretches before me, and I shove my way in front of the Chinese tour group. Despite the large 'No cellphone' sign on the wall, I pull mine out again. I should go ahead and book us into a two-bedroom Airbnb. Oz will appreciate it.

I open the Airbnb app and type in the criteria I want. A short list of available homes pops up. I scan the list. The third listing looks promising.

"Put your phone away!" a burly security man says, walking toward me. "Or I will take it."

I drop my phone into my bag. "No need. I'm done."

The guard clenches his jaw before continuing down the line of passengers.

As I creep closer to customs, the line divides into multiple lanes. An agent directs people to different lines. When it's my turn she sends me to the far right. I walk to my lane and wait. The customs agent checks my tourist card and passport before asking me the purpose of my visit. When he's satisfied, I'm waved through into a large room.

I press against the wall as people shove their way past me until an official-looking surly woman points at signs in Croatian and English directing me toward baggage claim. I hurry down a dimly lit, grimy hallway, eager to see Oz.

Like sardines, the baggage claim is packed with people. I dart around passengers looking for Oz, but he's not there. I immediately message him again:

--where are you?--

I move next to a dirty, gray pillar and press my back against it. As I wait for his response, I study the giant crowd again to make sure I haven't somehow missed him before taking a seat in an uncomfortable, orange plastic chair. There are only two options: he ditched me, or he's been detained. If he left, there's no point in sitting here; if he's been detained, it could be hours before he's released.

My stomach drops. Did he get tired of me and not want a confrontation? After all, he arranged to fly to Croatia without me. But why would he abandon me? We made plans to meet up. It makes no sense. He has to be detained. Or maybe he got in so long ago that he went into Split and planned to come back to pick me up?

I sit there for an hour until the baggage claim area is nearly empty. I continue watching the crowd and hoping my phone buzzes with a message from Oz. Desperate, I message him again.

I wait, but there's nothing.

With a sigh, I Insta-book an Airbnb with two bedrooms in case Oz turns up. I scan the baggage claim area again before gathering my suitcase and handbag and heading to the taxi line.

My phone dings as I wait for a cab, and my heart speeds up. But it's just a woman named Marika who owns the apartment I've rented wanting to know when I arrive in Split. I immediately message her back, telling her that I'm at the airport and ask for directions.

Because I'm waiting on an address from Marika, I let the person behind me skip ahead. After a few minutes Marika's response pops up on my phone with the address, and when it's my turn in line, I show it to the taxi driver. He punches it into his GPS and away we go.

As we drive, I can't shake the unease welling inside me. Oz wouldn't ditch me. He wouldn't. Something had to have happened to him.

The taxi flies down the freeway and into the chaotic maze of Split. Unlike in Marrakech, the drivers here try to use rules – but only the ones they like, so we're trapped between a tour bus and a delivery truck. My driver curses, lays on his horn, and kicks the car into reverse, hitting the bumper of the family car behind us. That driver yells out his window, to which my driver responds with a rude hand gesture.

Welcome back to Croatia.

Finally, the gridlock eases and my driver heads up a winding road – the wrong way. When I protest, he shoots me a dirty look, and I sink back against my seat. I'm going to die.

After a lot of mumbling, he halts abruptly, I tip forward, nearly hitting my head on the passenger seat. "Here," he says. "You get out now."

I pull up Marika's address to make sure I am indeed in the right spot, and satisfied it's correct, I pay the driver with a few *kuna* I had picked up in London. He leaves me standing on the sidewalk and continues driving the wrong way up the street.

Unsettlingly, there are still no messages from Oz. Has he ghosted me?

"Veronica?" A woman hurries down the street toward me. The light wind blows her brown hair back from her face, and she smiles as she approaches. When I nod, she says. "I'm Marika."

"*Drago mi je!*" I say in rough Croatian.

Confusion then amusement dances across Marika's face. "You speak Croatian?"

I shake my head. "Not really. *Samo mali hrvatski.* I lived in Zagreb for three years."

She claps her hands. "Wonderful! Welcome back!"

"Thank you for taking me on such a short notice."

Marika produces a set of keys. "My apartment is usually rented, so this is good luck."

"Indeed."

"May I help you?" She points at my bag.

"Oh, I'm fine."

Marika uses a keypad to unlock the front door and leads me up a flight of wooden spiral stairs to the second level. The interior is a little shabby, but not at all awful. She inserts the large metal key into the apartment door and steps aside. "Please," she says. "Welcome."

The gleaming white apartment is pristine. Not a scuff anywhere. It's spectacular with a small kitchen opening onto a living space with a couch and two chairs.

Marika moves toward the French doors that dominate the side of the room. "The view is lovely." She opens the doors, and the wind rushes in. "From here, you can see the Adriatic."

I wander over, and sure enough, the sparkling Adriatic spills out before me. Islands dot the view. "Beautiful," I say with awe. "I'm very lucky to find this."

"Yes, but I only have two nights. I have more guests booked. You understood that, yes?" Worry fills her eyes.

"Yes." I have no idea what I'll do after those two nights, but I have time to figure it out.

Marika guides me toward a short hallway. "The bedrooms are here." More pristine white walls and furniture and bedding in the side-by-side bedrooms. "The bathroom is here." It's absolutely spotless and with a bidet. Excellent. "If you need anything, my information is in the welcome magazine on the kitchen table. Please call me."

"I will."

After she fills out a form with my passport information, she asks, "Do you need a restaurant for tonight? Something in town?"

"That would be great," I say.

Marika's face lights up. She walks over to the kitchen table and opens a binder to a list of restaurants. "Here." She taps a name. "This is near the Palace and delicious. Traditional Croatian food and only a fifteen-minute walk."

Sometimes, living in Waterford, I forget how the majority of the world walks everywhere while we drive SUVs and live in spacious, sprawling homes. Why? Why do we choose to live like that?

"It sounds like exactly what I want," I say.

Marika nods and heads toward the door. "It is nice to meet you, Veronica. Enjoy your visit to Split."

"Thank you!"

After she's gone, I message Oz the address before hauling my bag into the bedroom and unzipping it on the beautiful light gray wood floor. I don't want the filth of my trip on the white duvet. There's no point in unpacking since I have to leave in two days, but I can wash clothes – something I desperately need to do.

Oz probably needs to wash laundry too, which means I should throw my load in now.

I separate my clothes into lights and darks and carry the light pile into the bathroom where the washing machine sits under the counter. Marika has left detergent which I appreciate greatly. I shove my clothes into the small front-loading basin and start the machine. European homes normally only have a washing machine, which means there must be a drying rack somewhere nearby. I search the small bathroom, but find nothing, so I go into the kitchen. Sure enough, there's a rack tucked between the wall and refrigerator. Good, I'll not only have clean underwear, but they'll be dry, too.

Where is Oz? I check my phone to make sure I didn't miss a message, but there's nothing from him. Lots of junk emails, but nothing from my friend. And if I'm honest, I'm more than a little worried, but there's nothing I can do until he contacts me.

It's nearly ten, and I need to eat, so I find my cleanest dress, strip off my traveling clothes, and put it on. Then I strap on a pair of sandals. People in Croatia dress to impress in the evening, and I don't want to stand out as a lazy American.

When I'm satisfied with my appearance, I grab my handbag and set out. Let's see where the night takes me.

The maître d' finds me a seat right away in the middle of the room – the spot where they place those who want to be seen. Normally, I'd love it, but at the moment, I'd rather not be front and center. But, I don't say anything and take the seat he holds out for me.

Fragrant orange trees tower over the outdoor seating area, and a wooden bar runs along the front. White tablecloths cover the square tables, and the chairs are a plush green material. Marika has sent me to a fine restaurant indeed.

I snap a few pictures of the liquor bottles lining the bar while waiting for my glass of red wine. This is the kind of place Pete would take me if he were here. He loves upscale spots and dives equally, but on the first night somewhere, he always tries to find the best restaurant.

Even though we've done nothing but fight since I've left, I miss Pete. Maybe I should call him tonight like he wanted? Perhaps, if he knew I'm in Croatia, he'd come.

The waiter sets down my glass of Croatian red wine. I haven't even glanced at the menu, but the waiter doesn't seem bothered. I sip the wine and smile. It tastes like Croatia – robust and earthy. The debit grape is one of my favorites, and I'm honestly surprised more people in the U.S. aren't using it. Pete often says that Croatian reds rival any Italian ones. Bonus that they are cheaper, too.

Pete. Why can't I do anything without thinking about him? I suppose it's normal, but it feels like an intrusion. My mind wants to forget him and all the good memories, but my heart can't. What does that mean? Am I forgiving him already?

I need to figure this out because my indecision is driving me crazy. Stay or leave. Forgive or not. I think one way; then I talk to Pete and change my mind completely.

I should text him to let him know where I am. I spin my phone around on its PopSocket, debating what to say. Finally, I simply text:

--*In Split. Hitting the old stomping grounds*—

I take a picture of my wine and send it along.

I wait. And wait. And wait. Finally, the waiter comes back, and I place my order of local fish and vegetables. I wait some more. No word from Pete. Maybe he wishes he could ghost me like Oz has.

Bored, I begin posting on Instagram. Maybe I'll do a story too. People always like those. I usually do videos because it's more personable, but maybe a pic of my wine would work. As I sit there debating what format and picture to use, the text alert on my phone dings.

The screen drops down with a message from Pete.

--*Jesus, Vee. You can't keep running. This needs to stop.*--

--*I'm happy here. I'm eating wonderful food and drinking Croatian wine. What's not to like?*--

--*Are you going to Zagreb too?*--

--*Maybe. Haven't decided yet.*--

Three dots appear, then disappear, the re-appear. I wait impatiently. My phone rings, and I answer it.

"Yes?"

"Vee, honey, I didn't mean to snap at you, but the kids and I are worried. Come back."

If I weren't in the middle of a crowded restaurant, I may act differently, but I feel constrained. "I'll come home when I'm ready," I whisper, my brain taking control over my heart this time. "And that's not right now. As for the kids, I'll text them that I'm fine. You can tell them whatever you want."

"They know. I told them."

I wasn't expecting that and inhale sharply. "Why?"

"Because I fucked up, and I need to own it."

It's a start. I run my fingertip along the edge of my glass. "They probably heard from their friends, and you were covering."

"I got to them first," Pete says. "I'm doing everything I can to fix this."

Is that what he thinks? Has he not listened to a word I've said? "You know, Pete," I say. "At first, I had a vision of you coming to Marrakech to be with me. I thought that would prove you knew you made a mistake, but you didn't do it. You left me alone, and now I think, maybe you're doing it because you're afraid of me." I pause. "Are you afraid of how I can take everything away from you? Is that why you keep begging me to come home?"

It's not until I say the words that I realize how true it is. Pete makes a good living, but I have more money. Plus, he has to disclose the affair to his job, or he could lose his security clearance...and his job. Pete stands to lose more than just me if this doesn't resolve the way he wants it to.

"I'm not afraid of you, Vee. I love you, and I think you still love me despite me being the shittiest husband ever. I'll even go to counseling if you think we need it."

"We need more than counseling." The waiter places my fish before me. The fragrant aroma of lemon and thyme fills my nose, and my mouth waters. "But that's a good step, and I'll think about it."

"So there's still a chance?" Pete says.

I glance to my left where a couple are locked in a deep, passionate conversation. Pete and I were once like that. Now? Well, we're two people who talk about things, but nothing of importance. I tell him about my day, he tells me what he can about his, and we roll on.

"There's a small chance," I say. "Maybe a larger one if you come here."

"Did you leave that guy in Morocco?" Pete asks.

"Oz?" I say, confused as to why Pete would bring him up. "No. I don't know where he is. We were supposed to meet up at the airport, but I don't think he's landed yet." I lie to make Pete angry.

"Are you a couple or something?" Jealousy creeps into Pete's voice, and I smirk.

"No. We're friends. That's it, but like I said, he's gone MIA." My voice sounds shriller than I want, so I soften it. "As long as I'm married, I'll never cheat unlike someone I know."

Pete's silent.

"Are you there?" I say.

"Yeah," Pete says. "What's his last name?"

"Why?"

"Because I want to make sure he's not a killer or anything."

I shake my head. "Dude, seriously. He's a harmless millennial."

"You don't know his last name," Pete says.

I grit my teeth. "Does it matter?"

Pete blows into the phone. "I want my wife to be safe."

I stab at my fish. "My food has arrived. I need to go."

"Vee, please be careful."

"I will be."

"I love you," Pete says.

"Wish I could say it back." I hang up.

The fish tastes as wonderful as it smells. Normally, I'd switch to white wine with fish, but the red is so delicious I can't refuse another glass. I eat most of my plate until I can't handle another bite and try messaging Oz again.

I wait a few minutes, but after not hearing anything, I wave for the check. Disappointment – or is it sadness – wells inside me. Oz should be done with customs by now even if he had been detained, so it's clear he really did ghost me. That's the best explanation I have.

12

"Ow!" Hot coffee burns my lips, and I set my cup down on the small balcony's bistro table. If I had my act together, I would have gone to a café and ordered a thick, strong Croatian coffee. But I slept terribly and didn't drift off until nearly 5am. Now, it's noon, and I've lost the entire morning.

Below me, the hum of traffic provides oddly comforting white noise. Cars skitter past each other, each one trying to jockey into first position. How aren't there more accidents? No one wears seatbelts, and everyone drives like maniacs.

I swirl my cup, trying to cool the coffee, and sip again. Perfect. At least something's going my way.

From my perch, there's an unobstructed view of the glittering sea and islands off the coast. Once, when we lived in Zagreb, Pete brought the kids and me to Split for a week. We took an apartment near the city center, and every day after sightseeing, we'd walk the kids to the nearby pebbled beach. Pete and I would share a bottle of wine while the kids splashed and built towers from rocks.

Those days seem so long ago, almost like it was someone else's life. We were so happy – until we moved to Waterford at my insistence, and I got caught up in the stay-at-home-wife social drama, and Pete decided to spend all his free time on the golf course with the guys. And my kids...well, they started sports and developed social lives of their own; they didn't need me anymore.

Basically, I worked myself out of my job as both a wife and mother. I rest my chin on my hand. Damn it. Here come the tears again. Why can't life be easy? Why couldn't Pete and I hit our stride and coast into old age together?

Why does this hurt so damn much?

Because you care. That's why.

A car honks, and another returns the favor.

Pete and I have been drifting apart for years, but I didn't want to believe it. I knew it when Elizabeth Mavery kissed him, and I knew it when he was on that awful Ashley Madison site. But I believed that he'd never leave me. For the most part, our lives were wonderful as long as I didn't ask, and he didn't tell. And it worked...until Eve.

The need to pick the scab overwhelms me, and I open my Google Photos, searching for pictures of Pete and me with the kids in Croatia. My throat burns as I scroll, seeing all our good times, but I don't stop. Tears run down my cheeks, and I sniff. We were so damn happy. Why did we have to ruin it?

I pause on a photo of me sitting on a blanket at the beach with the kids. Pete must have taken it. Lemonade light filters through the clouds, and we're all dressed in bathing suits. I hold my youngest in my lap and stare toward the sea. A bottle of wine lays on its side next to my bare thigh. It must have been a good day, but I have no memory of that particular moment. How much of my life is like that? I have the picture, but not the memory? And as I know all too well, pictures lie.

Unsure of what I want to find, I flip through the old photos until I land on a group picture from last Fourth of July. That's around the time Eve and her friends started hanging out with me and my friends. Sure enough, she's there, in the back near Melissa Foster wearing a giant smile and an emerald green tube top. Her blond hair is in a casual side braid, and she wears the Tom Ford butterfly-shaped sunglasses that were all the rage. I had the same pair.

My pulse thunders in my ears. Is this the day she met Pete? Did I unknowingly introduce my husband to the woman he'd cheat with?

If I had a physical photo, I'd x her out or tear it up like we did in middle school. Instead, I delete it. Then, I begin erasing every photo I have of Eve. I don't need those memories.

The sun sits higher in the sky now and casts a little light on the balcony. Soon, the shade will be gone, and with it, the coolness.

I should get out of the apartment and stop wallowing, but instead, I find the last picture I have of Eve and me together on my deck. It was a few days before the Memorial Day party. She had come to my house with her kids, and they ran wild while we – me, Stacey, Julia, and Eve – drank wine and planned our summer. I had snapped the picture on a whim, making everyone gather behind me for a selfie. Then I had posted it in all the necessary places with the hashtag 'goodlife.'

I was such a blind, trusting idiot.

I tap my text icon, and before I fully think anything through, I dart off a text:

--You conniving bitch. Hope you have fun with my friends and MY HUSBAND.--

Attach photo. Hit send. And...instant regret.

Nausea rolls in my stomach. Why did I do that? And if I'm going to do something, why do it when I know she's sleeping? It would be better to do it when she was possibly with others at the pool. Surprise her and make her a little off-balance.

Badly planned, Veronica.

I stare with anxiety and horror at my phone, waiting for the response dots to appear, but they don't. Frustrated with myself for being so emotional, I grab my coffee mug and head back inside. I dump my cup in the sink, scoop up my now clean clothes from the drying rack, and walk into my bedroom. I toss all the clothes on the bed. I hate doing laundry – that's why I have a laundry woman – and

Pete hates the mess I make with my clothes. Well, eff you, Pete. I'll be as messy as I want.

I stare at my clothes, at the unmade bed, at my suitcase flung open on the floor and drop to my knees. Here come the tears again, and I lie on my back as they roll down my face.

Why? Why? Why?

My navy blue dress billows around my legs as I walk along the waterfront toward Diocletian's Palace. Most of Old Split is built directly into the walls of the ancient Roman Palace, which makes it a crazy, living relic. People have carved out homes and businesses inside the walls while faux gladiators are all too happy to pose for pictures with tourists.

The Palace is at least 100 football fields wide and even longer, and without a drone, it's impossible to get a picture of the whole thing. It will probably take me a day or two to explore, and unlike in Marrakech, I feel comfortable going it alone.

Past a gelato stand with a line twenty deep, I turn right through a marble entry way and into the belly of the Palace. Shopkeepers shelling tourist trinkets call out to me, but I keep walking until I pop into an open air square. Marble columns frame each side of the cute square, but at the far end, a modern church looms like an ugly stepsister. Like much of the palace, uniformly cut pieces of marble cover the ground.

On the stairs to my right, a man displays watercolor paintings. When I stop to admire them, he tries forcing one on me, so I turn my back and snap a couple pictures of the hideous church. I'm not going to be bullied into buying something I don't want.

Mindlessly, I climb the stairs leading into a warren of winding, carless alleys. Laundry hangs on lines strung between windows, and TV antennas cling to the walls. New and old mingle effortlessly. New and old. Can Pete and I do that? Can we reconcile the past with the future? Would it work seamlessly like the Palace? Or would it be an ugly mess like the church in the square?

With nowhere to be, I walk. And walk. And walk. I pass the giant statue of Gregory of Nin, turn back into the palace, and continue until I find my way to another wide, old Roman road. This one is lined with posh shops and restaurants. I check the time on my phone. It's still too early to have dinner, but a light snack and glass of wine is always a good idea.

I read a few restaurants' menus before settling on one with a few other patrons on the gated patio. The host greets me warmly and ushers me to a front row table facing the street.

"Is this good?" he asks.

It's the prime spot on the patio. "Yes. It's perfect."

After I sit, he hands me the menu. "Only light fare right now. And drinks. Would you like a drink?"

"Do you have a wine list?"

"Of course."

He walks away, and I study the menu. All I want is a little cheese from the island of Pag and some crisp, white wine. Fortunately, both are available. I wave at the waiter, and he takes my order. I decide to try Oz once more on the off chance that he had been detained or my messages hadn't gone through. I'd really like to know what happened to him.

I also need to decide where I'm sleeping tomorrow. I could go to Zagreb, but then what? I don't know anyone who lives there anymore – like Pete and me, our friends were only on three-year assignments and are long gone.

A rowdy group of young people stop near me. The guys shove each other and laugh loudly. They wear causal beach gear and have British or Australian accents. The young women are dressed in much the same way and gawk at the store fronts. They move closer to me and begin smoking.

"Excuse me," I say. "Can you move?"

One of the guys looks down at me. His eyes dart from my face to my cleavage and back to my face. I don't mind, really – I'm used to men looking at me like that. "Oh. Are we bothering you?"

"You're blocking my view, and your smoke is drifting toward me."

A petite, dirty-blond woman wrinkles her face. "So?"

"It's rude," I say.

The waiter comes running out, shooing them away. "Go," he orders. "You can't stand here."

The petite woman rolls her eyes. "We can stand wherever we'd like. It's a public street."

"Please," the waiter says to me. "I can move you to a nicer table if you'd like."

I shake my head. "No. I'm fine here."

"Bianca," the first guy says. "Just move over."

"Why? Because an old lady wants us to?"

It takes everything I have to remain calm, but frankly Bianca is ruining my vibe; or maybe I need to lash out at someone. I stand and lean over the tiny railing separating me from the group. I tap Bianca on the shoulder.

"What?" she says, tossing her hair around like she's a supermodel or something.

"You're going to move, because if you don't, I'm going to dump my glass of wine over your head."

"What?" she sputters. "Who does that?"

"A crazy, old lady who has no patience for your nasty behavior."

Bianca spins on her heel. "Whatever." She motions to her friends. "Let's go find gelato."

When they're gone, I smile at the waiter. "See? They moved."

"Those Yacht Week tourists are terrible." He puckers his lips. "They never buy food, just stare and cause problems."

"Yacht Week?" I ask. "What's that?"

He splays his hands wide like Yacht Week is the bane of his existence. "It isn't a week – it's all summer. The trips are only a week, though. British and Australian - some German and Americans, too –

come to sail around the islands on catamarans. They drink too much and are disrespectful."

"Sounds lovely." I sip the delicious wine I didn't have to waste on Bianca. "It's a real problem?"

"Yes. There are too many of them. They're destroying Split. Hvar is even worse. Everyone wants to go there now."

When I lived here, the only people who visited Croatia were Germans and the Scandinavians. No one in America could point out where Croatia was on a map, but it's become a hot alternative to Greece and Italy.

"Is it only young people who do Yacht Week?" My interest is piqued, and to be honest, sailing around the islands sounds fun.

The waiter shakes his head. "No. It's all ages, but mostly younger. Sometimes, families rent private boats with captains."

An idea slowly forms in my mind. "How do you get a spot on a boat?"

He cast a wary eye at me. "There are places in the marina where you can go to find trips."

"Thank you," I say, dismissing him. As I nibble on cheese, I Google "Croatian Yacht Week." Dozens of companies come back, each promising the trip of a lifetime. I read reviews and search vacancies, until I decide upon a British company operating out of the Split marina. They're open until 8pm – plenty of time for me to finish my snack and walk down. Worst case, they have no spots, and I can move on to Zagreb...or maybe Paris. Yes, Paris is always good.

My phone dings.

I look down. The red number one hovers over my inbox icon. Probably junk mail, but still, I can't stand having unopened messages. I click my box open.

I shouldn't have.

It's from Eve.

Veronica-

If you want to harass me, I'd think twice. I know things. And I

know that if Pete really loved you, he'd be with you right now.
Instead, you're alone and bitter.

> *Better luck next time,*
> *Eve*

My hands shake, and I drop my phone onto the cheese plate. That bitch. That little, snake-in-the-grass bitch. I clench my teeth, holding back the guttural sound growing inside me. I need to go. Now. Before I have a complete public meltdown.

I frantically wave for the waiter. "I need my bill."

"Is everything okay? You didn't finish your meal."

The lump in my throat prevents me from speaking, so I nod. The waiter gives me a quizzical look before disappearing into the restaurant, and at the table next to me, a woman averts her eyes.

I'm making a scene.

I slump against my seatback. Eve hasn't said anything I haven't thought. If Pete loved me, he'd be here, not there with her – and definitely not going to parties and pretending everything is okay. He'd be hell bent on trying to fix our marriage, doing whatever I asked. Instead, he's sending me threatening emails from divorce lawyers and giving me excuse after excuse on why he won't come to me.

Is he simply giving me lip service while he and his attorney figure out the best way to take my money? Oh my God. What if he's actually tricking me into staying out of the country so that he can claim I've abandoned him? Would that even hold up in court?

Tears sting my eyes, and I reach under my sunglasses to dab them away. I can't do this to myself. I can't second guess Pete's intentions and my role and...well everything. I have the facts, and I know what I know. If there's a divorce, I stand to lose a lot financially even with my pre-nup, but I'll be okay. I have to be.

The waiter returns with the credit card machine, and I hand him my card without looking at the bill. After I push in my pin code, I bunch my napkin up on the table and stand. The Adriatic stretches across the end of the street, and sunlight glints off the rolling waves.

Out on the marble-paved street, tourists meander past, taking in the shops and reading restaurant menus.

If I weren't feeling miserable, it would be the perfect photo op and another opportunity to lie to the world about how amazing my life is. I could smile and wave and frame my life to crop out the ugliness. Fake it until I make it and all that.

But this is reality, and my life sucks right now. I've wrongly believed that if I could convince my social media followers and friends through pictures and posts that I was okay, I would be. But it's not working. If anything, I'm feeling worse.

The waiter hurries before me and opens the low, metal gate separating the café from the street. I pass through without a good-bye and out onto the marble street filled with tourists. The crowd presses down the slight hill toward the sea, and I follow along, casting side-glances at the predominately young women posing for pictures. Some even have their friends holding back other pedestrians in order to get the perfect shot.

I pause next to a storefront advertising women's fashion in the front window. Eve said I was alone and bitter. She's right about the being alone, but I'm not bitter. I'm angry, hurt, and very conflicted.

On the street, a girl in a strappy polka-dot dress twirls and poses. She smiles over her shoulder and extends her hand behind her like she's begging her picture-taking friend to follow her. But when the picture stops, she stomps over, grabs the camera – a fancy looking DSL type thing – shakes her head and angrily snaps at the photographer.

She resumes her spot on the street. "Try again," she says. "You blurred out the background too much. People need to see where I am, and it needs to look incredible. We need to sell it."

I frown as I watch her photoshoot for a good five minutes. A group of young women have cued up behind the photographer, like they're waiting their turn. All of them wear dresses and impractical, thin sandals with no support. One girl has a mirror and fixes her makeup.

Finally, the young woman checks the new images on the camera and nods her approval. She and her photographer blend into the crowd, headed toward the sea. The other young women rush forward, trying to get the perfect shot.

For a moment, I consider walking in front of them -- much like Amine had -- and taking a selfie, but instead I meander toward the harbor. Loneliness battles with my determination to prove that I'm okay.

I'm broken. I know it, and Eve knows it. And I'm sure she's told everyone in Waterford about my text. What was I thinking? Oh. Right. I wasn't.

What I need more than ever is evidence that I'm thriving, doing amazing things, and hanging with the best people. I need to do something that isn't poor Veronica, traveling alone, but rather "Look at Veronica! I'm so jealous!"

Rowdy shouts and singing fill the street as young people crowd the narrow space. Everyone laughs and flirts. They're having a great time. What a contrast I must be: old, depressed, and ghosted by the one person I've met on this trip.

Pete didn't chose me, and neither did Oz - and all I need is to feel wanted. If someone, anyone, would choose me, I would probably feel better.

A young man bumps into me, "Sorry!"

There's so much happiness and excitement around me. I need to tap into that and try to lift my spirits. Eating alone every day is getting old, and I doubt I can do it much longer.

I squint at the horizon toward where the harbor sits. Despite what the waiter said, Yacht Week sounds like it may be fun. Worst case, I get a week-long trip around the islands. Best case, I actually enjoy myself and no longer have to pretend to be happy.

It's time I started doing things because I want to - not because I'm trying to prove anything. And right now, I want to do Yacht Week.

13

White sailboats bob up and down in the harbor as I pull my suitcase over the wooden dock. The woman at check-in told me to go to Slip 53, which sounds far away. Despite wearing a sunhat, the sun beats mercilessly on me, and I want nothing more than to sit in the shade with a glass of rosé. But no. I signed up for one week aboard a catamaran with six strangers and no air conditioning.

I really am beginning to doubt my sanity. After all, what do I have in common with a bunch of twenty-something Yacht Weekers?

At the end of the dock, two walkways stretch like a 't'. I ponder which way to go, before turning left. Sunbathing seagulls scatter as I stroll, taking in the harbor. Unlike some bodies of water, the harbor doesn't have a pungent salty smell. It's not really fishy-smelling either. In fact, if I had to put a label on it, I'd say it smells like summer – sunshine and sunblock.

Techno music thump, thump, thumps out of different boats' speakers and shrieking Yacht Weekers dangle their legs off the sides of boats while passing drinks back and forth. Wonderful. I've signed-up for *Spring Break: Girls Gone Wild* Croatia edition.

To my surprise, no one pays attention to me as my suitcase

wheels click-clack over the dock slates. There's not even a glance. What's up with that? I thought European men were supposed to appreciate older women, so why am I suddenly invisible?

When I reach Slip 53, a hulking, white catamaran greets me. There's a net stretched like a hammock between the two sides of the ship's front, and the back has a pair of stairs leading up to a deck. High above it all sits the captain's quarters. Unlike the other boats in the harbor, it appears empty.

"Hello! Are you looking for someone?" A very shiny and perky young woman with a British accent asks. She holds a clipboard and wears a light blue polo while guarding what appears to be a gang-plank. I look her over. She's pretty, but who in their right mind willingly wears a polo?

I point at the boat. "No. I'm looking for Slip 53. Is this it?"

Confusion clouds the young woman's eyes. "It is. Can I help you with something?"

It's clear that she doesn't understand that I'm here for Yacht Week. "Only my luggage. I'm Veronica White. I should be on the guest list."

The woman's smile falters for a brief second before regaining her composure. "Oh! I'm so sorry! I thought, perhaps..."

"I'm too old to do Yacht Week?" I say, keeping my voice level even though I am annoyed. "I'm not, and I'm traveling solo."

She bobs her head. "Of course. I'm Katherine, your hostess for the week." She scans her clipboard. "Oh, you have the double room all to yourself!"

"Yes, I paid for my privacy." Katherine gives me an odd look, but I ignore her. "What room am I in?"

She taps on the clipboard with her unmanicured fingernail. "You're in cabin four, located at the front of the boat. Would you like me to carry your bag on?"

"No. I can handle it just fine." I pull my bag to the gangplank and lift it. "Will there be a safety meeting or something?"

"Once everyone has arrived, I'll go over policies and procedures."

Behind her a group of three guys and three young women make their way toward us. They walk in slow motion, like they're starring in a beautiful music video. One of them has a speaker that blares horrible music. Thank God I always pack earplugs.

"I think your shipmates have arrived." Katherine waves to them. "Welcome!"

The dark-haired young woman leading the pack stops right in front of Katherine. "Hi! Are you our hostess? I hope you are! You're so cute!"

Feeling incredibly old, I lift my bag and continue up the steps to the deck. Down below, the kids laugh and talk excitedly over each other. Their music keeps pounding out thumping bass, and not one of them has noticed me.

Well, that's definitely not going to work. If I'm going to live with them for the next week, they need to embrace me.

I pause on the deck, kick off my Tory Burch sandals, and lean over the railing so that the front of my navy maxi dress dips dangerously low. I throw my hands in the air. "Welcome to Croatia, bitches!" Six sets of eyes look up at me. No one speaks; they just stare. "What are you waiting for? Get your asses on the boat, and let's get the party started!"

One of the guys – the tallish one with amazing biceps -whistles at me, and I take off my hat and throw it at him. He catches it with a grin, and I wag my finger in his direction.

"You're already my favorite." I wink at him over my shoulder before continuing down the deck toward the interior of the boat. If I'm going to be the oldest person these kids have ever seen, I better show them I know how to have fun.

The clean interior is surprisingly large. There's a dining table with a banquette and a galley kitchen, and the refrigerator is stocked with sparkling and still water.

As I snoop through the cabinets, a thought hits me. I should have brought snacks or booze. The man who made my reservation said that all my breakfasts and lunches would be provided, but I'd have to find my own dinner. I should have filled in the blanks about alcohol. I'll see if my new friends have any, and if not, I'll buy some at our first port of call.

My berth is all the way at the front and the only room with a double bed. When I step into the cabin, a small private bathroom sits to my left and consists of nothing more than a toilet and a handheld shower. I pass it and squeeze into the small space in front of the bed. It's wedged between two walls -- one with a port window – and only has a top sheet and two pillows. Drawers fill the space underneath. The only way onto the whole thing is to climb up and over the bottom.

The accommodations aren't luxurious, but they'll do.

I toss my suitcase on the bed, unzip it, and remove my bathroom supplies before putting them in the shower. Then I carefully unpack my newly cleaned clothes and place some in the drawers and the rest in the minuscule closet across from the bathroom. Satisfied with how I've organized everything, I change into the white bikini I absolutely could not wear in Morocco and pull a short, green sundress over top.

Boisterous shouts ring out from the main cabin, so I crack my door eager to see what's going on. The young women stand near the banquette table, and the leggy brunette from earlier places her hands on her hips. Her dark hair hangs loosely down her back, and her ivory skin looks like she's never sunbathed. She's absolutely stunning. "I don't care," she says in an upper-crust British accent. "I am not sharing my berth with a random bloke. Emma, you do it."

The young woman I assume is Emma sighs dramatically. "Darling, I'll share," she says, her American accent peppered with a hint of British, like she's lived in both places. "But next time, you're with the riff raff."

The redhead laughs and slings her arm around Emma. "Good sport, Emma! Just don't bang him, okay?"

Emma blushes, shrugs away, and tucks a piece of her ice-blonde bob behind her ear. Large sunglasses sit perched on top of her head like giant bug eyes. "It was one time," she whines. "Can we let it go, please?"

"Hardly." The stunning brunette adjusts her bag onto her shoulder and pushes past the other two women. Her wide, blue eyes lock on me. "Well, hello! You made quite an impression, didn't you? Are you with the crew?"

I flash my best 'bitch, please' smile. "No, I'm Veronica, and I'm a guest." I walk into the main cabin where the young women stand. "I'm sorry, I didn't get your name."

She sizes me up, like she's searching for a reason to dismiss me. "Lydia."

I'm not about to let this Pretty Young Thing think she's running me. Oh no. "Nice to meet you, Lydia." I lean against the kitchen counter and pop my hip out so that I look even thinner. "I'll address the elephant in the room: yes, I'm about your mom's age; and no, I'm not going to be a buzz kill."

She stiffens. "At least you acknowledge it. My mother never would."

I press my lips tightly together to hold back a scathing remark.

The redhead shoves past Lydia. "I'm sorry," she says in her clipped British accent. "Lydia has terrible manners. We try not to let her out too often." She extends her hand. "I'm Stella. It's lovely to meet you, Veronica."

I can't figure out the dynamic between the three of them. I thought Lydia was the HBIC, but Stella ran right over her. There's no doubt Emma is the low woman, though. She bent over and took what Lydia dished out.

I shake Stella's hand and glance behind her. Lydia pouts out her lip, and Emma waits patiently for someone to order her about. There's a ruckus on the stairs as Bicep Guy bursts into the room. His shaggy, sandy blond hair isn't to my liking, but his arms are even more incredible close-up. He grins at me in a naughty way. "You," he says with a laugh. He has an accent too, but it's not quite British. "You are something else."

I throw myself into Party Veronica mode. "I'm here for a good time, and damn it, I'm going to have one. Are you in?"

"Absolutely, mate!" He steps aside and a much smaller, bookish looking man climbs down the steps followed by a lanky guy with closely cropped, brown hair. He carries an open box with what looks like bottles of alcohol poking out.

The seven of us stare at each other for a moment before I break the silence. "Did you bring booze? Because I need a drink."

Biceps jerks his thumb over his shoulder at Buzz Cut guy. "Daniel has everything we need." He nods at Lydia, Emma, and Stella. "If you ladies want wine, you're out of luck. We only brought the good stuff."

Oh, shit. They're going to go hard. My liver is going to die this week. "Tequila?"

"And vodka and whiskey." Biceps grins while Daniel places the box on the table and holds up a vodka bottle. "Everything we need is in this box. Guaranteed good time with great company, if I do say so myself."

The bookish man looks at me like I'm an expert or something. "I'm supposed to share a room with someone? Do you know who that would be?"

I point at Emma. "I think she's your bunk mate."

Emma's face falls. She doesn't even try to hide her disappointment. "We have bunks," she says in her weird hybrid-accent. "Don't get any ideas."

The guy stammers. "I...I don't have ideas. I swear."

Biceps slaps him on the back. "That's where you always go wrong, cousin. You should always think those things."

"Garrett," the poor guy says, blushing, "you should show the ladies respect."

"I'm being respectful! Aren't I ladies?"

Lydia bats her eyes. Ah. She's attracted to him. "He isn't being terrible."

A pleased smile forms on Biceps' lips. "I'm Garrett, by the way.

This," he taps the bookish man on the head, "is my cousin, Stephan, and that is my best mate Daniel."

"You're Australian?" Stella says.

"Daniel and I are," Garrett says. "Stephan is from Leeds."

Emma, still apparently disappointed that Stephan is her bunk-mate and not Garrett, huffs and walks away. Stella hides her grin behind her hand. "Have fun with her, Stephan," she calls. "Her bark is worse than her bite."

While the rest of them mingle, I inspect the box Daniel set down. It's filled with cheap, crappy alcohol. Jesus. I'm going to have to teach them, but what should I expect? Emma, Lydia, and Stella are maybe twenty-four, and the guys have to be no more than twenty-six. They must think I'm an withered, old lady.

I take stock of the girls. Lydia is gorgeous, Stella has an average body, and Emma looks like she tries hard to stay thin. None of them, though, have the body I do from hours spent running and watching my diet. A small tremble of satisfaction rolls through me. I may be twenty years older, but my body is twenty times hotter.

I lift a bottle of tequila and turn toward the group. "Why don't you all put your things away, and I'll pour welcome shots?"

Daniel beams. He's a bit ordinary looking, but not in a bad way – more like in an every man kind of way. He could easily be cast as an extra in a movie. "You do that," he says. "The sooner we get the party started, the better."

My remaining shipmates scatter to their rooms, and I search for something resembling shot glasses. The best I can find are drinking cups which means I'm going to have to eyeball it.

"Settled in alright?" Katherine says from behind me.

I turn around, tequila bottle in hand. "I think so. At least I am." I give the bottle a slight shake. "I'm getting our welcome drinks ready."

"After your drinks, join me up on the deck. We need to go over safety precautions before we can shove off." She's not much older than the rest of them, and I have a strong suspicion Garrett is going to be all over her if he doesn't have luck with Lydia.

Daniel steps out of his room and glances at Katherine. "Are you with us all week?"

"I am. I'm the hostess. I'll be making your arrangements and meals. Any questions you have, I'll do my best to answer them." Katherine still holds her clip board. "Enjoy yourselves. I'll see you in a few minutes."

After she walks away, Daniel eyes the shots hungrily. "Garrett," he yells. "Get out here. We're ready to party!"

Lydia appears first, then Garrett and Stella. I pass out the drinks while we wait for Stephan and Emma.

"Where is she?" Lydia huffs. "Why does everything take Emma so long?"

Stella smirks. "Maybe she has Stephan tied up already."

That piques Garretts interest. "Is she down for a little dirty play?"

Before Stella can answer, Stephan, followed by Emma, enters the cabin and stares at us in bewilderment which causes their friends to laugh. "What?" he says, glancing down at his khaki shorts. "Is something wrong?"

Poor guy. He's going to be the piss-on of the week. I hold out a drink for both Emma and Stephan. "Have a drink." When we all have a glass, I say to Stella, "We need a toast."

She nods and raises her glass. "To a fabulous week of new friends and fun adventures."

We clink glasses, and I pound the shot. It burns in the not-pleasant way that cheap alcohol does. "Ugh. That's mixer tequila."

Everyone stares at me, and I almost blush, but then I remember that I'm the HBIC here, and I need to make that known. "Katherine wants us up on the deck for a safety presentation or something."

Like an obedient dog, Stephan heads for the stairs while Daniel pours himself and Garrett another shot. The girls, because that's what they are to me, tail behind Stephan. For a moment, I consider following them, but change my mind and say to Daniel, "Hand me another."

Garrett grins as he hands me my drink. "I knew I liked you."

"Likewise." I pound the shot. It burns. All. The. Way. Down. And within seconds, my head feels woozy. "I need water. Anyone else?" I ask as I open the refrigerator and take a bottle of water that the yacht company so graciously supplied.

"I'll take one," Garrett says, and I toss him a bottle.

"Daniel?" I ask. He shakes his head. "Should we go up?" I ask between gulps of water. "Katherine said we couldn't leave port until she told us how to use the life vests."

The left side of Daniel's mouth ticks up. "Probably should."

I walk ahead of them, making sure to sway my hips a little bit more, and climb the ladder up onto the deck knowing full well that they can probably see up my short dress. I really don't care. Men want me. Women fear me. And that's the way it should be.

Blinding sunlight strikes my face, and I pull my sunglasses from the top of my head. Katherine, Stephan, and the girls stand a little distance away, chatting, and I make my way to them.

"We'll visit Hvar, Bol, and Vis," Katherine says like any of them understand what it means. "Tonight, we're not going into a marina, but the rest of the nights we will."

"Vis is where Tito had his military base, isn't it?" Stephan asks.

Katherine nods. "It is. We can arrange for a tour, if you'd like."

"That would be great!" It's the most non-embarrassed emotion Stephan has shown since I've met him.

"Right," Katherine says, taking stock of us. "Now that you are all here, let's go over safety issues." She rattles on, showing us how to use the life vests, but I check out. The harbor is gorgeous with all the rows of sailboats. I snap a few pictures, but Katherine shoots me a dirty look, and I stop.

She finishes her speech and hands each of us an itinerary. I glance over it – it's mostly a list of towns I don't recognize. "Will we get to explore Hvar at all? Maybe go to the night clubs?"

Katherine nods. "Yes, we can tailor your stay however you'd like."

I peer over the top of my sunglasses at my shipmates. "The night clubs on Hvar are amazing. You'll love them."

That perks Lydia up. She twists her dark hair at the base of her neck and says, "Oh, good! I was worried it was going to be marina parties all the time. I've heard Beyoncé goes to Hvar."

My phone rings, and I dismiss it. Pete can leave a message.

Katherine claps her hands. "Right, if you're ready, I'll tell the captain we can push off." She waves at some guys down on the dock. "Captain! We're ready."

One of the men breaks away and jogs toward the gangplank. Like Katherine, he wears a light blue polo. And like me, he's in his forties. He scans his passengers, and his hazel eyes lock on mine. I smile – something I do to disarm men. Confusion crosses his face, like why-is-she- here kind of confusion, but I ignore it.

"Nice to meet you, Captain..." I say.

"Eric." He's American and not entirely horrible looking. Okay, maybe he's quite good-looking with short brown hair and a fit body. His nose is straight, and he has a solid jaw. Definitely a week's worth of eye candy.

"Veronica," I say demurely.

My phone rings again. This time, I flip it over. I don't recognize the foreign number. My heart races. Did Pete come after all? "Excuse me," I say to the group. "I need to take this."

I move to a more private part of the deck and answer breathlessly. "Hello?"

"Veronica? It's me, Oz."

"Oh my God!" I scream. "Where are you?"

He laughs. "In Split. Are you still here?"

"I am." I knew he wouldn't ditch me. "I'm getting ready to leave for Yacht Week until next Saturday. I'm actually on the boat at the marina."

The captain nods at the rest of my group as if he has better things to do and heads toward the driving part of the boat, or whatever it's called. I guess he's eager to get going.

"Wait!" I yell, and Eric turns around.

I rush toward him as a half-formed idea grips me. "My friend is coming. He just arrived in Split, and..."

"He's not on the manifest."

"I know," I say. "But--"

"Veronica," Oz says into the phone. "I'll be right there. Get off the boat. We'll go to Zagreb."

"Eric, please consider waiting," I plead. "I've paid for two spots, and we can add him to the manifest."

The captain shakes his head. "We're sailing. If you're friend wants to meet us, he can join us at another port." He circles his finger in the air. "We're pushing off."

"Oz," I say, consulting the itinerary Katherine gave me. "Can you make it to Stari Grad or Hvar City? We'll be there in two days."

"I'll meet you in Stari Grad. There's a ferry out there, isn't there?"

"Yes."

The dock workers cast off the ropes holding the catamaran in place and the boat begins to move. "We're going. I'll text you at the next port."

"Okay."

"Bye," I say.

"I'll see you soon." Oz hangs up, and I fight the urge to press my hand against my heart. What am I doing? I'm married – maybe badly, but still. Why am I getting googly-eyed over some guy twelve years younger than me?

But I can't deny the relief I feel. Oz didn't ghost me. In fact, he wants to see me again.

Elated, I toss my hair over my shoulder and turn around. "Let's get some shots on the bow before we lose WiFi," I say to the kids. "I need Instagram photos."

Katherine holds up her hand. "No need to worry. We have WiFi on the boat. The password is written on the rules list in the kitchen. It should be attached to the inside of the cabinet."

Thank God. I'm not completely cut-off for the week. I walk down the deck toward the bow of the boat with a little bounce in my step. "C'mon," I wave to my shipmates. "Let's get pictures."

I pose against the railing. I could go with cheesy, "I'm the king of the world" photos, or I could do something sexier. I glance back at the motley crew I'm stuck with. I definitely need to go sexier. I beckon Daniel toward me, and he eagerly pounces. Good, someone on this boat finds me alluring. It's a start.

"Can you take a picture of me?"

"Sure," he says, reaching for my phone.

I hand it over, strip off my sundress, and drop it onto the deck. Daniel open-mouth gawks at me, but why am I surprised? I look amazing, and he wouldn't be a heterosexual male if he didn't appreciate my looks.

The sun sits high overhead. I lean against the railing and arrange my hair so that it hangs in perfect waves over my shoulders. Then, I push my right hip toward Daniel, creating a slight arch in my back. "Do I look okay?"

Daniel smiles. "Fantastic, love. Absolutely fantastic."

The others gather behind him, and Stella claps. "Whooo! Get it girl!"

All the angst of the past few weeks slides off me. It doesn't matter that Pete is a lying cheat. It doesn't matter that I'm twenty-years older than these kids. It doesn't matter that I'm alone. I can still have fun, and I'm determined to.

I pose while Daniel snaps the photos. Garrett whistles at me, so I turn my back to the camera and glance over my shoulder. I arch my back even more. Daniel is going to get a great shot of my toned ass, and I'm going to plaster that all over my social media so that Pete and Eve can see.

Lydia crosses her arms. "Are we going to do this all day?"

"Do you have something better to do?" I ask as my bitchy Waterford side unnecessarily rears its ugly head. "What I meant to say is, you can get your suit on and join me if you'd like."

"Really?" Lydia says snottily. "Tell me why I should pose for pictures with an old lady."

I can't help myself with this girl. "Worried you won't look as good?"

"No."

She stomps away, and I laugh. "Amateur."

"What was that?" Stella asks.

"Nothing." I say sweetly and step away from the bow. I stoop and pick my sundress up off the deck. After I slip it over my head, I smile at the remainder of my group. "Now, who's ready to party?"

14

These kids go hard. I mean, I go hard, but I don't have a twenty-something liver anymore. Daniel is the worst of them. He's been drinking straight whiskey since we boarded – maybe four of five glasses, not to mention the tequila shots – and somehow manages to stand upright with no signs of slowing down. He could out drink the men of Waterford, which I thought was an impossible feat.

"We're leaving," Katherine shouts from her spot on a smaller boat attached to the catamaran. "Everyone who is going to dinner needs to be on the tinder."

I sit snuggly between Daniel, who reeks of booze, and Stella while we wait for Lydia and Emma. "Are they always late?"

Stella sighs. "It's like herding cats with those two."

Katherine frowns. "What should I do? We have a reservation."

"Leave them," Stella answers.

Before Katherine can untie from the catamaran, the two young women appear on deck.

"Don't go!" Lydia whines. I'm beginning to think she's incapable of another other tone of voice.

"Get in the boat," Stella orders, and they climb down onto the swimming deck while clutching their shoes. Lydia mutters who knows what under her breath. How charming. Once they're onboard, Katherine shoves off.

The short ride across the tiny bay is uneventful. Katherine lets us off near a set of stairs leading up a steep cliff, and when it's my turn to walk up, I'm thankful I cut myself off after a second glass of wine. I have no idea how Daniel is going to make it up.

At the top, fragrant lavender fields flank each side of the walkway. I pinch off a few flowers and sniff.

"This is so gorgeous!" Emma says, turning around toward me. She, Lydia, and Stella walk slightly ahead of me, and the guys follow behind. "Are you picking flowers?"

I nod and hold out the crushed lavender. "It smells like Croatia."

Emma shoots me a strange look and hurries to catch up with her friends. Guess I said something wrong, but I don't really care. If she can't appreciate what she's experiencing, that's on her.

We crest another small hill, and a gorgeous low-slung wood and glass building appears. Next to it, rough-hewn picnic tables sit under a thatched-roofed patio. Several other diners enjoy their dinner, and the delicious scent of roasted meat causes my mouth to water.

A spritely, older man rushes toward us. He stretches his arms wide and beams. "Welcome!"

Garrett takes the lead. "Hello, there! We have a reservation for seven people."

The man nods and motions for us to follow him to a picnic table. As we arrange ourselves, a waiter brings out three bottles of wine. "The house specialty," the elderly man says. "Very good red."

Not one to complain about wine, I hold out my glass. "Thank you!"

The waiter gives me a generous pour, and I sip. The wine is earthy and full-bodied.

"You like?"

"Very much." I look down the table at my group. "It's delicious."

While he pours for my shipmates, another waiter carries a huge clay pot to our table and lifts the lid. Savory meat and veggies simmer inside. That's what I must have smelled on the walk up the path.

"What is it?" I ask.

"Lamb and vegetables," the waiter says. "Everyone shares."

Garrett immediate digs in with a ladle and dumps the contents on his plate.

"Ewww." Emma wrinkles her nose. "Is there anything else?"

"What's wrong with lamb and veggies?" Garrett asks between bites. "It's amazing."

She recoils. "I can't eat a baby animal!"

Oh, Lord. "Is it any different than eating an adult animal?" I ask. "You're still eating an animal."

She crosses her arms. "I'll have wine."

"Better find out if it's made from baby grapes," Daniel teases. Emma scowls at him, and I suppress my giggle.

Two hours later, most of the other diners have left, but we're still eating and drinking. The old man doesn't seem to care; he keeps bringing out more things for us to try, as if the amazing clay pot meal he gave us wasn't good enough.

Emma greedily gobbles up the cheese and figs, leaving scraps for the rest of us, and smacks her lips in appreciation. Then she pours herself another glass of wine.

I hold my empty glass up. "Would you mind?"

She obediently fills it, and Stella winks at me. For being the one in charge, Stella is certainly open to me taking the lead. Maybe it's my age, but she definitely defers to me, which means the other two should also. Lydia, however, is a tough, whiny nut to crack. She clearly doesn't like the attention I'm getting from the guys in our group, but she can fix that by being a bit more pleasant. No one likes a scowling sourpuss.

Elbows on the table, Stephan declares, "That was delicious!"

"And the company is pretty good, too!" Garrett replies with a slap on the back.

The waiter carries out some sort of berry dish drizzled in honey and presents it to the table. "You like?" he asks. "I bring it."

Lydia and Emma both eye the dessert with horror, so I answer, "That would be wonderful."

The grizzled man hurries away, and I lift my chin, enjoying my wine, the breeze, and the soft scent of lavender.

"Tell us about your friend who's joining us," Stella says. "What's she like?"

"Oz is a he," I rub my fingers together under the table. As excited as I am to have Oz join me, I'm nervous I may not hold up next to these younger girls.

"Your boyfriend?" Lydia asks in disbelief. Does she really think women my age can't have fun? Not that Oz is my boyfriend. But I am capable of getting men interested in me – Daniel and Garrett are two examples.

"No. Just a friend."

Lydia cocks her head. "How did you meet?"

I'm not in the mood for an inquisition, but I answer. "In Marrakech at a restaurant. We went to the Sahara together. You'll like him."

And she will. He's cute and sweet and everything that makes women interested. Lydia will try to make him her prey. I have no doubt about that.

"What's on the agenda tomorrow?" Stella asks.

Stephan – who I'm learning is a strict rule follower – says, "We sail for Hvar City then Stari Grad the next day."

I perk up. "Good! Oz will meet us there. And Stari Grad is so much fun!"

"Have you been here before, Veronica?" Emma asks, fiddling with the strap of her overalls. Underneath she only wears a crop top. She's trying to be fashion forward, but it's not a good look.

I nod. "Yes. I lived in Croatia for a few years."

Everyone stares at me.

"Are you Croatian?" Stephan asks.

I shake my head. "No, I'm as American as they come."

"Then why were you living here?" Lydia says. "This isn't exactly London or New York."

"Work. I lived in Zagreb, which is the capital and more inland. We would vacation on the coast though."

"We?" Lydia's eyebrows shoot up. "Are you a divorcée with a boytoy?"

It's been so easy not to think about the Pete mess since getting on the boat. There have been drinks and fun and people to distract me. Which makes thinking about him an intrusion even though he texted, 'You're on a boat?' after seeing my pictures.

"I'm not a divorcée. I'm on a solo trip." I pause to let my partial lie sink in. "I don't know where I'm headed after this."

"So, you've left your husband and kids – because I assume you have children – and are solo traveling the world with some guy named Oz? Sounds like marriage problems to me." Lydia smirks. "Let me guess: you read *Eat Pray Love*, and now you're searching for something more out of life?"

She's not going to wear me down. I'm better at playing a mean girl than she is; after all, I have years of experience. "My husband is indulgent, and I typically get what I want." I wink at Garrett for effect. "That goes for everything."

"Including side-guys and lavish trips." Lydia snorts. "It's so mid-life crisis that it's not even funny."

"Should we close out and head back to the boat?" Stella says, diffusing the situation. "We can play cards or something."

Since we're not in a marina, there are only three other boats tied up near ours. We're going to be each other's only source of entertainment tonight.

"Great idea, mate!" Garrett stands and stretches his arms overhead. "I'm going to test out the water."

"It's chilly and dark!" Emma exclaims. "You'll freeze."

He lets out a hearty laugh. "I'm a surfer. I'm sure I've felt worse."

The waiter rushes toward our table carrying a tray of dessert.

Shit. I forgot I ordered those. Oh well. "Sit, sit," he says. "More food for you." A younger waiter stands behind him holding a bottle of wine. "Drink this."

Stephan whispers in my ear. "We're paying for all this, aren't we?"

"Probably, so enjoy yourself."

He shakes his head as Garrett plunks down next to Stella on the bench. The waiter passes out the berry desserts, and Lydia pulls an ugly face. "They put something on the berries! Sugar! They put sugar on the berries."

I dip my finger in my dessert and taste it. "It's only honey."

"It's carbs." She pushes the dessert away. Can't blame her. It's bathing suit season, and a girl's got to watch what she eats or else risk having a carb belly.

Still, I bite into a ripe berry and exaggerate my chewing. "Oh, it's so good!"

"I don't for one moment believe you eat sugar," Lydia says. "In fact, other than your wine and the alcohol on the boat, I haven't seen you eat or drink much of anything."

It's true that I typically don't eat much, but the stress of the Pete situation has destroyed my appetite. Sometimes I'm ravenous, and other times, the thought of food revolts me. Tonight, I did eat most of my dinner. Well, at least a portion of it. Okay I nibbled.

"I had enough to feel full," I say.

"You'll probably vomit that miniscule bit up later," Lydia says. What is with this girl? Is she really that threatened by me? Granted, I probably could use a couple extra pounds, but I wear clothes well, and that's what matters most.

Stella shoots Lydia a nasty look, and Lydia purses her lips, but says nothing else.

After we eat – or don't eat – our desserts, the owner shuffles toward us with the check in his hand. "It's taken care of," he says. "The captain paid it."

"What?" Garrett and I exclaim in unison.

"The captain. It is part of your experience."

I try to remember if that's what the organizer told me when I signed up, but the wine has made my memory hazy. I glance at Stephan. "See?" I say. "It always works out."

Daniel offers Stella his arm, and Garrett does the same for Lydia, leaving Emma, me, and Stephan to bring up the rear. I'm not sure if they think those girls are easy targets or if they seem the most drunk, but I have to admit, I wish someone had chosen me.

The descent to the boat is steep, and I slip off my sandals so that I don't slip on the stairs. Half-way down, Lydia plunks down on a step. "I can't go on. I'm too drunk."

Garrett turns around and charges up the stairs. He picks Lydia up and slings her over his shoulder like it's nothing. She screams playfully, but I know better. She's perfectly fine. Maybe buzzed, but not so intoxicated that she can't walk. She wants attention.

I make it to the tender. It wobbles beneath me, and I lose my balance, careening into Emma. She braces me until I regain my balance. It's a short distance to our boat, and the tender pulls as close to the back stairs as it can. There's still a small gap between the boats, which may prove challenging in our current inebriated states.

Daniel jumps off first, offering his hand to Emma then Stella. Stephan steps off next, and he helps Lydia across. Only Garrett and I remain in the boat.

"Ladies first?" I ask.

He shakes his head. "I'll help you over."

I cross after him, giving him my hand. I nearly drop my sandals in the water, but manage to catch them before they actually fall.

Once we're all on deck, I take stock of the situation. Honestly, I've had too much to drink and need to sleep it off, but Stella and Daniel look ready to go. If I turn in before everyone else, I'll be "that old person." No, I need to power through if I want to have any fun this week.

Unlike me, Stephan has no qualms about turning in. "I'm going to bed," he says. "Do you want to use the bathroom first, Emma, or should I put a pillow over my head?"

"No. You go first. I'll be in shortly. I'm wiped out."

"It's the fresh air," Garrett says. "If you're not used to it and the sun, you'll tucker out fast."

"Don't forget the alcohol," I add, fighting back a yawn. "The amount we drank will bring the strongest down. Well, except Daniel. He's a beast."

Daniel laughs as he and Garrett disappear into the main cabin with Stephan following behind.

"What now?" I ask.

Emma lets out a loud yawn. "You know, I think I will turn in."

I nod. "Probably a good idea."

"We're going to the hammock," Stella says to me, pointing between herself and Lydia. "Join us?"

"I will in a few." Since others are turning in, going to bed won't make me an outcast. I'm about to follow Emma down, when Daniel pops up with a bottle of something and a few plastic cups. "You going to sleep?"

Emma nods. "I don't want alcohol poisoning my first night."

"Lightweight," Garrett teases.

Hushed voices drift from the front of the boat. I strain to hear, but the lapping of the waves against the boat drown out the actual words.

"I'm going to join Lydia and Stella," I say to the guys. "Why don't you two come?" I don't really feel like being alone with either the guys or the girls.

Daniel nods. "Good plan."

I navigate the narrow walkway to the front of the boat, and Stella spies me. She places her finger to her lips, and Lydia breaks midsentence. They were discussing me, and I can only imagine the things they've been saying.

"Can the geriatric join your group?" I ask.

Stella moves over on the boat-width hammock to make room for me. I try to delicately climb into it, but I stumble and somersault until

I land flat on my back. My dress bunches around my hips, but it's too dark for anyone to see anything.

"That," I say, trying to make the best of the situation, "is a talent you only develop as you age."

Garrett laughs. "Epic, Veronica. Very epic."

I don't feel epic. I feel old and tired, but it's important I stay out here. Daniel hands out the glasses and pours vodka into them. I really don't want any vodka. I want my bed.

"Cheers," he shouts.

Across the way, a passenger on another boat yells back, "Cheers!"

We laugh, and I lay back in the hammock with my glass resting on my flat stomach and stare up at the stars. There aren't as many as in the Sahara, but they're still beautiful. As the others chat, sharing stories about themselves, I allow the boat to gently rock me into bliss.

"Veronica? Come inside." Stella gently shakes my arm. "You're going to freeze out here."

I blink my eyes open. "Oh. Right. Good idea." I try rolling onto my side, but the pitch of the hammock tosses me onto my back again. "Oh, God," I moan. "I feel sick."

"You drank a lot. We all did," Stella says. "Try crawling out on your knees. That's what I had to do."

I flop over onto my stomach and press up onto all fours. The netting catches on my foot, and I yank myself free. Waves of nausea hit me, but I manage to crawl slowly toward the deck. Once I find my balance, I feel a little better. "Has everyone else gone to bed?"

Stella nods. "A while ago. We didn't want to wake you, but I couldn't leave you here even though Daniel said we should."

"Thank you," I say. "I'm sorry I passed out. That's not at all like me."

"It's fine. We didn't discuss anything major."

I straighten my dress. "I think he likes you."

"Who?" Stella looks at me quizzically.

"Daniel."

"Oh, well, too bad for him. I'm taken." She grins. "I didn't wear my ring on this trip because I didn't want to lose it, but I'm engaged. Emma, Lydia, and I are here on a hens week."

"Bachelorette party?" I say with surprise. "You're so young."

She laughs. "I'm twenty-seven. We've dated for five years."

"I guess that's plenty of time to know if he's the one," I say.

We sit on a bench near the cabin entrance. "What about you, Veronica? You say you have a husband, but you aren't wearing a ring. I can see the tan mark from where it was, though."

I can't tell her that I took my rings off as soon as I arrived home and left them on Pete's bedside table. "Same reason," I say. "I didn't want to get robbed."

"Have you been married long?" Stella asks. Interestingly, she doesn't ask about Oz.

"Too long." I immediately regret my answer when she frowns. "Oh, you'll know what I mean when you've been married twenty-odd years."

Stella's dreamy face glows in the moonlight. "I can't wait to be married that long. I want tons of children, and James does too. It feels like my life is finally beginning."

Oh, poor thing. Little does she know. Maybe it's the alcohol, but I can't stop myself from saying, "Your life begins when you want it too. Look at me. I'm forty-five. My kids are off to university. It's only me and my husband now. And here I am, on a boat in the Adriatic with a bunch of twenty-somethings, getting drunk."

She tilts her head. "Are you having fun, Veronica? Because, and I don't mean this with any ill will, but you have a cloud of sadness around you."

"I didn't know I wore my sadness like a cloak," I say.

"You are sad, then?"

"A little, but it's not going to stop me from having fun." I stand. I can't have this conversation – especially when I've been drinking. "We should go in."

Stella reaches for my hand. "Don't let Lydia bother you. She's always been the prettiest girl in the room, and she can't stand that she isn't here."

I shrug. "She has nothing to worry about. I'm twenty years older than her, and guys your age don't look at old ladies like me."

"Your bikini photo shoot proves otherwise." Stella pats her stomach. "My wedding is in two weeks, and I've been busting my arse trying to get svelte. I'm not naturally thin."

"You," I say staring into her eyes, "are beautiful. Don't think you're not."

"Thank you," she says. "Sometimes, next to Lydia and Emma, I feel like third place."

I sigh. "Have they found their soul mate?" I almost choke on the word. I no longer believe in two people being fated for each other. In fact, I think quite the opposite. There are millions of potential mates out there, but we often pick the worst one for us out of lust and obligation. "Are they married?"

Stella shakes her head. "Lydia can't commit to anyone longer than a month, and Emma...well, Emma has no luck with men."

"What's her deal?" I ask.

"Emma?"

"Yeah. Is she British or American?"

Stella chuckles. "She's very much American, but she's lived in London since university."

"What else?" I ask. "Is she an heiress or something? That hair makes me think you all are 'It Girls' working the scene."

Stella shrugs. "Lydia works in advertising, but not very hard. It's more of a hobby for her."

"She comes from money?"

Stella nods. "Old, aristocratic money. But Emma, she's American new money. Her dad is the CEO of some tech company in San Francisco. He made a fortune off IPOs."

I ponder that. They are three, wealthy young women sharing a boat in Croatia with strangers. It makes no sense. "So why not get a private yacht. A real one. Why are you doing Yacht Week?"

"Bucket list item. Plus, we wanted to have shipmates. I liked the randomness of it." Stella stares into my eyes, and it disarms me. "But what I want to know is how did you end up here?"

"It was a whim. A waiter told me about Yacht Week, so I went down to the marina and booked myself onto a boat." I pause. "I didn't know what to expect, but I thought getting out on the water would be fun." My head spins, and I brace myself against the wall. "I really do need to turn in if I have any hope of making it to breakfast."

"Veronica?"

"Yes?"

"You're going to be okay."

Right now I feel very far from ok, but I nod and head inside.

15

Morning doesn't treat me well. In fact, I swear I wronged it in a former life, and it's out for revenge. Still, I manage to drag myself from bed and into the bathroom without puking. I search through my dopp kit, find Excedrin Migraine, pop two pills dry, and pray my insides stay put.

Knock, knock, knock.

I startle and drop the pill bottle into the miniscule sink. "What?"

"Breakfast is ready," Stella says. "Are you going to join us?"

I stare at my reflection in the small circular mirror. Bloodshot eyes and a rat's nest of hair greet me. "I'm not very hungry."

"You should eat," Stella says from the other side of the door. "There are pastries, and carbs will help soak up the alcohol."

She has a point, but Jesus, how did I let myself get so wasted? "I'll be up in ten. Save me something light if Katherine wants to pack it up."

"Perfect! See you in a few." How can she be so awake after the amount we drank last night. Oh. Right. She has a twenty-seven-year old liver.

I brush the knots from my hair, then liberally spray it with dry shampoo. While I wait for it to absorb, I rub sunblock over my face and do my eyes. Finally, I work in the dry shampoo and brush my hair up into a high ponytail. If only I had Visine, I'd look normal. If I leave my sunglasses on, no one will know how hungover I am.

After changing out of the clothes I wore the day before and into my bikini and cover-up, I grab my sunhat and head out into the main cabin. No one is there, but voices carry down the stairs. I climb the stairs to the deck, and warm sunlight strikes my face. The fresh air fills my lungs, and my stomach settles a little. Food covers the folding table.

"There she is!" Garrett wears a tank top, exposing those gorgeous biceps of his. He may not be the smartest guy, but he is pretty to look at.

"I'm a slow starter," I answer as he moves over to make room for me.

Stella hands me a plate. "The chocolate croissants are delicious."

I wrinkle my nose. "Carbs aren't my friend."

She pushes a serving tray of pastries toward me. "Trust me, you need it today."

With a frown, I select the smallest croissant and take a few pieces of prosciutto and some melon. I glance around the table; everyone is in various states of being hungover, but I've got to be the worst. Daniel shovels food into his mouth like he's been on a deserted island for months. His sunglasses wrap around the top of his head, so clearly he's headache-free. How is that even possible? Bastard.

"What's the plan?" Lydia asks Katherine who walks toward us. Today, Katherine wears a white polo and khaki shorts. I wonder if she has one for every day? "I want to do something fun," Lydia orders. "You have planned something fun, haven't you, Katherine?"

I don't know how Katherine maintains professionalism with Lydia, but she very calmly says, "Captain Eric and I thought you'd like to take the paddle boards out this morning before we head to Hvar City. There, you can visit the city or take a tour of a lavender farm."

Emma sighs. "I think I'm sunbathing today. I don't have it in me to paddle board or tour another lavender field."

I pick at my pastry. "It's a lazy day for me, too."

"Does anyone want to tour Hvar City?" Katherine asks like a teacher speaking to her kindergarten class.

"I do." Stephan raises his hand and looks around our group. "The loggia and cathedral are important Croatian sites."

Daniel rolls his eyes, and Garrett punches Stephan on the arm. "If you paddle board with me, I'll go look at buildings with you."

"I agree." Stephan extends his hand. God, he's awkward.

"Is there any coffee?" I ask Katherine. If anything is going to save the day, it's coffee.

"Black or with cream?"

"Is it Croatian coffee?" I ask.

She nods.

"Then just sugar." Croatian coffee is thick and black, and absolutely not meant for cream. It's sacrilegious.

Emma and Lydia whisper to each other before standing. Lydia puts on a wide-brimmed hat. "We're going to the hammock," she announces as if that's her territory. "You have fun doing whatever it is you're doing."

Stella waves to them. "I'm going to lay out on the sundeck. Veronica, want to join me?"

I could use some color. Normally, I spray tan, but since running away from Pete, I haven't had one. Plus, that full-body scrub down in the hammam scraped off the last remnants of it. "Sure." I push my barely-touched food away. "Let me finish my coffee first."

I look out at the bay, only one boat is anchored with us now – the others must have left while I was sleeping. The crests of tiny waves sparkle under the bright yellow sunlight. Out of habit, I glance at my phone. It's only 10:30, but the heat already wraps me in an insufferable embrace. I'm going to have to jump into the cool, blue water at some point.

I run my finger over the phone screen before opening Whatsapp.

--Arriving in Hvar City today--

Oz immediately answers.

--Meet you in Stari Grad--

My heart sinks. I was hoping to see him today, but I'll survive. Katherine sets a mug of coffee in front of me, and I look up.

"Enjoy."

Steam swirls off the surface of the black liquid, and I inhale. Despite my best efforts, my mind flits back to a rainy afternoon in Zagreb. Pete and I sat in a corner café while our nanny watched the kids. I can't recall what we discussed, but I remember feeling complete. Happy. Like I was living my best life. And maybe I was. Maybe it's all downhill now. I sigh.

"Are you alright?" Garrett asks.

I sigh again. "It's my head. I have a raging headache, and the Excedrin hasn't kicked in yet, but the coffee should help." I blow into my cup. "At least I hope so."

He slides down the bench and away from me. "C'mon, boys, it's time to test the water."

Daniel stands and takes a bottle of whiskey off the table. How did I not notice that before? "Were you drinking that with breakfast?"

"In my coffee. A little Hair o' the Dog." He gives a slight smile. "Want some? It could help."

Is he really not hungover? I shake my head.

"Suit yourself," Daniel says before walking off with the other guys, leaving Stella and me behind.

She tilts her head. "I'll meet you on the sundeck?"

"Okay."

I sit there, listening to waves wash against the side of the boat and the splash of the guys jumping into the sea. Music from the other boat drifts across the water, but I can't make out any distinct voices.

Green hillsides slope into the water on three sides, making a cozy, protected harbor for us. It would be a romantic place for a vacation – if you didn't have to deal with drunk strangers. But there's no reason for anyone to know why I'm on Yacht Week or that I have a nasty hangover. All they need to know is that I'm on a boat on the gorgeous Adriatic.

As the boat rocks, I look up at the sky and find the best light. Using my phone as a mirror, I place my wide-brimmed hat perfectly on my head and adjust my sunglasses. Satisfied that I look like an heiress on the French Riviera, I snap a few selfies with the hills and sea behind me.

"Loving life in Croatia! Nothing beats a week-long yacht trip around the islands! Hvar City today and Stari Grad tomorrow." I geotag my favorite photo so it's easier to find and post it to Instagram and Facebook.

Within seconds, the likes start pouring in on Instagram. I study the layout of all my posts and weed out pictures that don't have at least seventy likes. When I'm done, my feed is a carefully crafted story of a woman having a fabulous life.

I can live that life. I can make it real. I need to keep trying.

Judging by the amount of sweat I'm covered in, alcohol must ooze from my pours. I prop onto my elbows, and sweat drips down my back. "I'm going for a dip." Stella lazily turns her head. Even though she's lathered in SPF 8,000, she's faintly pink. "Maybe you should get out of the sun," I say. "You don't want to peel on your wedding day."

She sits up and reaches for the bottle of sunblock. "I think I'll join you first." She squirts a blob of white goo into her hand and rubs it across her chest and arms. "But, you're right. I am getting burnt."

Next to my sexy white bikini, Stella's bathing suit is modest. It sits high on her waist and the top is a crop-top style. It's almost a tank-ini, except it's trying really hard not to be with its cute pompoms attached to the waist and bottom of the halter. Tankinis, after all, are what women wear when they've given up. Stella, at least, is still showing some skin.

I slip on my sandals so I don't burn my feet on the scorching deck and walk toward Lydia and Emma who lounge in the hammock. Both girls have plastic cups full of who-knows-what and rest so that their faces get direct sun. They're going to have so much sun damage when they're my age.

I slink past them toward the stairs. On the wet diving deck, I ditch my shoes.

"Veronica!" Garrett yells. "You coming in?"

"Will you save me if I drown?" I whip my ponytail over my shoulder.

"Of course!" When he's a few feet away, I hold by breath and jump. The chill of the water steals my breath. Against the heat of the day, it's refreshing, but shocking. It was silly not to have dipped my toe in first.

"You should have warned me!" I say, gasping. "It's cold!"

Garrett paddles up next to me, and I try to gracefully climb on, but there really is no way to pull yourself out of the water without looking ridiculous. "We need to go in soon," he says. "Katherine wants to make it to Hvar City today."

"Oh." I sit cross-legged on the board, behind Garrett. "We should go in then."

Up on the swimming platform, Stella waves. "Coming back?"

"Katherine wants to leave," I say.

She nods. "Captain Eric told me to get you out of the water, so we can pack up and go."

I had almost forgotten about Captain Eric. He must barricade himself in his quarters. "He actually came out of hiding?"

"He wanted to see how we were enjoying ourselves." Stella offers me her hand, and I clamber onto the platform. Daniel and Stephan wait to bring their boards in. "I told him we were having an exquisite time."

"And so we are," I say with a small laugh. I wring out my hair and twist it over my shoulder. "I really need to brush this mop, or it's going to be a mess – even with my keratin treatment."

"What's that?" Stella asks.

"Keratin?" She nods. "It's a treatment to make your hair smooth," I say. "No more flatiron."

"It takes a lot to be you, doesn't it?" Stella says in a non-accusatory way.

"If you only knew. Wait until you're my age, then we'll talk upkeep."

While the guys haul the boards into storage, Stella and I head to the deck. My cover up, hat, and phone lay on the ground, so I grab them and head toward the shade. Stella follows along. "Best to get out of the sun," I say. "Wrinkles and burns are the enemy of all women."

Stella stretches out on the padded bench. "Wrinkles equal wisdom."

"Says the twenty-seven-year old."

We sit in silence, and I focus on the light breeze and warm air surrounding me. The hills slip by, and a spray of water extends from the front of the boat.

Daniel comes barreling up the stairs toward us. "Drinks?"

"Vodka tonic?" Stella asks. "I bought all those bottles of wine last night, but I'm not in the mood for anything heavy. It's too hot."

"Red wine doesn't match well with these temperatures." I take off my hat and fan myself.

"Veronica?" Daniel asks. "Anything for you?"

"No," I say. "I'll get some sparkling water in a little bit." I still feel slightly off balance from my hangover.

Stella closes her eyes, and I take the opportunity to check my phone. First, Facebook. Some of my Waterford friends have to be up by now. And sure enough, I have fifty-seven likes already.

"Yachting! OMG!"

"You are AMAZING!"

"Pretty girl!"

And so on. I take a moment to like the comments before flipping over to Instagram. My chest pounds. I have 103 hearts, not the most ever, but definitely not bad. The comments though, are something else. All kinds of random guys commenting on how hot I am. It doesn't bother me though, because after all, celebrities have all kinds of crazies on their feeds. Not that I'm a celebrity, but I highly doubt anyone is going to fly to Hvar to stalk me.

"You're attached to that thing, aren't you?" Stella asks.

I hold up my phone. "Well, it is my only connection to my family and friends. I want them to see everything I'm experiencing."

Stella stretches. "But don't you feel like you're missing out by only seeing things through the lens?"

First Oz, now Stella. I thought millennials were supposed to love social media. "You have a point," I say. "But I really want them to know what I'm doing."

This seems to satisfy her, and she closes her eyes. And then...

"Stella!"

She bolts upright.

"Stella!"

"What the bloody hell is wrong with Lydia?" She jumps to her feet and runs toward the overhang to look at the hammock. "What?"

I can't see Lydia, but Stella seems pissed.

"Come down. We miss you!" Lydia's posh voice carries over the sound of wind rushing past us. The boat is at full speed, so she must be screaming. "Stop hanging out with old people and get with your mates."

Stella turns to look back at me. "I suppose I should go down."

I shoo her away. "I'll let Daniel know where to bring your drink."

"Thanks."

When she's gone, I place my legs on the bench and savor the shade. I'm protected from the wind, and it makes the day feel even more pleasant. I try to rest my mind, to let go of all the stress and anger I feel, but it's useless. I'm being gnawed alive from the inside out. This is what I hate: the alone moments -- those times when normally, I'd turn to Pete or call my so-called friends.

Like the waves crashing against the bow of the boat, my sorrow hits me hard. Stella can see it, and I'm sure everyone else can too. I'm the miserable, old woman in the front cabin. The outcast.

I fiddle with my phone, struggling against the urge to open it again. Stella is right, I do spend too much time on it. And yet, I can't help myself and tap it on. My finger hovers over the Facebook icon. I could look fast – just to see the comments. I don't need to scroll. I don't need to know what Eve has been doing.

But before I can stop myself, Eve's new profile picture fills my screen. She's at the pool, her long, blonde hair draping over her shoulder in mermaid waves and a little navy striped bikini sitting low on her hips. God, I hate her.

I keep scrolling through her page and the endless pictures of her with my friends. Every once in a while, Pete pops up in the background, but most are group shots with the prerequisite comments underneath.

Vomit rises in my throat.

"Where'd Stella go?" Daniel surprises me, and I drop my phone with a clank onto the deck floor. "Oh, sorry, I didn't mean to scare you."

I wasn't doing anything wrong, so why do I feel like it? "It's fine. I'm just jumpy. Not enough sleep last night."

Daniel nods. "You should get some water. Dehydration is no joke."

"Yeah." I collect my phone and jerk my head toward the stairs. "Stella went down to the hammock."

"Right. Well, cheers!"

Katherine said we would be sailing until mid-day, so there's time for me to nap. Otherwise, I'm getting in everyone's way. Garrett likes flirting with me, and Stella is nice enough, but the rest of them wonder why Grandma is on the boat with them.

My phone dings.

I stare at it, trying to comprehend. It's Eve.

--If you want to see what your husband says about you, read this.--

Dozens of 'downloading' icons fill my screen. My heart pounds against my ribcage, and my breath comes in short, ragged gasps.

The first screenshot loads, and I stare at it in horror.

--Vee doesn't like sex. She'd rather drink wine and be with her friends.--

--She's my roommate, not my wife.--

--She used to be fun.--

Eve's responses have all been strategically deleted. I don't wait for the rest to load; I've seen enough. I drop my phone on the bench and run to the railing.

"Veronica! What are you doing?" Stella yells. "Stop!"

I consider flinging myself into the ocean. I want all this to stop. I can't do it anymore.

Instead, I lean over the edge and puke.

16

I smash my face into a flimsy pillow to stifle my sobs. Every inch of my body aches, and my stomach bubbles and cramps. After my spectacular vomiting display, which I played off as motion sickness combined with a hangover, I've been locked in my cabin frantically refreshing my phone, trying to piece everything together.

How could Pete say those things? And why? I made him the center of my life, or at least I thought I did. And he's always been so good to me. Was it all a lie?

Did I believe my own bullshit?

Whether I like it or not, I need to accept that from now on, everything I do is on my own. The divorce is coming – maybe not immediately, but definitely when I get back. Pete has all but said it, and with those texts, what else can I believe?

Until Eve sent them, I didn't grasp how strongly I leaned toward forgiving and forgetting. I can't do that now. It wasn't one time with Eve. Hell, it wasn't even a two-time thing. Pete cheated over and over again and said vile things about me.

I roll onto my back. The stuffy, warm cabin air makes breathing difficult. With a sniff, I wipe my hands over my face and crawl off the bed. I check my reflection in the bathroom mirror, wash off my tear stains, and put my sunglasses on. Thankfully, it's still sunny, and I can hide my eyes.

Thankfully, when I crack my cabin door, silence greets me. The others must have decided to leave me behind and head into Hvar City. Good. It will give me a little more time to regroup.

My stomach quakes as I retrieve a bottle of sparkling water and a glass before climbing the stairs to the deck. Loud music and shouts hit me all at once, and even with my sunglasses on, I squint in the bright sunlight. Sailboats and catamarans jam every slip, and of course, half-naked, drunk people dance on their boats and crowd the dock.

If it weren't so hot in my cabin, I would go back down. But I need fresh air. I round the corner, and to my surprise, Katherine and Captain Eric sit on the shaded benches. "Oh!"

"Sorry. Did we surprise you?" Eric asks. Like Katherine, he's wearing khaki shorts and a white polo. He's attractive in a WAPSy, yachty way, if I were in the mood to notice things like that.

"Yes, but it's fine." I point at an empty seat. "Can I join you? I'd rather not be in the sun." I was hoping to be alone, but now I'm stuck.

"Of course," Eric says. "How are you feeling?"

Wonderful. He heard about my spectacular vomiting display. "Much better. I think being in the harbor is helping."

"We have sea sickness medicine if you'd like some," Katherine says with too much earnestness.

I shake my head. "I'll be fine. It was probably a combination of the sun and drinking."

"Happens to the best of us," Eric says with a smile. He places his open hand on a clipboard sitting on the table. "We're planning our course for the next few days, and I'd love to hear your opinion."

I pour water into my glass and place the capped bottle on the seat next to me. "I'm probably the wrong person to ask. My idea of fun and everyone else's is vastly different."

Eric chuckles. "How are you finding your shipmates?"

"Young."

"Most of our clients are," Katherine says. She looks away, like she said the wrong thing.

I give a half-shrug. "They're not bad, but I'm not sure I can keep up with their drinking for another five days." I glance at the shore. "Did they go into town?"

Katherine nods. "They did. They plan on eating dinner there."

Oh. It must be well after seven. I hadn't thought of dinner, and I have zero appetite. "I guess I'm on my own then."

Eric shakes his head. "Why don't you join Katherine and me? We're having sandwiches. Nothing fancy."

"Honestly, I don't know if I can eat."

Katherine and Eric exchange glances, and I know they're thinking about my puking incident. "A little food in your stomach will help," Eric says. "Trust me."

"You're probably right." I take a seat. "But it's not an insult if I can't eat."

"None taken." In the distance, someone screams, and there's a loud splash. Eric shakes his head. "I'd never get in the water here. We empty our sewage tanks in the harbor."

"Oh, gross." I wrinkle my nose. "Make sure you tell Garrett that. He may want to take another nighttime dip."

A dozen different songs fill the air, but most of it is thumping Euro-dance music that blends together. From the boats next to us, I catch snips of conversations in English and German, and a group of what I think are Chinese tourists passes by.

"The harbor is a mini United Nations," I say.

"Croatia is becoming more and more popular," Katherine answers. "This isn't even high-season. You should see it in a few weeks. You can barely walk through Split, and we battle for slips." She stands. "I'll get the sandwiches."

When she's gone, Eric folds his hands on the tabletop and leans towards me. "Aside from being sick, how have you enjoyed the tour so far?"

I smile politely. There's no need to complain about the lack of air

173

conditioning or that the bed is rock hard. "It's exactly what I expected."

Eric nods, and an awkward silence surrounds us.

"Do you sail year round?" I ask.

"After the season here, I move to the Caribbean."

"I do the same," Katherine says, popping up from below deck. She carries a plate of sandwiches, a bottle of wine, and a glass for me.

"What do your families think about it?" I ask, more because I'm interested in whether or not Eric has a wife and kids. Not that I'm interested in him, but rather, I'm nosy.

"My parents are supportive," Katherine says, setting everything on the table. "I love what I do."

Eric clasps his hands together and places them behind his head, elbows spread wide. "I'm not the settling-down type. And no, my parents are not supportive. They want grandkids." He laughs. "What about you, Veronica? How'd you end up on this boat? You don't seem to know anyone else."

Despite my best effort, my lip trembles, and I have to sniff to fight back tears. "It's not important."

"Is your friend still joining us?" Katherine asks.

"Yes, in Stari Grad."

"What's their name?" Katherine sits up primly. "I'll need it for the manifest."

"Oz."

"And his last name?" she asks.

I really should find out Oz's last name. "White."

"Isn't that your last name?" Katherine says, confused.

I nod. "It's a common name."

Katherine and Eric exchange a look, and she stands. "Excuse me. I need to use the toilette."

When she's gone, Eric strokes his beard stubble, and I fidget with the wine bottle. Neither of us say anything. When I can't take it anymore, I flip my phone over and open the camera app. "Can I take your picture? Maybe one of us together?"

It's the only way I know to how to cope – pose and pretend the miserable feelings don't exist.

"Sure."

I come around the table and sit next to Eric so that our shoulders touch. I snap away, then look at the shots. "We look cute!"

Eric shrugs without giving my phone a glance.

I set my phone down on the table and take another sip of wine. *Where did Katherine go?*

"So...you dock here often?" Clearly, I'm reaching for things to say.

"Every week." Eric glances over his shoulder. "Katherine must have gotten lost."

"Must have," I say. But seriously, she's been gone for at least twenty minutes. "Should I make sure she's okay?"

"No. She'll be back." Eric settles into the banquette. "In the meantime, let's enjoy the wine and company."

Is he flirting with me? And if he is, should I flirt back? I lift my wineglass. "To good company."

"To good company," Eric repeats. He sips and sets his glass down. "Now, tell me Veronica, why are you really here?"

I refuse to verbally vomit on Eric, so I tear off a piece of sandwich and pop it in my mouth. After I'm done chewing, I change the topic. "Should we wait for Katherine?"

Eric shakes his head. "She most likely went to lay down."

That's weird. "Why would she do that?"

"She needs to rest at some point," Eric says. "Plus, she needs to be up early to make breakfast."

"Oh. I didn't think of that." I frown. "But why didn't she wait until after we ate?"

The left corner of Eric's mouth pulls up. "If you must know, she wasn't supposed to be here, but I thought you wouldn't join me if I asked on my own."

My heart speeds up. He's flirting with me, and unlike my situation with Pete, I know exactly how to handle this. I smile coyly. "I might have said yes."

"And you might have said no."

I lean forward and wink. "Maybe, but now you'll never know."

"Won't I?" His eyes glint in the dwindling light.

Flirting comes naturally to me, and despite being married, it's something I do frequently. Men love it. Eric is no exception.

We eat and drink and flirt some more until Eric says, "Let's not play games, Veronica. You're a beautiful woman, and I'm not too shabby. I think we could have fun together tonight if you're interested."

Now, he's gone too far. It's not unusual for men to proposition me. Hell, there was a man in Waterford who tried to pay Pete for a night with me, and while it was flattering, Pete was appalled. I guess he's the only one who can step outside the marriage.

I frown at Eric. "Do you do this a lot? Have Katherine disappear while you try to seduce passengers?"

Eric shakes his head. "Is that what you think?"

"I'm putting evidence together." I run my finger over the lip of my wine glass. "You and Katherine seem to have plan."

"I asked her to leave, but that's it. There was no plan." Eric's even tone reminds me too much of Pete when he's trying to persuade me. "She has no idea that I'm interested in you."

As Yacht Weekers return from dinner, the noise level around us increases substantially, and I find myself raising my voice just to be heard.

"I'm flattered, but I can't accept your invitation." Pete had no qualms sleeping around, so why can't I? I have the opportunity, so why can't I seize it? Oh. Right. I have morals.

"Care for another drink?" Eric says smoothly. "My alcohol is better than the swill those kids are drinking."

I want to retire to my room for the night and stay away from the shit show that's bound to happen when everyone gets back. But part of me – a very large part – is flattered by Eric's attention. Another drink isn't a commitment. It will be fine. "Okay."

"We can hang out in the captain's quarters or here. Whichever you prefer."

If I go upstairs with him, everyone will know if they come back early. And it may give him the wrong idea. "Let's stay on the main deck."

"Okay. I'll be right back." A few minutes later, he returns with a bottle of gin, a bottle of vodka, and two real highball glasses. "Pick your poison."

"Vodka," I say.

He pours for both of us. I don't know how long we sit there, chatting about our travels, cracking jokes about Yacht Weekers, and sipping vodka, but eventually my shipmates burst onto the deck. The disappointment on Eric's face tells me it's a good thing they've returned, and that he had hopes of where the night may lead us.

"Hey, Veronica!" Garrett shouts as he lists to the right. "We missed you!"

"What are you doing?" Lydia narrows her eyes. "Did we interrupt something?"

"No," I say a little too forcefully. "We ate dinner here on the boat since you all ditched me."

Stella shrugs. "I tried knocking on your door, but you didn't answer."

"It's fine," I say. "I needed the rest."

Daniel lurks behind Stella. If he's had as much to drink as the rest of them, he isn't showing it. In fact, out of the six of them, he looks the most sober – even more than responsible Stephan.

"We're going to the hammock," Stella says. "Want to join us?"

"You know," I say with a yawn. "I'm tired. I think I need to go to bed."

"Okay."

Stella and the girls walk toward the front of the boat, leaving the

177

guys, Eric, and me. Stephan wraps Garrett's arm over his shoulder. "Daniel, help me get this one to his bed."

Garrett slumps onto his friends. "I'm fine," he slurs. "Perfectly fine."

"Do you see a lot of that?" I ask Eric as the guys drag Garrett downstairs.

"More than you know."

"My puking today wasn't out of the ordinary?"

Eric shakes his head. "Not at all." He leans closer to me, his breath warming the side of my neck. "You smell nice."

"Thank you." I turn my head slightly toward him. I could kiss him, and it would be easy. I could do it and get it over with. But I can't. I turn away.

"Can I come to your cabin later?" he asks quietly. "After everyone has turned in?"

"No," I say. I'm still married. I can't let this flirtation go any farther than it has. "I barely know you."

"So?"

"Oz is coming. Plus, if it's terrible, we have five days left together."

"Fair point, but at least consider it." I won't be considering anything. "Is Oz your boyfriend?" Eric asks.

"No." There's no need to explain our relationship to a stranger. I place the glass on the table and stand. Despite the wine and one glass of vodka, I'm not overly buzzed. "I need to go to bed. Good night."

Eric doesn't try to convince me to stay, and I hurry to my cabin and lock the door behind me. Exhausted from the sun and my conflicted emotions, I collapse on my bed and inhale deeply to steady myself. It would have been easy to sleep with Eric, but I've made the right decision. I know I have.

My phone dings. I haven't checked it since before dinner. Part of me wants to throw the damn thing into the harbor and lose all the drama it brings into my life. And yet, now that I'm alone, I have to look. I have to know what's happening. My homepage shows dozens of calls and texts from Pete. Each one more frantic than the next, but it boils down to one thing: Eve told him she sent me the texts, and Pete's claiming he was crazy when he sent them and that I shouldn't believe anything Eve sends me.

I'm tired, and I don't have any energy for this. I undress, wash my face, pop a Xanax, and climb into bed. Nothing is going to change between now and the morning, and I need to be on my game to deal with this.

17

--Stop texting me.--

--Not until I can talk to you.--

I stare at the screen. Pete won't stop badgering me, and his persistence is wearing me down. Damn him. And damn myself for being weak.

--I can't talk. I'm in the middle of the Adriatic.--

--And there's that. What the hell are you doing? We can't work things out if you're hanging out in Croatia doing bikini photoshoots with a bunch of kids.--

--I want a divorce.--

Three dots appear, disappear, then reappear. My stomach turns. It's the first time I've said it: I want a divorce.

--No, you don't. You're just hurt.--

--Stop telling me how I feel!--

There's a knock on my door, and I startle. "Yes?"

"Veronica? Are you awake?" Stella says from the other side.

I could sound drowsy and pretend she woke me up, but I answer, "Yes."

"We're going to play cards. Do you want to join in?"

We left Hvar City for Stari Grad earlier in the morning – a long day of sailing. After breakfast, I excused myself to get a nap, but really, I needed to deal with Pete blowing up my phone. Plus, I'm avoiding Eric. Not that he made me uncomfortable. I'm worried that in my current state of mind, I may do or say something to lead him on.

Then there's Oz. I'll see him in a few hours, and my heart is exploding from excitement.

"What card game?" I ask. In my stifling hot cabin, sweat dampens my clothes. I really do need to get out of here. Not only because of the heat, but also for my state of mind.

"Rummy," Stella says.

I fling the door open. "I love rummy. Count me in."

Stella wears a short, orange coverup over her bikini. Her gorgeous red hair is gathered in a messy top knot, and sunglasses are hooked over the collar of her shirt. A slick of zinc oxide is smeared down her nose. I would never be seen like that, but it works for her.

She glances behind me, at my unmade bed. "Did you have a good nap?"

"Not really. It's too hot." I fan myself with my hand.

"It is, isn't it?"

I point at her nose. "Who did that to you?"

She laughs. "Garrett. He said he was worried about me getting burnt before my wedding."

"At least he's thoughtful," I say. "Daniel, not so much."

Stella leans closer to me and whispers. "He's a bit..."

"Creepy?"

She grimaces. "I can't put my finger on it, but something is off with him. He drinks so much, and it doesn't have an effect. How is that humanly possible?"

"Watch yourself with him," I say quietly. "And the other girls should too. I don't like his vibe."

"We've already discussed it. No one is to be left alone with him. Ever."

"Good call." I take three steps back to my bed, pick up my phone, look at a screen full of texts from Pete and shove it into my sundress pocket.

"Your husband?" Stella asks.

"He's being a pain-in-the-ass."

"Oh."

I close my cabin door and stop off at the refrigerator for a bottle of water. The cool liquid feels amazing on my parched, cried-out throat. When I step above deck, everyone is gathered around the table waiting for us. True to form, Daniel has a glass of whiskey. The girls sip the wine they picked up in Hvar City, and Garrett and Stephan drink something clear – vodka or water, I can't tell. It's going to be another day of hard drinking, and I'm not sure if I can keep up.

The boat bumps against the waves, and a stiff breeze flutters the flags at the back of the boat. Katherine comes around from the other side of the captain's quarters, and when she spies me, she says, "Feeling better?"

I shiver. What exactly did Eric tell her? After all, she conveniently made herself scarce last night which makes me think that type of thing happens frequently.

"Yes." I slide onto the bench next to Stephan. "Naps do wonders."

Lydia fans the cards over and over again. It's annoying. "Are we going to play or not?"

"It should be a drinking game. Not rummy." Daniel says, slapping the table. "We're not a bunch of grannies."

"We can drink while playing." Lydia gives him a withering glance. I bet she eats the souls of men regularly. "We're going to play rummy. You're welcome to do something else."

While they argue, I sit back and soak up the fresh air. Being out here with others is a million times better than being cooped up in my cabin. I flick the ringer and vibrate off on my phone, so if Pete's texting, I won't know. I'm going to live completely in the moment.

The mid-afternoon sun shifts from directly overhead to closer to the horizon, and sea birds skitter across the water's surface, their calls lost to the wind. I may be crazy doing this trip with a bunch of twenty-something strangers, but being out on the water feels right.

As Daniel and Lydia continue their argument, Stella and Emma talk quietly, and Garrett looks bored. Only Stephan seems remotely interested in the fight. Katherine clears her throat. "Would you like a group photo?"

The bickering stops abruptly. Lydia gapes at Katherine as if she can't believe the 'help' would dare interrupt her. Before she can snap at Katherine, I answer. "Yes. That would be great. Use my phone."

I clear Pete's texts before handing the phone to Katherine. "Come on," I say. "Let's at least pretend we like each other." I shove Stephan so that he bunches into Emma. On the other side of the table, Garrett leans into Lydia and Stella. Daniel meanwhile, crosses his arms and scowls. "That isn't going to make a good picture," I say to him. "Try smiling."

"Okay, Ms. Sit-in-my-cabin-and-cry-all-day," Daniel says. "Don't think we haven't heard you. The walls are thin."

My cheeks burn, but I give a tight smile. "What I do or don't do is none of your business. Now get in the picture and try to pretend you're having a great time."

Daniel huffs before walking around Garrett and leaning over him. "Is this better?"

I nod. "Thank you."

Katherine holds up a finger. "One, two, three."

I make sure my smile touches my eyes. Hopefully, I look happy and not like a woman whose marriage is falling apart. Katherine hands back my phone, and I study the picture, searching for any sign of hysteria in my face.

"Is it good?" Emma asks. "If it is, can you send it to me?"

"It's cute," I say. "I'll WhatsApp it to you. Anyone else want it?"

All the girls do, but the boys seem disinterested. After I send it, I pull up Instagram. *Love these crazies!* I geotag the photo with Stari Grad and post.

"Are we playing cards or not?" Garrett asks. "Because I've lost interest."

"I don't know," Stella says.

Tree-covered hills slope down to the clear sea as the landscape slips past. Every once in a while, we pass a house, but this part of Hvar is mostly uninhabited and wild.

As we draw nearer to Stari Grad, there are more houses, more boats, and more beaches. This is party central on the island, and the kids are going to love the glitz and glamour of it.

And I'm going to see Oz. My pulse quickens.

Emma flips her cards onto the table. "I'm going to sunbathe. I've had enough of this."

Next to me, Stephan shifts uncomfortably. "We can still play if you want."

Emma shakes her platinum bob. "No. I'm done."

So much for the camaraderie of the first two days. Everyone is acting like siblings who've been locked up together for too long.

Stella finishes her drink. "I'm going with them."

Stephan's shoulders sag. Poor guy, he can't win.

"I'll play you," I say. "I love rummy."

He smiles weakly. "Thanks, but it's really only fun with more people."

Daniel scoffs. "We should play dice. That's a drinking game."

What is with this guy? I know Yacht Week is full of debauchery, but he's taking drinking to an Olympic level.

Garrett shoots Stephan a look, and he averts his eyes, but doesn't press the card issue anymore. "Let's get the dice."

Interesting. Garrett doesn't want Stephan to anger Daniel. I wonder why?

Mega yachts and simple sailboats crowd Stari Grad Harbor. This is where the rich and famous come to mingle with commoners and party. It's changed drastically since I first visited twelve years ago.

The girls perch on the bow of the boat, pointing at yachts and gossiping about who may be aboard while Eric carefully maneuvers our catamaran into its slip, and dock workers tie us off. Like in Hvar City, music blasts from boats, and shrieks fill the air. A quick glance around confirms that I bring the harbor's average age up by several years.

I shoot off a quick message to Oz:

--arrived—

I stand at the railing next to Emma in my black jersey dress and keep my hand pressed against my thigh to keep the dress from flying up. It's my most nightclub appropriate outfit: not too tight for daytime, but fitted enough for night.

I worked with Katherine to plan the evening: first diner, followed by a night club crawl. Even though the last thing I want to do is drink, Daniel's call-out has left me needing to prove I am not sad; I do not cry; I'm fun. But really, why do I care what these kids think? I'll never see them again, and yet, the need to fit in hits me hard.

My phone buzzes. Oz.

—where should I meet you?—

I give him the name of the first nightclub on our crawl and slip my phone into my bag.

"Veronica? Can I speak with you?" Eric says from behind me.

I turn around. He has his hands shoved into his pockets and looks a bit sheepish. "What's up?"

He motions me closer. "I'm sorry about last night. It was inappropriate."

He's apologizing for flirting with me? "You were fine. No lines were crossed that I didn't allow."

"Still."

"Still nothing. Everything is good between us."

He jerks his head toward the girls. "Care to ditch them and spend the evening with me?"

Does this guy not stop? "Oz is coming tonight."

"Right," Eric says with disappointment and a shrug. "I had to at least try."

My flirty nature rears its head, and I reach out to squeeze his hand. "I'm flattered." I spy Stephan behind Eric and take a step back. "Oh! Hi!"

Stephan ping pongs his gaze between the captain and me, and I smile like nothing out of the ordinary has happened.

"Am I interrupting?" Stephan asks.

"Have fun tonight," Eric says with a curt nod of his head.

I turn my attention to Stephan. "Of course you're not interrupting anything," There's just the right amount of pep in my voice. "Are you ready for an epic night? Katherine and I worked out the best clubs to hit."

Stephan wears seersucker shorts and a short-sleeved, button-up shirt. He fidgets with the collar. "Um. Yes?"

Oh, Stephan. You're never going to get lucky dressed like that. "That doesn't sound convincing."

"What doesn't sound convincing?" Lydia demands. Her perfectly straightened long, dark hair falls over her shoulders, and her eye make-up is ferocious. There's no doubt she's going to eat men alive tonight. Especially with her short, silver mini-skirt that barely covers her ass and highlights her long legs. A pang of jealousy hits me. I wish I could wear something like that without looking like I'm trying too hard, but those days have long passed.

"Nothing important," I say. "Are you ready to party tonight?"

Lydia rolls her eyes and walks away without the decency of a response. She joins Garrett and Emma near the railing. Emma channels a goth version of Anna Wintour with darkly drawn eyes and a platinum bob. She's actually very pretty, but beside Lydia she is more like the girl next door. Garrett, however, didn't get the dress code memo. He wears flip flops and a tank top, which don't get me wrong, shows off his physique, but it's not dinner or club appropriate. I guess he'll find that out when he can't get in anywhere.

Lydia and Emma chatter away while we wait for Daniel and Stella. I concentrate on the excited voices filling up the night air, and not on the butterflies in my stomach. Everyone in the harbor has the same plan as us, and the clubs are going to be packed. Thank God, I had Katherine make us a dinner reservation.

"Hi!" Stella sneaks up on us. A tiara sits securely on her head and a 'Bride' sash wraps around her torso. "Do I look ridiculous?"

"I think that's the point," Stephan answers.

Oh, Stephan.

"You look perfect." I kiss her cheek. "Like a bride-to-be ready for a night of fun."

Stella beams. She grabs my hands and twirls. "Are you excited to see your friend?"

I don't fight my grin. "Yes."

Next to us, Daniel clenches his flask. Despite a day of drinking, he doesn't lean or act buzzed at all. Instead, he leers at Stella in a hungry way, and a chill runs down my spine. He's so creepy.

"Stella, you looking for a last fling tonight?" he asks before swigging from the flask. "If so, I'm available."

To her credit, Stella remains composed. "No, I'm most definitely not."

"Well, you know where to find me."

Gross. Gross. Gross.

"Ready?" Garrett asks, stepping between us and Daniel.

"The ladies don't want to have fun," Daniel complains. "They can't take a joke."

I straighten to my full height. "You're disgusting, and it wasn't funny. You owe Stella an apology."

"Lighten up." Daniel heads toward the swimming platform where the gangplank is.

"Sorry," Garrett offers. "He's a pig sometimes."

I wrap my arm through Stella's. "Don't worry," I say. "I'll keep him away from you."

We exit the boat and weave our way down the crowded dock past rowdy boats and to the harbor entrance. Eric stands near the guard station talking to an official. He waves at us, and I immediately feel stupid going out for the night with a bunch of under-30's. I should be drinking wine and being the classy woman I know I am. I should have had Oz come to the boat instead, but if I change plans now, the kids will think I'm old.

"Which way, Veronica?" Garrett asks.

I pull up the directions on my phone and point. "Down that street and around the corner. Not too far."

We set out, eager to see where the night will take us. Garrett and I lead the way, with the others forming a loose group. Barking dogs run past us, and children play ball. The street is deceptively steep, giving my calves a killer workout.

Lydia squeals. "Look!" She points down over the low stone wall dividing the street from the houses. Compact houses sit below us on the hillside. "Do you see that?" A black goat meanders around someone's postcard-sized patio. "They have a goat in their yard!"

Of course, we have to stop and gawk. The poor goat bleats at us in the most pathetic way.

"He's going to be dinner," Daniel says, swigging from his flask again. "Goat stew."

Emma slaps at him. "Ewww. Stop. That's awful."

"It's the truth." He puts the flask back in his shorts pocket. "Did you think it was their pet?"

Garrett slings his arm around Daniel. "Let's go mate. No need to horrify the ladies."

We continue past the stone houses and stores until reaching the corner. "It's this way," I say, moving to the left. Sure enough, I spy the restaurant's sign halfway down the street. A group of about ten Yacht Week partiers stand underneath it. "This is it," I say, stopping. "Looks like it's popular."

Lydia frowns. "We have reservations." She pushes through the crowd to the door where a petite hostess stands answering questions. Lydia says something to her. The hostess shakes her head, and Lydia's face becomes more animated, until finally, the woman nods, and Lydia motions to us to join her.

"What was that about?" Emma asks.

"Just a bit of confusion. Nothing to worry about." We follow her through the arched doorway. We pass through a short, narrow hallway until it opens up onto a central courtyard with long picnic tables. There is no one else there, which is weird, given the trouble we had getting our table.

"Guess they don't want business," Lydia says, taking a seat and flinging her small bag on the table. "This place is dead."

"The tables may all be reserved," I answer as I sit in the middle of the bench nearest me. It's the best spot to participate in all the conversations.

"It doesn't matter," Stella says, trying to climb over the bench in a delicate and modest way, but her skirt keeps bunching up. She walks to the end of the row and inches her way over toward Lydia instead. The guys and Emma fill in around us, and the waiter leisurely strolls toward the table.

His eyes rest on Garrett. *Oh, no. He's going to get kicked out for his poor clothing choice.* But to my relief, the waiter only gives a disapproving smile. "Welcome," he says. "Tonight we have fish and vegetables."

Emma cocks her head. "That's our only option? Fish?"

The waiter nods. "We make one dish per night. Today it's fish."

"What kind of fish?" Lydia asks. "I only like certain kinds."

As the waiter launches into a description of the fish, Daniel downs the rest of his flask and sets it on the table. Even though he's two seats over from me, I can smell the whiskey on his breath. It's repulsive.

I turn away and try engaging Stephan in conversation, but he stammers, stares at his hands, and launches into a monologue on ancient Croatian maritime history. I tune out.

We spend the rest of the meal, drinking wine and making small talk. From what I can gather, some rule is made about bringing people back to the boat, but I think it primarily affects Emma and Stephan, and he has no chance of picking up a girl. Daniel and Garrett must have already discussed it, because they bro-fist bump. Stella and Lydia exchange disgusted looks, while Emma pounds her wine.

When the bill arrives, we pool our money and decide to head toward stop number one on our night club crawl – a supposedly hot spot near the marina. On our way down the hill, there's a beautiful view of the harbor that none of us noticed before. Emma holds up her hand, causing the rest of us to stop. "We should try for a selfie here."

The boys groan, but Stella and Lydia hurry to Emma's side. Stella beckons to me. "Veronica, get in here. You're an honorary mate."

"Are you sure?"

The girls all speak at once, encouraging me to get in the photo, so I do. Emma doesn't ask the boys to take the photo, instead she holds her arm out high and away from her to best frame us. "Veronica, stoop down a little bit. You're too tall."

I do as I'm told, and Emma takes the photo. She looks at it. "One more."

We resume our positions, and she takes another. This time she's satisfied. "What's your Instagram, Veronica? I want to tag you."

I spell it out for her and add, "It's Veronica White – one word."

Emma shows us the picture. It's cute, but I look like I'm with women who could possibly be my daughters.

"Are you a mother?" Lydia asks as if reading my thoughts.

"Yes."

"A housewife?" she probes.

I shrug. "I don't work a nine-to-five job, if that's what you mean. But I'm afraid I'm a terrible housewife. I have people who do most of it for me."

Lydia's eyebrows tick up. "Oh?"

Maybe it's the wine, but my tongue is loser than normal. "You know: housecleaner, laundry lady, lawn guy. When my kids were younger, we had a nanny."

"What *does* your husband do?" Lydia asks hungrily.

"He works for the U.S. Department of State." What I don't say is that he frequently works for the CIA too – because I'm not supposed to know about that.

That should be the end of the conversation because Emma and Stella walk down the hill with the guys, and I follow. Lydia, however, has a different idea. "Is that why you lived in Zagreb?"

I nod. "We've lived in a lot of places. Perk of the job."

She pauses mid-step. "How in the world are you affording this trip? Weren't you in Morocco before this?"

"I'm not poor, if that's what you mean. I have my own money."

I step away from her, eager to end the conversation, but she persists. "If you never worked, how can you have your own money?"

I turn to face her. "You tell me," I say with a hint of annoyance. "Stella said you're old money. I'm sure you didn't work for any of it."

"Touché." Lydia grins. "You're an American heiress, then?"

I roll my eyes. "I grew up in Zurich. My father was in banking."

"I knew it." Pleased with herself, she runs off to join the others. I hang back. Did I tell her too much about myself? Does it really matter?

When we pass the harbor, I seriously consider going back to the boat and messaging Oz to skip the club, but then I remember that I'm playing Veronica White, party girl tonight. I'm fun, and not a woman who spends all day alone crying.

18

Where is Oz?

Sweat rolls down my neck and into my cleavage. I dip lower and shake my shoulders, pretending that I'm not at all anxious. When I'm as low as I can go without flashing my underwear at everyone, I rise slowly making sure to keep my partner's eye contact. I run my hand up my leg and torso before placing it on his cheek. Euro dance music blasts from the speakers, and he gazes at me hungrily. When he tries to grab my hips, I step away, out of reach and wiggle my finger.

It doesn't matter who this guy is. Right now, I want someone to dance with while I wait for Oz. Where is he? He hasn't responded to any of my many messages.

"Get it, Veronica," Stella shouts over the pounding bass. I turn my back to her and shake my butt, which she playfully smacks. All those mornings I spent busting my ass and doing squats have paid off.

Europeans have the best dance clubs, and this one is no exception. Even better, I'm not the oldest person here – there are men and women who are easily in their fifties dancing alongside the younger crowd. I spin around toward Stephan and Emma, who awkwardly bob to the music, and grab their hands.

"Dance!" I order.

The DJ drops the bass, and the crowd yells in appreciation as strobe lights pulse around us. I toss my hair around, letting the cascading vibrations of sound flow through me. As I wave my hands in the air, the guy I was dancing with re-appears. He leans in close and reeks of cheap beer. "Do you want a drink?"

Once again, I glance around the dancefloor looking for Oz. It's boiling hot in here, and I'm a sweaty mess, but I'm not stupid enough to let a strange guy buy me a drink in a nightclub. "I'm fine."

"Come," he says, pulling at my hand. "One drink."

I yank my hand away. "I said I'm fine." I scowl, but he persists by placing his hand on my shoulder. I tense before slapping it away. "Leave me alone."

He shouts in some foreign language that I don't understand and walks away. Stella gives me a knowing look, and satisfied that my stalker has gotten the hint, I close my eyes and sway to the pulsating music.

The music shifts to that old Korean hip hop song everyone loved, and I open my eyes. Lydia and Garrett have disappeared, Emma looks bored, and Stephan does some weird jerky moves. At least Stella and I are having fun. I step closer to her and adjust her tilted tiara. She laughs and twirls, her red hair fanning out behind her.

Near the bar, Daniel hands a woman with brassy blonde hair a baby bottle of champagne, and she sips through the straw while making doe eyes at him. She's a bit plain, but maybe that's his MO – go for the plain girls because the pretty ones, like Lydia and Stella, have better options.

The song changes, and I swing my hips around before bouncing up and down. I whip out my phone. "Selfie!"

Stella grabs Emma and Daniel, and they crowd around me. Stephan reaches for my phone. "I'll take it."

"I want you in it," I say. "Get behind me." He reluctantly squeezes into the shot, and I snap the picture. It's cute, and it looks like I'm having the time of my life. I show Stella. "It's definitely going on Facebook," I say.

She shrugs. "I like Snapchat and Instagram better."

"Right. Kids usually do," I shout over the music, my voice blending with the noise around me. "I'll make sure I post it there too."

Little lines form between Stella's eyebrows. "Don't look, but there's a guy staring at you. At first, I thought I was wrong, but now I'm confident he's checking you out. And not in a subtle way."

I don't turn around. "I'm married. He can look all he wants, but that's it."

"Oh! I think he's coming this way." Stella grabs my arm and pulls me deeper into the grinding crush of dancers, but I turn my head, curious to see who's been admiring me.

Our eyes lock, and I squeal. "Oz!"

I break free of Stella's grasp and run toward him. He lifts me up and spins us in a circle. With no hesitation, I plant a huge kiss on his cheek.

"I've been waiting for you!" I say breathlessly. "Where have you been?"

He sets me down and grins in his lopsided way. He's shaved since I've last seen him, and it makes him look even younger than normal. "Wow! If that's the kind of welcome I get after a few days, I'd love to see what you'd do if I'm gone for a month."

With a smile etched on my lips, I shake my head and laugh. "Don't you dare go away for a month!"

Stella tilts her head. "Are you Oz?"

"I am." He offers his hand.

"Stella." Her gaze darts between us. Apparently, our age difference is confusing. Or maybe it's that I'm clinging to Oz, unwilling to let him go of him. Either way, it actually makes me self-conscious.

Oz squeezes me closer, and his lips graze my ear. I try not to think about that, but my heart races.

"Drinks or dancing?" he asks as his warm breath washes over the side of my face.

"My feet need a break," I say, spinning playfully away from him and motioning with two fingers for him to follow me. "Let's get drinks. Stella?"

She shakes her head. "I'm going to dance more."

As Oz and I wind our way toward the bar, Lydia and Garrett try slipping past us looking rumpled and breathless. I roll my eyes and laugh.

"What?" Oz asks, leaning into me again.

"Lydia and Garrett. They probably hooked up in the bathroom. I can't see it ending well."

Oz shrugs. "Not your problem."

He's right. It's not. I lift my face so that I look up at him under half-closed lids. My pulse races. How is it possible to have missed someone I barely know, or be so excited to see him? "I can't believe you're here! I thought you ghosted me." We slide up to the bar next to Daniel. He nods in greeting, but doesn't say anything, so I turn my back to him. "Or, I thought, maybe you'd been detained."

"I was."

"What?"

"Detained."

"Why?" I say with a frown.

Oz shrugs. "They never really said. Just kept me in a room for a few hours then let me go."

I furrow my brow. "They gave no reason?"

"None."

"But they took your phone?"

"And claimed it went missing."

"Typical." I tap on the countertop. "But how did you find my number if they took your phone?"

He raises his eyebrows, and I melt slightly. "You wrote it in my notebook, remember? The night we met?"

"Well thank God for that, or we may have never seen each other again."

Oz presses his hand into the small of my back. "I would have hunted you down on Instagram." He pauses. "I'm enjoying our time together too much."

My heart sputters. Did he...Yes. He did. I move so that he can't see my face. "Oz..."

"I know. There's a husband."

"There is." If I were fifteen years younger and single, Oz would be my victim. But I can't drag him into the insanity that is my life.

"A guy can dream."

The bartender stops in front of me. In my current state of too-many-vodka-tonics, I can't remember the Croatian word for water, so I ask in English. The bartender fishes behind the counter and emerges with two liter-sized glass bottles. I laugh. "Oz, can we split one?"

"Sure."

I take one of the bottles off the bar and wave away the second. Oz gets two plastic cups, and shouts something over the music to Daniel. I frown as they laugh and slap each other on the upper arm. What could they have been saying? To my surprise, Daniel follows Oz and me as we snake our way through the dancing crowd toward a quieter corner.

My head spins from a night of drinking and the excitement of seeing Oz, but I'm definitely not sloppy drunk. No, tonight that honor belongs to Lydia, who is now making a complete ass of herself on the dance floor by trying to keep other women from coming within a three-foot radius of Garrett.

Oz sets the cups down on a small high-top table with no chairs. He motions me over, and I plunk the water on the table. Daniel rests against the wall. The brassy blonde woman he was with has disappeared. "Where'd your girlfriend go?" I ask. "You seemed to be having fun."

Daniel half-shrugs. "I don't really care."

God, he's callous. "You ditched her?"

"I guess." He swigs from his glass and finishing it off, sets it hard on the table. "Can I get some of that water?" He grabs the bottle and pours it before Oz or I can stop him.

Oz taps my cup. "Have you been watching your drinks? I heard these places are ripe for date rape drugs."

"No one is going to drug the old lady," I say. "But yes, I'm being vigilant. I'm only drinking what I get directly from the bartender and not leaving it alone."

"I saw a video," Daniel says. "Of a girl who had roofies dropped in her drink while she was dancing. Didn't even know it." He narrows his eyes. "Think about it."

"Maybe you should be more concerned about the other girls. Like I said, no one is going to drug an old lady. But Emma..."

Daniel pours water into my cup, and I take a large, heavenly gulp. Its coolness is in direct opposition to the oppressive heat in the room. I drain the cup and refill it. Maybe I should have kept the second bottle.

Out on the dance floor, my friends huddle in a tight group. Occasionally, one of them glances toward us. Emma is the most obvious. She can't stop looking at Oz. It doesn't surprise me because he's definitely cute. What are they going to think about Oz sharing my cabin? And is he going to want to stay with me after what he confessed?

"They're staring at you, mate," Daniel says. "Probably trying to figure out why you're with Veronica."

"I'm with Veronica because she's the best woman I know."

Embarrassed, I finish my water and start glass number three. I'm overly dehydrated from the vodka tonics and dancing.

Daniel raises an eyebrow. "How *do* you two know each other? Because you seem very chummy for being random travel partners."

I start to speak, but Oz cuts me off. "We're international people of mystery. We operate on a high-level and can't disclose our connections. In fact, you're in danger just knowing that we know each other."

Daniel scowls. "That's the best you have? You can't answer the question?"

"That's the truth, and now we may have to kill you," I say, touching Oz's arm. "What do say, can he live or not?"

"I think he can live as long as he tells the others our story."

Daniel huffs. "I'm going to get another whiskey. Do you want something?"

It's the nicest he's been to me, and honestly, I'm surprised. "A vodka tonic. Oz?"

"I'm good with water." He pours the remainder of the bottle into his glass and shakes the empty bottle. "Maybe some more water?"

"Be right back." Daniel walks away.

When it's only Oz and me, I say, "He's interesting. I can't figure him out."

"Seems like a normal guy, but do you think the others are going to be as nosy?" He points to my shipmates. "I don't want another police interrogation."

"No. Stella's cool. The rest of them are...I don't know...young?" Cigarette smoke wafts around us, and I cough. That's the only down-side to European clubs – everyone smokes. I clear my throat.

"And how are you surviving Yacht Week?" Oz asks with a hint of amusement.

I roll my eyes. "Apparently, I'm the oldest person to ever do it."

Stella and the others join us. "Hey, Oz. This is Emma, Garrett, Lydia, and Stephan. I see you already met Daniel." She points at each person as she says their name. "You're joining us for the rest of the week?"

Did they plan the group attack? On one hand, I'm glad they're looking out for me; on the other, I'm a big girl.

Oz winks at me. "Only if Veronica will have me."

Daniel returns and hands Oz and me our drinks. Despite feeling dehydrated, I take a few large sips. The vodka hits the back of my throat with a burn. I really should have asked for water.

Lydia frowns. "Does anyone want to go out on the patio? It's getting hot in here."

"So take off all your clothes," I sing, and Oz laughs.

She stares blankly at me. "Excuse me?"

"It's a song," I say, feeling my age. "It was a big party song in the U.S. ten or so years ago."

"I guess I'm not old enough to remember," Lydia snarks.

"Veronica isn't old. You're just inexperienced." Oz slings his arm around my shoulders, and all the anxiety I've been holding on to disappears. I let out a laugh before covering my mouth. Lydia shoots daggers at us. I ignore her, but she's right. It is hot in here, and the cigarettes and sweaty bodies reek. I take a step forward toward the patio door and sway. I bump into the table.

"Whoa, there." Oz catches me. "You feeling okay?"

I nod. "I'm fine, but I think I need to get outside for some fresh air."

Stella peers into my face. "How many drinks have you had, Veronica?"

I count off on my fingers. "Maybe 4 or 5 over seven hours? Plus what we had at dinner. I've lost count, but nothing out of the ordinary. I'm a seasoned drinker."

Lydia huffs dramatically. "This is supposed to be Stella's hen party, not the Veronica is drunk again party."

I grit my teeth, but it makes my head hurt. Jesus, did I really drink too much?

Oz grabs my elbow and the water bottle and guides me toward the patio. Euro ravers crowd into the narrow garden space, and there's no way standing around like a sardine will make me feel better.

I try to spin around to head back inside, but I lose my balance again. Garrett grabs my arm. What the hell is wrong with me? "I think I should go back to the boat."

"Is it that bad?" Stella asks with concern.

I try nodding, but damn if my drinks haven't caught up to me, and my head spins. "I'm old and need beauty rest." The rest of my group looks conflicted. "Hey," I say. "You don't need to go back. It's only..." I fumble with my phone, "two. Have fun! Be young!"

Oz frowns. "You're slurring, and I don't want to leave you alone."

I wave my hand. "I can get back to the boat by myself, Oz. Stay with the kids. They'll show you back, won't you guys?"

He wraps his arm around my waist. "Uh, no, you can't go alone. How about I walk you back? The party will always be here."

Lydia lounges against the door frame, dragging on a cigarette. "If he takes her back, we don't have to leave."

Oz glances at Lydia then Stella. "I can get her back to the boat. What slip are you?" I totter again, and Oz holds me tighter. "She needs to go back. Now."

They say something, but I can't understand any of it. Shapes dance around me, and my vision fades in and out. "Did I drink that much?"

Oz leans in close to me. "What?"

"Drink?" I slur.

He hands me a bottle of water. "Here you go. You need to hydrate."

I spill the drink down the front of my shirt. My lips aren't working, and my face feels numb. I want to say something, maybe tell Oz that this isn't right, that I didn't drink enough to feel like this, but he's scooped me up and is carrying me through the crowd and out the exit. I rest my head on his shoulder.

We're walking down the street.

We're stumbling down the street.

We're...

Vomit spews out of my mouth, and my stomach clenches. The vile smell overwhelms me, and I puke. Over and over again until I'm dry heaving. When I'm positive I have nothing left in my stomach, I flop onto my back and moan. My head pounds like I have a migraine, and I shield my eyes from the small stream of light pouring through the port window.

"You can't lie on your back, Veronica," Oz says as he pushes my hair out of my face. "If you pass out again, you could choke to death."

I moan. "Dying sounds pretty good right now."

He helps me onto my side and picks up the serving bowl I've been puking into. "I'll be right back."

I'm too sick to even be mortified. I try closing my eyes, but waves batter the boat, causing it to rock more than normal. "Are we sailing?"

Oz sticks his head out of the tiny bathroom. "We left port a few hours ago. We're headed to Vis."

I pull my knees into my chest and wrap my arms around them. For a moment the pain in my stomach eases, but it doesn't last. How did I let myself get this drunk?

Oz comes back into my room with the bowl. He crawls up the bed and sets it next to me, before rubbing my back. "It's going to be okay, Veronica."

My throat burns. "What happened?" I ask in a raspy voice. "I don't remember anything."

"You passed out on me when I was carrying you back to the boat."

The catamaran is supposed to be more stable than a sailboat, but it feels anything but. I struggle not to vomit again. "I never pass out. Never."

Oz stretches his long legs out next to me. If he's bouncing the bed, I can't tell. "I spoke to everyone. No one knows how much you drank."

I clutch my queasy stomach. "I honestly don't know either. I lost count."

"You wouldn't black out like that or be this sick if you'd only had a couple of vodka tonics and a few glasses of wine over the course of a long night." He's not accusatory, but rather concerned sounding.

I try pushing myself up to sitting, but I'm too weak. "Are you saying I was drugged?"

"No. I'm saying you may drink too much from time to time."

I let that rattle in my head for a moment. "I'm not an alcoholic."

Oz rubs my back again. "No one is calling you an alcoholic."

I scrunch my brows together. "Then what are you saying?"

"I think you binge drink." Oz frowns. "I've seen you down bottles of champagne. That's not normal."

I glare at him. "How much I drink is none of your business."

He inhales sharply. "I'm saying something because I care."

"I've been with my husband for over twenty years. He's never once expressed concern." The boat pitches, and I groan. "I think you need to mind your own business."

Oz presses his lips together in a grimace. "I also think you've suffered a traumatic event and may not be acting in your best interest."

My head pounds, and I squeeze my eyes shut. "Stop. Just stop."

"If you say so."

My stomach gurgles.

"Do you want something light to eat?" Oz asks. "I'm sure Katherine can find some bread."

"I'll try it, but I can't guarantee I won't puke again." Beads of cold sweat dot my brow while heat races up my spine. I'm definitely detoxing.

Oz pushes the puke bowl toward me before gently sliding off the bed. "I'll go get you some food."

He pulls the door shut behind him, and I try my hardest not to move. I haven't felt this sick in years. Maybe Oz is right? Maybe my drinking is out of control?

I dig my fingernails into the bed and fight the vomit boiling in my stomach. No, there's nothing wrong with me. I like a glass or two or three. All my friends do too. There's nothing wrong with that.

But maybe I am out-of-control? Maybe I am dealing with the trauma of Pete's affair by drinking myself into a stupor. I close my eyes. Either way, I need to get myself under control.

19

I wait to come out of my cabin until my shipmates have left for Vis. When I finally do venture above deck to find Oz, we're anchored in a small harbor with a few other boats. I'm happy not to have a rowdy group around – my head still hurts, and I'm a little shaky.

"Hey!" Katherine says, looking up from the card game she and Eric are playing. "How are you feeling?"

I shrug dramatically. "Better."

Eric places his cards face down on the table. "We were worried about you. We thought you might need medical attention."

I bristle. "What?"

"It's not unusual," Katherine says in her clipped accent. "Happens every year at least once."

I flush hot. "But not to the old lady on the boat."

"It can happen to anyone," Eric says.

I scan the sun deck, but find it empty. "Do you know where Oz is? He isn't answering my messages." He wouldn't have left me alone to go into Vis, would he? Since our fight, we've been dancing around each other, and I hate it.

"Oh! He's down on the hammock reading. Do you want me to get him?" Katherine says.

I take a seat under the canopy. I may not be sick anymore, but I'm not 100% either. "Would you mind?"

"Not a problem." Katherine leaves her cards face down on the table and heads toward the rear of the boat.

A gentle breeze moves hot air over my body, but it feels pleasant. I'm finally not sweaty or miserable in my cabin. If I were at home, I would probably call Stacey or Eve and see if they wanted to sweat the alcohol out in the sauna, but I'm not home. I'm thousands of miles away in a foreign country with a guy I barely know taking care of me. Plus, being around Eve is the last thing I want.

"You didn't tell me you had a husband back home," Eric says.

"How do you know that?"

"We asked Oz, and he said you have a husband who should be notified if we needed to seek medical care, but he doesn't know his name. Or really anything about you."

I bite my lower lip. "Don't judge. Oz is just a friend."

"Who's sleeping in your cabin." Eric raises his eyebrows.

"We're just friends, and jealousy doesn't suit you."

"Hey, Veronica," Oz says, interrupting us. He's wearing the same green t-shirt he had on the day we met, and the stubble on his chin is trying to grow in, but it's nothing like the beard Pete can grow. God, why am I thinking about Pete?

"How are you feeling?" Oz walks toward me.

I tilt my chin up to look at him. I've twisted my dirty hair into a loose braid that drapes over my shoulder, and I play with the end. "I've been better, but I'm not dying anymore."

"That's good."

"Excuse me." Eric stands. "I have some preparations to make."

The boat bobs on the soft waves like it's trying to lull me back to sleep. When Eric is gone, I say, "You didn't have to stay behind with me. You could have gone with the others. I understand. You've played nursemaid enough."

"I couldn't leave you." Oz rakes a hand through his hair. "I was worried about you. I've never seen anyone that sick." He squints into the bright sun. "And besides, our shipmates probably would have left you for dead in that club if I hadn't been there."

He has a valid point. I may not remember anything, but I can only imagine how annoyed Lydia must have been. Stella, however, did come check on me a few times to give Oz a break. "They're not all bad."

"Right. Only that Daniel guy." Oz spits out Daniel's name.

"What has Daniel done to you?"

"He was alone with your drink." Oz clenches his fists. "I've thought about it, and you may be right. Maybe you were drugged. He kept talking about date rape drugs and stuff."

"Really?" I say. "I don't remember." It's unsettling how there's a big, black hole where my memory of the night should be.

"If you were drugged, you wouldn't remember, and you'd be violently ill." He studies my stunned face. "Even Eric mentioned it."

"You're kidding right?" The idea that Daniel would drug me is unnerving. Why would he?

"Not at all. You did drink too much, but this was something more than drinking."

Katherine rounds the corner. "Sorry to interrupt, but would you like to go into Vis today? I could arrange a Jeep tour of the island for you if you're feeling better, Veronica."

Oz studies me. "I'm game if you're up for it, Vee."

Asking Oz to miss out because I was careless with my drink is unfair. "What would it entail?"

"A ride around the islands with stops at scenic overlooks, and if you want, a tour of Tito's submarine tunnels."

I vaguely recall Stephan being excited over Vis being Tito's military base. "Would we run into the others?"

Katherine shakes her head. "Most likely not. They left a few hours ago."

My stomach no longer flip flops, and if I take Excedrin, my headache may ease. "Can I shower first? I'm disgusting."

"Of course. I need to make the arrangements, so you have at least an hour."

"Are you sure?" Oz asks me. "I don't mind hanging out here today." He holds up his tattered paperback copy of *The Unbearable Lightness of Being*. "I was reading in the hammock and chilling."

"It's fine," I say. "Katherine, can you book the tour?"

"Of course." She retreats around the corner.

When we're alone, I point at Oz's book. "You keep reading that over and over again, don't you?"

"It's one of my favorites."

"What's it about?" I ask.

Oz shifts his weight and pauses before speaking. "It's pretty philosophical, but I guess at its heart, it's about love and sex and how they can exist independently."

I frown. "So someone can have an affair, but still love their spouse?"

Oz looks away. "Something like that, but there's more."

"Why do you like it?" A twinge of hurt permeates my voice. "Do you think affairs are perfectly fine?"

"On the contrary. If anything, by the end of the book, I think the reader comes away with a stronger sense that sex and love are intertwined."

Not wanting to debate the deeper philosophical meaning of a book I haven't read, I say, "I'm going to shower."

"I'll be in the hammock," Oz says. "Reading my book and learning how not to treat women."

I give a slight shake of my head as I walk away. Oz has a way of surprising me. Sure, he's a millennial who is living a life of adventure, but he's deeper than that. I've gotten so used to superficial conversations with Pete and my friends that I forgot people actually enjoy thinking about difficult topics.

A half-hour later, I emerge from my cabin with my freshly-scrubbed hair pulled into a ponytail. Oz and Katherine sit at the table chatting. "Hey," Oz says when he spies me. "Katherine has put together a great trip for us."

"Awesome," I say. Now that I've showered, I'm eager to get off the boat. I've been cooped up for too long. "When do we leave?"

"The Jeep is waiting outside the marina," Katherine says. "So, as soon as you're ready."

I've already packed my bag, and I pat it. "All set."

"Then let's go." Oz stands. He's switched into tennis shoes. When did he come into the room? While I was showering? I didn't even hear him.

We exit the boat and head toward the marina entrance. "Thanks for being a good sport," Oz says. "I'm really excited to see the sub tunnels."

I reach down and squeeze his hand. "I owe you after what you've done for me."

He squeezes my hand back like it's completely natural that we're holding hands. When Oz spots a Jeep with the words 'No Bullshit Vis Tour,' he guides me in that direction before dropping my hand. "Hi!" he says to the bald man leaning against the jeep. "I'm Oz, and this is Veronica. I believe you're taking us on a tour?"

The man flicks his cigarette to the ground. "I'm Bruno. Hop in."

Soon we're flying up the sides of a steep hill, and I pray we don't career over the cliff. If the bus in the Atlas Mountains was a 10 on the fear scale, this is a 20. Every time I gasp or shriek, Oz either rubs my thigh or holds my hand. As we go, Bruno spits out bits of historical trivia, but I'm so focused on not dying that I can't concentrate on anything he says.

Finally, Bruno careens to a halt in a dirt parking lot. "This is Fort George. The British built it in the 1800's, but now it's a restaurant and nightclub. Many people have weddings here. Follow me."

Oz and I walk behind Bruno into a courtyard. Tables and chairs are set up out on a patio. Bruno shows us around the inside, giving us some history before leading us to the patio. It overlooks the sea, and gnarled trees surround the space. It has a beautiful, Mediterranean vibe, and I understand why a bride would want her wedding here.

Oz threads his fingers through mine and pulls me close. "Care for a dance?"

I giggle. "Is it a waltz or a rave?"

"A little of both." He leads me through a few steps before letting go and jumping around with his fist in the air. "Can't you hear the sick beat?"

I bounce up and down to the imaginary music, not caring if Bruno thinks we're insane. "And that bass drop!" I shout.

Oz grins and hugs me close. My heart bangs against my ribs. "Slow dance," he whispers in my ear. Without thinking, I rest my head on his shoulder, and we sway back and forth to our mutual unheard song. Being in Oz's arms feels right – and a little bit dangerous.

"Can I take your picture?" Bruno asks, breaking our trance.

Oz shakes his head. "Not mine, but I'm sure Veronica would like one."

I don't understand Oz's aversion to photos, but whatever. I hand Bruno my phone and lean against a tree. He doesn't give me a warning before firing off shots and tossing my phone back at me.

"Next stop, Tito's submarine tunnels." Bruno walks briskly back through the courtyard and to the Jeep. Once again, he drives wildly up the hillside before descending. He parks off the road near a concrete structure and jumps out. While Oz and I exit the vehicle, Bruno rummages through the trunk and produces three hardhats with lights attached. "Wear these," he says. "It's black inside the tunnels."

I put on the hat he hands me and scurry after Oz and Bruno. Bruno halts at the edge of the concrete entrance. It's at least twenty feet wide, and a narrow strip of railing-less walkway disappears into the dark.

"Stay on the path," Bruno orders. "It's a steep drop. Sometimes, men will jump from here, and sometimes they die. We don't want you to die today."

He's not making me feel any better. It's a good thing I can't see the drop, because I wouldn't be able to continue on.

Oz turns to me. "You okay?"

I don't want him to think I'm unadventurous. "I'm fine."

We stride into the dark tunnel with only the headlights illuminating the narrow path. Bruno stops and shines a flashlight in a room. Why the hell did he just get that out? "This is where they kept the TNT," he says. "Tito liked blowing things up."

He gives us a brief look into the room before moving on. We wind through the tunnels in the pitch black, stopping every so often to look at graffiti or a room with cut wires. I'm sure Stephan loved this, but it's all the same to me.

Eventually, we emerge on the other side of the tunnel from where we entered. Bruno leads us up and over the grass-covered tunnel, and I slip coming down the steep hill. Oz waits for me before we pile back into the car. Once we're settled, Bruno kicks it into reverse – all the way up the hillside until he comes to an intersection. This trip is not for the faint of heart.

Our tour continues past the American war memorial and airfield until we reach a small chapel at the highest point on the island. "It's still a functioning chapel," Bruno says. "Please be respectful."

It's literally a 12x9 room with an altar, icons, and hundreds of candles. Oz and I look around, spending an appropriate amount of time inside then exit.

"Look," Bruno orders, pointing across the sea. "That's Italy." Sunlight glints off the Adriatic, and in the distance, the coastline of Italy rises like sleeping giant. "Take your time walking around," Bruno says before leaving Oz and me alone.

Oz grabs my hand, and I sigh. Touching him is natural.

Stop it, Veronica. Even if there was something between you, you're married.

We wander toward a small railing overlooking the sea. "It's beautiful," I say. "I'm happy we did this."

"The driving aside?" Oz jokes.

"Well, there is that. What's up with you trying to kill me on bus and Jeep tours?"

Oz turns so that he's looking down at me. Our eyes lock, and hundreds of bouncy balls ricochet around my stomach. "This has been one of the best days on my trip," he says.

I grin. "Oh? You like danger?"

"I like spending time with you." His hand travels up my arm and stops below my elbow.

"This could be dangerous." I hesitantly rake my fingertips over his stubble. What am I doing, encouraging this? "I'm...well, you know my situation,"

Oz nods. "I do, but tell me you don't feel the same way."

I should lie. I should tell him that he's only a friend. I should send him away. Instead, I lean closer to him. "You're what I need right now."

"Only right now?"

I look away. As much as I want to encourage him, I can't. "Oz...I can't lie to you. You know I have a husband and life waiting for me. I don't want to hurt you."

"Let me make that decision for myself."

He is an adult, and so am I. It would be so easy to rebound with Oz, but then what? I go home to Pete and carry this secret for the rest of my life? No. It's unfair to Oz.

"You barely know me," I say, my voice shaking.

Oz rests his hand on my shoulder. "I know you're funny and kind and smart. I know you want something more than what you have at home."

If he had witnessed my behavior when I first got on the boat, he'd think none of these things. Hell, if he saw me in Waterford, he'd run. "Oz, I'm a terrible person. Trust me on that. I'm basically Lydia, but with wrinkles and years more experience."

"Who do you want to be, Veronica?" He places his hand flat against my chest. "Deep down inside, do you want to be an older version of Lydia, or do you want to be the woman you've shown me?"

I want be the woman he thinks I am, and not the mean, cynical bitch I know I am. I want a life that exists beyond drinking, shopping, and gossip. I want to be a better version of myself.

"I...I think we should head back." I turn toward the parking lot. "I can't do this right now."

Gravel crunches beneath my feet as I hurry away. Oz doesn't know anything about me beyond what I've shared. He doesn't know the way my friends and I revel in others' downfalls, and he doesn't know how shallow I am. It's like he's only viewed me through my favorite social media filter. I slide into the backseat of the Jeep and buckle myself in. Oz glances at me with concern, but doesn't say a word.

On our way down the hill, Bruno rattles off more facts while I keep my eyes fixed on the countryside and my hands tucked under my thighs. Oz asks Bruno questions and keeps his distance from me. I don't like it at all.

2 0

Oz and I politely declined Bruno's invitation to join him and his family for dinner and instead returned to the boat.

The sound of laughing floats toward me. "They're back," I say to Oz. "Are you ready for the invasion?"

Oz glances up from his book without answering. He hasn't been ignoring me, just like I haven't been ignoring him, but there's a distance between us that wasn't present earlier today. Does he wish he could take everything back, or get off the boat and never see me again?

Lydia bursts onto the deck followed by Emma and the guys. All of them are buzzed and staggering. I give a silent prayer of thanks that I missed their excursion.

"You're alive!" Garrett shouts. "I thought we lost you."

I force a chuckle. "I'm still here. Groggy and tired, but still here."

Katherine joins us with her clipboard in hand. She's made herself scarce while it was only Oz and me. Can she see what I don't want to acknowledge? Is the attraction between Oz and me that noticeable?

"We'll sail back to Split tonight. I'll arrange a dinner for you." She taps her board. "Tomorrow morning everyone needs to clear off the boat by 9am."

"Can the harbor master hold luggage?" Lydia asks. "Our flight isn't until three."

"For a small fee," Katherine answers. "I can help you with that tomorrow." She nods at the horizon. "Captain wants to raise anchor now. Is everyone accounted for?"

We confirm, and Katherine walks away.

The sun still sits high in the sky, and there's very little shade under the canopy. In fact, I'm pretty much hogging it all. Lydia adjusts her sunhat. "It's hot," she says in a nasally whine. "I'm going below deck."

"It's miserable down there," I say. "It's much cooler up here."

She huffs and flounces onto the banquette. "Says the woman in the shade."

Stella puts her hands on her hips. "Leave Veronica alone. She's had a rough couple of days."

"Fine." Lydia flutters her hand as if waving the conversation away and pulls her hat over her face.

Daniel has gone below deck, probably to get drinks, and Oz moves in that direction, but I shake my head. Our earlier conversation about me being drugged worries me that Oz may confront Daniel.

"You know, Veronica, it's weird that you have a husband, but are traveling with Oz." Emma folds her hands in her lap and stares at me.

I gape at her. Does she have no decency? "What business is that of yours?"

Oz walks back toward me. "It's none of their business," he says. "Ignore them."

"Where *is* your husband?" Lydia asks with a smirk. "Was I right? Are you divorced?"

"No." My neck muscles tense. "My personal life is no concern of yours."

Lydia narrows her eyes. "It's weird there aren't any pictures of the two of you on your Instagram."

I hold up my hand. "Okay, if this is going to be an inquisition, I'm out, but if you must know, my husband can't have social media. He can't be on public feeds. Having even one public picture with him is a no-no."

"Oh! That's right," Stella says. "I forgot he works for the U.S. State Department." She gives an understanding nod. "Are you enjoying your holiday, Oz?"

Thank God we're dropping this ridiculous conversation. Oz sits next to me and our legs graze against each other. I pretend that it's perfectly normal, but it isn't. Not at all. I want him to touch more of me even though I know I shouldn't.

"Things got better when I found Veronica again. And we had a great day on Vis today." Under the table, our bare legs touch in several more spots. Is he doing that on purpose? My pulse races.

"You went out? Just the two of you?" Lydia says. "How sweet."

Thankfully, Daniel reappears before I let loose on her and hands out plastic cups while holding a bottle of cheap vodka.

"No thanks." My stomach clenches. "My liver needs to regenerate."

Daniel sneers. "That's weak, Veronica. C'mon." He shoves a cup at me. "Have a little."

Oz swats Daniel away. "Leave her alone. She doesn't want to drink."

The boat bounces over the waves, and it's becoming harder for the guys to stay upright. Garrett grips the edge of the table, and Stephan leans into a metal pole. Daniel slides onto the banquette next to Lydia. He pours some vodka into her cup, and she makes a big deal about sipping it. Emma purses her lips, but like everything else about Emma, her mood flits away quickly.

For the rest of the ride into Split, we divide into two groups: Daniel's and mine. Stella moves back and forth between us, but everyone else – except Oz – is with Daniel. I'm not surprised. I'm the old lady who can't handle her alcohol. Oh, and my friend is being a pit bull. Yeah. I'd ignore me too.

When we arrive in Split, the sun has set, and there's a slight chill in the air. Katherine gathers us together, and with her clipboard, she goes over check-out policies. I tune her out until she says, "I've made dinner reservations for you. I hope that's okay?"

My growling stomach thinks that's more than okay. "Where?"

She hands me a card with the name and address written on it. "It's a nice place near the harbor, and only a short walk."

Oz leans into me and whispers. "Do you want to eat with them, or do something on our own?"

"It's the last night. We should go if they don't mind." On the other side of the boat, Stella laughs at something Stephan said. He blushes and looks away. Poor guy, he's so freaking awkward. "I'm going to change," I announce. "Dinner is in an hour. Let's all meet back here in thirty, okay?"

Garrett flashes me a thumbs up, and Lydia says, "That's so early!"

I'm not going to miss any of them...well, maybe Stella, but the rest of them have worn me down. I duck below deck with Oz in tow. My cabin is immaculate – all of Oz's stuff is out of sight, and the bed is neatly made. It's oddly weird having Oz stay with me because it feels natural.

"How do you want to do this?" Oz asks.

"Can you wait in the lounge?" I'm not about to strip down in front of him after what happened on the tour.

He sits at the small kitchen table, and I shut the cabin door behind me. I change into my cleanest dress before touching up my makeup. Satisfied I don't look like I spent two days with the worst hangover of my life, I open the door.

To my surprise, Stella and Oz are locked in a quiet, but heated conversation. When Stella spies me, she stops talking, but Oz grins like nothing is wrong. "Looking good, Vee."

"Thank you." I study them, but decide not to pry into their conversation.

Stella squares her shoulders. "Are we ready?"

"I am," I say. "Oz, you good?"

He looks down at his dark navy shorts and Adidas tennis shoes. "This is about as good as I can do. I need to find a laundry."

"Tell me about it," I say with a laugh. He's acting like himself, and that puts me at ease. "My clothes are stiff."

When we've all gathered above, the vibe is different than the first night on the boat. Wistful, maybe? Or even sad. Or maybe we're all just sick of each other.

Dinner is uneventful. Daniel drinks heavily, Stella and the girls flirt innocently with our waiter, and we make pleasant conversation. After we pay the bill, Daniel suggests we hit one last nightclub. Against my better judgment and Oz's advice, I agree to go.

I walk ahead with Stephan, answering his questions about Croatia the best I can. We turn the corner, and rowdy, drunk tourists barrel down the street shouting. I jump out of the way, and Stephan does the same. They continue past us, unaware that they nearly ran us over. I look at Stephan and shrug.

Then I hear it: familiar voices yelling. I spin around toward the back of my group. Daniel and Oz have stopped in the middle of the street, and Daniel has Oz by the shirt collar. Shit.

I hustle toward them. "Hey! What are you doing?"

Daniel shakes Oz before pushing him away. Oz totters backward, regains his balance, and rages. "He's overstepping."

Oz is always so composed. So calm and mellow. This side of him is...well, he's clearly upset. What on earth did Daniel say?

"If it's not true, then why are you so upset?" Daniel narrows his eyes.

Stella forces herself between them. She places a hand on Daniel's arm and the other on Oz's chest. "Stop it."

Daniel puffs up. "No one else is saying it, so I will." He jabs his finger at Oz. "Why don't we talk about how Veronica was drugged?"

"What?" I sputter. "Why do *you* think I was drugged?"

"I'm a bartender," Daniel says. "I've seen roofied women, and you were definitely roofied" He jerks his chin toward Oz. "My money is on this guy. Shows up half-way through our trip and is free-loading off a woman who is having marital problems. You're an easy target."

Oz rocks on the balls of his feet like he's about to pounce. "Apologize."

Stella holds up her hand. "From what I understand, you were alone with Veronica and her drink, Oz."

Daniel smirks. "See. We all agree. Something is off, and everything points to you."

My mouth drops open. "Are you accusing Oz of drugging me, Stella?"

She shrugs. "It is interesting how he showed up right before you got sick."

Oh, God. I suck in my bottom lip and shake my head at Oz who looks like he's going to attack Daniel. His eyes flash. "Nice theory," he says. "But you were also alone with her drink, Daniel."

Daniel glares at him.

"Oh? Did you forget about that?" Oz taunts.

My stomach jitters. "Look, I'm fine now, and nothing bad happened. That's what matters."

"He's a grifter." Daniel points at Oz, and Oz slaps his hand away. Shit. I throw myself between them and form a wall with Stella. "Motherfucker. Don't touch me," Daniel hisses.

"Oz," I say, softly, hoping to diffuse the situation. "Let's have drinks just the two of us."

Without an answer, he spins around and tears off down the street. I start to go after him, but Stella holds me back. "Let him go."

"Oz has no reason to hurt me." My voice sounds hysterical – even to me.

"Maybe not," Stella says slowly. "Or maybe he does."

"What are you saying?" I ask, as blood pounds in my ears. "Oz is my friend."

Stella cocks her head. "Is he really? You're – and forgive me – at least ten years older than him. You recently met and barely know him. Daniel is right – Oz is very likely taking advantage of your fragile state."

I pull myself to my full height. "I am not fragile. My husband may be a cheating asshole, but I am stronger than you seem to think." I turn around and wave over my shoulder. "Have fun tonight."

"Veronica! Wait!" Stella shouts, but I keep going. I weave in and out of the crowd and walk and walk until my feet ache. My brain spins. Oz is not manipulating me. Not at all. Those moments on the island today were genuine, and he's been respectful of my wishes.

Of course Stella is going to side with Daniel; Oz is the newcomer and popped up out of nowhere. I'd be suspicious too. But what they're accusing Oz of is ridiculous. He's harmless and the least dangerous person I know. Besides, if Oz had drugged me, why would he take care of me? And he had ample opportunity in the desert to attack me. He didn't.

I slowly make my way back to the harbor and the boat. Katherine has left the lights on, but the interior is quiet. I assume she and Eric are in their quarters since it's well after midnight. I climb downstairs, into the lounge area, and head toward my cabin. To my surprise, Oz isn't there. His stuff is, though, so he's going to have to come back at some point.

I change into a yoga pants, sports bra, and tank top and climb into bed. I lay there for a few minutes, unable to get the fight out of my head. There's a side to Oz I haven't seen – one that's fiercely protective of me.

Ugh. Why does this have to be messy?

Loud voices carry into my cabin, and curious, I hurry to the door. Garrett and Lydia stand in the lounge area, propping up a very drunk Daniel. Emma and Stephan huddle together near the stairs. Stella brings up the rear.

"What's going on?" I ask.

Lydia lets go of Daniel, and he falls forward until Garrett gets a better grasp on him. She stops right in front of me. "Daniel got us kicked out of the club."

I cross my arms and a satisfied smile slinks across my face. "Oh? The guy who never gets drunk can barely stand. Funny."

"C'mon, Veronica. We didn't make fun of you," Stella says.

"No, you accused Oz of drugging me and being a con man."

Daniel's head rolls side to side. "I..."

"You're drunk. Stop fighting it," I say. I turn to Garrett. "Put him on the sofa."

Garrett lies Daniel down, before crossing his arms. "I know my mate, and he doesn't get sloppy drunk."

"I guess it's a night of firsts for him." I'm seething about them running Oz off.

"Don't be a bitch, Veronica," Lydia says in her haughty way. "We get it. You're mad about the Oz thing."

Normally, a snappy reply would readily come to my lips, but I have nothing, and to my relief, Oz creeps down the stairs wearing a sheepish look. "Hey," he says. "I'm sorry about earlier."

"Don't be," I say. "They haven't apologized for anything." I glance at Daniel, and a thought nibbles at me. What if he drugged himself to make it seem like he was innocent? And what if he did actually drug me? There's no way a simple hangover would last two days.

"What happened to him?" Oz points at Daniel.

"He's drunk," I say with a smirk. "You guys should go to bed. We have to be off the boat at 9 am," I say to my shipmates. "Daniel will be fine here. Leave him with some water and a bowl."

I grab Oz's hand and pull him into our cabin. When I close the door, I lean against the bed. He raises his eyebrows.

"What?" I ask.

His eyes light up. "You're kind of hot when you're mad."

I should shut him down, but instead I press the back of my hand against my forehead and fake swoon. "Why thank you."

Oz steps closer to me, and I have no desire to move. He inches even closer. I lean into him, and he smiles in surprise.

"Where did you go?" I rest my hand on his chest, trying to stop whatever is about to happen even though my heart is screaming that this feels right. There's a faint, pleasant smell of whiskey on his breath.

"I walked around, had a drink at a bar, and came back here." He puts his hand over mine, and the hairs on my arms prick up. "What about you? How was the club other than Daniel getting wasted?"

"I wouldn't know. I walked around too and never made it to the club." *He's too young for you. Stop this now.* I pull away and lean back on the bed with my hands supporting me. He could kiss me now, and I wouldn't mind. "Everyone is talking about us."

"So? You'll never see them again."

"What's going on here?" I ask. Maybe this is all in my head. Maybe he's just a nice guy who wants me for a traveling buddy and that's all. I could almost convince myself of that, except he's told me he's interested.

Oz grins sheepishly, and I melt a little more. "Nothing that you don't want to happen. I will never pressure you to do anything that feels wrong to you."

It would be easy to kiss Oz – he's a willing, attractive man. But what would that say about me? Am I no better than Pete?

I fight the butterflies in my stomach. If Oz makes a move, I won't say no, but I'm not going to initiate.

"I'm not ready," I whisper, more for myself than for him. "I like you – maybe too much. But I am married, and my life's a mess. And-"

Oz places his hands on each side of mine on the bed and leans over me so that our faces are inches apart. My lips part in anticipation, but he pulls back and stands up. "Your husband doesn't deserve your loyalty."

"I don't want to talk about Pete." Whatever spell Oz has on me breaks, and I climb up onto my side of the bed. "Are you tired?"

"A little."

I pat his side of the bed. "Lay down with me?"

"Is that a good idea?" There's a breathlessness to his deep voice. "I could sleep on the sofa."

I don't want him to go. In fact, I desperately want him to stay. "Daniel is there."

"Right." Oz climbs onto the bed fully clothed. He positions himself a respectable distance away from me, and I hit the light switch. Blackness engulfs us, but I'm keenly aware of his body. If he reached over...

His hand darts out and wraps around mine, and I savor the connection. It takes everything I have not to roll onto my side and move closer to him so our bodies touch in twenty-seven different places.

Eventually, Oz softly snores, and my restless brain plays with the idea of waking him. But then what? In his sleep, he squeezes my hand tighter, and my breath catches. What is he dreaming about? Me? Someone else?

I blink into the darkness debating my options – not even the gentle rocking of the boat soothes me. Maybe it's time for Oz and me to go our separate ways. If we don't, does that mean I am willing to let the inevitable happen?

How do I say goodbye to the one thing that brings me joy right now?

21

I am forty and standing on a balcony in Nice overlooking the sea. The wind keeps blowing my hair, and I'm laughing while trying to tuck it behind my ear. I have on a tiny, pink bikini and wedge sandals. They make my long legs look even longer.

"Just this way, Vee," Pete says. "Look at the camera."

I turn to face him square on. He's bare-chested, and his palm-tree print swim shorts sit low on his hips showing off his well-defined abs. It's in moments like this that I realize how attractive my husband is. I've always been drawn to him, but he's aging so well. There are a few gray spots in his scruffy five o'clock shadow, and his hair is a little thinner than it used to be, but his mischievous blue eyes have never changed. And that smile, it still charms me.

This trip has been heavenly. No kids. Just us celebrating our anniversary. Our hotel room overlooks the town square and the sea. Pete spared no expense.

I frown and pose with my hand on my hip as the warm Mediterranean air washes over my skin and sends my hair flying again. My gaze keeps drifting to the bottle of Nicolas Feuillatte rosé champagne waiting to be opened.

"Smile, Vee. Show off those dazzling white teeth of yours."

Pete has always been in awe of my smile. I keep telling him it's blindingly white because I gave up cigarettes and Coke years ago. He tells me it's good genes because our kids have my beautiful smiles.

After striking a sassy pose, I flop sideways onto the chaise. Pete keeps clicking away, taking pictures of God knows what. When I glance over my shoulder, he's grinning. "Ass shots," he says and laughs in his deep, hearty way.

He flashes the screen at me, and I point at my thigh. "Too big," I say. "Too jiggly."

"Workout more," he answers.

Our skin is bronzed and salty from swimming in the sea, and I'm exhausted from spending the day on the beach drinking champagne. It's a content kind of sleepy. The kind that only comes after a particularly wonderful day.

Pete bends over me and kisses my shoulder. I roll onto my back and take his face between my hands. When his lips met mine, he tastes like salt and strawberries. His breath is flavored with champagne, but mine is too, so I don't mind.

"Wait a minute," he says and disappears into our room. When he returns, he kneels next to my head.

"What are you doing?" I ask.

Pete lifts my left hand and slips a large diamond ring over my knuckle. "An upgrade," he explains. "All the women in Waterford have larger diamonds, and I thought you should have one too."

My wedding band is a plain platinum band, and next to it, the diamond looks enormous.

"It's bigger than Karen's." Satisfaction rolls through me. "Everyone is going to be jealous." I admire the way the diamond catches the light. "I should Instagram it."

Warm fingers skim the back of my hand. "Veronica? Are you okay?"

I groan as the last fragments of the dream evaporate.

"Veronica?"

I blink, trying to make sense of where I am. On a boat. Not with Pete, but with Oz. "Oh. I'm...yes, I'm fine." I yawn and am very aware of my morning breath. "Is it time to go?"

"In a few hours. You were moaning in your sleep."

I stretch and pull the thin sheet higher up on my chest even though I'm fully clothed and it's boiling hot in the cabin "We should get up. Are you hungry?"

"I'm worried about you," Oz says, moving his hand up my arm and sending chills down my spine. "You don't seem like yourself."

The anxiety from last night rushes back, and my hands tremble. "Hey," he says, touching my cheek. "Maybe we should leave before everyone else gets up."

Waves slosh against the boat, and cars honk up near the Promenade. I'm in Split with Oz. Not with Pete. Oz. There is no diamond ring. No ass shots. No long vacation in Nice. Just me shoved into a catamaran with six strangers.

I lift my gaze. Early morning moonlight streams through the port window, and Oz's eyes appear darker, more mysterious than they do during the day.

"Hey." He must have brushed his teeth because he smells like peppermint. "What's going on? You seem off."

My chest rises and falls as the dream wedges into my mind. Pete and I have been playing a game of keeping up appearances for much too long. Unfortunately that life with him is my real life, and I can't deny that it's not.

"I think it's time for me to go home. Pete and I have a lot to work on, and running around the world with you isn't helping any of it."

"Are you sure?" Oz sits up, and bumps his head on the top of the cabin.

"Not at all," I whisper.

"Maybe," he says softly as he moves one hand to my shoulder.

"Maybe you should live in the moment. Take advantage of what's right in front of you."

My pulse thunders in my ears as I sit up and face him. "Oz--"

His warm, peppermint lips press against mine, and I yield into him. Without hesitation, I grasp the back of Oz's neck, my fingers playing with his hair, and kiss him harder. I devour the sweet taste of peppermint on his bottom lip, and Oz's hand skims the sliver of skin between my top and pants. The yoga clothes I wear form a flimsy barrier between us and can easily be removed.

Do I want that?

"Is this okay?" Oz asks breathlessly when I pull away.

Guilt nibbles what's left of my conscience. Pete did worse with Eve. This is just a kiss. "Yes."

"You're amazing, Veronica." Oz brushes my tangled hair from my face. "Don't think that you're not."

I turn slightly away from him. "I don't feel awesome. Not anymore."

"Because of the kiss?" He says, his voice full of regret. "I'm sorry. It won't happen again."

I twist to cup his cheek. His stubble pricks my fingertips. "I like you. Too much. And that scares me."

He falls back onto his pillow. "I thought..." His voice shakes. "No, I don't want to get between a marriage. You need to do what you need to do. But I hope we have a little more time together. I'm not ready to give you up."

I fall onto the bed next to him. "I don't know what I want, and that's not fair to you."

"I'm prepared for whatever road this ride takes me on." He stretches his arm under me, and I crawl into his side.

Even with my reservations, this feels right. But sometimes, what feels right is all wrong, and this is one of those times.

I slip off the boat before the others are awake. I don't need to say goodbye to any of them. I wish them the best, but really the trip went on four days too many.

"Veronica?" Oz stands on the swim platform and stares down at me standing on the dock. He glows in the early morning sunlight. While I packed, Oz sat above deck, waiting for me.

"Are you sure you want to go home?"

"No." I sit my rolling bag upright with the handle sticking up. "I'm not sure of anything."

"Then give yourself a little more time."

"With you?"

"Selfishly, yes." He walks down the gangplank until he's mere inches from me. I don't trust myself to hug him. That one kiss was enough, and I worry I'll cave and not go home if I don't walk away right now. And I need to go home. I've spent enough time hiding from my issues.

Seagulls squawk, but other than the that, the harbor is silent, and Oz's voice carries. "One week," he says. "We'll go to anywhere. Your choice. Just don't leave yet."

"Nice?" I ask. "Would you go to Nice with me?"

"Anywhere." His eyes plead with me to stay.

Nice would be the ultimate fuck you to Pete.

"Sounds nice." He wiggles his eyebrows. "But seriously, if it means one more day with you, I'll gladly go wherever."

Maybe I'm insane, but a smile stretches across my face. "Go get your stuff."

"Really?"

"Go before I change my mind."

Oz plants his hands on my shoulders and kisses my forehead. "Thank you."

When he disappears back onto the boat, I pace the dock debating on whether I should tell Pete that I'm headed to Nice. I could be a total bitch and let him find out when Eve shows him my Instagram pictures, or I could give him a heads-up over text.

--Going to Nice with Oz—

22

Oz shields his eyes against the sun with one hand and flags the waiter with the other. We're sitting on our hotel's private beach in Nice. "Let's get a bottle of Taittinger." He plucks up the water bottle we've been drinking from the ice bucket. "We're out of water."

We've been laying in the sun since 1:30 and haven't had anything alcoholic to drink. It feels like a major accomplishment. "If you want," I say, rearranging myself on the sunchair. "I need to watch myself though. Don't want my binge drinking to rear its head."

"I'm sorry I said that. I over stepped." The corner of Oz's mouth ticks up. "But, c'mon, Vee. We're in the south of France. If you can't drink champagne here, where can you drink it?"

"Fine," I say. "I'll have one glass, but that's it. I need some food in my stomach though, or I'm going to die." Despite not drinking today, my liver still hates me.

After Oz orders the champagne, he reclines on his lounge chair and places a towel over his eyes even though our umbrella provides full shade. When his chest rises and falls regularly, I assume he's asleep. His skin has turned a deep, honey brown – a color I can only achieve via my once-weekly spray tan sessions. Before he can stop me, I snap a quick picture.

He really is a beautiful man.

Desperate not to veer into that territory, I click open a few apps, but there's nothing new. Facebook is the same old, same old; Instagram is boring; and my news feed is depressing. As I'm about to set my phone aside, a message from Pete pops up, and my insides jitter.

--You alone?--

I glance at Oz. He's still asleep.

--Yes.--

--You're in Nice?--

--Yes.—

Why is Pete giving me an inquisition over text? I drum my finger against my bare thigh while I wait for his response.

--Where's Oz?--

Oh, seriously? That's what he's worried about.

--sleeping—

--where?—

I sigh. Of course he suspects the worst.

--on the sunbed next to me--

Three dots appear, so I stare off at the ocean. The wind has picked up, and waves crash into the pebbled beach. I glance to my left at Oz; he still hasn't moved.

--Vee, I'm going to call you, but you need to be somewhere private--

A lump forms in my throat. Chatting via text is one thing, but having an actual conversation with Pete may kill me.

--Okay. Give me five. Let me call.--

I swing my legs off my chaise and tug my coverup over my head. Then I slip into my Tory Burch sandals and head toward the beach's restaurant. There's a quiet area near the locker check that's close to the bathroom – just in case I need to lock myself in a stall.

The only person there is a worker manning the lockers. I lean against the wall and call Pete. A sick feeling bubbles in my stomach. Pete and I haven't spoken in over a week. I turn my back to the entrance, and when Pete answers, I speak softly into the phone. "What's going on?"

"Vee, I need to know if you're still with Oz."

I sigh. "Honestly, is this why you're bothering me?"

"My wife is running around Europe with some guy half her age and posting it all over social media. Of course I fucking care."

"Your wife was publicly humiliated by your mistress," I hiss. "You have no right to judge me."

"You're being a spoiled bitch." Ah, so the nice Pete has disappeared.

"I'm not the one who stuck my dick in a skanky ho."

There's silence on Pete's end.

Shouting erupts behind me, and I spin around. A tiny woman carrying a tray of glasses flashes angry eyes at another server. She's accusing him of being lazy, I think, and he in return is calling her an old cow.

I press my back into the wall, half interested in their fight.

"Is everything okay?" Pete asks with a twinge of worry.

"Just some servers arguing." I sigh. "I can't talk to you if you're going to be mean."

Pete blows into the phone. "I'm jealous, okay? Is that what you want to hear? I fucking hate that guy, and the thought of him touching you is killing me."

I could deny his implications, but I don't.

"Are you there?" Pete says frantically.

"Yeah."

"You don't have anything to say?"

"We're not sleeping together, if that's what you mean." After what Pete did, my kiss with Oz is insignificant.

"Well that's something."

The woman and waiter have finished their argument and gone in different directions. "If you'd have come when I asked, I would have never met Oz."

"You're blaming me?" Pete says, his usually calm voice raising.

I inhale and exhale loudly into the phone. "Funny how that works."

"This isn't the same," Pete says. "Eve was a one off. She--"

"Don't lie," I snap. "It was more than once. She said as much."

Pete's jagged breath comes across the phone. "About that--"

I shake my head. "Until you can be honest, I don't want to hear anymore." I hold the phone away from my ear and can hear Pete frantically talking, but I hang up. I'm done forcing myself to believe his lies.

When I return to my seat, Oz is sitting up, eating a strawberry with his closed notebook in his lap. "Where'd you go?"

I take off my coverup and heave myself onto my chair with a sniff. "I was talking to my husband. He likes to make me feel miserable."

Oz lowers his sunglasses so that he's peering over them at me. "I'm sorry. Do you want to talk?"

"You don't need to hear about it." My heavy heart presses against my ribs. "But basically, his affair is my fault."

"What?" Oz asks in disbelief. He drops his notebook into his backpack, before giving me his full attention. "He said that?"

"Not today. Before I left." I rub my eyes. "Apparently I didn't give him enough undivided attention."

Oz frowns. "I'm sorry he's blaming you for his bad behavior."

I touch the back of Oz's arm, and electricity trills through me. "You're not a consolation prize, you know."

"Just Mr. Right Now?" he asks.

I've never felt more connected mentally to anyone in my life. "We're friends. Maybe more."

He presses his lips tightly together before saying, "Good thing I'm a patient guy."

He's so different than Pete, and I'm terrified he's only my rebound guy – albeit, a sweet, caring rebound guy.

We sit there, not talking, for another good ten minutes. Everything Pete says rushes through my mind, and I fight the frantic feeling building in my brain.

"Oz?"

"Yeah?" His head drifts lazily toward me.

"Let's get in the water." I flip onto my side so that I'm facing him. "It's getting too hot."

"Sure."

I shove my phone into my bag and stick that under my chair. The beach club has laid carpets over the pebbled beach along all the walkways, but the water is covered in rocks too, so I slip on the ugly water shoes I bought from the shop across the street.

I lead the way past the other sunbathers to the water's edge. It's high tide, and when the waves pull out, the sharp drop at the water's edge is exposed.

Oz stops behind me, wraps his arms around me, and rests his hand on my shoulder. "Have I told you how gorgeous you look in this white bikini?"

I snort. "I'm pale as a ghost."

"Maybe I'm into hot, ghost women."

I playfully slap at his arm. "I'm going in." He releases me, and I walk into the water. The waves crash into me and knock me off balance. I grapple to find my footing, but another wave hits me, and I go under. So much for being graceful.

"Are you okay?" Oz asks, pulling me to my feet as I sputter.

I adjust my suit and push my knotted hair back from my face. "I'm fine. We need to get out a little farther where the water is calm."

Since my hair is already wet, I dip below the surface and swim away from the shoreline. When I pop up, my feet touch the rocky bottom, and I wave to Oz. "Come out."

He wades toward me, and I let the gentle waves carry me toward him. Oz embraces me. "You look like a mermaid."

"Oh?" Every nerve in my body tingles. "Is that a good thing?"

He releases me, but not before I catch a glimpse of desire in his eyes. Thank God we booked two rooms.

A little farther out, a speed boat pulls two parasailers high above the water before dipping them into the Mediterranean. The parachute sends them back into the air, and their feet dangle. "Let's do that," Oz says with excitement. "It looks fun."

I tense. "No. I'm afraid of heights remember."

He pokes me gently. "Try."

The thought of being strapped into that contraption freaks me out, but I don't want to disappoint Oz. "I can watch you."

He scoops me up in his arms so that I'm cradled against his bronzed chest as he walks toward the shore. "I'll never force you to do anything you don't want to." When we get closer to the water's edge where the rough waves crash into the land, he places me down. "It's going to be ugly getting out. You might want to crawl."

"Crawl?" I will look like fool scrambling up the step shoreline.

"Trust me." A wave knocks into me and shoots me toward the pebbled beach. Oz reaches me and gives me a hand. "See?"

Taking his advice, I crawl up the shoreline until I'm out of the water. "Now what?" I ask as I fix my bathing suit. "Should we call it a day?"

"We should have a bottle of Taittinger waiting for us."

"Ah, right." If I drink, I'm in danger of throwing caution out the window, but crisp, cool champagne sounds delicious. Especially with the juicy, plump strawberries that come with it. "Let's finish our bottle and head back to our rooms to get ready for dinner."

Oz widens his eyes. "I'm game for whatever."

I sigh. That's exactly what worries me.

23

"Let's play a game," Oz says as we stroll the maze-like streets of old Nice, searching for a bar or restaurant that appeals to both of us. "We'll go in separately and pretend we don't know each other. Then I'll start sending drinks to you and flirt."

Since leaving the beach, my stress over Pete has lessened and lightness fills me. I link my arm through Oz's as we walk, enjoying the connection. Maybe our age gap makes us look strange together, but I don't care. I like him, he likes me, and everyone else be damned. Thankfully, no one really pays us any attention. We're simply two more tourists crowding the small city.

"Should I act interested or play hard to get?" I ask, liking his idea.

Oz half-shrugs. "Your choice, but you do enjoy making me work for things."

I blush. Why does he make my knees weak? It's like I'm twenty years old all over again, and a cute boy has asked me out – I want to bounce around and act like a fool. But, of course, I can't do any of that. I'm forty-five, and well, I'm supposed to be classy...and married.

We stop outside a small bistro and study the menu. It's nearly ten-thirty, and the place is packed. A waiter rushes forward. "Bonsoir."

"Bonsoir," I say. I always speak French in France. It's polite even if Oz doesn't understand. "Do you have a table for two?" There's no space for us to play Oz's game here. We can eat and then find a bar.

"Yes, but it is not a good table. Nothing outside."

The waiter speaks to me in French, and I translate for Oz. "Are you okay with that?"

He nods. "I'm starving. The beach gave me an appetite."

I chuckle. "What you mean is that you need something to soak up all that champagne."

He laughs and lifts his finger at the waiter. "We'll take the table."

The waiter guides us toward the back of the restaurant near the stairs to the bathroom. The chairs are arranged so that both face out into the main room. The waiter holds out one of the chairs for me before handing us menus.

I'm in no hurry to order food, so I set mine down. Actually, I have dry champagne mouth and could use some Vittel.

"Not hungry?" Oz asks.

I shake my head. "A little, but let's enjoy ourselves." I nod toward the crowded room. "These are perfect seats for people watching."

"They are," Oz says with a grin. "Check out the couple to your left. They look miserable. What do you think their deal is?"

They're around my age, but wear their middle agedness like thick tires around their torsos. The woman keeps pouting out her lower lip, and the man stares off into space. "Anniversary trip?" I say. "But headed toward divorce."

"Why do you think that?" Oz asks.

All those times Pete and I have sat quietly in restaurants not talking, but rather on our phones, come back to me. Occasionally, we'd read something out loud to the other, but mostly we didn't talk much. "They don't know how to talk to each other. Their kids are most likely grown, and she's sad because she spent every minute wrapped up in her kids."

"You know this because..."

"It happens a lot to my friends. They give everything to their kids and forget to nurture themselves and their marriages."

"Hmmm." Oz waves for the waiter. "Vittel?" he asks me.

"Yes, please."

After the waiter is gone, Oz says, "And the guy?"

"Resentful because he's spent his life working and now, he feels stuck paying for college and whatnot."

"You're good at this," Oz says.

"I've been around a lot of unhappy couples." The waiter returns with the bottle of water. I wait for him to pour and leave. "It's easy to lose sight of who you are as an individual when you've been part of a couple for so long."

Oz shifts uncomfortably in his seat.

"What?" I ask.

He hesitates and plays with a bead of water sliding down his glass. "Is that what happened between you and your husband?"

I cast my eyes downward. "Pete and I...no. That's not what happened. He didn't feel I was enough." I fold my hands together and take a deep breath. "But he was wrong, wasn't he?"

Oz reaches over and pries my hands apart. "You're enough. Don't ever think you aren't."

Tears sting my eyes, and I blink. "He hasn't chosen me. I've given him every chance to come to me to work things out, and he refuses."

Oz clenches his jaw, looks away, and then looks back at me. "It may be time to move on."

I lift my chin so that his warm eyes met mine. "To you?"

"Maybe." He leans closer to me. "Pete can't see what he's losing, but I can see what a treasure you are. You're smart and funny and have a kind heart."

"Are you sure about that?" I don't want to tell him that at home, I have a reputation for being a bitch.

Oz sits back and smiles. "Absolutely. Anyone can see it."

I press my lips tightly together to hold my soft sob inside. This, right here, is what I want – not Pete or Waterford or being the prettiest member of the Bitch Brigade, but this. I've waited years to feel alive again, and now that it's here, I'd be a fool to let it go.

"I want to leave my husband," I blurt.

Oz startles. "Really?"

"I...yes. I'm sure of it. I'm tired of allowing myself to be treated like a pretty ATM."

"What?" Oz asks. "I'm not following."

I rest my chin on the back of my hand. "All of our money is mine. Pete makes a decent salary, but I have a trust, and that's what pays the bills and funds the fun."

"You have a trust fund?" Oz's eyes grow large. "I knew – from your Instagram – that you have a charmed life, but you have a trust fund?"

I nod. "And I don't want Pete to get a penny of it. As long as we're married, I control everything, but if we divorce, I believe he can make a claim to it."

"No pre-nup?"

"There is, but Pete could make a strong case for exorbitant spousal support." Maybe it's the alcohol, but my tongue feels looser than normal.

"You really have a trust fund?" Disbelief fills Oz's voice. "Really?"

"Yes." I trace the condensation trail on the table, spreading the water everywhere.

"So, you're stuck." Oz frowns. "There has to be a way around this. Some way to keep your husband who cheats on you from getting anything."

"If you can come up with a way, let me know." I sip my water, letting the cool crispness soothe my dry throat.

For the next two hours, we dance around the subject of whatever is going on between us. Finally, we ask for the bill, and I insist on paying. It only seems right given what I've disclosed. "You can get the next one."

"Vee, you can't keep paying for me." He rubs the back of his neck. "Even if you are an heiress."

I hand the waiter my card. "Yes, I can."

Oz objects again, but I press my fingertip against his warm lips. "Shhh."

That stops his protests, but once we are out on the street he says, "Drinks are on me."

"Deal," I slip my hand into Oz's. Maybe it's forward, but his warm skin comforts me. We head out of the old town and back toward the beach. There's a bar not far from our hotel that I noticed on our way to dinner, and I lead Oz there. "I'll go in first," I say. "That way we can execute your plan."

He laughs and kisses my forehead. "This is why I'm so thankful I found you again. Parasailing aside, you're game for anything."

Am I really? I've always thought of myself as reserved and collected. Level-headed, but a party girl. Maybe that's what he means: I know how to have fun.

"Meet me inside?" I say.

Oz holds up his hands. "I'll be in in ten minutes."

The tiny bar isn't anything special. French pop music blasts from speakers, and a few couples sit at the bar, but mostly the patrons crowd around high tops. There's one empty chair next to a paunchy elderly man, and I take it.

"*Bonsoir*," he says in South-of-France accented French. "*Parlez-vous français?*"

"*Oui, mais je prefere l'anglais.*"

He clicks his tongue. "*Je ne parle pas l'anglais.*"

"*C'est dommage.*" I don't want to waste time talking to an old man; however, if someone around my age wanted to chat, I'd welcome it. Make Oz work a little for my attention.

Speaking of Oz, he's taking his time coming inside. I reach for my phone, but it isn't in my bag. I tear the top open and begin putting everything on the counter, trying to find it. Oh shit. Did I leave it at the restaurant? Or the hotel? My heart pounds. I still have my wallet, so I wasn't pick-pocketed, but where the hell is my phone?

I push away from the bar, nearly toppling my stool, and rush outside. I search the street, but Oz is nowhere to be found.

Where did he go? I know we said we were going to space out our arrivals, but he should have come in by now. Heat rushes through me. The last time he didn't show up, he went missing for days.

I pace in front of the bar for what seems like an eternity. Unable to wait any longer, I start walking briskly back toward the restaurant. Hopefully, if I left it on the table, someone turned it in.

"Veronica! Where are you going?" Oz calls from behind me.

I spin around and glare at him. "Where were you?"

He holds up his hands. "Whoa. I grabbed a Coke at the café on the corner. I wanted to give you some time before I came in so it wasn't obvious we are together. Remember?" He steps closer to me. "What's wrong? You're shaking."

"I can't find my phone." Nausea builds inside me. "And I need it."

Oz grabs me and pulls me tightly against his chest. "It's okay. We'll retrace our steps."

"What if I was pickpocketed? My phone has all my contacts, financial information, and passwords. It would be easy to steal my identity."

"You have FaceID, don't you?"

I shake my head. "No, I haven't upgraded my phone in a few years."

"Shit." Oz exhales loudly. "Let's head back to the restaurant. Do you remember having it there?"

I shake my head. "Maybe I left it in the room? But that's so unlike me."

"So is not checking your phone every ten minutes. Are you sure you didn't have it at the restaurant?" He furrows his brow. "Actually, I don't remember you having it."

I fight the panic gnawing at me. "I would have taken a few pictures." I grimace. "How could I lose it and not realize it?"

"It's probably at the hotel. And if not, we'll figure out how to lock it."

I cast my eyes to the ground. "Pete will have to do it. I don't know how, but our phones are linked together."

Oz presses his lips together. "We'll only call Pete as a last resort."

We hurry through the winding old town streets until reaching the restaurant. I rush toward the first waiter I spot, and in careless French, ask if anyone has turned in my phone. Oz meanwhile heads toward our empty table to search the area around it.

The waiter shrugs. "I don't know," he says in French. "Let me ask."

As he confers with another waiter, I spot Oz crawling around on the ground. Diners stare at him before resuming their meals. The waiter comes back. "I'm sorry, but no one has your phone."

I'm going to be sick. Absolutely sick. Heat rushes into my head, and I sway.

"Veronica!" Oz shouts, not caring about the other patrons.

I grab onto the back of the nearest occupied chair to steady myself. My phone is my lifeline. All my pictures, all my social media – if I can't find my phone, I'm going to lose everything.

"Veronica!" Oz says again, rushing toward me. "I found it!" He holds my phone out in front of him. "Hey, are you okay?"

"You found it?" My voice trembles.

He beams. "It was under the table. I guess they don't sweep often." He wipes his hands on his shorts. "Gross."

I grab my phone, throw my arms around Oz's neck, and plant a string of kisses across his face. "Thank you! You saved me."

He returns my kisses with one on my lips, and I'm not sure if it's the adrenaline from losing my phone or Oz kissing me in public, but my heart races, and I feel dizzy. I clutch his arm. "Let's get out of here."

"Still want to play our game?" Oz asks with a hint of mischievous in his voice. "Or, if you want, we can go back to the hotel and have a drink there."

There's something exhilarating about the chase, and I don't want to stop now. "The bar," I say. "You need to work for me."

He gently touches my face, and my heart sings. "I'll gladly bust my ass for you."

To my disbelief, I'm at a loss for words. It's been so long since Pete's flirted with me, and Waterford men don't count – they'll flirt with anything. But this...it feels completely different.

"The man at the end of the bar bought this for you," the bartender says in French while handing me a glass of champagne. "It's what you've been drinking." I turn my head slightly and smile coyly at Oz. He raises his glass of whiskey in my direction. "Do you accept it?" the bartender asks.

"Yes. Tell him *merci*."

There's a group of American tourists next to me, and one of the girls squeals, "Oh my God! That's so cute!"

I sip the fresh glass of champagne. Cute. Ugh. I don't want to be cute. I want to be the sexier, older woman who gobbles up men for breakfast. "What do you think?" I ask her. "Should I invite him over?"

"You have to! Doesn't she, Molly?" The girl draws her friend into the conversation. "He's totally into you. And he's really good-looking."

Molly nods her overly highlighted head. "Do it. Wave him over."

I glance down the bar, but Oz is scribbling in his notebook and doesn't notice me. "I think he's busy."

"Then go over there," the first girl says. She shoos me with the back of her hand. "You may regret it if you don't."

I take another sip and study Oz. Objectively, he's insanely attractive in a millennial way. He glances up from his notebook and smiles devilishly at me.

"What are you waiting for?" Molly says, pushing on my arm. "Oh! Nevermind. He's coming here!"

I turn toward the bar, pretending that I'm indifferent to the situation. "Shhh," I say. "I don't want him to hear you."

"Hi," Oz says in his sexy, deep voice.

I pivot on my barstool. "Hello."

"I'm Oz. I bought you that drink." He's so effortlessly confident. "Thank you."

Molly interjects herself. "Tell him your name."

If this is her wingwoman game, Molly has a lot to learn. "I'm Veronica," I say extending my hand. "Nice to meet you."

"And your friends?" Oz asks as if he really has no clue who I am. I do appreciate that he didn't imply they were my daughters, because really they could be.

"We don't know each other," the first girl says. "I'm Jane." She flashes what I suppose is a pretty smile, but Oz ignores her.

"Can I sit with you?" Oz asks me.

I pull out the stool next to me, bumping Jane in the process. She doesn't take the hint that it's time for her to move on. Instead, she plants herself firmly.

"Oz...what an unusual name," she says. "Is it short for something?"

Funny, I never thought to ask him that. He's always just been Oz.

"No," he leans his back against the bar. "It's what my parents named me."

"It's such a cool name," Jane says, batting her eyes.

"My mom was a big *Wizard of Oz* fan," he says indifferently. I frown. He's never told me that story.

Jane twists a piece of her highlighted hair around her fingertip. "I *love* that movie!"

WTF? Did she want me to call him over so she could move in on Oz. That's so not going to happen.

"Thank you for the drink," I say.

"Not a problem."

Jane steps closer to Oz and grazes his bare arm. I resist swatting her away. "You should buy me a drink, too."

Well, isn't she an aggressive little thing?

"You know, Jane," Oz says. "I really want to talk to Veronica, but I promise to return your friend in one piece."

Jane recoils. "First, she's not my friend. We just met. And second – really? She's old."

"I prefer mature," I snap. "And I'm still hotter than you. So gather yourself and move along. Oz isn't interested."

Molly grips Jane's arm. "Let's go. He clearly has a thing for old ladies."

Oz shakes his head as they walk to the other end of the bar where a few guys closer to their ages stand. When they're out of earshot, Oz says, "Better luck next time, ladies."

"Stop it," I say, pouting. "They called me old."

Oz brushes his fingertips over the back of my hand. "Hardly old. And definitely hotter."

"Good answer." I drain my glass. "I'm tired of this game. Should we go back to the hotel?"

He flags the bartender. "I was hoping you'd pick me up and take me to some fabulous hotel overlooking the beach." He laughs. "Lucky me, you're making my dreams come true."

I slug his arm lightly. "Get the bill."

While we wait for the bartender to close our tabs, Oz places his hand on the small of my back, and I shiver. I know I shouldn't be doing this, but I can't help myself.

The bartender hands us the bills. "Let me get both," Oz says, reaching for his wallet. "It's only fair after you picked up dinner, heiress or not."

I don't argue, and he flips a credit card onto the counter with the bill. It's a United Airlines card.

"Is that how you're able to afford all these flights?" I ask, even though it's really none of my business.

If he's uncomfortable, Oz doesn't show it. "Yeah. I mean, I have the money from selling the house, but I pay for almost everything with my card and cash in the points. It adds up fast and has great perks."

I have a Citigroup Chairman card, but I can't tell him that – not that Oz would know what it is. It would do nothing but once again underscore how different our lives are.

After paying, we walk outside. A light sea breeze kicks up and the palm trees rustle. This is the time of night I love – the darkness and emptiness give off a magical quality.

Or maybe it's the 70,000 glasses of champagne I've had over the course of the day.

Halfway back to our hotel, Oz stops and spins me toward him. My breath quickens as he stares into my eyes. "It's going to be hard to say goodbye to you, Veronica."

Wind whistles around us, sending my hair flying into my face. Oz pushes it away with the softest touch. My chest rises slowly, and my pulses races. "We have time."

"Not enough," he says, lifting my chin. His deep brown eyes find the center of my soul, and I can't look away. "I knew the first time you smiled at me, Veronica, that I'd fallen madly in love."

I close my eyes, and his whiskey-flavored lips find mine. The rush is too hard to ignore, and I grasp the back of his neck and pull him closer to me. He moans when my tongue darts between his lips, and his hand rests on my hip. "Veronica--"

I'm insane, but I can't stop myself from covering his mouth with my hand and giving a sly smile. "Don't say another word. Just enjoy the moment."

"Maybe I want longer." Moonlight softens his sharp features, making him look more vulnerable than normal. Our connection is electric. "Maybe you can give me longer."

I rub the naked spot on my ring finger. I may still be married, but Pete is the one who broke our vows. He doesn't deserve my fidelity. "Maybe I can."

24

"Goodnight." I stop outside my hotel room door. The walk back to the hotel has been...pleasant? It's like I've known Oz for years, but my conflicted heart wouldn't let me enjoy it. "I'll see you for breakfast?"

Oz glances up and down the hallway before playfully pinning me against the wall and nibbling my neck. "Vee, let me come in."

I swallow to wet my dry mouth as excitement and disappointment tear at my heart. If I let him in, what does it mean for Pete and me? And more importantly, what does it say about me? "Oz..."

He presses his fingertip against my lips. "Don't think."

He gives me puppy dog eyes, and I flip the key card over in my hand as my heart bangs against my ribcage. Before I can talk myself out of whatever we're doing, I reach behind me and tap the key against the lock, and the door clicks open. "Come in." I push the door open. "We can have a drink on the balcony."

We both know why he's coming in, but I can't say it out loud. Being with Oz has always been easy. The conversation flows, and we get each other. But right now, a silent awkwardness has settled over us, and I need to break tension. I grab his hand and yank Oz into the room.

Housekeeping left the lights on when they did turndown service, and three more macarons and a bottle of Vittel sit on the small table. Oz moves toward the table, selects the pistachio macaron and offers it to me. I decline and toss my handbag on the chair.

Oz eats half the cookie in one bite. "Oh, man. That's delicious."

"You should try Ladurée in Paris. Those are the best." I dart my arm out so that I barely miss touching him, but am near enough to be flirty, and grab the bottle of water. "Let's go outside."

With the water tucked under my arm, I slide the door open, and rowdy cheers drift up from the square below. There's some sort of concert going on down there, and I wanted to check it out as we walked back to the hotel. But I want whatever is going to happen with Oz more.

Humidity and salty, ocean air rush in around me. I collapse on the nearest lounge chair and shift so that my legs look their best. It's not at all comfortable, but Oz will appreciate it. I tilt my head upward and stare up at the retractable awning. "We could open that up and see the stars."

Oz sits next to me on the lounge chair, his hip touching my bare upper thigh where my dress has pulled up. He takes the water bottle from my hand and places it on a side table. "If you lift the awning, people may see us."

I raise my eyebrows. "And what is there to see?"

"This." He leans in and plants a trail of kisses along my collarbone.

A soft moan escapes my lips. "Oz."

"I thought..." He pulls back. "Do you want me to stop?"

Insanity. That's the only explanation I have for my behavior. "No."

The only things between me and my marriage vows are a flimsy black dress and my dwindling willpower.

Oz's hand skims over my thigh and under my dress where he gently rakes his fingers over my stomach. I shift and wrap my leg around his waist, pulling him closer to me. He tugs his t-shirt over his

247

head, exposing his six pack, and I run my fingers through the soft patch of hair on his chest. He groans.

Don't think, Veronica. Live in the moment.

My dress lands on the ground next to Oz's t-shirt. He reaches behind me and unsnaps my bra. When I'm topless, Oz cups each of my breasts.

"Perfect," he says, and I blush. I'm used to men commenting on my body, but this is raw and more intimate.

"Someone may hear or see us," I whisper.

"The music is too loud." He kisses the top of my breast. "We'll be quiet, and as long as no one has binoculars, we're good."

I fight the slight nauseous feeling in my stomach. I can do this. I dip my fingertips under the waistband of Oz's shorts. "Take these off." I sound more confident than I feel. "They're in the way."

Oz stands and slides his pants off. I bite my lip. This is happening.

When he lies back down next to me, he slides my panties off, and I'm completely naked. His hand rests on my hip.

"I want you to enjoy this." He bends and flicks his tongue over my stomach. Then lower. And lower.

I gasp and lift my hips. His fingers explore even lower. "Don't stop."

He chuckles. "I have no intention."

He kisses the inside of my thighs, and I roll my head to the side. Sex with Pete is usually married maintenance sex. Nothing spectacular, but not bad. Just a way to get our needs taken care of.

This isn't maintenance anything.

I clench the lounge chair cushion and force my hips up.

"Relax," Oz says. "Let me please you." He wraps my leg over his shoulder. "Enjoy yourself."

I close my eyes and do as I'm told.

I stretch my hand onto the far side of the bed and touch Oz's bare back. It's weird having another man in bed with me – exciting, but weird. Nothing like when we were on the boat.

"Are you awake?" I whisper.

He doesn't answer, so I sit up and clutch the stiff white sheet against my bare chest. We left the curtains open, and sunlight sparkles off the harbor. It's another beautiful day. Another day where I'm going to pretend my life isn't veering out of control.

I draw my knees to my chest and rest my cheek on one knee. Things are going to be different between Oz and me now. It's inevitable.

In hindsight, we've been careening down this path since the day we met. I lied to myself when I forced thoughts of Oz from my mind. He was never too young for me, and I've always been attracted to him.

I glance at the clock. It's still early – I should try to fall back to sleep, but my chin quivers, and I struggle against the tears forming in my eyes. How could I do this? It felt so right in the moment, but now...

This was all a mistake.

As I slip off the bed, I'm very aware of my nakedness. Normally, I enjoy the male gaze, but now I'm hoping Oz stays asleep as I quietly walk down the short hallway to the bathroom. I softly close the door and lock it.

What does this mess say about me? Am I really that desperate for attention that I'll fall into bed with the first guy who is interested in me?

I sink to the floor, pulling one of the white terrycloth robes with me. Oh my God. We didn't use a condom. What if...No, I won't go there. I curl into a ball and try to fight back the hundreds of disaster scenarios flitting through my mind.

Pete hurt me, but I'm embarrassing myself running around with a guy twelve years younger than me. Behaving like this isn't going to heal my marriage. I don't know what will, but I know it won't involve me being unfaithful. Yesterday, I wanted a divorce; today, I am thinking about healing my marriage. Why is my head doing a 180?

I can't fight my feelings anymore. But before this goes any farther, I need to confront whatever is waiting for me in Waterford.

With a sniff, I pull myself up and walk toward the massive tiled shower. There's a large rainfall showerhead attached to the ceiling and a handheld unit mounted to the wall. I study the handles, trying to figure out what they do. Finally, I crank one, then the other, and water sprinkles down from the ceiling.

I have to leap backward so the cool water doesn't blast me. I wait, outside the spray, dipping my toe in every once in a while to see if the water is warm enough. When it reaches the right temperature, I immerse myself and let the water wash away the negative feelings building inside me. I slowly wash my hair, scrubbing my scalp and taking care to really soap the ends. As I wait for the conditioner to soak in, I rub shaving gel on my legs and shave.

When I'm done, I wrap myself in a robe and my hair in towel. With my hand, I wipe away the steam fogging the mirror. My reflection startles me. Everything about me looks like it did yesterday, but I feel completely different inside. Dangerous maybe? Out of control? Secretly excited? Thoroughly disappointed in myself?

What is wrong with me? I should be thankful someone finds me interesting and desirable. Pete may not have chosen me, but Oz did, and he's here unlike Pete, who refuses to come to me.

I brush my damp hair into a low bun and carefully apply my make-up. Yes, Oz has seen me puking and with tear stains on my face, but men like when women take care of themselves. And if I'm honest, I want Oz to want me. I don't want this to be just a one-time thing.

My hands shake a little as I slip the bathrobe on. I didn't bring clothes into the bathroom with me and walking around naked in front of Oz feels weird.

I quietly pull the door open so that I don't wake Oz if he's still asleep. I slink down the hallway toward my suitcase and peer around the hallway corner toward the bed.

The bed's empty.

"Oz?" I walk past the disheveled bed and toward the balcony. My clothes cover the cement floor. "Are you out here?"

He's not.

I purse my lips and take in the crime scene. The white duvet hangs off the side of the bed, and an empty bottle of Veuve sits on the side table. I vaguely remember ordering it and remember drinking it even less. With a shake of my head, I step back outside and scoop up my dirty clothes.

Oz must have gone to his room to shower and change.

I dig through my suitcase, find my cleanest dress, and make a mental note to have my things sent out for washing today. The sun floods the room, and I sit at the small table. Crumbs from Oz's half-eaten macaron cover the surface. With a quick flick of my hand, I brush them onto the floor.

How awkward is it going to be between us? Will we act like nothing happened, or will we act like a couple? What's the right protocol after you hook up with your friend? And do women my age hook up? Is that a thing?

My phone beeps. I swivel my head. Where did I leave it?

It beeps again, and I search around the table. Another beep. What the hell? I pull open a dresser drawer, and my phone flashes at me. There are dozens of alerts and messages from Pete, but nothing from Oz.

My heart sinks at the sight of Pete's name. What I've done is no better than his whatever-it-was with Eve. I check the time on the last message – it came over four hours ago. Pete must have sent it before he went to sleep...around the time I was in bed with Oz.

My stomach clenches. *Don't go there, Veronica. Pete didn't think about you.*

Before I can drive myself crazy, I open WhatsApp and jot off a message to Oz.

--hey let's get breakfast--

He probably feels as awkward as I do. Or maybe he knows it was all a mistake. After all, I'm too old for him despite his claims to the contrary.

I glance at my phone. Nothing.

I wait.

And wait.

And wait.

After twenty minutes – because what guy showers for more than twenty minutes?—I grab my room key and head to Oz's room. I gently knock on the door.

Nothing.

Maybe he's getting us breakfast?

Doubt nibbles at me. It's annoying more than anything, but I can't ignore it. Oz regrets everything and doesn't want to see me. I slink back into my room and fall onto the bed. Why did I have to mess this up? Why?

My phone dings, and I hold it over my face to see what Oz said, but it's only stupid shopping emails.

I glance at the room clock. It's been almost two hours since I woke up. Where the hell is Oz?

With growing unease, I message him again. Maybe I'm going too psycho after a one-night stand, but I don't care. It's weird that he's been gone so long and isn't returning my messages. And if this is the end of our time together, he owes it to me to say so to my face.

My stomach rumbles. I can sit here waiting, or I can go eat some-thing. Either way, Oz will come back when he feels like coming back. I don't need him to think his disappearing act has me worked up, so I should get on with my day.

I wander out to the balcony and pose against the railing. I frame myself on the phone screen so that the bay stretches out behind me. For having very little sleep, I look amazingly refreshed. Make-up does wonders. After I snap the selfie, I post it on Instagram.

Unable to deny my hunger any longer, I head back into the room and put my shoes on.

Where's my bag? I stare at the spot on the dresser where I left it.

Why isn't it there? I frown, trying to remember if I dropped it some-where else, but honestly, everything is a bit blurry. I look behind the TV. I search the ground. I look in my suitcase, on the bed, out on the balcony. Nothing.

What the fuck?

I rip the top dresser drawer open. It's empty.

I tug the next one open. There's a passport. I flip it open, and my picture stares back at me. Why is my passport in the drawer? If I take it out of my bag, I always lock it in the safe.

So why is it here? And where is my goddamn purse?

My heart races as I destroy the room. I strip every sheet off the bed and pile them in the corner. I crawl around the floor. I check the safe and even look through the spare pile of linens.

Where is Oz? Could he have taken my bag?

Vomit strikes the back of my throat, and I run for the bathroom. Nothing comes out no matter how hard I wretch.

No. Oz wouldn't travel with me for weeks only to sleep with me and steal my wallet. Someone had to have broken in while I was in the shower.

I run cool water over my wrists while struggling to get my breath under control. When I'm composed, I lift the house phone and call down to the front desk.

"Mrs. White? How can I help you?"

"I think my room's been broken into." As I speak, I realize how stupid I sound. No one waited outside my room until the exact moment I climbed into the shower.

"I'll send security right up."

"Thank you." I pull the phone away from my ear. "Oh, can you do me a favor? Can you please ring room 803. My friend isn't answering his door."

The receptionist click clacks on her keys. "I'm sorry. Mrs. White, I have no one in that room."

"Of course you do. We checked in together yesterday. Room 803."

"Room 803 is unoccupied."

My chest seizes. "He didn't check in?"

"I'm sorry, but I don't have anyone in that room."

"Oh my God."

Someone bangs on my door. "Mrs. White? It's hotel security."

I slam the phone down and cross the room. When I yank the door open, two very French looking security guards stand outside.

"There's a problem, Mrs. White?" the older one asks me in French.

"*Oui*," I answer shakily. "My wallet and money are missing." I don't mention Oz. There has to be a reasonable explanation for his disappearance.

"May we come in?"

My mind blurs a little. "Of course."

They walk down the short hallway toward the table and stop. "Is anyone with you?"

"My friend Oz, but I have no idea where he is at the moment."

The younger of the two guards gives the other a knowing look. "Did you recently meet?"

"No." This is ridiculous. Oz had every opportunity to rob me on the boat and in Morocco. Why would he wait until he slept with me? "We've been traveling together for several weeks."

"Please, sit." The older guard motions to the nearest chair. "What can you tell me about this man? His last name, perhaps?"

"I don't know it," I stammer.

"You've been traveling together, but you don't know his last name?"

I nod as the realization that I know next to nothing about Oz hits me. The younger guard scribbles on his notepad while I speak.

"But you've been traveling together? For weeks?"

"Yes."

"And what is the nature of your relationship?" The older guard is no-nonsense.

I refocus my gaze and lie. "We're friends."

"Your wallet and money are missing, but your passport and phone remain?"

"Yes."

The older guard nods. "I'm afraid, Mrs. White, that you are the victim of a crime. This man – your friend – he stole from you."

Rationally, it makes sense, but why would Oz travel with me for weeks only to steal from me now when he had ample opportunity before today?

"That's not possible," I say, wanting to deny the truth. It wasn't until last night that I told him about my trust fund. Conflicting thoughts form in my mind: he did really like me battles with he only liked me for my money.

"Perhaps – and I don't mean to be indelicate – but you should inform your husband. You do have a husband, don't you?" The guard nearest me crosses his arms.

"My husband?" I stare at the guards with confusion. "I'm not sure I understand. Why does my husband need to be involved?"

The younger guard flips his notepad shut. "You have your passport, but no money, is that correct?"

I nod.

"You're going to need money to get home. Are you able to cancel your credit cards before they're used?"

I hadn't thought of that. "All my banking is on my phone," I lift my phone and tap the screen on. "I can do that now." I scroll to my finance folder. "What the hell?" I stare at the screen in confusion. "It's gone."

"What's gone?" the older guard asks.

"All my banking information. My passwords and banking apps are all gone." Panic gnaws at me. This can't be happening. "Oz did this?"

"Does your husband have access to your accounts?"

"Some of them."

"I would call him immediately," the older guard says.

I tilt my head back and stare at the ceiling. I will not cry. How could I be so stupid? And now Pete is going to know.

"Mrs. White?" the younger guard says.

"Yes?"

"Would you like us to call the police? They will investigate, but if you don't have his name, it will be difficult to locate him."

"His name is Oz."

The older guard looks at me with pity. "No, Mrs. White. That's who he wanted you to believe he was. Who he really is, is a mystery."

25

The first thing I notice isn't the flowers, but rather Pete's newly shaved face. I haven't seen his scruff-free face in nearly five years, and he looks different – like a version of Pete that isn't quite right.

His eyes zero in on me as I stand in the doorway. I bite my bottom lip as he holds yellow roses out like I'm the winner of a beauty pageant. If Pete knew me, he'd know I hate yellow flowers. Orange is my favorite. I stare at them, and when I don't immediately accept them, Pete hangs his head.

"Hey," he says. "I guess this isn't how you wanted to see me?"

I nod and take the flowers. A maid walks past, unaware of the drama playing out between Pete and me. When I called him, I didn't give him all the details – only that my wallet had been stolen and that I needed him to cancel all my cards and block charges to our joint accounts. Then I told him where to find the account numbers and passwords to my private accounts so he could shut those down too. After he did all that, I asked him to come. And this time, under the guise of getting me out of France, he agreed.

"Are you not speaking?" Pete asks.

I step aside so he can enter. "I'm tired. It's been a rough two days."

"Let's get you home." Pete doesn't try to kiss or touch me, and I'm thankful. If he's furious about the missing money, he's not showing it...yet. "We can check you out in the morning. There are flights to D.C. tomorrow. We'll have a layover somewhere since there are no direct flights."

I've practiced how to tell Pete about the whole disaster for the past day, but now that he's here, I'm more nervous than I anticipated. I pause next to the table, place the flowers down, and point at one of the chairs. "Can we talk first?"

He drops his backpack on the floor and sits backward on the chair while resting his arms along the top. He's 100% in fix-it mode. "What's up?"

What's up? That's the best he has? We haven't seen each other in weeks, and he thinks we can hop on a plane and return to Waterford like nothing has happened. Unbelievable.

I should have called my parents and avoided having to see Pete. They would have given me money and helped me access my trust fund. But that would have required me admitting my stupidity... and infidelity. "Thank you for coming. I know you didn't have to, but--"

"Vee, of course I'd come. You need me." There's a slight air of victory in his voice, and his blue eyes dance. "I'm not going to leave you penniless in Europe."

Heat rushes down my spine. I haven't missed the way Pete makes me feel, and he's acting so gallantly when he's not. In the past, I would fall for this routine, but not now. I see him more clearly. His luster wears away when he's not surrounded by his Waterford country club friends.

"Considering how you refused to come until now proves differently."

The corner of his mouth drags up. "I didn't come because you were otherwise occupied with Oz."

Blood rushes to my head, and I grab onto the edge of the table before I topple over.

"Whoa," Pete says with what could pass for genuine concern. "Are you okay?"

I lift my chin. "I'm fine. Once we get the financial stuff sorted, I'll be perfectly fine."

"The bank is working on it," Pete says, not making any sort of move to help me. "I've filed a complaint with them and a police report back home."

"We'll get our money back?" I ask. If we do, maybe this can all go away.

"Someone hacked our accounts and wired two million dollars into a Maltese account. I guarantee you, our bank has every available person working on this."

"Oh."

Pete scowls. "We're out two million dollars, and all you can say is 'oh'?"

"What else should I say? I've already apologized for losing my wallet."

Pete ignores me and glances over his shoulder like he's looking for someone. "By the way, where is this Oz guy?"

I pace between the sliding door and the table. "He's not here."

"He left?" Pete says, his smirk growing more prominent. "You ran out of money, and he left. I didn't see that one coming."

The sick feeling in my stomach returns. If I tell Pete the truth, he's going to hold it over me – even if I only tell him a half-truth. I don't have to admit sleeping with Oz, but I do need to tell my husband about Oz's involvement in the theft -- only because it impacts him too.

"He took my wallet."

Pete's eyes pop open. "What?"

"Oz is the one who robbed me." My dry throat aches.

"You've got to be kidding me." Pete pushes off the chair and stands. He grabs me by the shoulders and stares into my eyes. "How did that happen? And how the fuck haven't you filed a report with the State Department yet? He's a U.S. citizen, right?"

My chin quivers. "Yes."

"Everything? Your passport, too?"

I shake my head. "No, only my wallet and financial information."

"How the hell did that happen?"

I close my eyes. "He took it while I showered."

Pete drops his hands. "I'm not going to draw conclusions, but I'm sure there's a story there." He stares over my head and out the sliding door. "There's a police report?"

"Yes."

"Okay. At least you did that." He clenches his jaw. "I'll have INTERPOL put an alert out on his passport. As soon as he tries to use it, he'll be detained. What's his full name?"

"I don't know."

"You don't know? How the hell do you not know?" Pete tosses up his hands. "What's his Instagram account? We can hunt him down that way."

I shake my head as tears form in my eyes. "He doesn't have one."

"He's a fucking millennial. How is that possible? Did that not raise any alarm bells for you?"

"He doesn't like having his picture taken...It struck me as odd at first, but he was more interested in living in the moment than doing selfies."

Pete crosses his arms. "Vee, I've been patient. I've let you run all over the place with that guy. I've tolerated the questions about your Instagram pictures. I've even covered for you with the kids when they asked who Oz was. You owe me some answers."

I blink away my tears. "I owe you? Have you forgotten you slept with Eve?"

"You're going to go there again?"

I give him withering look. "You humiliated me."

"You've done the same." Pete grabs my wrist. "Don't think you haven't. I've been batting cleanup for you, and now your boy toy has cleaned out our bank accounts. Nice."

My mouth drops open. "Are you serious? Cleanup for me? What the hell do you think I do all the time?" When he doesn't answer, I add, "I run around behind you and convince the world that you're not a piece of shit."

"Name calling is beneath you." Pete lets go of my wrist and walks over to where my half-packed suitcase sits. "We can't go home until you make the necessary reports."

"I told you, I've already filed a police report."

Pete blows out a burst of air. "That's not enough. You have to file an INTERPOL report, or do you want him to get away with this?"

What do I want? The image of sweet, caring Oz conflicts with Oz the conman, and I'm not ready to accept that version of him yet. "Of course I don't want him getting off, but is it necessary to involve the U.S. government?"

"If we want our money back -- all two million of it."

I exhale loudly. Oz can travel for a long time with that kind of money, and if he's smart, he'll keep transferring it to new, untraceable Maltese accounts. "What do I need to do?"

Pete's already on the phone. He holds up his finger, silencing me, and steps outside. I sit at the table and play with the fresh macarons house cleaning left. How did Oz know my favorite was pistachio?

"Okay." Pete walks back inside and continues his take-charge routine. "We need to go to Paris, to the embassy, and they'll take your statement in person. Thank God he left your passport."

"I have copies stored at home and in my suitcase," I say softly. "It would have been fine."

Pete rubs his hairless chin. "You know, the passport thing puzzles me. So does him leaving your phone."

It puzzles me too, but I don't let Pete know that. "He deleted all my banking apps and password list. Remember? That's why I needed you."

"Yeah, but how did he get into your phone in the first place?"

I've thought hard about this. Oz told me he's a hacker, and maybe that's how he got into my phone, but the night at Bo Zin, I rattled off my password. "I may have given him the password once."

"What?" Pete stares at me in disbelief. "Why would you do that?"

"He was taking pictures of me, and my phone locked."

Pete shakes his head slowly. "Wow. He must be good. That thing never leaves your hand."

"I don't want to do this right now," I snap. "I know I messed up. I don't need you reminding me of that."

"Fine." Pete sits opposite of me. "We leave in the morning, so let's grab some dinner. When's the last time you ate?"

I shrug. "I had some fruit yesterday."

But Pete isn't really paying attention and is lost in his phone. "There are a few flights to Paris tomorrow morning. Let me book one."

I leave him to go sit outside. Cars honk over the hum of typical city noise. I stretch out on the sun lounger and stare into the darkening sky. Pete hasn't said he's happy to see me. In fact, all he's done is blame me for everything.

Does he not understand that we wouldn't be in this mess if he had been faithful? Why is he incapable of accepting any responsibility? I know I was stupid; why can't he say he was too? I guess he would argue his indiscretion didn't put our family in financial jeopardy, so therefore, it isn't as big of a deal.

Has he always been like this?

After a while, he shoves the door open and sticks his head out. "All booked. Our flight is at 10:20. I didn't book us to D.C. because I don't know how long we'll need to stay in Paris."

I keep my gaze fixed on the sky.

"Hey, are you okay?" Pete says gently. I almost believe he cares.

"Yes. I'm just overwhelmed."

Pete stretches out on the lounger next to mine. He sighs. "We've really fucked things up, haven't we?"

PICTURE PERFECT LIES

"You fucked them up," I say flatly even though I don't want to fight. In fact, I want to sleep and wake up and be done with everything.

"You made it worse," he says.

I roll my head so that I'm looking directly at him. Pete wants something, but he's waiting for the right moment to pounce. Best to beat him to it. "What do you want?"

"Dinner."

"And then what?" I don't feel like playing twenty questions.

"This isn't all my fault." Pete's blue eyes pierce through me. "You're not exactly acting thankful that I dropped everything and flew to save you."

I can't do this now. I can't deal with his blame game. "Let's go get dinner."

"Good idea." Pete extends his hand, and I gingerly take it. Regret immediately hits me. Unlike in the past, there's no comfort in Pete's touch, only sorrow. I want to yank my hand away, but that would only anger him more. So, despite my reservations, I let him guide me inside.

"Where are your shoes? Or did Oz steal those too?"

I glare at Pete. "Cute." I walk around to the other side of the bed and slip on my sandals. "I need to use the bathroom."

Once inside, I close the door and pause in front of the mirror. I've aged five years since Oz left. Granted I've had a horrible two days, but the lines around my eyes are more pronounced, and my laugh lines weigh my face down. If I thought Pete didn't find me attractive before, he must find me repulsive now.

I sigh. Why the hell do I care? Women age. It's perfectly fine. And if my husband is so shallow that he can't accept that, maybe the problem is him and not me. Haven't I learned that Botox doesn't make a man faithful?

I close my eyes, and Oz's goofy lopsided grin wedges itself into my memory. How could he let me believe he cared? Is my choice in men so awful that I can't spot a conman – especially after Stella and

263

the others warned me? Or am I so self-centered that all it takes is a little flattery to gain my trust?

An easy mark – that's what I was. I should have known when he didn't show interest in Lydia. After all, what thirty-three year old guy wants to be with a forty-five-year-old woman? Hell, what forty-five-year-old guy wants to be with a forty-five-year-old woman? Not many. Oz should have been drooling over Lydia, but he never gave her the time of day. I ignored every red flag.

A little sob rolls out of me. God, I'm stupid. If only I had listened to my mom and gone home to Pete. But I can barely stomach the sight of Pete, and I absolutely don't want to go back to Waterford.

"Vee? You okay?" Pete knocks on the door. "Are you crying?"

I wipe the back of my hand across my face. "I don't love you."

"What?" Pete says, swinging the door open.

I move as far from him as I can and press against the bidet. " I can't love you. Not after what you did. I can't let it go." Tears roll freely down my face. "I wanted to try. In the beginning, I thought maybe if I saw you, I could get past everything, but I can't. I tried pretending, but this time, it didn't work."

"Stop." Pete steps closer to me and pushes my hair off my face. "You know there is no one in this world that I love more than you."

"You said horrible things about me to Eve."

Pete shrugs. "I was crazy. That's all that was."

"So you can sleep with Eve, but still love me? Is that what you're saying?"

"If you want to put it that way," Pete says, calmly. "What I did with Eve is completely independent of how I feel about you."

Is this like Oz's book? Can Pete really separate his love for me from his sexual adventures with Eve? I study his face. No, it's not possible. Oz said that by the end, the reader realizes the two acts are intertwined. Pete's actions show he doesn't love me.

"I don't believe you."

"I'm here, aren't I?" His fingertips trail down my jaw, and I fight the horrible shiver racing down my spine.

"What if I don't love you anymore? Then what?" My chest tightens.

"I'm going to fight for you, Veronica. If you want it, I'll fight."

"I'm tired of fighting," I say, pushing past him and out the door. "And I'm tired of empty promises."

"We've never really tried." Pete reaches around my waist and pulls me so that my back meets his front. "We can't live without each other. You know that."

Once, I would have believed him. I would have thought he was being romantic. I shake my head. "I seem to be surviving just fine without you."

Pete laughs. "Vee, you're stranded in a foreign country with no access to money. That's not exactly doing fine. In fact, it's kind of worse than fine."

I can't really argue with that.

I let Pete sleep in bed with me, but on top of the duvet. Long after he's completely asleep, I toss and turn. So much has happened, and my brain can't process any of it. I stare into the dark, trying to calm myself, but all I think about is either Eve screwing my husband, or the tender way Oz held me before robbing me blind. Neither one is a soothing image.

Since I'm not getting any sleep, I slip out from under the covers, grab my phone from the side table, and step onto the balcony. I might as well as read the news.

Why am I lying to myself? I want to look at pictures of Oz. I need to see if I missed something.

I curl up on the lounger and pull my t-shirt over my bare knees. I only have 51% battery, but that will give me a few hours. My finger hovers over Instagram. I can't bring myself to open it. The thought of seeing how happy I was with Oz makes my stomach churn. Instead, I pour through Facebook, looking for any sign that my old friends will welcome me back into the fold. Nothing extraordinary stands out among the pictures of parties, pools, and drinks. This is why I'm going home? To be friends with vapid women and a wife to a man who doesn't deserve me?

No. I'm going home because it's expected of me. Women like me don't get divorced. We suck it up for the kids, our image, and our lifestyle. I've been sucking it up for far too long, but what other option do I have at the moment? I tried running away and look what happened.

I set my phone next to me on the chair and close my eyes, listening to the sound of the waves crashing into the shore. Oz conned me, but I can't help but believe there were genuine moments – like when he saved me from the waves, or when he cared for me when I was sick on the boat. Was he really that great an actor? Or did I put so much of myself out on social media that figuring me out was a piece of cake.

I open Instagram, and the number 10 hovers over the heart. I click it open. It's nothing exciting, only a bunch of likes on my old posts. My last post – one of Oz dozing on the beach in Nice with a hat pulled over his face – is a few days old. The comments are typical: He's adorable! How fun! Wish I was there!

If I had only known.

I bash my hand against the lounge cushion. I was so stupid, and yet, I still want everything we shared to be true.

With my heart pounding, I open WhatsApp. Maybe Oz has messaged me back, and this is all a mistake.

"What are you doing?" Pete flicks on the balcony light. "Why aren't you sleeping?"

"Insomnia." I casually close the app. "Why are you up?"

He runs his hand through his hair. "I haven't slept much since you left." He stands over me. "Anything good on social?"

Pete hates my social media obsession. "Not really," I say. "Just the normal stuff."

He glances at his watch. "It's three in the morning. Come back to bed."

Not knowing if Oz has messaged me is going to kill me. "I'm not tired."

"You know I'm supposed to be the one with jetlag." Pete frowns. "You really should come back to bed."

Reluctantly, I stand and start to head inside, but Pete darts his arm out.

"What?" I ask.

"Give me a chance."

I open my mouth, but snap it shut before anything scathing comes out. "I'm going to sleep."

Pete follows me like a puppy into the room. He waits until I'm under the covers than slides in next to me. "Is this okay?"

No. No, it's not. "It's fine."

He rolls closer to me and pecks me on the forehead. "Goodnight, Vee. I love you."

I cringe. I don't want his love or empty promises. I want action, and Pete did nothing, not one thing, to show me he wanted me. He didn't come to Morocco. He didn't fly to Croatia. He partied with our Waterford friends and only texted when it was convenient. He didn't come until our money was at stake.

Pete doesn't love me. He loves the idea of me.

2 6

Pete shoves my suitcase into the overhead compartment along with his backpack while I climb across the row to the window seat. He always lets me have the window seat because I love photographing the tarmac and view from above. Today, however, I leave my phone in my bag. I don't even place it in the seatback.

"You're not going to listen to music?" Pete asks. "Did Oz steal your AirPods, too?"

I scowl. "Enough. I get it. You're pissed."

"And you don't seem pissed enough." Pete manspreads as much as he can in the narrow seat, forcing me to cram closer to the window. Lucky for him, the aisle seat is empty.

"You should move over," I say. "They've closed the door. No one else is boarding."

Pete narrows his eyes. "If that's what you want." He flips up the center arm and moves. "Better?"

I turn away and watch as we pull away from the gate and to the runway. As the plane climbs higher, I place my hand against the window. Nice and the Mediterranean stretch out before me, but unlike when I landed, there's no sense of excitement. No wonder. Just pain and worry and anger.

The flight is uneventful as is the train ride into Paris. Pete and I have been here so many times that we used to discuss buying a second home in Le Marais neighborhood – not far from Notre Dame. It was our retirement dream: own a pied-de-terre in Paris, a place big enough for us and maybe two guests in case the kids wanted to come visit. But now, I don't want to be here.

"I told Dan we'd come straight to the Embassy. We'll need to transfer to the Métro."

"What stop?" I ask, trying to sound like I care.

"Concorde."

The Paris suburbs fly past as the train rushes closer to the city. Green space gives way to poor neighborhoods until we enter a dark tunnel. Before we stop, Pete and I head toward the exit and the baggage rack. He hands me my suitcase.

The station is a study of orderly chaos – people, luggage, and buskers all mingling in a way that is distinctly Parisian. We find our Métro line and press through the crowd.

"You're unusually quiet," Pete says as we exit the Concorde station.

"Just thinking." I dodge a man rushing down the stairs and blink as I step into the sunlight. Oppressive city heat engulfs me. Paris isn't humid, but it is a boiling hot concrete jungle. "Can we walk on the other side?"

Pete nods and crosses to the shady side, and we walk the rest of the way to the embassy in silence. Cement barricades fill the space in front of a tall, metal fence. "This way," Pete says. "We need to enter over here."

Due to Pete's job, I've been to many embassies and know we're going to be thoroughly searched and relegated to a waiting room. "We have an appointment?"

Pete nods. "Dan said he'd take care of us as soon as we arrived."

I have no idea who Dan is, but Pete must have worked with him in the past. Pete's like that – contacts, many that I don't know, all over the world. "What will I have to do?"

"Make a statement and give as much info as you can. I've sent over the pictures of Oz from your Facebook and Instagram accounts, but he's really good at not having his face photographed. I'm hoping they can pull something from his profile shot."

My heart clenches. "How did you do that? You don't have social."

"Says the woman who was posting so that I could see what a wonderful time she was having without me." When I stare at him blankly, he adds, "Oh, c'mon, Vee. You know damn well I monitor you."

After being screened, Pete and I are allowed into the embassy. It's an ornate French building that shows off all the money and power of the United States. We're led to a private room with comfortable, high-back chairs and a giant, polished mahogany desk.

"Mr. Talin will be right with you," our young escort says.

When we're alone, Pete leans into me. "Tell him everything. Every detail. It's the only way we'll catch Oz."

I am not going to say a word about sleeping with Oz, at least not with a witness. Unlike Pete, I'm not into embarrassing my spouse.

Dan Talin bursts into the room. He's a large man – taller than Pete – and broad. Pete stands, and they clasp each other on the back. "How's it going?" Dan says. "I haven't seen you in ages."

"I'm stateside now. No more overseas appointments."

Dan nods. "This is Veronica?"

I remain seated. "Yes. Nice to meet you, Dan."

He lumbers around the desk and tosses a file folder on the top. It lands with a thud. Dan arranges himself behind the desk and folds his hands. "Pete told me a little about what happened, but I wanted to hear it from you. All details are important."

I inhale and launch into my story. Dan takes notes as I speak, and every so often, stops me and asks for clarification. "Let's go back to when you first met. Can you tell me about what you were doing before you arrived at NOMAD. Do you think he followed you?"

I shake my head. "He was already there."

"It was a chance encounter?"

"Yes."

Pete interrupts. "You were posting all day on Instagram."

"So?"

"Pull up the post with you and the monkey." Pete taps the desk. "I want to see it."

I do as I'm told and hand the phone to Pete. He clenches his jaw and shakes his head. "She told the world where she was going." He reads from my phone, "*Had an amazing time in the souks today. Met this little guy. Going to NOMAD for dinner tonight. I'll let you lovelies know how it is.*" Pete places my phone on the desk. "You geotagged it too. Anyone with half a brain who was following the location could find you."

"What are you saying?" My vision blurs. "I gave Oz the information to target me? That he was waiting for me?" I shake my head. "He had no idea where I would be seated, and it's a crazy vertical restaurant with lots of nooks and crannies."

"But he would have recognized you, and chances are you would have gone to the rooftop for a photo since that's what you like to post on your account." Pete pushes his tongue against the back of his top lip, puffing it out. "You set yourself up, and the rest was easy."

I want to vomit. Or cry. Maybe both. I grab my phone and scroll through my Instagram photos. There are pictures of me all over the world; pictures of me with my friends; pictures of my favorite wine; and to my horror, a picture of me holding a box of Ladurée macarons: *pistachio are my favorite!*

"He used everything you posted publicly to get to know you better," Dan says. "It's what a conman does, and it's why you should never geotag or make your accounts public."

I smash my hand over my mouth. No wonder it felt like I had known Oz for years – he had stalked my social media. From the first minute we met, he'd been planning to steal from me. Or was it the minute I divulged my trust fund?

I sit there for a minute, digesting my stupidity.

"We've already contacted INTERPOL," Dan says. "They're going through the plane manifests into Croatia, but without a last name or an actual date of entry, it will be hard to find him." He presses his lips together. "Can you tell me anything about him at all, Veronica? Where he's from, perhaps?"

I hesitate. The thought of Oz sitting in a jail cell causes my lip to tremble. He stole from me, and I should be livid, but part of me doesn't want him to rot in jail. I want to remember him how he was with me: gentle and sweet. The thought of having to see him in prison clothes and confront my own stupidity and the realization that it was all a con is too much. I want it to go away. Yes, I'm putting a two-million-dollar price tag on my pride, but I can't drag this out. I want it done.

"Veronica?" Dan asks.

"Sorry, I don't know much about him, and what I do know, I've shared."

Dan focuses on Pete. "I'm afraid without a picture or a name, it's going to be hard to find him. INTERPOL can try to get the Maltese bank information, but that could take years and lawsuits. It may end up costing you more than you lost."

"What about camera footage of Veronica entering the Marrakech airport with him?"

Dan frowns. "There is no camera footage."

Pete bangs his fist on the arm of the chair. "Damn it, Veronica."

Dan closes his file folder. "I wish I had better news."

Pete shoves his chair back and stands. "Thanks, Dan. It was good seeing you again even if the circumstances aren't ideal."

"Yes, thank you," I say stiffly. I will not cry. I won't. I turn my back and dab the corners of my eyes with my fingertips.

Dan shows us out and when Pete and I stand on the sidewalk outside, Pete glares at me. "Well, at least your Instagram has gotten more likes than you ever dreamed of."

"What does that mean?" I snap.

Pete snorts. "Everything you do, Veronica, is for show. But it bit you in the ass this time. You'll need to tap your trust fund to pay back our accounts. I'm not paying for this."

As much as I want to remind him that it's all my money, not his, I hold my tongue. Because the truth is, Pete's right. I've spent so much of my life keeping up appearances and being the woman that people expect me to be that I lost sight of myself. If I couldn't Instagram a party, it wasn't worth attending. If my hair didn't look on point, I couldn't be photographed. If I couldn't get the highest number of likes or loves, it was a waste of my time.

In some ways, I'm no better than Oz. The only difference is my con hurts no one but myself.

"Do you want to do some sightseeing before dinner?" Pete asks. "I booked our flight home for tomorrow morning, so we have the rest of today."

I honestly don't want to do anything other than curl into a ball and let myself be miserable. My plan to prove to the world that I'm okay backfired. I look up at Pete through swollen lids. "I'm tired."

"We're not sitting around the hotel. It's not even going to be dark until at least ten. We have plenty of time to do stuff." Pete offers me his hand. "C'mon, get up."

I study him closely. A faint stubble has returned to his jawline, making him look more like the Pete I know, and he wears a pale blue, long-sleeve dress shirt with the sleeves rolled up and jeans. He looks exactly the way I've taught him to look. Casual, but pulled together. A European sensibility in an American body. But no matter how hard I try to see it, Pete looks a hell of a lot less shiny than he does in Waterford.

"Vee, let's go."

I yank the covers over my head. "No."

"Stop acting like a child." Pete tugs on the sheet, but I hold it firmly in place.

"I don't want to go out. You can go do your own thing. You're good at that."

Pete sits next to me, and I lower the sheet so that my eyes peek out.

"I had hoped we could sit outside somewhere and talk," he says.

"About what?" I ask. "I really don't want to hear any more digs about Oz."

Pete shakes his head. "About us and our next moves. When we get back to Waterford, what's our plan?"

I push up to sitting and lean back on my hands. "I haven't completely decided to go back yet."

"Don't be ridiculous. What will people think if you don't come back?"

I shrug. "I'm pretty sure I no longer care."

Pete raises his eyebrows. "Of course you care."

I lean forward. "Not really. The kids aren't there, and there's nothing holding us to Waterford. I could go anywhere." I stop and correct myself. "We could go anywhere."

"Like where?"

I shrug. "I don't know."

"Get up, and let's go have a drink. We can discuss it there." Pete stands. "I'm not going to let you lay here and wallow."

"Fine." I stand, and Pete places both of his hands on my shoulders. He gazes into my eyes until I turn my head. "Stop it."

"What? Can't I look at my gorgeous wife?"

I slip on my shoes. "Is that all I am to you? A trophy? Do you think any woman would look at you the way they do now if they knew all the money belonged to me?"

"Don't be crass." Pete holds the hotel room door open.

He may seem composed, but I can tell from the tone of his voice that I've touched a nerve. Pete's always had a fear of people finding out that I'm the one financing our lifestyle. It injures his fragile masculine pride.

We walk in silence to a bistro a few blocks away. The waiter shows us to a patio seat near the smokers. "Excellent," Pete says. "I love a little lung cancer with my *poulet roti*."

I study the menu, anxious about having any sort of meaningful conversation with Pete. Since nothing appeals to me, I order water.

"That's it?" Pete asks. "You've barely eaten since I've been here. You're going to waste away."

"You like me thin."

"I like you healthy," Pete answers.

"Right. Because a diet of Adderall and champagne is healthy."

"Stop it."

I settle back into my chair and watch tourists and natives wander past. Every so often I catch a snippet of conversation from the tables near us, but mostly, I let my mind wander. Without Pete, I'm unable to stay in Europe since I have no debit or credit cards at the moment. That means I need to go back to Waterford if only to get my affairs in order.

Next to me, Pete digs into his chicken. He's on his second glass of wine and showing no sign of slowing down. His phone dings, and he takes it out of his pocket and frowns. "I have to take this. I'll be right back."

When he's gone, I distract myself with my phone. The first thing I do: change all my security settings to private. I don't need to be an influencer; I don't need likes and loves; and I absolutely do not need everyone knowing every move I make.

Once I'm done with that, I open my camera roll. How strange. It opened in the middle of my roll. I swipe down and squint at the screen in confusion.

The last picture is a handwritten note in a back-slanted scrawl.

--It's not what you think--

I glance down the street to where Pete stands out of earshot and try to get my thundering heart under control. When did Oz write this? While I was in the shower? After he decided to rob me?

Blood pounds in my ears. A little way off, Pete waves his hand like he's agitated, but since I can't see his face or hear him, I have no idea what's going on.

If it's not what I think, Oz, what is it? I fold my napkin and place it on the table.

The waiter rushes over. "Are you finished? May I clear the dishes?"

"Yes." I stare at Pete. Something feels wrong. "I'll be right back. That's my husband. I need to ask him if he wants another drink. I'll leave my bag."

"Oh, no, Madame. There is no need. I trust you."

God bless the French.

I walk out the gate separating the patio from the sidewalk and creep up on Pete.

"You're being ridiculous," he says in a harsh whisper. "I told you I need to bring Veronica home. I can't leave her in Europe without money. That wouldn't play out well." I stand behind him, waiting for him to notice me, but he's too wrapped up in his conversation. "No," he says. "Of course I love you, but things are complicated."

I spin around, anger raging in my veins, and return to the café. If I confront him, what advantage am I giving up? But damn it, either that was Eve, or he has a new plaything. Or maybe he's always had multiple. Whatever. He's a confirmed ass, and he hasn't changed at all.

I press my tongue against the roof of my mouth and breathe deeply. Pete stomps back toward me with a forced smile on his face.

"What was that about?" I ask. *Let's see if he can carry on the charade.*

Pete gives a half-shrug, but doesn't meet my gaze. "Work stuff."

"Uh huh." I fight back the scathing remarks ready to pour out of me. "Do you want more wine? The waiter asked."

"No. Let's get the bill. I'm tired and want a nap. Maybe we can walk around later after we rest."

"But I'm not tired."

"Oh, hell, Vee. Can you please stop being difficult?" His face softens. "You're not making this reconciliation easy."

"Is that what we're doing?" I'm going to hold all my cards until I have to show them.

"It's what we agreed to. Remember?" Pete's fingers reach out and graze my the underside of my arm. "Let's go."

My phone dings, and I excitedly look at the screen, hoping that it's Oz. My heart pounds, but it's not WhatsApp.

"Who is it?" Pete demands.

"Stacey." How odd that she's texting me now. It's like Eve told her to call me. Why else would she ask if Pete and I are having a romantic time in Paris? I grimace. "It's Waterford girl nonsense. You know how it is."

Pete shifts his eyes to the left and down. "What nonsense?"

"As if you suddenly care."

He glares at me before taking out his own phone and typing a message. I sit back and study the man I married. He thinks he's so damn sneaky, but I'm smarter. I've always been smarter, and I'll always be one step ahead of him. If he's even contemplating divorce, I'm going to slam him with papers the minute we step off the plane in D.C.

Oz was right about one thing: there has to be a way out of this mess. I just have to figure out what that is. A chill races down my spine, and I twirl a piece of hair around my index finger. Can I completely blow up my life and go against everything I've been taught about marriage? Maybe not two months ago, but now – yes, I certainly can.

"I'm ready," I say after Pete pays the waiter. Attorney. Divorce. Finances. I swallow the lump in my throat. "Maybe we can go to Notre Dame tonight. I love how it looks lit up." I lace my fingers around his. "Truce?"

Pete stares at our entwined fingers. "I'd like that."

Liar.

2 7

We trudge past baggage claim and out into the humid D.C. air. Sunlight strikes my skin, and sticky sweat immediately dampens the back of my neck. Summer is oppressive here.

Pete and I barely spoke on the flight home, and the silence I once found so comforting now unnerves me. I wanted Pete to say something meaningful to me, to convince me that coming home is the right thing to do, but he watched movies and slept.

"I'm in the daily lot." He walks toward the bus stop without waiting for me.

"No Uber?" I say as I scurry to keep up.

"I knew I wouldn't be gone long." He says this with the confidence of a man who always gets what he wants.

"What if I didn't want to come home?" I ask.

Pete chuckles. "I love your spirit, Sweetheart, but you weren't really in a position to stay."

I grit my teeth. I don't want to be here, and I especially don't want to be in Waterford with Pete pretending we live a charmed life. But until I figure out a plan, I'm stuck. And unfortunately, anything I transfer from my trust fund to our mutual accounts becomes communal property, and Pete has equal rights to it. That's why he has me make a large withdraw every January 1st – he wants access to my money.

We ride the bus to the daily lot, and after Pete places my suitcase in the back of his black BMW, he opens my door. I can't bring myself to speak, and instead, crank up the radio's volume. He gives me a cautious look and guns it out of the parking lot and onto the highway. He zips in between cars, switching lanes without signaling, and I clutch the side of my seat. Pete's reckless: with his driving; with his life; with my heart.

How ironic is it that I'm the one who threw caution to the wind and got swindled?

I rest my head against the back of the seat. Pete opens the sunroof, and a blast of air sends my hair flying. "Can you shut that? I don't have a scarf."

"I like it open."

I gather my hair in my hand and twist it over my shoulder. If Pete won't budge on an open sunroof, what else will he dig in on?

We exit the highway and head down a tree-lined street leading into our posh Northern Virginia suburb. Like all other rules, Pete believes speed limits don't apply to him, and he flies down the winding streets.

He stops in front of our perfectly-manicured lawn. It's been freshly mowed and the hedges are uniformly squared. The porch lights illuminate the red front door of our gray two-story home even though it's only four in the afternoon. Pete and I fought when we bought this house. I thought it was too large, but he wanted the 'successful' American Dream. To him that meant a 6,000-square-foot house with five-and-a-half bathrooms and six bedrooms for four people. Never mind that I had to use a significant portion of my yearly annuity to pay for it or that I wanted something more practical; Pete had to have it, and like everything else regarding him, I caved.

"Welcome home." Pete jumps out of the car and retrieves my bag.

When I don't move, he opens my door and says, "Don't be difficult. I thought we were trying."

With a heavy heart, I walk up the driveway. Pete opens the front door, and I brush past him before dropping my carry-on next to the stairs. The house is silent, but what did I expect? Now that the kids are off to college, it's just Pete and me. No buffers, and nothing to ease some of the tension between us.

I kick off my shoes and spin around. "What now?"

"What do you mean?" Pete furrows his brow.

"What do you want me to do? How are we going to do this?"

"You can start by deleting every photo you have of Oz. I want them off all your feeds." Calm, collected Pete actually sounds a little jealous. "They're useless, and we gave everything you had to the State Department and INTERPOL, so delete them."

"Maybe I don't want to." I cross my arms. "Maybe hanging out with Oz was the best time I've had in years." I can't stop myself. Pete's smugness is asking for me to smack him down a notch or two.

"Oh? Well that's great - if you're into conmen who steal your money." He walks closer to me. "Everything you did with him was a ruse to get you to trust him. An illusion. Just like his name."

"Like you? All you like me for is my money. It's why you stay. Admit it."

Pete recoils. "Is that what you believe? That I only love you for your money?"

My emotions snowball. "You've cheated on me numerous times. I know, so don't deny it." I pause and watch Pete's face grow red. "But I forgave you as long as you came home to me and didn't do anything publicly embarrassing. Everything changed with Eve."

"Are you really putting your husband of twenty-three years in the same category as a conman? Really?" Pete juts his chin out. "That's rich, Veronica. Absolutely rich. Do you want to know about Oz?"

"What do you know?" I try to sound calm, but my insides turn to Jell-O.

Pete snorts. "Oz probably ran his scam all over the world. I wouldn't be surprised if he wined and dined women from Sydney to Nice, and you are nothing more than another stupid woman who fell for his charms."

"So you've got nothing except insults to hurl at me?"

"Oz isn't even his real name." Pete rocks back on his heels.

I blink. "What?"

"No one with a U.S. passport named Oz entered the EU when you did, so lover boy lied to you about that too."

I clench my jaw and close my eyes. Oz isn't Oz. Who is he?

Pete touches my arm, almost like he cares about me. "It may take a while, but INTERPOL will catch him, and when they do, you'll have to testify."

"What?" I don't hold back my surprise. "Dan didn't mention that. How long have you known?"

"Does it matter?" Pete says. "If they get the bastard, we'll get our money back."

"How long?" I shout. The thought of seeing Oz again stabs my heart. "How long have you been hiding this from me?"

Pete shakes his head. "I'm not hiding anything."

"You didn't want me to know."

"I wanted to see if you'd fess up to having an affair with him, but you're good. You kept your cards close." Pete keeps his voice steady. "But I'm better, and I checked the hotel records. No Oz was on record, and no one checked into the room next to you, which means he stayed with you. Does that sound right?"

I am not going to give Pete anything he can use against me, so I heft my carryon over my shoulder. "I'm going upstairs to unpack and shower."

"Fine. I'll let you know when the scumbag is rotting in a jail cell."

Before our fight escalates, I climb the steps and turn left at the top and walk into my bedroom. My mind whirls. Oz isn't Oz. He even lied about that.

I lean against the wall and bounce my head off it. I want to close this chapter, forget about Oz, and move on. But something about the whole situation feels wrong. There's his note, plus he left my cell phone and passport. Nothing adds up.

Maybe that's the beauty of his con.

But here's the thing. Even though Oz is a shit, he showed me a life beyond Pete and Waterford, and his betrayal helped me see my toxic relationship with outside validation. I'm changing in a good way because of him.

For that, I'm forever grateful.

28

"Veronica! Oh. My. God! You're home!" Stacey rushes toward me, her chestnut extensions swinging loosely around her shoulders. "Look at you! You're so tan!"

I plastered on my I'm-so-excited-smile before walking into the crowded clubhouse, and now it feels etched onto my lips. "Hey! You look great, too!"

Pete loops his arm around my waist. "Vacation suits Vee well."

Ah, so that's what we're calling it. Vacation.

"I'm so completely jealous," Stacey says. "Marrakech looked amazing! Julia and I were saying we should do a couples' trip there. What do you think? Is it worth it?"

There is only one rule to living successfully in Waterford, and that's always be perfect. Because as soon as you show any sign of weakness, the sharks circle. And honestly, there's nothing the women of Waterford love more than watching one of their own sink. "I wouldn't go for more than a few days. Croatia and Nice were much better." Pete tightens his grip on me. "Did you see those pictures?"

Stacey nods. "I did..."

C'mon, Stacey, ask who the guy was. C'mon...

"Did you hear about Christina? She got a DUI! How mortifying, right?" Stacey grimaces.

I half-shrug. "I'm surprised more people don't have them to be honest."

Pete pecks my cheek. "I'm going to get drinks. A vodka tonic?"

"Sure," I answer. "Stacey, do you need something?"

She holds her half-empty glass up. "I'm drinking the same."

When Pete's a good distance away, Stacey leans into me. "Okay, so tell me all about the guy in the pictures. Who is that?"

I open my mouth, but close it. It would be so easy to spread stories of my illicit romp through Africa and Europe, but I have more self-respect. Plus, Pete's not here, and I really only wanted to make him uncomfortable. "Just a guy I traveled with for a while."

"Well, he's yummy – even if he never showed his face! With those abs, I don't know how you kept your hands off him."

Careful, Veronica. Anything you say will be used against you. "I'm married. Of course nothing happened."

Stacey nods vigorously. "I told the girls that, but you know how they are. All gossip, all the time. But I knew you wouldn't whore it up."

"Should we get a table?" I ask, eyeing the Saturday-afternoon crowd. "Or do you want to stand by the bar."

"Oh, I ate before coming up." I resist rolling my eyes. Everyone knows Stacey doesn't eat.

"Okay. Let's go to the bar. Pete should have our drinks by now." We move closer to the men crowding the bar and wait outside of the crush. "Who are you here with?"

"The girls." Stacey shifts her eyes. "They're out on the verandah."

Eve's here, but Stacey doesn't want to say it. "I'll meet you out there."

"Okay." Excitement creeps into Stacey's face.

After she walks outside, I skirt around a table to the exterior door and shove it open. Eve's cackle hits my ears as soon as I step onto the verandah, and I swivel my head in her direction. She's perched on the arm of a chair wearing a maxi dress and surrounded by my old friends – which, let's be honest, aren't people I want to be friends with anymore.

Her back is to me, and she's too involved in her story to see me approach. I stand off to the side, listening to her detail the horrors of her last bikini laser treatment. Slowly, the other women begin to stare at me.

"Hey!" I say. "How are you guys!"

Eve freezes, and her mouth drops open.

Tracey McGraw jumps up. "Veronica! You're back!"

"I am." I scan the group. It's the usual suspects. "Can someone make a little room for me?"

Kate pats the wide arm of her wooden chair. "You can sit here."

"Thanks. How is everyone?" I arrange myself so that Eve has a direct view of me, and she shifts uncomfortably. For the first time since Oz left, a laugh tickles my throat.

"It's the same old, same old here," Julia says. "But your adventures looked amazing."

"Where's Pete?" Eve interrupts. "Did you come with him?"

"I did." I smile pleasantly before going in for the kill. "He's inside talking to Lyndsay Meyers. She looks particularly cute today."

"Excuse me," Eve stands and all but runs inside the building. No doubt the thought of Pete talking to any other woman upsets her.

I spend a few minutes, half-listening to the women of Waterford gossip when my phone dings. Out of habit, I flick it up to see the screen. My heart stops. A red number one hovers over WhatsApp. No one has ever messaged me there except Oz. "I need to pee. I'll be right back."

There's a nervous silence followed by whispers as I walk calmly away. Either everyone knows Pete and Eve aren't done, or my former friends never expected to see me again. My money is on a combination of the two.

When I'm at the other end of the verandah, away from everyone else, I open the app. My pulse races as I speed read the message.

--Call this number—

It's a foreign number with a country code I don't recognize. I copy and paste it into my contacts then delete the message. With a trembling hand, I dial the number and hold the phone to my ear. After a short silence, it rings twice.

"This is Maxim. How may I help you?" The voice is heavily accented, and I can't place it.

"Um...hi. My name is Veronica White. I was told to call you."

"Mrs. White. I've been expecting your call."

"Who exactly is this?" I ask.

"My name is Maxim Xavier, and I'm with *Credite Malta*."

"A Maltese bank?" I say with surprise. The only people who do business with Maltese banks are the ones with something to hide – and Oz.

"Yes. We're handling an account for you."

"For me?" I say quietly. "There must be a mistake. My money is held in Swiss accounts. Not Maltese."

"Ah, but this isn't your account. However, we were told that you'd contact us with additional instructions, and we are to execute them without question upon verification of your identity."

What the hell? What exactly has Oz done? "Instructions?"

"On how to handle disbursements."

"Oh, I see." But really I have no idea what's happening. What game is Oz playing now? "What do I need to do?"

"Would you kindly answer a few security questions so I can provide you with service?" Maxim asks patiently. I wonder if he gets this type of thing a lot?

"Of course." Rationally, I know this could all be another scam of Oz's, but my gut tells me it isn't. I should trust Maxim.

"What is your favorite macaron?" he asks. A harmless question Oz already knows the answer to.

"Pistachio."

"And your favorite flower?"

"Orange roses."

"Last question, Mrs. White: what was the name of the redhead on the boat?" That's an Oz question. One-hundred percent an Oz question. My heart flip-flops.

"Stella."

"Very good." Maxim sounds pleased. "Now if you will, I have two million U.S. dollars that I need your instructions for. We're happy to hold it, but perhaps you'd like it wired to another account."

I stare off at the river, trying to make sense of this strange turn of events. "Whose name is on the account?"

"Mr. Samuel Ossing is the holder, and you are a signer."

"Samuel Ossing?" Ossing...Oz?

"Yes. Is that a problem?"

"No."

"What would you like to do with the money, Mrs. White?"

My mind churns. Oz once told me he worked as a hacker. Is that how he knew Maltese bank accounts are difficult to discover? Does he funnel money to them often?

"Mrs. White?"

"Is it possible to open a new account and transfer the funds in to it?" I need to make this as hard as possible for Pete to find.

"Of course. Mr. Ossing has already given us permission to do that. I assume you want to be the sole owner?"

"Yes."

"Very well. We already have your identification information, and we will complete the transaction by end of business Monday. Is there a contact number we should send the account information to?"

I pause. If it's sent to me, Pete will be able to see it if he subpoenas my records. I take a leap of faith. "Please send it to Mr. Ossing. He'll share the information with me."

"Very well. It was my pleasure to assist you, Mrs. White."

"Thank you," I say before hanging up.

I stare at my phone in disbelief. Oz found a way. He stole from me, set up a bank account in a country that has notoriously lax banking laws with the money he stole, and gave me access to it.

I bite my lip and tilt my head back to look at the beautiful, bright blue sky. I palm my phone, trying to think of what to say.

--I called--

--and?—

--Thank you—

There are more people on the verandah now, and with shaky legs, I weave between a few golfers until I spot Pete at the far end of the bar talking to his friend Tom. My and Stacey's drinks sit on the countertop.

"Hey," I say, calmly snaking my arm through his. "I thought you were going to bring these out before the ice melted." I smile up at Pete in what I hope looks adoring. "Oh, hey, Tom! How are you?"

Tom runs his eyes over me, stopping briefly on my breasts before finishing off on my lips. He leans forward and gives me a hug and kiss on the cheek. "Veronica, you're back."

I wag my finger. "I hope you kept Pete out of trouble."

Tom holds out his hands, palm side up. "I tried."

"Can I steal Pete?" I pick up the vodka tonics. "I promise to return him in two seconds."

"I can't resist a request from a beautiful woman."

I flash Tom a smile before lifting my chin toward the exterior door. "Pete, help me take this to Stacey."

My husband, because that's what he still is, follows me outside. Instead of turning toward the girls, I move to the other end of the verandah and around the corner.

"Where are you going?" Pete asks.

I put my drink on the empty table nearest me. No one comes down here, so we have a little privacy. "You asked me that the last time we were here. Do you remember?"

"What?" Confusion clouds Pete's face.

"Memorial Day. I was standing here, and you asked where I was going." I turn so that I look out over the golf course and point to the cart path below. "Stacey was there, going on about Eve."

"Oh, right."

"Seems like a long time ago, doesn't it?" I pivot so that I face Pete directly. "Time heals all wounds and all that bullshit."

"What are you talking about?" Pete leans against the railing. "You're not making sense."

My heart pounds. I lift my glass and bring it to my lips. The vodka burns as I swallow. "Ask me again."

"What?"

"Ask me where I'm going," I say.

Pete rolls his eyes. "Where are you going, Veronica?"

"Away from here." I place my hand on Pete's cheek and smile sweetly. "I'm done with Waterford."

"Vee, don't be ridiculous. Our life is here now, and everything has blown over. Look how the girls treated you. They're happy you're back."

I raise my eyebrows. "Eve wasn't happy."

Pete sips his old-fashioned. "I'm not surprised."

Now's the time to strike. "She seemed rattled, and she especially didn't like the idea of you talking to Lyndsay."

Pete tilts his head. "We'll talk about this at home."

"Oh?" I lift my eyebrows. "Is there something to discuss?"

He huffs. "You announced we're leaving Waterford. Where do you propose we go?"

I love how he assumes I want him to come with me. "Not us. Me."

"Are you serious?"

My emotions get the better of me. "You haven't stopped sleeping with Eve."

Pete pales. "I...yes, I have. It's over. I told you as much."

"Really?" I cross my arms. "Because I bet if I went inside and confronted her, she'd say differently."

Pete hangs his head. "Don't make this into a thing."

"So, I'm right."

"You were running around with Oz, refusing to come home. What the hell did you think would happen?"

"You think a good way to prove your love is to keep doing what drove me away in the first place?" I am surprisingly calm as I study the landscape. "That's the stupidest thing you've ever said."

"You're back now, so things have changed. Eve knows that." Pete doesn't apologize. "She'll leave us alone."

"I'm leaving." I shove past him. "I'm going home, packing my bags, and leaving."

"Vee, wait. You sound crazy. Don't make rash decisions."

But I'm done waiting for Pete. Listening to Pete. Believing Pete.

EPILOGUE

TWO YEARS LATER

My phone dings as I stroll down the narrow street toward Hôtel de Ville. My work day ended twenty minutes ago, but when you run your own company, you take calls when they come. And since my write-up in *Condé Nast Traveler*, I've been busier than ever.

I answer in French. "Bonjour. Veronica's Wine Tours. How may I help you?"

"*Parlez-vous anglais?*" The woman's voice is decidedly American.

"I do. How can I help you?"

"My girlfriends and I would like to take the trip you outline on your website to Champagne with the chocolate tasting."

I stop outside a tiny pizzeria and step aside so that I'm pressed up against the cool, stone building. "When were you thinking?"

"Tomorrow?"

It's short notice, but I am a miracle worker – even during the height of the summer season. "You're already in Paris?"

"Yes."

"Can you send me an email with your contact information and

itinerary choice, and I'll pull something together. Realistically, it would start around 1pm since you will need to take the train out. Would you like dinner also? I know a lovely Michelin-starred restaurant."

"That would be wonderful!"

I rattle off my email address. "I'll get back to you by ten tonight with all the details."

After I hang up, I drop my phone back into my handbag. Once she emails me, I'll start pulling my contacts to see who's available, but right now, my attention is on getting to dinner.

The square in front of Hôtel de Ville is being set up for a summer concert, so I can't walk straight through, and instead skirt the edge toward the Seine. All around me, Le Marais hums with excitement. I pause at the dock running alongside the river and savor the sight. In the distance, the top of the Eiffel Tower peeks above historical buildings. Down below on the bank, the city has set up small sandy beaches with chairs and games, and they're full of people.

If someone told me two years ago I'd be living in Paris, I would have said they were crazy. But here I am, not only living, but thriving. Not surprisingly, my divorce from Pete turned ugly, but in the end, I got exactly what I wanted: my freedom and my self-respect – even if he did secure a ridiculous amount of spousal support.

I cross over the river and wind my way through the labyrinth streets of the Latin Quarter until I reach Rue des Artes. A few blocks up, I turn right toward the restaurant.

A man in slim cut jeans and a fitted green t-shirt rushes toward me. He's polished in a carefree way and carries a bouquet of orange roses.

A smile dances across my face as he nears me. How did I get so lucky?

"I hope you weren't waiting long. I got held up at work." Oz holds out the flowers and kisses me softly on the lips.

This is real life. Not social media likes and loves. Not outside validation. I don't need men to tell me I'm pretty or worthy of attention. I'm no longer pretending to be someone I'm not.

I'm Veronica White, and I'm going nowhere except where I want to go.

THE END

ABOUT THE AUTHOR

Mia lives in Northern Virginia with her husband, children, and cats. When she's not writing, she's practicing yoga, traveling, or drinking ridiculous amounts of green tea.

She's been known to eavesdrop a time or two.

ALSO BY MIA HAYES

The Secrets We Keep

All The Broken Pieces

Made in the USA
Middletown, DE
29 November 2020